Also by the author
BALLOON TOP

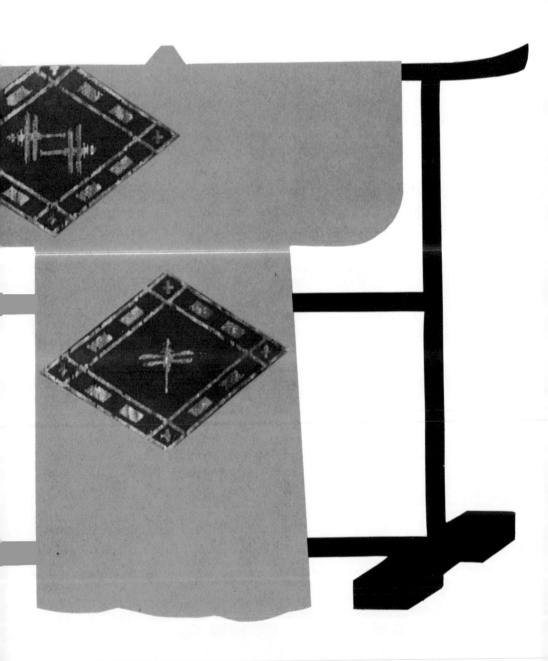

THE HOUSE OF KANZE

A NOVEL BY

NOBUKO ALBERY

SIMON AND SCHUSTER / NEW YORK

This novel is a work of fiction. Names, characters, places and incidents either are the product of the author's imagination or are used fictitiously. Any resemblance to actual events or locales or persons, living or dead, is entirely coincidental.

Copyright © 1985 by Zeami Holdings, Inc.
All rights reserved
including the right of reproduction
in whole or in part in any form
Published by Simon and Schuster
A Division of Simon & Schuster, Inc.
Simon & Schuster Building
Rockefeller Center
1230 Avenue of the Americas
New York, New York 10020
SIMON AND SCHUSTER *and colophon*
are registered trademarks of Simon & Schuster, Inc.
Designed by Edith Fowler
Manufactured in the United States of America

1 2 3 4 5 6 7 8 9 10

Library of Congress Cataloging in Publication Data

Albery, Nobuko.
  The House of Kanze.

  1. Zeami, 1363–1443, in fiction, drama, poetry, etc. 2. Japan—History—1333–1600—Fiction. I. Title.
PR9515.9.A5H6 1986   823'.914   85–30305
ISBN 0–671–60520–8

ACKNOWLEDGMENTS

THE DISTANCE that separates me from my motherland made research very difficult, but my task was greatly eased by my scholarly bookworm uncle Tadao Yagi, who looked out for and sent me numerous books on the noh theater and Ashikaga shogunate, and Mr. Kunio Watanabe, kabuki expert and hardworking producer of plays for Toho Theatres, who organized a five-hour marathon seminar for me, when I was back in Japan in March 1984, with Professors Noboru Miyata of Tsukuba University and Kiyoshi Hirai of Tokyo Kogyo University and Messrs. Shimpei Matsuoka of Tokyo University and Keiichiro Tsuchiya of Meiji University—a highly stimulating evening which provided me with much valuable background information on the everyday life of the period. My grateful thanks to all.

Also, my deep gratitude to Mrs. Yoshie Aihara, my history teacher at Kobe College High School, who helped me clarify historical data by correspondence, and to Miss Keiko Omoto of the Musée Guimet, Paris, who has patiently helped me find books and pictures relevant to the era at the museum's excellent library.

And above all, my inexpressible and fondest thanks to my husband, Donald, whose support, constructive criticism and suggestions have been invaluable and inspiring throughout.

7

To Dame Ninette de Valois
and
Dame Margot Fonteyn,
with profound admiration and affection

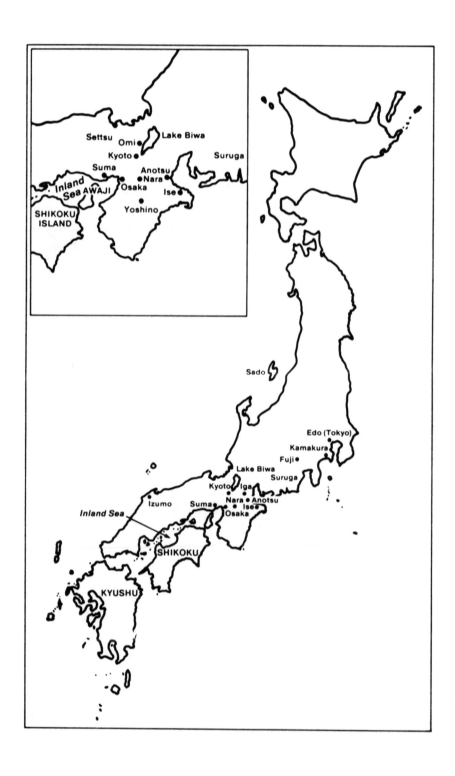

CHARACTERS

THE ASHIKAGA SHOGUNS

Takauji	1304–1358
Yoshiakira	1329–1367
Yoshimitsu	1357–1408
Yoshimochi	1385–1428
Yoshinori	1393–1441

THE KANZE

Kiyotsugu Kanami	the first master of Kanze; shogun's Companion-in-Arts
Tamana	his wife
Fujiwaka Motokiyo Zeami	son of Kanami and Tamana; the second master of Kanze; shogun's Companion-in-Arts
Yukina	Zeami's wife
Juro Motomasa	eldest son of Zeami and Yukina; the third master of Kanze
Goro Motoyoshi	second son of Zeami and Yukina
Saburo Motoshige Onami	adopted son of Zeami; the fourth master of Kanze

PRINCIPAL MEMBERS OF THE KANZE TROUPE

Toyodayu Toyojiro Toyosaburo	three generations of *shité* (principal role) players
Homan	*shité* player
Hotan	Homan's son; *shité* player
Raiden	*shité* player
Raido	Raiden's adopted son
Raiman and Raizen	Raido's sons
Kumazen	*waki* player
Suzume	Kumazen's wife
Kumao	Kumazen's elder son
Kumaya	Kumazen's second son
Sazami	Kumazen's daughter
Ogame	kyogen player; Fujiwaka's tutor-cum-nanny
Kogame	Ogame's son; kyogen player Juro Motomasa's tutor-cum-nanny
Meisho	flautist
Meiroku	Meisho's disciple
Ippen	big-drum player
Jippen	Ippen's disciple; big-drum player
Fuzen	hand-drum player
Jumon	small-drum player
Hachi	stagehand and entrance-fee attendant
Sango	all-purpose menial of the troupe

1

FUJIWAKA LISTENED to the din outside for a fraction of a second: village children howling and jeering.

"What's that base stupid look? The right foot over the left, idiot!"

A leather-bound whip tore past the little boy's knee. The father, a tall, wiry, handsome man in his mid-thirties, stalked in menacing circles around his son with thunder between his brows, his supple spine and the arches of his feet curled like a cat's.

"Please, Master, remember his age!" Ogame slid forward on his knees, picked up the whip and reverently handed it back to Master Kiyotsugu. Ogame, the kyogen* comic who, many in the Yamato province believed, could purge them of a fox demon by simply making it tumble out with laughter, was Fujiwaka's tutor-cum-nanny. It was he who taught the boy to read and write, as he was the troupe's only literate member apart from the Master himself. The other members of the troupe, seated in a row against the

* Farce performed between sarugaku noh plays as comic relief for the audience. Kyogen actors, always unmasked, also appear in noh plays as characters of the real and present-day world.

flaking clay-and-straw walls of the room, cowered lower over their work of tending their musical instruments and costumes. Privately they likened the Master's irate outbursts to the erupting Mount Fuji and feared them as much. It was not unusual for Kiyotsugu to break a dozen whips in a week.

"His age? Were he a month-old tiger, he'd have the mettle to eat a deer; were he a spineless little worm, he'd know how to creep the day after he was born! I'd rather not have a son at all if he couldn't shut his ears to a bit of noise outside and concentrate on his lesson. Do the turn again, Fujiwaka, right foot over . . . now, hips—sink your hips way down; grind yourself into the earth as you turn. Not low enough—look!"

To illustrate his point, Kiyotsugu poked the six-year-old lightly in the shoulder with the handle of his wip. The boy tottered a few ungainly steps, his lips trembling and his eyes bulging with tears, but clutching for life at his grimy, child-sized fan, he managed to regain his balance. He stood erect, hot tears pouring from the wide-open eyes set dutifully on his father and master.

"Before I brought him to you, Master, he'd had a long flute lesson with Meisho, blowing his little lungs out. In my humble opinion, he's done a good day's work. Now, now, stop sniffling and chewing your tears like that, little master."

Ogame waddled to and fro between the father and the son, expertly overplaying his nanny part.

"You spoil my son rotten, Ogame. All right, let him go and play." Kiyotsugu walked back to the spot where he had left his fan and dropped straight-backed to sit with folded legs. Fujiwaka in his short, hurried steps returned to the center of the squeaking uneven wooden floor, sat down and, placing his fan parallel to his kneecaps, bowed to his father and to the fan, the symbol of his art, till his excited hot forehead touched the polished wood. Then he darted toward Ogame, who quickly led the child out of the bare, large room which the Kanze household called, with a special quiver in their throats, "the stage room." Kiyotsugu watched his son disappear with an amused wry grimace, then clapped his hands—three dry sharp claps.

Immediately, Meisho held the flute to his lips; Ippen sat on a low stool behind his big drum, scratching his forehead with his sticks; Fuzen put his hand drum on his left knee, his hardened fingertips caressing the ox hide of the drum, and Jumon hoisted his small drum onto his right shoulder, wetting the delicate stretch of the colt hide with his saliva. The acne-faced young Hachi hurried about, urging haste on those engaged in arguing the bill with a mask maker or cutting wood for the kitchen fire. The main rehearsal was about to start.

Hardly had Ogame finished tying the strings of his straw sandals when Fujiwaka leaped out of the house. The first thing he saw was a village boy with a blue quilted waistcoat walking triumphantly on *his*—Fujiwaka's—bamboo stilts, guarded by a tight circle of village boys, whilst the children of the Kanze troupe sulked in morose, voiceless protest.

Kogame, the five-year-old son of Ogame, to whom Fujiwaka had entrusted the stilts, was beside himself at the sight of Fujiwaka.

"I couldn't . . . Fuji-chan, they threw me down, just wrenched them out of my hands . . . I couldn't . . ."

"They are *mine*! My new stilts!" Fujiwaka bellowed. "Ogame made them for *me*."

In the sudden hush, Fujiwaka was disquieted to see every face turn on him. He swallowed hard.

"Fuji-chan!" Kumao, fifteen years old and the oldest of the company's children, quickly came over and seized Fujiwaka by the sleeve. "Don't shout at them like that!"

"They are not yours, and I want them back!" Fujiwaka yelled, stretching his neck like a cock declaring the morning.

"Listen to the dancing beggar's son," retorted the blue-quilted waistcoat as he hopped toward Fujiwaka, soaring three feet above him. "*My* stilts, Ogame made them for *me*, huh? Who the devil d'you think you are? They're far too good for the likes of you. I bet Ogame stole them. My father says your lot are no better than thieves, beggars, murderers, lepers and hide merchants* and if you weren't chattel belonging to the Kofuku Temple, he'd burn down your house tomorrow. *My* stilts, damn you, dirt!"

The bully arched like a windblown kite above the players' children, who gathered behind Fujiwaka in a tight, cowed cluster. Fujiwaka, trembling and suddenly cold all over, dashed forward and grabbed hold of the stilts. Before the village boys had time to pounce on him, Kumao and other Kanze boys yanked Fujiwaka

---

* Because of the Buddhist prohibition against taking life, men engaged in killing animals to obtain such products as fur, hide and oil were considered to be godforsaken outcasts and untouchables.

back, but not quite quickly enough: the blue waistcoat, with a precarious balance, lifted one foot off the stilt and kicked Fujiwaka in the face. "Let go, you untouchable! There, eat my shit!"

The boys huddled around Fujiwaka, who lay curled up on the dusty earth with blood slowly spilling from his right nostril and bore on their rounded backs spittle and repeated insults from the village boys, Kumao holding his hand cautiously over Fujiwaka's mouth to prevent him from replying.

"NEVER MIND, little master; I'll make you a new pair, just like the others," said Ogame as he spread a strip of old cotton soaked in herbal infusion on the ripening bruise on the side of Fujiwaka's face. The house being overcrowded, Ogame had taken the boy to the narrow passage outside the Master's room under the dilapidated low-hanging thatched eaves, where however low the late-afternoon sun bowed, its rays did not penetrate far enough to dry out the dank, mosslike odor that permeated the place. Wooden pilings that raised the floor a foot from the ground were impotent against the notorious humidity of the Yamato basin.

"What does it mean—untouchable?" asked Fujiwaka, feeling safe and cozy as he nestled in the crook of Ogame's crossed legs, his haven of security for as long as he could remember.

"Verily, this is a Terminal World indeed. Fancy, a boy of your age asking me such a question!" squealed the kyogen comic. Acorn-sized and bald at thirty-seven from, so he claimed, worrying too much and too far ahead, Ogame was an orphan who had been brought up in a monastery, and he took great pride in using esoteric expressions he had overheard amongst the monks.

"What's Terminal World?" Fujiwaka was always curious about new words, which he collected and chewed as more privileged children of his age would toys or sweets.

"Two thousand years after Shakamuni's death, this world as we know it began crumbling into evil decay, which learned people call the Terminal World, and we've been in it now for more than three hundred years. I am telling you, little master, the end isn't far." Ogame rotated his bulging goldfish eyes as he dropped his voice. "Just look around and you'll see what I mean: Buddha's teachings go unheeded; sins multiply unrepented; evils strut main streets; sons kill fathers and servants their masters; monks maraud and turn moneylenders; famine, plagues, earthquakes, tidal waves and fire after fire, yet nothing will stop mighty warlords from warring, soaking rich fields in blood, cutting down more trees, removing more stones to build more fortresses. So, what do we have? More floods and more wars. More rice to feed the armies means more levies. Can you blame poor peasants for leaving their rice land and turning into bandits or beggars in the cities? If they have any wit they shave their heads, put on ink-blackened robes and call themselves monks.

"You ask why we are called untouchables, eh? I'll tell you. Infinitely merciful Buddha, with his own hands, put us—you, me, your father, Toyo, Raiden, all of us—on the Way of Art. You may well ask, is that a nice place to be? Maybe not. Many may argue it's the lowest of the low amongst living creatures, to be performers. But don't forget, Buddha put us there, and we actors live in service to the gods. Without us, who'd sing and dance their words? Who'd plead with gods for rain and rich harvests, for enlightenment and forgiveness? We don't plant rice, we don't trade, we don't run amok with swords, *but* we do show other men the grace of Buddha. We tell them, don't cry, this life here is not important. What matters is the one after this. So, *of course,* we're not like other people! We, the humblest leeches of temples and shrines, though called untouchables, beggars and dung-worms, by singing, dancing, giving happiness to thousands of miserable souls should be the first amongst holy herons and peach blossoms to be allowed into Heaven of Blissful Peace. No wonder others think of us as strange and dangerous and don't want to touch us!"

Drunk on his own florid words, Ogame remained choked in silence for a while, as was his intent little listener.

"But honestly, Master Fujiwaka, who could blame this world for turning upside down, eating its tail like a serpent, when we have two suns over our heads? Naturally, things that are unthinkable happen: some years ago in the middle of the night the hills around Kyoto rumbled, and the sound of galloping horses in the sky lasted an hour. Without a breath of wind, balls of fire in the shape of a heart darted about and fell on the Kiyomizu Shrine. Soon we'll hear cicadas crying in the snow of January or the moon dropping into our well. 'Watch where you're going, clumsy moon; you've broken my pulley rope!' I bet you, it'll soon come to that."

Fujiwaka squealed with laughter. The child had such a delightful way of laughing, like a bagful of crystal beads shaken by angels, that Ogame, smiling and shutting his eyes, listened to it awhile.

"The two suns in one sky" was the popular way of referring to the period known as the Era of the South and North Courts, and this political abnormality of two reigning emperors had existed in Japan for more than thirty years when Fujiwaka was born. In 1336 an ambitious warlord, Takauji of Ashikaga, manipulating the discontent of the warrior class against the autocratic and reactionary Emperor Godaigo, chased His Imperial Majesty out of the capital, set up Godaigo's young cousin as the new emperor, declared himself shogun and thus began the Ashikaga shogunate, which was to last for two hundred forty years.

Emperor Godaigo, who believed in his divine right to rule as passionately as he despised the upstart shogun and his puppet emperor, continued to assert the sole legitimacy of his court, which now lurked in severe discomfort in the mountains to the south of Kyoto, maintaining that he was the one who possessed the Three Divine Wares, the ultimate symbol of the sacred and inviolable right to rule Japan, handed down through an unbroken imperial line for ninety-six generations.

Since that time, the country had been torn and bled by incessant strife between the North and South Courts—the former propped up by the armed might of the Ashikaga shogunate; the latter a rallying point for a number of nobles, clergy and warriors who for various reasons resented the Ashikaga ascendancy.

"But, Ogame, before the End of the World comes I do want to get to Kyoto and play there," said Fujiwaka after a long, pensive grimace. He was worried that he might have arrived too late on this earth to reach the capital city of Kyoto.

"O Buddha and eight million and eighty thousand gods," Fujiwaka, eyes closed, prayed aloud, banging Ogame's thighs with both his fists, "please make me a good actor. I want everyone who comes to see me to smile and sigh, without knowing why, Aha! and to become nicer and happier and live longer. Then, afterward, I want winged goddesses to come fluttering down and tell me, 'Fujiwaka, no one plays as well as you except your father; so we'll now take both of you to the capital.' "

"Ah, yes, the capital, little master . . ." sighed Ogame wistfully, and they both lifted their eyes beyond the moss-green eaves.

●

To Kyoto, where in Fujiwaka's mind the winged goddesses lived, his father, whom he worshiped, had never been allowed to come, let alone commanded to bring his troupe. Every member of the troupe regretted this as starkly as if he had had one leg missing.

Under the all-powerful sway of the Kofuku Temple in Nara, the capital of Japan till 794 and now the capital of the Yamato region, there were three other sarugaku troupes besides the Kanze: the Komparu, the Hosho and the Kongo. It was the duty of all to offer performances at both the patron temple and the Kasuga Shrine* as well as at their tributary temples and shrines spread widely in the Yamato. Known collectively as the four Yamato sarugaku schools, they were no more than small provincial troupes which managed to survive from hand to mouth on a grudgingly scant subsidy, and having had no opportunity to be appraised by the capital's connoisseurs, they had no choice but to accept being considered "just a poor man's dengaku."

Dengaku, literally meaning "music of the paddy fields," had its roots in the coarse but rousingly humorous and acrobatic dance and music performed in the rice fields at the time of planting and harvesting—meant to inspire the peasants to work harder by keeping them happy and invigorated.

Sarugaku, on the other hand, had always been "music of the gods," developed from religious rites, with benedictory or didactic messages sung and mimed and danced. Since their disparate origins in the far past, influencing and feeding each other, dengaku and sarugaku had remained the cherished entertainment for the hardworking, gullible and god-fearing common people of towns and fields, whilst the emperors and the nobility, who "lived above the clouds," had despised their indigenous forms of musical theater and patronized exclusively the archaic court music and dance imported from China within their so-called Ninefold Forbidden Enclosure.

The situation would have remained static, neither dengaku nor sarugaku having preponderance over the other, had not the warriors surged onto the national scene of power, those "boors

* By this time the Japanese had blithely developed their ways to avoid conflict between the atavistic Shintoism (the Way of Gods) and the imported new religion, Buddhism. The Kasuga Shrine, built in the tenth century, came under the direct management of the Kofuku Temple, and to this day the two religions have survived in serene cohabitation.

and hairy apes of the hinterland" whom the aristocrats, loath to leave the flowering capital of Kyoto, had been employing at their vast estates in remote provinces as guards, tax collectors, self-appointed militia to engage in constant border strife and to bully the peasantry.

Having usurped more and more power from the enfeebled and increasingly indebted imperial court and absent noble land-lords, Takauji of Ashikaga, from the eastern marshland, finally set up his samurai government in Kyoto in the early fourteenth century, and in order to discourage his swashbuckling vassal daim-yos* from scheming against his shogunate in their distant wild provinces, the first Ashikaga shogun ordered them to reside in the capital. A daimyo who left the capital without the shogun's per-sonal permission was immediately branded a rebel. Whenever a daimyo with the shogun's permission departed from the capital, he was required to leave his heir in his place as an honored hos-tage. This caused a new and large population of samurais to find means to divert themselves in the strange and big city, and wealth-ier daimyos competed against one another in building sumptuous mansions equipped with huge halls to enjoy the wide variety of entertainments the capital could offer. It was only natural that these warriors, finding the court entertainment punishingly boring, should instead be captivated by the more immediately appealing and spectacular dengaku rather than the sarugaku. With fanatic support from both the first and the second Ashikaga shoguns, den-gaku had swiftly become the pet entertainment of the new power and consequently the craze of the whole capital: a subscription performance on the dried-up bank of the Kamo River in 1359 had been so massively attended that the scaffolding of the loges and galleries collapsed, causing hundreds of deaths and injuries.

When the ten-year-old Yoshimitsu succeeded his father and became the third Ashikaga shogun, his far-seeing chancellor Hoso-kawa encouraged him to continue supporting dengaku in order to strengthen in the public's mind the independent spirit of the sho-gunate vis-à-vis the Emperor and his court.

Taking their cue from the shogun and his chancellor, not only the daimyos and warriors but even the once-supercilious no-blemen vied with each other in support of various dengaku com-

* daimyo: a warrior who has fought his way up to become the feudal lord of a province.

panies, for by then the aristocrats could no longer collect the taxes due them from their remote estates without the shogunate's military assistance, as more often than not it was the shogun's own vassals who were filching the money or the tribute of rice due the noble landlords who, so precious and effete, would not dream of visiting, let alone personally supervising, their estates.

No wonder, therefore, that while the Kanze sarugaku troupe lurked in poverty and neglect in an obscure village in Yamato, the dengaku actors strutted in the capital covered with honors and in luxury. The news reached even the little village of Yuzaki that the boy shogun, on the advice of Chancellor Hosokawa, had made Kiami* of the dengaku main troupe a Companion-in-Arts—a title designating artists of exceptional merit who were handpicked and in personal service to the shogun. The actor now walked the streets of Kyoto followed always by an attendant carrying a small damask-covered cushion on which rested a jeweled sword received from a wealthy daimyo. The possession of swords was of course out of the question for a mere entertainer, but with his fame and the protection he enjoyed from the highest in the land, Kiami got away with this illegal act of ostentation, he who had started life as a baby left outside an itinerant juggler's tent and who remained illiterate to this day.

Kiyotsugu ruefully repeated to his troupe:

"There is the Time of Male, when nothing can fail but success feeds upon success; and there is the Time of Female, when even superhuman efforts bear no fruit but just rot in ignominy. It is the law of the universe. Don't fret, don't be discouraged, hang on, sit it out and a Time of Male will come, perhaps one day soon. . . ."

But he himself was far from resigned to wait and see out the Time of Female. No, he would kick and shake and thunder out of it. His combative, forthright character was manifested in his high, candid forehead, brows angularly drawn, a straight high-winged nose and large, piercing double-lidded eyes. He was tall, five feet ten inches at least, which was rare in those days amongst his class of people, and built on a tree of hard good bones, with hips and

---

* The religious title of *ami* was conferred on outstanding artists to circumvent the rigid social class barrier. Once called *ami,* heads shaven and mostly clad in priestly attire, the lowly-born artists became somehow "classless" and could then serve and mix amongst the people of high social rank.

spine that would have looked good on horseback. People wondered how he could manage to appear so meltingly frail when he played a woman's part and so airborne and bulkless as a ghost, for when he played a demon he seemed to grow double in wrathful mass and many swore that the metal-studded eyes of his mask actually rolled.

When the veteran actor Toyodayu described Kiyotsugu as a samurai with a fan as his sword, he was not far off the mark. Kiyotsugu was a fighter, a creator who saw his way of art as a long uphill road with so many ambushes and life-or-death battles along the way. In him this sense of perpetual combat ignited a thousand flames of creative force, but at the same time made him excessively severe and exacting with his disciples.

"The strictest discipline and a meek heart at lessons" was his company motto, and he expelled anyone who willfully disobeyed the Kanze house rule never to indulge in drink, flesh or gambling.

"What confounded conceit for an actor!" His stepbrother, Master of Hosho, who loved all three sins, smacked his tongue in amazement when he happened to hear of Kiyotsugu's three commandments. "What does he think we are? Saints? Eunuchs?" He then began assiduously to try to persuade Meisho, the tippler flautist and notorious womanizer, to leave the Kanze and join the Hosho.

But Meisho would rather have broken his flute in two and spent the rest of his life in drunken stupor than desert Kiyotsugu.

"For no one else in the world would I willingly forgo wine till nightfall," declared Meisho, who had begun drinking too much rough, unwarmed wine at so early an age that his nose had turned red and coarse-grained in his thirties.

Kumazen, the *waki** player who had been with Kiyotsugu ever since the latter had left his adoptive father's sarugaku company in Iga province, was a recalcitrant and prickly northerner who loved nothing better than to contradict Kiyotsugu and reply to his question by a surly counterquestion. Others called Kumazen "Twisted Navel," ascribing his character kink to his mother's difficult labor. But he was a brilliant *waki* in support of Kiyotsugu as a *shité*,† and if Kiyotsugu should ask for his life, he would have

---

* Supporting role. *Waki* players are not masked and play only *waki* roles.
† Leading role. *Shité* players alone may play principal roles, lead the chorus and serve other *shités* as *koken* attendant-cum-understudy.

retorted: "Why ask, Master? Take it: it's yours. Tut—fancy *asking*
me for it!"

With thirty-one men, women and children bearing their hard
life with such unshakable loyalty and devotion to their master,
Kiyotsugu found every small sign of the troupe's penury and obscurity a singeing reminder of his own failure. He suffered an excruciating hesitation when, for example, on a rare occasion his
wife, Tamana, brought him the only bit of salted fish in the house.
It took her time to persuade him to eat it, saying that on his health
and good work thirty-one others depended and that she had overheard Kumazen scolding his wife, Suzume: "Don't ever come to
me dithering about empty stomachs and tatters and leaks and rats
and lice! Haven't our children grown up immune to colds and epidemics thanks to them? How dare you, woman, complain when
our master, a Buddha-blessed genius if ever there was one, is
breaking his bones night and day to get us to the capital? With a
little more patience and hard work we'll get there, all right. You'll
see. You'll see."

And no one could have accused Kiyotsugu of not trying hard.
"A master-actor who cannot write plays to suit his company is a
duelist without a sword" was his belief, and he not only adapted
the old anonymous plays but wrote a prodigious number of new
plays to which he added his own music, choreography and direction. Amongst a class of people who were generally illiterate Kiyotsugu was an exception: he would gladly walk for a day and a
night to visit a learned hermit or perform without fee at a private
banquet if afterward he was allowed to study rare books imported
from China or containing old poems, many of which he later
worked into his narratives and lyrics. He also went to great effort
to spy on his rivals' performances, both sarugaku and dengaku
and, unabashedly stealing others' plots or characters, improved
them. In return, he was perfectly indifferent to his sarugaku colleagues' freely copying and performing his plays. Whenever Toyodayu grumbled that the master was generous to a fault, he laughed.

"Why worry, Toyo? By the time they've learned my last play,
I'll have written something ten times better."

It was not only the arrogance of an exceptionally talented and
prolific artist that made him say this: he was becoming increasingly dissatisfied with the present state of the traditional sarugaku
entertainment. He believed that dance and music must be coher-

ently and intrinsically linked with the story. "If drama is the bone, dance and music must be its skin and flesh." He envisaged plays richer in dramatic suspense, employing characters and subjects of everyday life instead of always gods and demons from the mythological past. But, alas, easier said than done. Blessed with a pitilessly accurate ear, he was only too aware that the sarugaku music, all luscious melodies and long breaths of cooing, however effective in creating a desired ambiance, was hopelessly underpowered to build dramatic tension or to drive a dance to a thrilling climax.

"I'm getting heartburn from the overcooked noodle of our sarugaku music. It's so limp, so flaccid. I confess I'll soon be falling asleep playing demons, gods and once again demons!" He fretted and worked many long nights, burning dry more rapeseed-oil lamps than the household could afford; but since the annual retainer paid by the temple was a mere pittance, he was at the same time obliged, as the master of the troupe, to keep his loyal men and women alive by catering to his provincial audience with a diet of demons and sapless music.

In between their official engagements in Yamato province, adult members of the troupe with Kumao, five years senior to Fujiwaka, as a child actor went on the road on foot. Pulling handcarts, they sought permission to perform at provincial shrines and temples on festive days, and when such occasions were lacking they performed where they could—on dried-up riverbanks, outside a town dignitary's tiled gate or simply at a wide crossroads.

When the troupe returned from what they called with much affection "the mud road," putting a brave face on the often appalling conditions of provincial touring, Kumao, looking wizened and gray from the accumulation of unwashed grime, dust and fatigue, proudly told the other children of his mud-road adventures:

"In Uji some spectators paid for their entrance with azuki beans, and Hachi started a fire in a brazier behind a stone lantern outside, and those of us who weren't on stage watched over the beans simmering in a covered kettle. That night as soon as we found a deserted Fox Deity shrine outside the town limit, Hachi made a delicious sweet-bean paste. With Father giving me a bit of his and Master a good half of his share, I ate till I felt as full as I had never been before. Then in the middle of the night I woke up with a horrible toothache, but really painful, in my right cheek. I screamed and woke up. Guess what it was! A mouse. No, a rat. Could have been a weasel even! It'd come to eat a bit of the bean paste stuck on my face. Next time, I tell you, I'll wash my face clean if we take shelter in one of those abandoned old shrines again."

The children, who had been salivating copiously, so envious of the feast Kumao had consumed, burst out laughing delightedly that the greedy rascal had been duly punished. Yes, unlike the drab, cramped and fidgety everyday life in Yuzaki village, where the player children were obliged to live like skulking rodents avoiding the village bullies, the mud road seemed an open, freer space where they could perhaps stretch their spines and hold their heads a little higher without being slapped down: "What, a saru-gaku monkey strutting the main road like a shogun?"

The wives and daughters of the troupe, who remained in Yu-zaki, worked assiduously sewing kimonos for the village women, plaiting reed and straw into mats, sandals, baskets, hats and cloaks. Even Master's wife, Tamana, who was slowly recovering from two stillbirths, joined the other women and often stayed up till long after the midnight bells from the nearby Jozen Monastery, sitting on the hard wooden floor of the stage room. On such nights Ta-mana kept open the sliding screens that separated the stage room from the Master's family room—the only private room in the house, used by day as a sitting and dining room and by night as a bedroom, with Fujiwaka's sleep mat laid at the foot of his parents'. As he lay on the thin, battered mat, he could watch his mother fling up long wild tails of straw which rustled and shuddered on the floor, spreading a piquant scent of the sun and the wind of the last summer, which was rapidly absorbed into the stale humidity of the dank old house.

In the faint glimmer of a rapeseed-oil lamp he could see how her eyelashes cast long shadows on her pallid lean cheeks. From time to time she would look up in his direction and smile shyly in reply to the child's intent, doglike gaze. In her thirty-fourth au-tumn, her smiling eyes looked sadder with their trailing fine wrin-kles. —When I grow up and play a goddess, I'll have a mask carved like Mother when she smiles at me. A smile that makes me feel like crying and asking for forgiveness.—

"Couldn't I help, Mother!"

"No, Fujiwaka, you're too young. Sleep," replied Tamana in her lovely lilting voice, with which she used to sing at her father's roadside puppet performances.

Every night Tamana heard her son mumble his prayer asking

Buddha and all the gods to grant him health and sound limbs the next morning so that he would not miss his lesson. Even when he was stung by a wasp on the eyelid, which swelled up to obstruct his view, he refused to skip his lesson, insisting: "Father taught me to bury my eyes in my hips; I know exactly where I am on stage without seeing."

The child heard his father castigate his senior actors who, when masked and hardly able to see through the two tiny eyeholes pierced in the wooden masks, tended to take small, cowardly steps whenever they felt they were approaching the limit of the stage.

"An actor who hasn't the guts to risk falling off the stage will never go far."

Thereafter, whenever he had a chance to rehearse on a real raised stage belonging to a temple or a shrine, Fujiwaka asked Ogame to bind his eyes with a thick band and let him go on stage. The child never once flew off the stage into the waiting arms of Ogame or Hachi despite the wind-raising speed with which he turned the corners or charged toward the front of the stage—an art that was to excite his audiences till the last performance of his long career.

Aside from his training as a *shité*, under Meisho's expert coaching Fujiwaka made rapid progress both in flute playing and in breathing, which helped him to acquire remarkably sustained phrasing for such a young boy, his bell-like child's voice pouring out of his small chest with a seemingly inexhaustible supply of air.

By the time Fujiwaka turned eight, even his harshest critic, Kiyotsugu, had to admit that there was in his son not only an exceptional talent but an inherent grace and poise which even with the eight million and eighty thousand gods' blessing one could not have hoped to find so complete in one human parcel. The first time Kiyotsugu let Fujiwaka play the part of a little princess chased by a demon, it was at a shrine in Iga province. Costumed and wigged, but unmasked because at his young age he was deemed not yet soiled by earthly passions, he was so very much a princess and so touchingly true in her anguish that when Kiyotsugu as the demon menacingly approached the child, the entire audience cried out in protest.

Being a perfectionist with a staggering capacity for work, Kiyotsugu tended to be unimpressed by his son's tenacity of purpose, which struck everyone else as being out of all proportion to the child's age. When Ogame demurred that perhaps it was a little too early for Fujiwaka to start learning hand-drum playing, Kiyotsugu remarked drily:

"When I was eight, on top of all that Fujiwaka is now learning, I was practicing acrobatics and was made to drink a cup of straight vinegar every morning, as it was believed to make the bone more supple. I could in fact manage ten consecutive somersaults with a long, trailing lion wig. No learning is begun too early, and none is wasted."

Kiyotsugu went further: in his opinion, learning for an actor had no frontiers. Disregarding the sanctimonious frowns from the elders in his company, he allowed the eight-year-old to go amongst the motley throng of passing entertainers to whom both Kiyotsugu and Tamana had not the heart to refuse shelter from rain or cold. They willingly offered the itinerant performers the Beaten Earth— a large bare area under a sagging thatched roof beyond the kitchen. There the hedges of costume baskets, farming utensils and chests of sundry necessities for touring were strategically lined up against the sharp teeth of the predominantly northeast wind which combed the house in all seasons. During the Middle Ages, when traveling from one province to another involved endless formalities with certificates and pass levies, the so-called "floating weed" untouchables were allowed great freedom of movement, as they were not considered to be normal and respectable citizens worth counting. Roaming the whole country as they ceaselessly did, the entertainers were often the first to know what was new and afoot. Kiyotsugu told his son to learn any new tricks or steps from the itinerant entertainers, who were held in much harsher contempt than even sarugaku actors.

ONE LATE afternoon in the monsoon month of June, after two whole days of steady gentle rain, the leaden sky turned black and a downpour began. Seeing a picture-story teller, a group of *sumō* wrestlers and a blind fortune-teller with his young daughter being led into the Flat Earth, Kogame and Kumaya, bored stiff after such a long spell of rain, alerted Fujiwaka at once.

The three friends were listening to the storyteller vividly describing the flooding of the Yodo River he had just passed, when there arrived a band of dancers and musicians led by an entrancingly attractive woman some years younger than Tamana, full of

gay, abandoned laughter, with a touch of the rogue in her dark
eyes. Both her kimono, tucked up boldly into her waistband, and
her underkimono, wet through from the driving rain and clinging
tightly to her sinuous hips and thighs, seemed to be in garish taste
to Fujiwaka's eye, so used to his mother's subdued tone of colors.

When this young woman announced herself as Omina, the
kusé dancer, everyone in the Beaten Earth brightened up: Oh,
so this is the Omina trained by Hyakuman, who according to a
legend, died a Bodhisat saint for having given so much joy and
solace to so many. Whilst the buzz of recognition was making the
round, Omina threw off her sodden straw rain cape and shook
down a thick mass of glossy black hair, flashing a jaunty, almost
impertinent grin at the surrounding faces.

"So much rain, mildew's growing on my eyelids. Dance for us,
Omina!" someone yelped from the dank semidarkness.

"Let's see what you learned from Hyakuman, girl!" the *sumô*
wrestlers, emboldened, clamored their support.

Omina's musicians, girls just as gaudily dressed and coiffed as
Omina and her dancers—the only difference was the dancers'
sparkling hair decoration in the shape of a crescent moon—let out
what to Fujiwaka sounded like urgent shrieks for help. Simultaneously drums and bells and wind instruments responded with
a breathless, irregular and totally chaotic rhythm as if everyone
were going her own way. The music they produced had an uncontrolled energy and attack the like of which Fujiwaka had never
heard. He felt his skin tauten like wet leather.

Into this stirring din Omina leaped like an unleashed beast
with both her arms thrown high, dropping her ample kimono
sleeves to the roots of her shoulders, which unabashedly exposed
the inner white of her upper arms. Her steps, now anticipating,
now dodging and tripping up the music, caused her feet to jolt
and stamp in frenzy, like sesame roasted on a quick fire, but all
the while her chest and spine retained the utter serenity of a bird
on a suspended glide.

The room, till then dreary with a leaden light grudgingly
reflected from the raining sky, was jerked into life, a lair of shim-
mying and clapping warm bodies. Fujiwaka could not keep still;
his trained muscles quivered in response to the music's assault. He
swayed his body and clapped his small hands. It was then that his
eyes struck upon a face across the room. His father's. He swallowed

a cry and stared at the face so transfigured: the half-open mouth was warped to one side, and Fujiwaka could feel that he was scarcely breathing; his unblinking eyes burned with a kind of intensity peculiar to hunger or hatred or murder. He had never seen his father's face so raw, so lusting, so devoured by a passion. Now and then, Kiyotsugu winced and visibly writhed as if Omina were dealing him a body blow or nauseating him.

It was Omina who cut short Kiyotsugu's ravished agony. Sighting the master of the Kanze behind the crowd, she suddenly fell flat on her knees with her head bowed in apology and embarrassment, gasping for air and pushing up wild strands of wet hair from her face.

"I didn't know you were here, Master Kanze. Please forgive me if my vulgar roadside romp has offended your eyes—though I must confess I love dancing the way I do!" She grinned with a cocky little nod to herself.

"So should you, and so did I," Kiyotsugu said as if his mind were a thousand miles away, and suddenly, for no apparent reason, he burst out laughing like a child who has just found out he can swim.

Born of the people, of their hard life, absorbing innumerable folk traditions through the ages, the *kusé* music was a rhythmic vindication of their tough survival. Like weeds from under stones, their songs had the buoyancy and vigor that neither a rake nor fire could eradicate. Year after year, it rebounded with even tougher resiliency.

Having dutifully served the music of the temples and gods for so long, Kiyotsugu felt the *kusé* rhythm make his blood run in reverse, and he felt intuitively that he could work it into the sarugaku music, whose melodious beauty and eloquently sustained pauses would atone for the raw and hectic beats of undiluted *kusé* music. —Even if I am not a large enough vessel to achieve this fusion, at least let me try.— Kiyotsugu prayed for Buddha's blessing. He had no illusions; the task would be formidable.

When Kiyotsugu told his wife to tidy up their room, as he would like to receive the *kusé* dancer there, Tamana thought her husband was either drunk or out of his mind. As the daughter of a provincial hand-puppeteer, she had always been charitable to anyone of the same precarious profession in need and trouble; but as an honest wife and mother, she could not approve of the brazenly courtesan fashion in which the street dancer was dressed, coiffed and smoked in heady incense.

Expressing her disapproval by an overornate politeness, Tamana apologized for the cracked cups and the absence of sweets in the house and placed the pot of roasted barley tea on the rough floorboards between her husband and Omina, who in her turn slid off a straw-braided cushion in an obsequious fluster and scraped the floor with her damp hair in deep bows.

"Madam, oh, please don't . . ."

"Madam" from the famous dancer disarmed the mistress of the house at once, and she softened to the degree of calling the woman of flamboyant notoriety "Omina-san."

Ignoring the fatuous female courtesies, Kiyotsugu went straight to the point: "Would you do me a great favor? Teach me *kusé* music, Omina-dono."

After an incredulous hush while Omina with difficulty adjusted herself to the honorific "dono," normally used only between equal and respected colleagues, she slapped at her own breast with a cavalier insouciance.

"Why, Master of Kanze, I'd be delighted to! No, no, no trouble at all, and do not think of payment. I'm honored to teach you, Master Kanze. Never mind what my troupe won't be earning. It's the monsoon month; how many dry days do we get to dance in the street?"

She stayed throughout the rainy month in Yuzaki and taught Kiyotsugu and his musicians and elders. On the rare dry days she sent the rest of her troupe to nearby towns to perform and gave the entire takings to Tamana. "Go on, Madam, let's have some treats: beans, dried fish and some sweets for the little ones, eh?"

She was simple, generous and gallant. Children adored her; adults accepted her as one of themselves. As was often the case with a woman known for amorous excess, in the company of respectable wives and mothers she turned into a dedicated and willing servant, friend and companion, so intent to please that whenever she was not working with Kiyotsugu she helped cook, sweep, mop, carry water and even mend children's clothes, and she bullied her dancers and musicians to do the same. Omina—she who was unquestionably the best in her own field, on whom many rich and powerful men were rumored to have squandered money and favor and for whom Nanami, the shogun's favorite Companion-in-Arts, had written and composed.

The day before her departure, with her impulsive generosity Omina sold to a passing merchant her string of murky orange beads, said to be from neither China nor India but somewhere even farther distant, and spent the money on more than enough food and wine for both the Kanze and her troupe. She and Meisho drank much less than Kiyotsugu, but both of them got drunk and flushed, whilst Kiyotsugu remained utterly sober, looking pale and tired. Tamana, who neither drank nor ate much, sighed heavily all evening and gave Omina a pincushion stuffed with her own hair collected after each hair washing.

Omina in return promised she would write to Madam from every town she visited, adding with dry, self-mocking laughter: "That is, if I can find someone who can write."

Then, her eyes more sensual and challenging in drunken recklessness, she stared at everyone in the room, rolling her weight from left to right.

"Listen, I want to say something to all of you Kanze disciples! Your master, here, hates flattery. But never mind, I'll be gone tomorrow, and what I say is the truth and may Buddha be my witness. I've heard Kiami, whom the entire capital from the young shogun to a waffle vendor worships as a god of music; I've seen Icchu fly across the stage and disappear into the roof; I've traveled widely enough to know all the greats in the provinces, such as the famous Inuo in Omi; but if you ask me on whose shoulders the tomorrow of our profession depends, I swear on the tomb of my mother it's on your Master's. If I were you, I'd rather starve and die for him than have it easy under a Kiami of this world. There, now, I've said it. And you, Madam, you must surely have been a Bodhisat in your last life to have merited both Kiyotsugu-dono and Fujiwaka."

Omina burst into incoherent sobbing before falling fast asleep. As this was always the case with Omina when she got drunk, her dancing girls gently covered her, and everyone went to sleep.

The following morning when Omina left with her troupe, all the Kanze women and children walked a long way with the departing friends and waved goodbye till they became unrecognizable dots on the dusty summer road.

As the house, emptied of the lighthearted hubbub of the kusé dancers, was beginning to be reinvaded by the familiar mildewiness, Kiyotsugu summoned his men to the stage room.

"I'm going to ask everyone a very great favor— I should say a great sacrifice. Kiyotsugu of Kanze, like this, kneels before you and begs you all to work with me the way I lead you and to bear the hardship that will accompany my decision. I do not want to go on tour till we have caught the new music by the neck and I'll have written at least five new plays using it. I feel the music in me; I can almost hear it. But to bring it out in sounds and beats, to make all of you sing it and dance to it, we'll need months, seasons, maybe a year. Will you try with me? Will you help me?"

Kiyotsugu was an irascible, unbending tyrant whose pride and integrity in all his work made life for his disciples far from easy and often intolerable. There had been times when they had wistfully sighed amongst themselves, "Were we under, say, Master of Hosho, that easygoing jovial drunkard stepbrother of our master's . . ." but now, in front of them, Kiyotsugu was bending his proud spine, asking them to come and fight with him. Every one felt his abdomen rise with emotion: life was hard no matter how one lived it, so one might as well suffer it for this man, with this master.

From Toyodayu and Raiden to Hachi, in one guttural exhalation everyone dived his head, vowing his obedience to Kiyotsugu.

THAT SUMMER even the notoriously vile heat of the Yamato basin seemed frightened to intrude beyond the low-hanging Kanze eaves. From early morning till late at night there was hardly a prolonged enough silence for the cicadas and crickets to be heard. With income drastically decreased, the wives warily measured every ladleful of thin gruel, burned less rapeseed oil and darned and darned again over an old patch. Everyone, even the youngest children, listened anxiously to the tone of the master's voice spilling out of the stage room: Is he anywhere nearer his new music today? Will he ever get there?

As Tamana seemed nowadays to manage with only one frugal meal a day, Fujiwaka was made to eat his bowl of thin millet-and-wheat gruel alone in his parents' room at midday. Before, he used to resent having to eat alone, away from the other children, but now it was a privilege, for he was sitting only a few yards from the scene of his father's battle. He chewed the tough fiber of pickled turnips slowly so as to cause the least noise in his tiny skull, straining all his attention on the least sound emanating from behind the warped and yellowed sliding screens. He heard his father counting out the tempo, hurrying on the tardy chorus, challenging, cajoling and all too often groaning in bleak despair.

Kiyotsugu insisted on hearing and seeing the music in dancing human bodies and on coordinating the cumulative and assembled effects of voices and instruments, which obliged him from the start to work with the whole company; it was a time-consuming and in terms of manpower a costly way of working out something which at that early stage was still a vague light glimmering in his mind alone.

"Can't you hear? Can't you hear? Hand drums, you must leave room for the dancers to breathe and stretch. And Ippen, what's the matter with you—you're just banging it like regular raindrops!"

"But, Master," Ippen panted, scraping the perspiration from his forehead with his drumstick. "Didn't you just a while ago tell me to keep to our usual eight-beat and not to be led astray by the chorus? I don't underst—"

"I didn't ask you to understand! What's this *understand?* Why must you understand when all I'm asking of you is to listen, idiot, listen and feel? If you can't feel it, shave your head and beg in the marketplace: you'll make a better living that way. You stick much too often to the hanging bottom of the chorus like wet underwear. Follow your own eight-beat, but breathe the *kusé* rhythm. Picture to yourself two carp swimming in the same direction, weaving in and out around each other, but not on top of or bumping into each other."

"I don't think we'll ever get this *kusé* music tamed into our old sarugaku way. It's like asking a nightingale to sing like a woodpecker," a surly voice spoke up, not from amongst the word-shy musicians, but from the chorus. It had to be Kumazen, who, as a *waki* player, had no business being there but had volunteered to learn Master Kiyotsugu's new way.

"It may well be, Kuma, that it is quite impossible," said Kiyotsugu leniently; he always had a larger bag of patience with Kumazen.

"I didn't say it was impossible, Master," retorted Kumazen, the Twisted Navel.

"Yes, you did. But, Kuma, let's not forget that we're slightly more resourceful than your woodpeckers and nightingales. We've suffered long enough the same old seven-five-and-twelve syllables spread on the same old eight-meter. It's high time we got out of the rut. There is a devil and a hellfire in *kusé* music, and we must use it to wake up our drowsy goddess of sarugaku music. We've got to! I am not afraid of failure; I'm willing to risk!"

"Who said I'm afraid? Of course I'm willing to risk. You make me sound as if—"

"Now, now, Kuma, and Master, and everyone . . ." Toyodayu, always a mediator, narrowing his folded-umbrella shoulders even narrower, strained his long stringy neck out of his shabby collar. "If we want to get on a Kyoto stage before our last tooth drops out and our hands start shaking, we must cut the cackle and work. No other way. Let us go on, Master. Eh, Kuma? Shall we, everyone?"

Toyodayu beamed till his slits of eyes disappeared behind the wrinkles of his weather-beaten face.

"Right, from the beginning!"

Kiyotsugu was up before anyone else, flexing his bamboo whip impatiently. And so it went relentlessly on, an inch of progress only too often followed by two inches of despair.

2

In the Buddha-forsaken Terminal World, as Ogame often remarked, people became pathologically superstitious, seeing evil omens everywhere. Temples and shrines grew richer and mightier, feeding on the lifeblood of millions of fearful people who, both during their lifetimes and after death, eagerly donated their possessions, from a bunch of wildflowers to a vast provincial estate; and of all the temples in the land, the Kofuku had probably been the wealthiest and most influential for longer than any other.

It owned estates not only in the fertile Yamato province but throughout the country. The privileges and immunities which generations of astute priests had obtained from the court were profuse, and there was no limit to their sanctified license and arrogance, backed up by an immense corps of armed monks who were for the most part mercenary drop-outs and misfits from all walks of society.

Both the court and the shogunate had proved impotent to stem their armed religious power: whenever a massive contingent of the Kofuku monks stormed into the streets of Kyoto—their heads wrapped in gray gauze, armored under their priestly ink-dyed robes, brandishing their swords and lances and prayer beads with unveiled menace and chanting outrageous demands—the shogunate, knowing too well the value of such Buddha-blessed militias in time of war or border strife, generally made haste to advise the emperor to give in to most of their demands.

Kyotoites bolted their front doors and huddled in their back rooms, whispering. "Mention an armed monk, and even a baby will stop crying."

The Jozen, one of the principal Kofuku monasteries, which had a high proportion of armed monks with those engaged in purely theological studies and meditations, was just outside the Yuzaki village. The monastery's chief abbot, Daijo, had a long cicatrice stretching from the corner of an eye to his chin, and the mere mention of his name made those whose livelihood depended on the Kofuku Temple catch their breath and turn cold. Before he forsook the world and took the tonsure, he had been one of the Ashikaga generals most feared and detested by both his enemies and the men under him.

Fujiwaka was nine when at the annual harvest thanksgiving performance at the Kasuga Shrine, he played a wisteria spirit, neither male nor female, ageless and elusive, in a pale mauve-and-green costume. Beside the towering demon played by Kiyotsugu, the boy's diminutive figure was so chaste and yet seductive that the chief abbot was seen to have saliva leaking from the corner of his loose mouth. He wasted no time in sending a messenger down to the players' house.

"Consider this command an honor. Have the boy washed thoroughly, give him clean clothes and send him to the monastery before the Hour of Bird."*

KIYOTSUGU TOOK a deep breath and held it for a long while, his eyes fixed on his son's dimpled small hand—no larger than a maple leaf—then spoke drily, almost severely, for he feared he might otherwise not be able to say what he had to say. What father, a king or an untouchable, would find it easy to prepare his nine-year-old son for a rape by an elderly monk? Every word he uttered to Fujiwaka was coated with the blood of his own humiliation.

"I hoped against hope that my son would be spared . . . but remember, we are entertainers. If our patron temple requires a

* About six in the evening.

service from us, we cannot refuse, we must offer it, whatever that might be. The pain, you'll grow used to. I had to do it; so did Toyo. So, probably, did Raiden. Keep your heart meek, body at ease; and the rest, forget. Give pleasure to others, ask none for yourself: that is the karma of our profession."

As Fujiwaka came out of the room he found his mother squashed very small in the corner of the corridor, crying with her face buried in her sleeves, but hearing him, she started to her feet and took him to the kitchen, where Ogame was squatting alone beside a large wooden pail of water from the well. With a clenched jaw as if she had a toothache, and avoiding Fujiwaka's eye, Tamana undressed him and scrubbed him all over with a tightly squeezed wet cloth. As Ogame handed her a clean but heavily darned undergarment and Fujiwaka turned his back toward her, she saw the child's shoulders scrubbed red, and each small enough to fit inside her rounded palm. She dropped her head to her chest, shaken by fierce sobs.

Ogame took over the dressing of the child and combed and tied his hair. Finally, as he held the paper lantern in one hand and the child's hand in the other, Tamana took a dismayed step backward, stuffing her mouth with the end of her sleeve.

"We must go now," said Ogame, bowing gravely to his master's wife, who could manage only a jerky nod.

For once Ogame was incapable of his usual funny remarks. Grim and speechless, back bent, he did not slow his preoccupied, quick pace till they reached the wide, cypress-bordered main road that led to the monastery gate. There, Fujiwaka let go Ogame's hand and looked back toward the house. It was already dark, with a thin sliver of a moon hanging in the blue-black gusty November sky. The house itself was only partly visible behind the crumbling mud-and-hay wall, and as they had to economize severely on lamp oil, it squatted there like an eyeless black vulture.

"Why weren't Kogame and Kumao there when we left? Where have they gone to play so late?" Fujiwaka spoke for the first time that evening.

"Oh, those brats. Anywhere, little master. They're just useless kids!"

—Am I no longer just a kid? No longer a brat?— Fujiwaka asked the question again and again on every step till they reached the immense monastery gate.

Ogame took the boy to the kitchen entrance. Bowing and

mumbling like an irresolute fly, Ogame cowered before a low-ranking monk engaged in cooking, who had a soiled towel tied horizontally across his forehead, red and sweaty from the hot fumes of a gigantic iron kettle.

"If you'd be so kind as to allow me to wait here . . . in case . . . in case my little master is dismissed earlier . . . He is, after all, only nine . . . that is, if I may . . ."

"Dismissed earlier?" The plump short monk whinnied with derisory mirth. "With this pretty face and the downy neck, your little dancing master won't be dismissed that early. Leave the boy; you've done your duty. If you must wait, wait outside the main gate. Now, get going!"

In the mess hall where Fujiwaka was told to go, he saw six other boys carrying crockery and cushions and hot charcoal. Aged somewhere between seven and fourteen, most likely to be either orphans or "the weeded mouths," fed and lodged in the monastery like guard dogs or falcons, they were of a coarse and under-developed ugliness. They all stared at the newcomer with a malevolent curiosity, and Fujiwaka could feel their hostile gaze like a hot iron on his back.

They are jealous of me, he thought, because I have a father to teach me and a mother to clean and darn. But then, why should I be here amongst these boys? Fujiwaka suddenly felt like crying.

A loud gong sounded and the boys fell on their knees. One of them cracked his knuckles nervously. Presently came a noise as if a hundred carriages were crossing a loose wooden bridge from the two covered corridors that connected the dining hall with the other buildings. Monks filed in, clad bulkily in layers of black, gray and white, their bulbous shaven heads gleaming, their heavy tread shaking the legged trays on the floor and clattering the cups and bowls.

His father had said merely, "The Jozen monks have just come out of their hundred-day penance" and had not explained how that had anything to do with Fujiwaka's service; but the sheer volume, weight and size of the warrior monks choked the boy with a cold terror he had never known before.

The one who appeared most particularly repulsive, with loose red lips and a long scraggy scar straight down one side of his face, sat down on a long dais and summoned Fujiwaka to serve him wine. Feeling quite sick, even faint, from apprehension and unidentifiable disgust, Fujiwaka gripped his body in the basic dance posture his father had whipped him into and pulling in his stomach, contracting his anal muscles, he walked down between walls of fuming, hungering masculinity and sat down beside the abbot's raised dais. Child of barely nine though he was, Fujiwaka was already an entertainer, disciplined to the core to please others' eyes; unconsciously he carried his body with the poise and grace of a professional, which, coupled with his striking physical loveliness, could not fail to stir even the stunted sensibility of the men used only to battlefields and religious purgations, both equally savage and inhuman. As Daijo fondled the player boy whenever he had one hand free of food or wine, his knuckly hand so clumsy and big over the boy's delicate eyelids, ears, lips, nape, waist and hips, the majority of monks felt their desire vault and mouths salivate, but a few, knowing to what the abbot's caressing of the child was leading, found the scene intolerable, ate their food quickly and slipped off to their cells.

At the end of the meal, Daijo told the monastery boys to clear away the legged trays and ordered Fujiwaka to dance and sing "something vernal and amatory." Not understanding the abbot's words, Fujiwaka stood up, bewildered and hating the dishevelment of his hair by Daijo's sticky hands, for his mother had always told him, "Even in tattered rags, so long as you wear your hair neatly, people will respect you."

He began dancing and singing a short piece Omina had taught him about a boy perched on a tree by the river who caught fish by playing his flute. Many of the monks guffawed and protested at such a fairy-tale entertainment, and Daijo, screwing up his face, either irritated or impatient, grabbed hold of the boy and, carrying him with one arm over his hipbone, unceremoniously strode out of the hall, leaving the monks to do what they pleased with the mealy-faced boys who had finished clearing away the trays.

—Father told me, heart meek, body at ease, body at— Fujiwaka repeated to himself as Daijo, breathing hard, shut the beautifully painted sliding doors behind them and threw the boy onto a fragrantly new straw mat, spread in the middle of the clean bare room. —I won't watch, I won't smell, I won't hear so that I'll have nothing to recall or to tell anyone. Shan't tell Mother and Ogame. Nor Kogame or Kumao. Father, I don't have to; he knows. He knows—

With his eyes crushed shut and his teeth grinding till they could have sparked a light, as his immaculate boyhood was being manipulated, brutalized and taunted in endless obscene acrobatics, he went on repeating:

—Father had to be dirtied like this. Toyo too. Raiden too. We are entertainers . . .

Fujiwaka was a fastidiously clean child. Drenched as he was in the sickening opacity and odor of animal secretion, finding himself so detestably filthy all over struck him as far more unendurable than the pain and soreness; and throughout the night it was not so much his pride or sense of duty toward his parents and the troupe as purely and simply the physical discipline of his art that preserved him. As Daijo's noxious-smelling urgent body crushed his little bones into the floor, his inflamed cheeks against the cool of the straw mat, his thick eyelashes grazing the mat's silk binding, only once did Fujiwaka open his beautiful long eyes. He stared at the regular weave of the young green straws and thought at once of his mother sitting with her straw work by a faint lamp when his father was away on tour.

—Could I help, Mother?—

—No, Fujiwaka, you're too young. Sleep—

Suddenly, and for the first time, tears brimmed in his eyes and throat. I'm no longer too young. I'm big enough to help. Father will finish his new plays and we'll all go to Kyoto to play them.

Ogame had sat outside the gate all night. At dawn, seeing a little bundle of human refuse tottering uncertainly toward him, he jolted to his feet, stifling a moan so terrible that it ran back inside and burned his guts. With his stained porcelain face averted, Fujiwaka thrusted into Ogame's hands a sack of soja beans and a few rolls of cloth. His hair was matted and dirty, and on his neck Ogame saw bulging red bruises crawling like long worms. When Ogame drew in a breath in search of something to say, the boy's furious black eyes flashed, petrifying Ogame's tongue at its root, refusing to be comforted, imploring him to look away; his pride was his only strength. Fujiwaka, showing a rigorous little of the soreness and pain, walked alone and ahead of Ogame, who, more bent than the child by the weight of the beans and cloth, followed at his heel.

Just as Fujiwaka turned off the cypress-bordered road, with

the house standing straight ahead of him, a strain from a single flute shot at him through the grayish morning air. The child knew his flute teacher's unique voice. Meisho, who rose earlier whenever he had a hangover, was playing his flute to cure it.

In all his life, Fujiwaka could not bring himself to speak about his homecoming on that frosty November morning. All he could ever manage was "Meisho saved my life once." Too affected to say a word more, he would hold his breath and wait for the pain to pass, his eyes focused far away as if he were trying to hear Meisho's flute again.

When Fujiwaka's small feet suddenly stopped and remained nailed to the dusty earth, Ogame looked up anxiously. He saw Fujiwaka's swollen lips part, his eyes blink as if coming out of a blindness and his dirty pale face open to the music like a flower to rain. Turning to Ogame, the face seemed to ask: Do you hear it, do you hear it? And on it such pathetic force, such triumph.

"Meisho," sighed Ogame, he too listening with his chin lifted and eyes half shut. "That's your father's 'Songs of the Western Isles' he is playing."

To his consternation, Ogame saw the child sprint, throwing his skimpy legs and arms forward with random, desperate speed. Ogame shook his head, smiling; then, with a short kyogen yell he began trotting after Fujiwaka—or rather, toward Meisho's flute music, as he was blinded with a gush of tears: he had not been the little master's nanny without understanding the working of his heart.

Fujiwaka's duty at the monastery was confirmed as every third night for two months from immediately after the monks' hundred-day purification period, then as up to ten nights in each month till their next penance. The reward was grain, cloth and even some rice, all of which, despite the circumstances under which they had been obtained, were keenly appreciated. The effect of Kiyotsugu's decision not to go on lucrative provincial tours had been alarmingly felt in the Kanze household.

On the mornings when Fujiwaka returned from the monastery—at the hour when normally the clatter and buzz of the waking household danced to the tune of the temple bells and the crackling din of ducks and chickens in the backyard—the boy was washed and put to bed, in a windowless small room where the valuable masks and costumes were kept. Tamana would creep into the dark room and without saying a word gently stroke her little son from outside his sleep cover; the entire household hushed their breath, drew shutters slowly and scolded young children in whispers, and Kogame and Kumao treated Fujiwaka as if he were a wounded soldier returning from the battlefield, ran errands for him and saved the last persimmon left on the tree for him. On such mornings Kiyotsugu was willing to let his son go on sleeping, but after a few hours of deathly-deep sleep the boy crawled out of the mask room, dressed and watched his father work; and when his turn came, he learned with a concentration that almost made him cross-eyed, and when given a difficult step he would repeat and repeat it till Kiyotsugu had to restrain him.

"Mind, Fujiwaka, don't stamp through the boards."

In that winter, Kiami of the dengaku school had the high honor of performing at the Houn-In in Nara with all the costumes lent by his numerous aristocratic supporters. Kiyotsugu took his son to see the performance. As Kiami walked on the stage in a hemp wig, clad in a magnificent damask garment, singing in a voice as introverted as an echo from a deep cavern, Kiyotsugu noticed his son tauten, grow taller then remain utterly immobile till Kiami made his slow exit.

"Father," he said afterward, "when Kiami sang 'Long ago in the great capital I lived in splendor' so simply, so straight at us, straight from . . . here!"—he searched with his spread-out child's palm somewhere from heart down to stomach—"I understood him. I'll never forget it. He *is* a great artist."

Kiyotsugu took a long side look at the child's intense little face and thought: Not an ordinary parcel I have here. It takes a lark, not a thrush, to know a nightingale. Buddha have mercy and let me live long enough to give him everything I can!

3

When Kiyotsugu felt sure of his grip on the new music, he began working alone, and the house was at once swallowed up in an expectant hush. On the evenings when Fujiwaka was not at the Jozen Monastery, he would fall asleep listening to his father mumbling and chewing his lyrics and beating the rhythm of his new music by slapping his thighs.

One evening when Fujiwaka was serving at a "tea-drinking bath," a fad in which the Kofuku high priests often indulged themselves, Daijo, the scarred chief abbot, made Fujiwaka share his round wooden bathtub and, fondling the boy, asked him what treat he fancied most.

Fujiwaka replied without hesitation: "Tea from China!"

The extravagance of the request and the eagerness of the child's flushed little face demanding it so disarmed the abbot that he screwed up his sweating red face in a grin and said to everyone's amazement, "So be it. Give the boy the best tea from the gardens of the Ming Emperors!"

Fujiwaka came home panting with excitement, holding a

small tea caddy as reverently as if it were a mask by the great Shakuzuru.

"Father, tea, the best tea from China! I hear it makes your head clear and fills it with delicious thoughts."

Kiyotsugu shut his unslept bloodshot eyes to hide his emotion and after some moments said with a smile he had not shown for many months, "Soon, Fujiwaka, I hope you won't have to go to the monastery. I have almost finished the first of my new plays."

It took him another month before he was satisfied with *Bewitched in Saga,* his first masterpiece exploiting the new music; then he wrote six more in a month. Since that rainy afternoon in June when Omina and her troupe had danced in the Beaten Earth, more than a year and a half had passed. Snow was now melting on the sunny hillside, and early buds lifted their furry little heads on peach branches.

Kiyotsugu made preparations for an extensive tour which would hover very near the capital, nearer than he had ever dared attempt before. In the meantime, he rehearsed with the speed and vigor of a tumbling boulder, to which his troupe responded with inspired dedication. The children too caught the fever: they learned by heart every new play, overhearing or peeping at the rehearsals through small tears in the sliding screens. They would sing and dance excerpts from these plays at every idle moment, even when they stood in a queue for their turn to use the skipping rope or at the well to draw water to wash their muddy feet.

Spring came early that year in the Yamato basin; Kiyotsugu could tell from the way his palm felt damp against the bamboo bones of his fan as he danced.

"Soon we'll be on the road—muddy, lumpy, thawing earth everywhere," Kiyotsugu sighed one night very late, as Tamana massaged with her thumbs deep into the wire-hard muscles on the back of his neck. "Tamana, I do so want a floor!"

"To take to the road?" asked Tamana, her voice somewhere between a giggle and a gasp of incredulity. She had never heard of such an extravagance: a floor for the mud road!

"Everywhere we go; on the riverbanks, in marketplaces, at main crossroads and at temples and shrines. We are the youngest and least known of the sarugaku troupes outside the Yamato region; in the provinces it is often very difficult for us to get permission to perform on temple or shrine stages. What I am creating needs a space of make-believe, cut out from the rest of the world. All I need is just a simple platform to emphasize: this *is* Kanze's special world! You couldn't imagine how desperate it is to have to dance a heavenly maiden while kicking up clouds of dust or rattling stones underfoot on a rough riverbank."

Kiyotsugu, having listened to his own sonorous complaints, was so upset, almost enraged, that he turned around and glared at his wife as if it were her fault that he could not possess the wonder of boards under his dancing feet.

Tamana could not confront her husband's unhappiness or disappointment without somehow feeling herself guilty. She covered her mouth and blinked her eyes rapidly at him, apologetic and pensive. The husband and the wife looked at each other like this in silence for a while, before Tamana gently turned Kiyotsugu around and began massaging his neck again.

Almost a month passed. The departure was imminent. One afternoon, Kiyotsugu was working with his men on the Beaten Earth floor, making a tall structure with sliced bamboo which was to be a piece of mobile scenery representing a cave where a hermit lurked, when Hachi darted in, his acned face glowing in red excitement.

"M-m-ma-master! It has to be a mistake!"

"What is a mistake? Calm down and talk in proper order."

"Two huge rolls of rush mats have been delivered on a handcart pulled by a man whom I've never seen before. He said they're for you, Master. He dumped them there and has gone."

Sure enough, the rolls of thick rush mats lay against the crumbling mud-and-straw fence outside the house, shining arrogantly in fresh rose-yellow in the setting sun. Kiyotsugu quickly undid the hempen cords that tied up the rolls and had them spread side by side on the ground. Each roll was composed of three good-quality rush mats, sewn together and neatly bound at the edges with black linen bands.

Stupefied by the size, the quality and the sheer unexpectedness of their arrival, those who had followed their Master outside the house stood agape gazing at the spread-out mats.

Only after some moments was Kogame's husky voice heard, ever so gently, almost in a wish: "Isn't this . . . a stage?" Then, he yelled insanely, "It is! It *is* a stage! A portable stage for the road!"

Men, women, children—everyone—dropped to their knees to feel any part of the traveling stage. Children, having flung off their sandals or quickly cleaned their bare feet against the hems of their clothes, stepped onto it, timidly at first, then jumping and screaming wildly; and their parents were much too wonder-struck themselves to order them to get off the clean new mats. Fujiwaka, who was to be taken on the road for the first time, naturally took a more possessive and professional interest: he danced a few steps, then walked on the smooth black linen edge of the mats, singing at the top of his lungs the new song his father had written for him, with Kumao and Kogame, also chosen for the road company, following on his heels, jabbering each his own line.

No one noticed Kiyotsugu slipping back into the house. He went through the dark kitchen and found Tamana outside by the well, squatting in front of a round wooden tub. A white and indigo-blue cloth wrapped her head and was tied on the nape of her neck. Hearing Kiyotsugu's footsteps, she began vigorously scrubbing the clothes inside the tub. Kiyotsugu walked straight up to her and snatched away the cloth from her head. Her hair, tied at the back with some leftover pieces of costume material, was cut barely an inch below the knot.

"A midwife in the village," Tamana said finally, "is paid by a wig shop in Nara to find women who'll sell their hair. After that, I went to see Himi."

Tamana spoke the name of a well-to-do hide merchant's son, cursed since early childhood by the incurable illness popularly called "shriveled legs," whom Kiyotsugu had encouraged into carving masks. The young man had both talent and the tenacious application often found amongst the deformed, and although he was a confirmed misanthrope, he worshiped Kiyotsugu and was devoted to Tamana. From time to time he would send his young menial to Yuzaki village to beg Tamana to come and just sit and watch him work. The young man's father, a harmless but uncouth man, often teased Tamana that his son was head over heels in love with her.

"Himi paid the rest and arranged everything," she continued, neither turning back to face her husband nor completely removing her hands from the tub. "He said he'd just carved a mask in the likeness of his dead mother and wants you to have it and write a play for it one day. He wishes you a great success on the road."

Tamana took her hands out of the water, dried them on the edge of her apron, waited, listened. When the silence behind her became too menacing, she turned, still squatting, on the springy balls of her feet and covered her mouth with her damp, cold hands.

Kiyotsugu stood there with the cloth from her head squashed over his face, his big hand like a rake across it. He stayed immobile for a long time. Then, suddenly dropping his chin to his chest, he gasped bitterly: "Why do I take you for granted like this? Why haven't I stopped a second to take notice of your hair? Sharing a sleep mat as we do night after night, why haven't I touched you for so long? Tamana, I am a monster. I can do only one thing well, but that isn't to make you happy. Hair is a woman's joy and pride. . . ."

Tamana had been prepared for an outburst of anger: "You, woman, how dare you! I'm the master, I'm the husband. Did you think I was such a rotten incompetent sluggard that I had to wait for my wife to sell her hair to . . . ?" She was perplexed beyond her wits. She sidled up to him and, standing below him like a castigated pupil, began apologizing in a chippering hurry.

"We are very sorry, Himi and I, that we couldn't get you a wooden stage—far beyond our means. Of course rush mats won't last as long as wooden boards, and probably after a couple of tours they'll tear and rot; besides, they won't be of any use on a wet ground. . . . But, husband"—Tamana cocked her eyes at him with an infectious bright smile—"you *can* put rush mats on uneven ground! Boards, you can't!"

With an exasperation so loving and so impatient, Kiyotsugu hugged his wife in his arms, stroked and stroked her truncated hair, with big tears rolling down his cheeks. Kiyotsugu loved his wife. She was his wife and the mother of his only son, who meant to him more than just a child and a growing life: the continuity of himself and his art. In Fujiwaka he saw Tamana, and he loved both his child and its mother all the more. Yet in the love Kiyotsugu offered her, there was always a touch of remorse. When he made love to her, even now after nearly fifteen years of married life together, he felt a twinge of compunction as if he were somehow taking an unfair advantage of his own wife. She was just as unselfish, grateful, rapturous in physical encounter as in any other ways with him. She was satisfied and satisfactory, as wife.

Only, he could not quite stop reproaching himself as if he had been unkind or hurtfully unfaithful to her—which Buddha knew he had not been, not so far. . . .

HAVING ALWAYS dutifully carried out all the performances required by the Kofuku Temple, Kiyotsugu had little difficulty in obtaining permission to take his troupe on an extensive tour. The temple's authorities were not unaware how small a retainer they paid the troupe. Once the official permission from the parent temple had been granted, the Jozen Monastery could hardly obstruct Kiyotsugu from taking his son with him. The chief abbot, Daijo, showed unexpected generosity by sending down a small wicker case of clothes for Fujiwaka for his journey; it included a kimono made of fine cotton cloth woven at one of the Kofuku-owned estates.

Come April, the stage mats were rolled and put on the sturdiest of the handcarts; and with the costumes mended, masks repaired and repainted, the company's new repertory rehearsed to near perfection, such a hope as they had never before dared conceive tingled in every disciple's heart: this time, will the road to Kyoto open at last for us, somewhere, somehow?

On the morning of the departure, Tamana in her best kimono, her short but rich black hair tied with new silk, solemnly struck flints over Kiyotsugu's and Fujiwaka's heads in front of the family altar, praying for their health and safety on the road, as did every other wife over her departing husband's or son's head. When Tamana had finished strapping on Fujiwaka's back a pouch filled with a change of clothes, herbal medicine, a wooden comb and some salt to clean his teeth, then tying two pairs of sandals she had woven herself around his waist, the child, topped with a large mushroom-shaped straw hat, looked like an ambulant junk heap, as did Kogame.

In the first blush of the sun as pale as if filtered through the thinnest slice of watermelon, the mud-roaders set out with four handcarts loaded with the stage mats, costume baskets, props wrapped in weird shapes, cooking utensils, braziers and carpentering tools. For the first few miles the travelers marched in the atmosphere of a flower-viewing picnic, which quickly evaporated, however, as the sun rose higher and the roads became ruttier. More frequently than was agreeable, the good people traveling the same road ordered the herd of entertainers to step aside and let them pass first, often pushing the actors off the road into paddy fields and sometimes too near one of the ubiquitous manure ponds.

By the time Nara, of innumerable temple roofs and spires, was half a day's walk behind them, both Fujiwaka and Kogame found even their small pouches weighing like rocks on their backs and their dusty feet chafing painfully against the plaited straw of their sandals; and as the road began winding up the hill, leaving the flat-bottomed Nara basin, and the red evening sun was shooting into their eyes below the rims of their hats, the boys were dropping behind the others—even though Kumao, sixteen and considering himself an adult, had volunteered to carry both Fujiwaka's and Kogame's pouches. Kiyotsugu stopped the handcart loaded with costume baskets and told the two boys to climb on top. With a grateful whimper they clambered up and were soon fast asleep, with Ogame and Kumao walking vigilantly alongside, lest their limp bodies start rolling from the handcart as it bumped along.

It was past the Hour of Boar* when the troupe arrived at the Miwa Shrine, where, in order to secure the best positions in the shrine's grounds for the three-day rice-planting festival, many groups of open-stall merchants and entertainers had already installed themselves, either sleeping like thrown logs beside their barrows and carts or boiling water and cooking gruel on small braziers. The sky was roughly scrabbled with flying clouds, into and out of which sailed the moon as slim and curled as a baby worm in the black spring earth. Owls in the firs and the cedars hooted, and the mountain stream skirting the shrine compound was just as clamorous as the wind-stirred bamboo forest, in front of which the Kanze troupe had decided to sleep the night and to spread their proud new stage mats in the morning, if the fine weather held out.

After Ogame had made Fujiwaka and Kogame wash their faces, hands and feet in the cold stream, they felt so wide awake and intimidated by the black night and the strange noises it contained that they held on to Ogame's arms and sleeves with both their hands as they lay trying to sleep their first night out on the mud road.

* Ten o'clock at night.

IN YAMATO, where people had always lived in benign intimacy with demons and hobgoblins, Kiyotsugu had been most appreciated for his bravura demon acts, but on this tour the audience saw him in immediately recognizable and comprehensible human characters such as a warrior, a widow, a courtesan or a novice. They became so involved with the characters that they listened with bated breath and forgot to applaud and yell their appreciation during Kiyotsugu's performance; but at the end their enthusiasm knew no bounds, and they went home humming the most catching of the tunes. For many days that followed they tapped the rhythm of a particular *kusé* number that had caught their fancy and urged their relatives, friends or travelers going in the same direction as the Kanze troupe to make sure of seeing Kiyotsugu of Kanze in his new plays. They called his new-style theater the Kanze's noh in order to distinguish it from other sarugaku schools' work with which they had long been familiar, perhaps overfamiliar.

In a jostling marketplace or on a riverbank by a ferryboat landing, a crowd would quickly gather for the Kanze's noh performance, often six or even seven rows deep. They became so absorbed with what each character had to say that if, as was only too frequently the case, a juggler of swords and burning torches or a so-called miracle-ointment peddler, envious of the Kanze's large audience, raised his voice aggressively the spectators themselves turned and berated the disturbing one. At temples, priests in charge of festivals were seen discreetly applauding behind the crowd; and the shrine priestesses came in their full white-and-red finery to take a look at the Kanze's performance whenever there were no paying customers to engage them for a danced prayer.

The word of mouth traveled far and fast: by the time the troupe moved on to the Tamba province and reached the Shinomura fair, a letter from a local merchants' guild was awaiting Kiyotsugu's arrival asking him to give a special performance at the mansion of one of its members.

Hachi, who collected entrance fees at public performances, wailed blissfully at the rush of eager customers, "Truly, it's no less than a miracle, Master! When I see so many customers coming at me, extra arms seem to grow from my shoulders; and there I am like a ten-armed Buddha, grabbing their coins, rice, beans, salt or whatever."

After each performance, Hachi counted aloud and Ogame wrote down the various takings, which greatly surpassed the amount and the quantity they had been accustomed to. Most of the surplus of money, rice and grain was regularly sent back to the women and children waiting at Yuzaki village by a couple of younger disciples, who then brought back the news from home and a new supply of sandals, which the troupe wore out at an alarming speed. The three boys in the company learned for the first time in their lives not only what it tasted like to eat fresh fish and rice without other grains mixed in it but what it felt like to be satiated.

With the income far exceeding their frugal needs on the road and at home, Kiyotsugu took—and to the weary young disciples who had been pulling and pushing the handcarts in turns it seemed truly providential—the bold decision to acquire two bullocks and a cart to carry the heavier part of their load. After much haggling in the next few villages they passed through, Kiyotsugu finally made the purchase, and thereafter on rainy days or after dark the two younger boys were allowed to travel on the bullock-drawn cart sitting on the carefully wrapped rush mats.

Taking advantage of their additional transport, Kiyotsugu had some bamboos cut and three shapely young pine trees dug up from the roadside and planted in wooden tubs. Thereafter, whenever he performed outdoors he had both the rush-matted acting area and the area where the musicians and the chorus sat delimited by hempen cords tied to tall bamboo corner pillars. He also had the three pine trees placed in a straight line, either at a right angle or diagonal to the stage, to suggest an entrance bridge.

It was a pathetic imitation of the great Kofuku stage, but Kiyotsugu was immensely pleased and proud of his world within a world, and when the rainy month of June obliged the troupe to take refuge in a large deserted temple in his native province of Iga, which they shared with other roaming groups of entertainers and peddlers who came and went, he had the leaky roof temporarily repaired and set up what he called his Kofuku stage to rehearse the new plays he had written on the road.

Hearing from a couple of *sumō* wrestlers where the Kanze were sheltering from the monsoon, Omina and her *kusé* troupe made a detour, as Omina archly put it, "to worship Master Kanze's Kofuku stage complete with pines and bamboo corner pillars." He showed her the bullocks and the cart and the floor mats, zealously kept clean and frequently mended and aired. Omina responded heartily to Kiyotsugu's childlike enthusiasm for all his new equipment, and when he suggested to her that she step onto his stage and dance, she slapped her chest, blushing and blinking incredulously.

"What, me on your Kofuku stage? Me, a *kusé mai-mai*?"*

The entire Kanze troupe shouted their approval.

"Well!" Omina laughed, showing her good large teeth. She quickly dusted her feet with the ends of her sleeves and jumped onto the rush-matted stage. Old Meisho, who confessed that somehow wine went to his head faster in Omina's presence, picked up his flute and played in concert with Omina's girl musicians. Afterward, Kiyotsugu and his elders performed one of his latest plays, *Motomezuka,* inspired by Himi's exquisite mask which, although said to have been carved in memory of his dead mother, looked uncannily like Tamana. Behind this mask Kiyotsugu played the woman who, loved by two men and not knowing which to choose, kills herself; by the time the performance was over, every *kusé* dancing girl was drowned in tears as if it were her own tragic romance that had been told. That evening, Omina drank a little too much and wept as she repeated:

"Kiyotsugu-dono, with such a play in your repertory, why despair, why fret? After the rains you'll surely be in the capital!"

Rains stopped at last; fields began blazing with wild poppies, and nights became brighter with uncountable fireflies.

"If only I had the talent to laze," sighed Omina as she put on her leg covers against the dust and mud of the road, "I'd live happily ever after in a place like this, eating what's there in the field and sewing by the light of fireflies."

"But it won't always be early summer, and you'd be bored to death if you weren't ceaselessly on the move and dancing," said Kiyotsugu, staring at Omina's large traveling hat which he held in his hands.

"True," said Omina, laughing. "Born poor and a nothing, all my life I'm being harassed by obligations of gratitude to others. If I said, 'Right, sir, I'll come back here and dance on your ancestors' day,' I'd get there if it killed me. In my next life perhaps Buddha will make me rich and ungrateful."

---

* A derogatory term for a dancer.

After her noisy departure with her girls, which plunged every-one—adults and children alike—into despondency, Kiyotsugu gathered his elders aside and in a low whisper discussed their future plans. Having hovered around the capital's gates for months with what seemed indisputable success at performance after performance, they had not received a single inquiry, let alone an invitation, from any of the shrines or temples or great houses of the capital.

Kiyotsugu wanted to barge boldly into the Kyoto suburbs, but the elders persuaded their impatient master to push on to the cooler heights above Lake Biwa and to arrive in time for the two-day festival at a shrine famous for protecting travelers from danger on land and sea; for unlike the cold-shouldering capital, the shrine's official in charge of the festival had let it be known through an Iga post-horse keeper, who had long been a committed fan of Kiyotsugu, that the Kanze troupe would be welcome to share the shrine's stage with a local sarugaku troupe long in service to the shrine but lamentably substandard in recent years.

On the morning after their arrival, while Fujiwaka was being rehearsed by his father on the raised stage, Kogame, as was his habit, went reconnoitering, and as soon as Fujiwaka's rehearsal was over, he grabbed him by the wrist and began pulling him.

"Come, Fuji-chan, there's a monster. If we go now, the man said he'd let us watch it for nothing."

The word "monster" and the corresponding expression on Kogame's face promised something quite horrific. Fujiwaka sped after his friend. A soiled, mildewy tent not much taller than Fujiwaka was pitched on the ground, with a painted board hung over its low entrance:

THE SLUG MAIDEN, NATURE'S UNFORGETTABLE FLUKE
HIDEOUSER THAN THIS YOU'LL FIND NOWHERE ELSE!

Next to this tent, three young girls dressed in goddesslike flowing robes, two juggling painted balls and one holding a lighted lamp, were walking tightropes in their high-heeled wooden sandals.

"Don't go in there; it's rubbish. Stay here, rich boys!" yelled the girl with the lamp, her small pale face rigid from concentrating so much on her feet on the tightrope.

Kogame stuck out his tongue at the girl and clasping Fuji-waka's hand tighter, pulled him into the monster's tent.

Inside, it was suffocatingly heavy, dark and stinking of cheap wine.

"Wait in the corner till some paying customers turn up," a gruff voice said with a heavy northern accent.

In the light spreading from the slim triangular opening in the tent Fujiwaka saw a round wooden tub crudely painted in red and white stripes with two small wheels attached to its bottom. He could see that the tub was not empty, but could not discern exactly what sort of monster lurked inside it. The ripe red nose of the man who sat next to the tub, on the other hand, was quite visible, and as Fujiwaka's eyes grew used to the darkness, he saw a flabby middle-aged man with wispy dirty hair hanging from somewhere unidentifiable on his balding head. He had the coarse, weak face of a drunkard and seemed to be suffering an acute hang-over. Waiting for a customer to arrive, the man began asking the sarugaku children questions about the various tolls and controls they had passed, about the rumors of highwaymen and slavers, and about the comparative affluence of the towns the troupe had played in. The boys replied in childish blunt monosyllables, as their en-tire attention was riveted on the mound inside the tub.

Finally, when two travelers, bending low over their canes, entered the tent and without complaint paid up to see the Slug Maiden, Fujiwaka and Kogame sat up, their eyes gleaming with anticipatory horror.

The man lit one mean oil lamp and, taking out a bamboo flute from his dirty sleeves, blew a melancholy, seductive strain on it. Tiny white hands came out of the mound and with undulating, unhurried movements stroked the earth.

The tub rolled forward and arrived within the low light of the lamp. The mound trembled a little, and out of it grew up-ward two pieces of flesh that looked like a pair of chewed-off tallow candles. The tiny hands kept pushing the earth, and the tub turned round and round with those disgustingly undefined lumps of flesh standing upright, till suddenly they leaped out of the tub and after two somersaults landed on the ground. They were trun-cated thighs, and above them sat an abnormally short torso topped with a small girl's head, with the hair and the eyebrows shaved off. Her eyes were not just shut, they were shut in that obliterating, cruel way which was immediately recognizable as sightless. Standing at full height, she could not have come up to Fujiwaka's waist. Her face was normal, it could have been said even regular-featured, but with her head and brows shaven, her eyes wiped out by blindness and clad in a bizarre costume of tight-fitting flesh-colored vest with a sort of man's loincloth to show off her chopped thighs, the wretched creature could not have appeared more grotesque and obscene.

When she began singing in a piercing, randy-cat voice and made some pathetic attempts at dancing, now standing on her stumps, now upside down on her hands, Fujiwaka nudged Kogame. With a nod to each other, they sneaked out of the tent.

Once outside, they gasped out the fetid damp of the monster's den and avidly gulped in the midday heat, their eyes watering at the blazing light on the white of the gravel. Without speaking to or looking at each other, they ran as fast as they could back to their elders. Fujiwaka felt he had swallowed a bellyful of poison-ous filth; that the Slug Maiden was a professional entertainer just as his great father was, the former exploiting her raw physical de-formity, the latter his acquired art, frightened and deeply humil-iated him.

"It is indeed a Terminal World we live in!" Fujiwaka imi-tated Ogame's cliché and felt a little better, but remained cheer-less and without appetite all day. At the performance later in the day, he played with such ardor that Kiyotsugu whispered to his son during their first exit together, "Watch out, Fujiwaka—it's a raised stage today. If you fly off, Ogame won't be there to catch you."

After two days of exceptionally encouraging response and good business, the Kanze troupe began packing, and as they were to leave at the crack of dawn the next day, Ogame told the two children to wash themselves in the stream as soon as they finished eating their gruel. Kogame, however, tired and lazy, fell asleep by the fire with the chopsticks and empty bowl on his lap. Fujiwaka, taking Kogame's bowl and chopsticks as well as his own, went alone to where the spring water burbled out from the chilly over-grown hillside and formed a shallow pond before narrowing into streams which ran down to the shrine grounds. He washed the bowls and chopsticks, then scrubbed himself with a worn loofah and filled his gourd with water, ready for the next day's journey.

Only after he had finished dressing and cleansed his mouth did he recognize the tub with two small wooden wheels, half-hidden behind a cedar tree.

Fujiwaka jumped back a step and felt icicles of fear stand on his head.

"Beautiful boy," came a soft voice. Tiny hands patted the ground, and the tub rolled forth. To Fujiwaka's immense relief, the Slug Maiden had her head wrapped in the manner of a nun, and a grimy loose jacket covered her flesh-colored vest and part of her torn thighs. With startling accuracy, the blind girl swerved the tub toward Fujiwaka and stopped only a few steps from where he stood petrified.

"Beautiful boy," she said again in a voice so different from that demented animal shriek Fujiwaka had heard the day before. "Don't be frightened. Look at me; what could I do to hurt you? I am only thirteen or fourteen. You are very beautiful, very special: I know; I can tell."

"How? You can't see!" Fear made Fujiwaka yell aggressively.

"I can tell how lovely you are by the way people speak to you. Even Father, that drunkard you saw, had a strange way of changing his voice with you. The other boy isn't special. You are!"

"You have such a nice voice and a funny northern accent that make me want to listen to you, so why did you have to sing like that? I hated it. It was dreadful!"

Fujiwaka was surprised that he could and wanted to speak to the monster girl, and what was more, speak truthfully. She had that bitter authority of someone totally wretched and beyond remedy or hope. He somehow felt he would be ashamed of himself, would feel himself a coward, if he did not speak the truth to the freak.

"For a living, little boy," she laughed, her colorless chapped lips showing bad teeth. "What we do for a living, eh?"

"When you laugh like that you don't look like a slug, and I'm not scared of you." Fujiwaka squatted before her tub, put down the bowls and chopsticks, and looked at her small, pale, young—indeed, very young—face which reminded him of a mask before it was painted and eyeholes pierced. "I only feel like weeping for you, and for myself."

"For you too? But why? You have everything."

"Everything? And nothing. We are entertainers and depend

so much on other people. Father has been working all his life for someone important to see us and bring us to the capital."

"No one has?"

"No one. Have you been there, to Kyoto?"

"No; Father says there are already too many cripples much more horrifying and impressive than I am."

"Were you born like this?"

"No, I walked into a fox trap. One toe, two toes, then both legs rotted. So they had to cut them off. Eyes? In our village small children went blind all the time after brain fever. Nothing special. Oh, yes, before that I could see and run and skip."

She laughed, slapping affectionately at her stumps, which stretched, incompletely and incongruously, just long enough to balance her torso upright.

"You are so merry; you don't complain!" Fujiwaka exclaimed in amazement. "But why? It's ridiculous. You are a monster. You ought to be sad and angry."

"But, beautiful boy, I was. If you only knew!" She laughed again.

"You laugh!" Fujiwaka gasped, and he felt a pain at the base of his neck. He was trying hard not to cry. He had never felt so horribly sad and miserable; yet the strange thing was that at the same time he felt happy, filled with merry lightheartedness. How was he to understand or explain this? She was the hideouser-than-any monster, yet there she was, soothing him, consoling him: It's all right, beautiful boy, it's like this.

"You are ridiculous!" Fujiwaka repeated gravely.

The Slug Maiden tilted her head a little better to hear the tone of Fujiwaka's voice, then said, modestly but triumphantly, "You like me!"

Fujiwaka was not at all sure he wanted to confirm that he *liked* such a horrid monster, but it was true—he did feel such a tenderness toward the Slug as he had never experienced before.

"I want to give you this." Fujiwaka pulled out from under his clothes the talisman his mother had hung around his neck, a small bit of wood with a few holy words written on it. "From the Kasuga Shrine in Nara." He put it around the Slug Maiden's neck.

"I'll never take it off, and never forget to pray for you so that you'll get to the capital."

Again, with the urge to cry in the root of his throat, Fujiwaka remained speechless, but looked at the freak with a bright, sad smile. Yes, since endless time the blind and the crippled have been said to possess Buddha's nature in them and to receive His special favor in their next lives, for Buddha has chosen them to bear the miseries of the world during their lifetime on this earth. If *she* prayed for us, Fujiwaka thought gratefully, we might be able to get to the capital.

"It's growing dark." Fujiwaka stood up, picking up the bowls and chopsticks. "We start early tomorrow. I must go."

Clasping the talisman in both her hands, the Slug Maiden lifted her face toward Fujiwaka, and what she said startled him, as it was precisely what he was thinking of saying.

"Don't say 'See you again.' I want you to reach the capital, stay there and never beat the mud road again like me. Beautiful boy, thank you for the talisman, and good luck!"

Fujiwaka walked away and did not wave to her, as he knew she could not see. He turned back only once; she was still there in the same posture, with her face lifted, and in the gathering darkness her closed eyelids seemed to glow, two lotus blossoms.

4

SUMMER WAS breaking in thunderous showers. The troupe had been traveling for four months, and the fact that their success on the road had singularly failed to coax even one invitation from the capital made the usual wear-and-tear fatigue of the mud road all the more insupportable. Kiyotsugu began glumly contemplating that there would be no excuse for not returning to Yuzaki village for the harvest-season obligations at his patron temple and shrine.

Had I hoped for too much? Too high, too soon? Was I mistaken in believing that I had created something truly new, exciting and worthy?

Kiyotsugu was a fighter, an optimist, aggressively confident of his talent; therefore, all the more intense was the dejection he had to suffer. Watching his father, Fujiwaka felt his own little shoulders shrivel. Since his night duty at the Jozen Monastery, he had intuitively begun to understand what it was like to have a Way: that uncanny feeling of someone holding his hand and leading him in the dark; that compulsive sense of mission which could make him insensible to many of the sordid miseries of this world. Had he been an ordinary boy, without the discipline of the lessons and the Master to return to, he would have drowned himself in the pond behind the monastery, as several boys had already done. In his childishly simplistic but obsessive manner, he believed that the Way of his art would eventually take him to the capital and that once there, he would never have to return to night duty at the Jozen Monastery. What, therefore, he felt for his father, seeing him crumble in humiliation, was not mere sympathy or commiseration: no, it was far more personal and desperate, an urgent cry of panic:

"If you fail now, Father, I perish too!"

Omina, who was then touring in the neighboring province of Settsu, sent Sango to repeat her message verbatim:

"I keep hearing about the tremendous success you are having. Surely, you must have received an invitation to the capital by now. Please let me know when it is to be, as I am determined to be there."

Kiyotsugu broke down at last:

"Tell Omina-dono, Sango, perhaps Kiyotsugu of Kanze didn't have it in him. . . . We shan't, I don't think, be invited to Kyoto this time. . . ."

The first typhoon that threw out summer and shoved the autumn sky-high was quickly followed by another, and on many typhoon-hit nights Kiyotsugu was obliged to lodge his troupe in a few large bare rooms at modest inns. Loath to waste hard-earned money on further fruitless roaming, Kiyotsugu finally made up his mind to take the troupe on the homeward journey.

Once decided, he moved quickly and, hurrying his men and bullocks, arrived at the Fox Deity shrine, some twenty miles outside the southern gate of Kyoto, just in time for its five-day festival, where he knew he could obtain permission to perform.

Immediately after their second performance, a jaunty plump man in his fifties, with a gleamingly shaven head like a priest's but dressed with a dapper, understated chic and carrying an elegant slim sword, appeared at the outbuilding of the shrine which served the troupe as their stage door, kitchen, dressing room and storeroom—altogether an appalling jumble of discarded footwear, clothes, braziers, cooking utensils and all the usual theatrical properties.

"My name is Nanami. Announce me to Kiyotsugu of Kanze."

Hachi hesitated for a moment, staring curiously at the incongruous combination of the visitor's sword and tonsured head, but Ippen, who was tying the strings of his straw sandals on the entrance step, jerked to his feet. He grabbed the young man's shoulder.

"Wait; stay here. I'll go and tell Master!"

In the back room, Kiyotsugu was naked except for his white loincloth, but on hearing that Nanami, one of the shogun's famous Companions-in-Arts, was at the stage door, he flew into whatever clothes were lying around him and ran out, still tying his waistband.

Nanami returned Kiyotsugu's deep bow with a mild, amused grin.

"Omina sent me a messenger. She knows that just about this time every year I come this way to visit my old protector's tomb. So I've made a detour to see what she calls Kanze's noh."

Kiyotsugu, nearly twice as tall as Nanami, dropped to the ground, his knee striking a dry hard noise against the temporary wooden flooring.

"And?"

"In fact, I was here yesterday as well."

"And?"

"Not bad," Nanami said with a teasing glint in his eyes—he who was said to enjoy the shogun's esteem and trust for his impeccable taste; born the illegitimate son of a nobleman and versed in all fields of the arts, Chinese and Japanese, poetry, music, painting, pottery and games of incense, tea and flowers; a man who set the fashion in the capital and had once created three hundred poems in a night just to keep himself awake under an exquisite full moon.

"Quite impressive what you've achieved here with your *kusé* music. I'm said to own a better pair of ears than most men and dogs, but I would never have thought of marrying sarugaku and *kusé*. That had to wait for you. In the capital, as you know, one has endured year in, year out a staple diet of dengaku, and one has become, to say the least, a little weary of it," he said in an elegant slow munching way, perfectly anticipating Kiyotsugu's response:

"Do we stand a chance, if . . . ?"

"Perhaps; but don't forget, dengaku has been the entertainment of the capital for so long, and the capital teems with the most gifted and celebrated artists who have for so long enjoyed the shogun's patronage, which they will fight by means fair and foul to retain. You can just hear the howl of protest against permitting a sarugaku troupe into Kyoto, let alone the youngest and to them the least known of the four Yamato schools. I can't promise; but I'll try.''

Trailing behind him a thick cloud of precious foreign incense, Nanami left the dressing room, and Kiyotsugu followed him down the white pebbled path out of the shrine grounds.

"Oh, I almost forgot: would you like to put to music the lyrics I've just written for Omina?'' asked Nanami as he reached his waiting palanquin.

"Nothing would please me more,'' replied Kiyotsugu.

"Good. Here they are. I'll send word to her that you've agreed to do it. She'll be pleased.'' Nanami neatly folded himself into the palanquin. "Hope we'll meet soon, Master Kanze.''

Within four days of Nanami's visit, a messenger-priest was sent from the Daigo Temple in Fushimi, a prosperous town almost next door to the capital, with an orally delivered command that the Kanze troupe offer seven performances at the temple's famous annual festival, as apparently the temple's official dengaku troupe had been found wanting in recent years.

On the morning following their arrival in Fushimi, as Kiyotsugu and the elders of his troupe, all dressed in formal dark *hakama* and *suho*, hurried their way to the Daigo Temple office to complete the formalities, passersby and apprentice priests sweeping the ground stared at Kiyotsugu, who cut an arresting figure by his exceptional height, good looks and supple carriage. The advance word of mouth on the Kanze's noh had already reached the town.

"Not at all like dengaku, I hear,'' the theater-loving suburbanites were saying. "The music, I gather, could make the crippled skip.''

"The spirit of the moment seems favorable to us here. Would that the Time of Female at last loosen its grip on us!'' said Kiyotsugu more to himself than to others.

"Don't let us forget, though, Master''—Kumazen drew his bushy brows together in a bellicose frown—"we're breathing down the back of our dengaku friends here. I've told my boys to sit in the Flat Earth and keep their eyes and ears skinned for the dengaku-paid hecklers.''

"Besides, the Fushimi audience have an unattractive reputation," Raiden added glumly. "At the slightest provocation they jeer, hiss and throw their straw seat mats or broken fans at actors."

It was no wonder that on the first day of the performance the entire company felt needles in the air they breathed. After the ritual opening work, *Okina,* in which Toyodayu, thanks to his seniority in the company, always took the title role, he whispered to Kiyotsugu as they passed each other in the dressing area. "Unnerving, Master—so quiet, narrow-eyed and testing out there."

"At least that means they're curious, intrigued. Not a bad sign," said Kiyotsugu curtly under the mask of a young maiden, and he sailed onto the entrance bridge. By the time he made an exit for a quick change of costume in the middle of the play, he had the audience—from the young mother in the Flat Earth with a baby strapped dangling on her back to the high clergy and the town's dignitaries in their loges—like a ripe berry in the hollow of his hand.

Later, when the five-colored curtain swayed open to reveal Fujiwaka's doll-like figure, there was a hush of incredulity. As he slowly slid onto the stage to dance, sing and speak with such immense dignity, presence and skill, a long guttural exclamation issued from the entire audience.

At the close of the first day, thunderous applause fell on the stage. "I don't care if it's not dengaku. I loved it!" summed up the general attitude of the people who would normally despise anything not originating from the capital.

Early next morning, deaf to the unmistakable hum of success in the air, Kiyotsugu was seen putting his troupe through an even harsher drill than usual. He forbade Hachi to open the barrel of wine that had been sent in with the compliments of the silk merchants' guild.

"We have nothing to celebrate, not yet. Besides, who knows it isn't from our dengaku friends, that barrel? So far, so good, but don't forget it is Kyoto we have to conquer, not Fushimi. Now, once more, go on!"

It was on the fifth day that Hachi reported to Kiyotsugu: "I'm sure they are the dengaku lot, scented and dressed silk on silk. And the one with his head shaven, more like a lecherous hermit, with a gold-splattered tea caddy hanging from his sash, must be the famous Companion-in-Arts Kiami."

Kiyotsugu, hearing this, let out a delighted short chuckle—

the first time he had shown any mirth on this tour. But he added sternly: "If they think our work is any good or too popular with the audience, they'll cause trouble for us. Think how easy for them to bribe the stagehands employed directly by the temple. Before every performance check the stage floor and look out for rusted nails and patches of wax. Trust no one; take nothing for granted."

On the seventh day there was not a space left in the Flat Earth even to slip a cat into, the heat of the spectators' enthusiasm matching the fluke return of summer weather in late September.

Kiyotsugu was in the middle of the *kusé* dance, with the chorus and musicians in concerted crescendo, when a shrill scream tore through the warm evening:

"Fire! Fire!"

By the time Kiyotsugu had his mask removed by Kumazen directly on the stage, the flames were visible, climbing from beneath the wooden scaffolding at the extreme end of the fan-shaped loges. The intense red waves of fire moved fast, but were still confined to a small area. The priests on guard duty pounced on the fire and, despite the panic-stricken chaos amongst the audience, proceeded to extinguish the fire with laudable efficiency.

The whole troupe stood stupefied on the stage, gazing vacantly in different directions. The smell of the burnt wood and straw stung the eyes, and young apprentice priests carrying pails of water darted to and fro like blackbirds. The crowd, who till only moments earlier had breathed in enraptured union with the stage, had rapidly disappeared. No one of the company wished to express aloud his strong suspicion, but in the back of their minds, all saw a dengaku conspiracy in dripping fresh ink. It was an age of superstition and unreasoning fear; nothing would be easier than to smear the name of the Kanze with an ill-omened fire.

Kiyotsugu turned his head, feeling a sting where the perspiration had half dried, and saw Nanami at the edge of the stage. And Omina, straw-hatted and with a large traveling pouch strapped on her back. Fujiwaka and Kogame yelled her name and rushed up to her, and she knelt and hugged both their heads inside her sleeves.

Nanami came forward and said in a soft voice, "Better not say what you're all thinking. Suspect, and be on your guard. That's enough. There are matters of far greater import on which to concentrate your minds."

Kiyotsugu held his breath.

Omina whispered to the boys, "Listen!" Her lips as they touched Fujiwaka's earlobe were hot, but the child went ice-cold all over.

"I have come today as an official messenger from the shogun's household office," Nanami said.

Everyone who was not already seated knelt down at once at the mention of the shogun, squaring his every limb and bone.

"On the seventh day of May next year at the Imakumano Shrine in Kyoto," continued Nanami, giving full value to each word, "the Kanze troupe is commanded to open the three-day subscription performance. On the first day, the shogun will grace the occasion with his august presence. The shogun's chamberlain will be informing the Kofuku Temple of this honor, and Kiyotsugu-dono, you are to send me your program and the names of your performers before the end of the year."

The significance of the shogun's Companion-in-Arts addressing himself to Kiyotsugu with the honorific *dono* was not lost on the awestruck actors, and Kiyotsugu pressed his hands on the floor covered with burnt ash and began sobbing incontrollably—a thing which his disciples had never witnessed before; and the love and proud devotion that this crying giant, this genius, their master inspired in them were like stabbing pains in their chests. Fujiwaka's heart too would have burst with insane joy, had it not been for Omina's arms which so tightly embraced it and the hot tears that rolled down from her chin to his head.

5

BACK IN Yuzaki village, hardly had Kiyotsugu shaken the journey's dust from his feet when he hurried to the Jozen Monastery.

"What? Have you quite lost your head? A sarugaku beggar
demanding to see the chief abbot?" an armed monk yelled at
Kiyotsugu, and tried to kick him in the hips.

Kiyotsugu leaped back in time and said in one fierce breath,
"Yes! Kiyotsugu of Kanze is here to see the chief abbot, Daijo, for
I think he would be interested to know that I and my troupe have
the honor to perform for the shogun in May at the Imakumano
Shrine!"

At the mention of the shogun's name, Kiyotsugu was admitted
to see the chief abbot, the untouchable performer prostrate on
the hard wooden floor of the corridor and Daijo on his dais at the
extreme north end of the room.

"True what I've just been told?" asked the gruff but nasal
voice.

"Yes, every word of it; and I have come here also to entreat
with you on behalf of my son, Fujiwaka. As a professional and colleague dedicated to the same art, I am convinced beyond any

doubt that the boy is a material blessed with Buddha's as yet unknown miracles, which, I hope—with your most essential help—
the capital will be able to discover when he performs beside me
for the shogun next May. One day he will bring honor and renown to the name of the Kofuku Temple. As you were the first
to recognize an exceptional quality in him, I embolden myself, as
his father and teacher, and beseech you, please, with Buddha's
infinite mercy, to release him from the night service and let him
devote himself entirely to his art and art alone."

Kiyotsugu's breath, soughing against the floorboards, echoed
all the humiliation, despair and supplication of the father whose
boy had to be served up like sweetmeats to quell the carnal hunger wrapped in priestly robes.

"Have I heard you correctly, master of a beggars' circus?"
Daijo's voice drawled incredulously.

"Yes, and for good!"

Above Kiyotsugu's prostrate head the silence was deep as
Daijo absorbed both the flattery and the insinuation contained in
Kiyotsugu's speech—and not least the implacable determination
he detected in the sarugaku entertainer's voice.

"I see no blasted reason why I should," grumbled Daijo.

"Of course you have no reason to. You have all the right and
all the overwhelming power and means in your sole hand to *not*
release Fujiwaka. The easiest, the most natural answer for you to
make is 'No.' That is why I beseech you to resist it! Have pity on
a father and a son whose only strength is that they are so abjectly
powerless."

Kiyotsugu had an uncanny intuition that his arrow had not
landed in a void.

"Lift your face," ordered Daijo. Kiyotsugu not only lifted
his face but raised his eyes so defiantly that he felt his upper eyelids dig into his brows. Daijo was even more hideous than had
been rumored, a mass of indolent, hedonist flesh, from which a
pair of intelligent hard eyes gleamed. The two men stared at each
other.

"Hmm—I often wondered from what sort of loins the kid
had sprung. Couldn't believe his being just a riverbank beggar's
son. I won't give you away: tell me, are you a samurai deserter
turned entertainer, eh?"

"No, an orphan brought up by entertainers."

"Hmm." Unconvinced, Daijo licked his fleshy, pendulous lower lip; then across his ugly face flitted a warped, almost friendly smile. "When all seems lost and death is hanging on one's nose tip, one throws oneself on the enemy. Sometimes the power of desperation can prove stronger than fate or sword. The case in point is what you've just done to me. If we were fighting with steel-bladed swords, I'd be lying at your feet bleeding."

Daijo suddenly jangled his strings of beads with violence.

"So be it. Your son gave me his first flower and served me well. All changes, all passes; one mustn't cling to anything in this life. I grant him my permission to return wholly to his calling. All the best."

Daijo flicked his fingers, and his two attendants instantly shut the sliding doors, leaving Kiyotsugu to gaze at the ink painting on them of four tigers leaping out of a bamboo forest.

The triumphant father could not recall when he had last run so fast; his overeager steps tore off the straps of his straw sandals. Tamana and Ogame, who had been waiting by the roadside half-way from the house, started to their feet at the sight of Kiyotsugu flying toward them in bare feet.

"Fujiwaka is discharged! I have the chief abbot's permission!"

Tamana devoured her husband's broad grin, but still incredulous, put her palms on his gasping chest.

"Not even a night in a month? Never have to go?"

Forgetting Ogame's presence, Kiyotsugu squeezed his wife in his big impulsive embrace; but the poor woman went on asking timorously: "Never? Not again? Does this mean Fujiwaka can . . ." and when she reached home, she had to be made to lie down and drink one of her strong herbal infusions.

THAT FROM that day onward he would be allowed to do only what he loved most, what he had been born for! Fujiwaka could hardly believe such bliss to be possible or lasting. Then he thought of the Slug Maiden, her heartbreakingly cheerful voice, her strangely illuminated eyelids, and a profound gratitude filled him: for wasn't he at last reaching the capital thanks to *her* prayer? And did not there lurk, behind his father's and his own advancement, tens of thousands of unfulfilled prayers from the "floating-weed" entertainers and freaks like her? Rapturous but at the same time gnawed by a morbid fear that he too might one day degenerate into a roadside curiosity, he vowed to work harder, harder than ever before.

Every morning he woke up much too early, aching with impatience to start another day of work—only work, and no monastery duties. But sleeping as he did at his parents' feet and knowing that his father, working on his new plays for the Imakumano performance, had gone to sleep hours after anyone else in the house and that Mother would always wait up for Father, darning or pickling turnips, Fujiwaka would try very hard to go back to sleep; but no use—he could not keep his nose from itching with a tune and his toes from wriggling. He would gingerly stretch his leg till his foot touched his father's, which, Father being so tall, always stuck out of his scant cover. Listening attentively to Father's heavy, regular breathing, Fujiwaka would keep his toes ever so lightly in contact with Father's big foot; he would sigh and shut his eyes, his face wreathed in a big grin, believing that some of Father's immense genius could be transmitted to him this way.

As he slumbered again, he recalled regretfully what Mother had recently said: "You're growing up so fast, Fujiwaka, soon you'll have to sleep alone in the mask room."

Now that I *can* sleep every night at home, Fujiwaka prayed, please, Buddha, let me sleep always at Father's and Mother's feet!

All his friends were growing up too, and as fast. Toyojiro, adopted son of Toyodayu, was twelve; Hotan, five; Kogame was ten; Kumao, seventeen and Kumaya, ten. There was little discrimination separating the boys in the troupe: Fujiwaka, aside from a few privileges such as taking meals alone in his parents' room or being taught by Ogame to read and to write, had grown up in unfettered intimacy with his future subordinates. But as they began receiving adult training and going on stage, each in his different capacity—Fujiwaka, Toyojiro and Hotan as *shité* players; Kogame showing impressive talent as a comedian-dancer in kyogen, and Kumao and Kumaya being rigorously trained by their father in *waki* roles—although they remained the best of friends, the professional discrimination, unwritten and therefore all the more insidious, began putting them on different levels, making them respect one another's rank and obligation in the theater with no one actually having to tell them.

Kogame, for example, without being taught, waited on Fujiwaka at rehearsals and like a dutiful attendant looked after Fujiwaka's socks and fans after each lesson. Kumao already had the self-effacing yet dignified manners of all good *waki* players on and off stage and always let Fujiwaka, six years his junior, pass through the doorway first and never spoke to him whilst standing.

Hotan, a *shité* player, made a quaint request to Fujiwaka:

"Fuji-chan, one day when I am almost as good as you and can be made your *koken*,* will you please faint in the middle of a performance so that I can step into your part?"

"Oh, no, silly, I shan't, I tell you—I shall never faint. Not on stage!" protested Fuijwaka, whilst Kogame, Kumao and Kumaya, who in their lower-graded capacities would never be allowed to understudy a *shité* player, listened with due respect and distance.

In return, Fujiwaka perfectly naturally assumed the responsibility of his position and began teaching other boys to read and write. As every available resource then had to be spent on preparing for the Imakumano shogunal performance and paper was exorbitantly expensive, he taught them by drawing in the sand with sticks.

AFTER THE New Year, Kiyotsugu began chucking away half what he had created and even some of the work he had already begun rehearsing as well. Women sewed till their fingers bled, while children took over much of their work and Hachi walked countless miles with his master's detailed and exacting instructions to dye houses. It was Tamana who took copies of Kiyotsugu's new plays to Himi so that the crippled mask carver could understand what masks were needed for which characters. Covered with chips of hinoki wood from head to toe, Himi would beg her not even to mention the cost of his masks: "First, let us send Kiyotsugu-dono to the capital armed with the best masks I can carve. We can worry about the rest later." And he would not hear of receiving a penny toward the money he had given her to buy the rush mats.

That winter Omina did not take her troupe down the mild Inland Sea coast as in other years, but toured in and out of the Kyoto-Nara area and frequently dropped in at Yuzaki village with her faithful Sango alone in tow, having arranged for her dancing girls various performances in the city of Nara. Her visits were as

---

* A stage attendant in black costume, unmasked; always performed by someone almost equal in art and rank to the *shité* on whom he attends, as in case of emergency the *koken* must take over from the incapacitated *shité* and finish the performance.

eagerly awaited as a rare day of warm sunshine, not so much for the most reliable and up-to-date news of the capital and the many sweets for the children she brought as for the infectious joy and energy she carried with her. With her disarming bossiness she ordered Tamana to take a rest and herself stood in the kitchen preparing copious meals.

She cajoled Kiyotsugu and Tamana to share the wine she had brought with her, repeating, "Nonsense! If a man says he can't write with a bit of wine in his head, I tell you, he's no man for me. And listen, Madam, wine will do you much more good than that nasty herbal concoction of yours. I'm a slut, but *not* because I tipple; you're a lady, but *not* because you don't. Come on, let us hear your lovely giggle, eh?"

Whilst Omina was a type of drinker who turned lachrymose, Tamana with a little wine began giggling; the more she giggled, the more enchantingly and helplessly embarrassed she became and giggled even more. But Kiyotsugu always knew when to intervene and restrain Omina.

"Tamana has had all she can take. She's bewitched by you and will do anything you tell her to. Now, stop bullying her and instead show us your new work."

Omina would laugh with roguish abandon, leap to her feet and with her legendary snow-white skin glowing in the color of a sunset, dance and sing the latest work written by Nanami, composed by Kiyotsugu and choreographed—or rather, improvised—by herself. In that tiny master's room, hemmed in by trays, cushions and the folded knees of Kiyotsugu, Tamana and Fujiwaka, Omina danced as if she were an eagle with an entire sky at her command, free, wild, yet so cunningly in control.

Without quite knowing what the word meant, Fujiwaka knew he too was bewitched by Omina from the intense emotions, glad or sad, which her noisy, unpredictable arrivals and departures aroused in him. But then, everyone else seemed to be affected by Omina: Father, Mother, children, adults—even the five cats, who were kept sufficiently hungry to catch rats and mice in the house and for whom Omina made the habit of saving her fish bone. After her usually early-morning departures, everyone found the rest of the day unbearably long; Fujiwaka thought Father's whip cracked with uncalled-for irascibility, and Mother offered long prayers morning, noon and night for Omina's safe journey.

Nanami too breezed in and out of Yuzaki village, bringing

with him some rolls of beaten silk or brocade strips, sometimes money and always invaluable advice.

"Kiyotsugu-dono," began Nanami nonchalantly one day, "you have said yourself, an actor must keep his heart meek and open, have you not? Then, listen to me. I suggest that *you* play the leading role in *Okina** when you open at the Imakumano."

"What, I?" Stupefied, Kiyotsugu stared at Nanami's imperturbably smiling ruddy face. It had long been established that in *Okina* the oldest actor in the company—"the older, the nearer to the gods"—regardless of his art, should play the lead.

"If I broke our age-old tradition and played the part myself at forty-one, I'd be buried under the most damning criticism."

"Never mind what the mildewy blockheads might or might not say. If you fail to captivate the shogun's first glance at Imakumano, you'll remain forever just another village entertainer attached to the Kofuku Temple, nor will you be given another chance like this. Make no mistake, the shogun Yoshimitsu is the most enthusiastic and generous patron of all forms of art, but an awesome critic and an exacting, impatient devil of a spectator. His intolerance of anything mediocre and stale is only too painfully known to us, his Companions. I have witnessed many instances when, the entertainment having hardly begun, the Great Tree simply walked out. Unless you catch his attention from your very first entrance, you've lost him for the rest of the day, perhaps for the rest of your life. That is why I repeat that you, Kiyotsugu-dono, at the zenith of your career should play Okina." Nanami then casually added, "And what if you let Fujiwaka be your mask carrier in *Okina*, eh?"

---

* The word *okina* means "old man"—in fact, a god of longevity. *Okina* is the oldest, holiest play in both the sarugaku and the dengaku repertories, and the actor who portrays Okina must observe a strict purification regimen prior to the performance.

6

THE THIRTY-SIX crowns of the Higashi Mountains which encircled Kyoto shimmered like an emerald diadem; young green leaves shook their impatient frail fingers as if trying to reach the cloudless sky, made even brighter by the exultant singing of a myriad of birds.

From the heights of Imakumano, Fujiwaka stood on his toes and strained his eyes, but could not see the limits of the capital, which sprawled far into a blurred horizon, with innumerable temples and fire-watching towers soaring over the low ripples of baked black tiles and thatched roofs. The capital was far more immense and more wondrous than he had ever imagined.

"This morning, Father took me to bow to the stage," he had written to his mother, who for reasons of health and economy had remained in Yuzaki village. "I don't know why, but touching the most beautiful and smooth floor I had ever seen, I burst into tears. Mother, I am frightened. I have wanted so much to come here!"

No expense and trouble had been spared. The shogun was shrewd and ruthless, taking after his grandfather, Takauji, the founder of the Ashikaga shogunate; he had a cunning way of *hon-*

oring his wealthier and more powerful daimyos, men who might be a potential military threat to the shogunate, by giving them the depletingly expensive task of financing and administering charity performances. On this occasion, the proceeds were to be dedicated to renewing the roof of the Imakumano Shrine, severely damaged by a typhoon in the previous autumn, and the three-day event had been assigned to the eminent daimyo Lord Akamatsu, who, in his fertile province on the Inland Sea, had amassed a colossal fortune from farming, mining, fishing, salt and wine making and seaway trading. And certainly His Lordship would not have liked to risk offending the shogun and the ancestral gods of the Imakumano, in that order of importance, by being seen to be stinting.

"If only I could paint in colors to show you what a magnificent stage we are to perform on here. For the four corner pillars of the stage, Lord Akamatsu had more-than-a-hundred-year-old cedar trees cut down in his province and had them transported by sea and river. I cannot imagine how men brought these huge tree trunks ashore and up the steep hills!" gushed Fujiwaka in his letter to his mother. And it was not only Fujiwaka who was struck dumb by the extent of the luxury; the roof of the stage which cut the blue of the sky with thrilling precision was covered with scented hinoki bark, and all the Kanze actors stood agape at what seemed to them a shocking extravagance.

To the east and the west of the stage, temporary wood-frame buildings, hung with billowing white curtains, were constructed for the festival officials and the actors; and the passage connecting the dressing area to the entrance bridge of the stage was screened with a rich purple silk with the Akamatsu crest painted in silver. Immaculately white and fine gravel encircled the stage. Painstakingly raked in a swirling wave pattern, the gravel gave the impression of a pure stream separating the stage from the Flat Earth, where there jostled from the early hours of the day of the performance the theater-loving townspeople and low-ranking samurais and monks who could not afford the expensive seats in the loges.

"Look there, little master—those on the Flat Earth, they can be a terror!" whispered Hachi, squashing his face into the narrow gap between the curtain and the entrance-bridge pillar. "And quite right they should be hard to please, for an honest carpenter or a fan maker would have to pay two whole days' wages for a space just large enough to wedge his bottom in. And on the left of the shogun's loge, see the one kept empty? That's the loge reserved for gods, the guests of this festival."

"Hachi! Haven't you gone for the salt yet? And you, little master, no time for gawking at the audience—hurry, hurry, you must get sewn up." Ogame, already in the costume for *Okina,* with cranes and pines, symbols of longevity, painted on it, hustled Fujiwaka back to the dressing area. In the center of the frenetic but curiously hushed coming and going stood Kiyotsugu, majestic in an ornate brocade robe with copious square sleeves over a massive *hakama* divided skirt. After the seven-day abstinence that had been required of him in order to play the sacred role of Okina, he looked gaunt, with the strings of his tall lacquered hat biting tightly into his cheeks, and his eyes stared from deeper inside his skull.

Omina was kneeling before him with the sleeves of her kimono tucked up unceremoniously with a well-worn crepe string, several threaded needles stuck in her collar and a pair of scissors shoved inside her obi. Tamana had entreated with Omina to accompany the troupe to Kyoto: "You know the people, the streets and the way of the capital. Your presence would be much more valuable than mine. It's costly to feed a useless mouth in the capital, and in any case I don't know if I could withstand the strain of the journey."

Omina dexterously sewed up the folds of Kiyotsugu's outergarment so that the line of his costume would not slacken during the performance. Pressing her forehead into Kiyotsugu's abdomen, she cut the thread between her sharp teeth; then, sliding back a few yards, she scrutinized Kiyotsugu's appearance with an intent grimace as she narrowed her myopic eyes. With a satisfied big grin she nodded to Kiyotsugu and turned her attention to Fujiwaka. She scratched her scalp with the needle a few times to grease its point, then with an unexpected force gripped Fujiwaka's collar and plunged the needle into the stiff layer of silk. Fujiwaka was shutting his eyes in reaction to the potent exotic scent Omina wore, when she halted her needle and whispered, "Listen—a hush in the Flat Earth. The nobles and daimyos have started arriving!"

The Kanze troupe, who had never played before such an exalted public, held their breath; some began muttering prayers in front of the small altar that traveled everywhere with the troupe.

First swaggered in daimyos in order of rank within the sho-

gunate hierarchy, brazenly showing off their favorites clad in sumptuous garments. The multicolored splendor of their attire against
the red rugs and tiger skins that adorned the privileged loges drew
sighs from the Flat Earth.

Following the warlords, in filed a row of pale moons, the
shaven heads of the prelates of the capital's great temples and
monasteries; then, as the people down below swayed to right and
to left, rolling on their chafed knees, to have a better look, the noblemen, referred to in common parlance as "those who live above
the clouds," emerged and took a long time to settle down, for
court etiquette dictated the most cumbersome procedures and order of precedence even when they were outside the Ninefold Forbidden Enclosure as guests of the shogun, whom they privately derided as "that jumped-up bandit."

Hachi rushed into the dressing area, rattling the floorboards
under his overvehement tread.

"The shogun has arrived!"

Kiyotsugu nodded to Toyodayu, who had the honor today of
acting as the master's *koken* attendant. Toyodayu went up to the
altar, with a solemn bow took down a wine urn, lacquered cups
and rice and brought them over to Kiyotsugu, who drank wine
and put a few grains of uncooked rice on his lips. Toyodayu then
sprinkled a handful of salt over his master to purify him. Whilst
the other performers in the play were given the same ritual, Kiyotsugu looked for Fujiwaka, and when their eyes met, the father
with a nod shut his eyes. The son felt calmer at once.

Four musicians and Toyodayu walked onto the entrance
bridge; then the chorus, led by Raiden, entered the stage and
took up their position. Each time the five-colored silk curtain was
hauled up by two young disciples at the entrance bridge, a vapor
of massive expectation gushed into the dressing area.

Finally came the turn for the actors' entrance. Fujiwaka, as a
mask carrier and herald, called poetically "one who removes the
dew from the path," went on first. As he took his first step onto
the bridge under the fluttering silk curtain, the spectators, incredulous, leaned forward, narrowing their eyes at the apparition of
such uncanny beauty. Fujiwaka was not tall and did not promise
to grow to his father's stature, but the proportions of his slim, supple body, the way he held himself and let his long slanted eyes lead
the inclination of his head could turn the viewers' saliva into

honey. Till the stir of excitement both in the loges and on the Flat Earth subsided, Fujiwaka, with a sangfroid rare for someone so young, stood his ground with utter immobility, then unhurriedly slid forward.

When, following the miniature enchantment of Fujiwaka, Kiyotsugu entered, his soaring carriage and haughty head making his unusual height appear even more impressive, the audience gasped again. Kiyotsugu, gauging the buoyant, welcoming spirit of the audience, slid serenely to the center of the stage, where he put on the mask offered to him by Fujiwaka and danced, as noble and gigantic as an old oak tree, the dance which despite the absence of a spectacular show of gymnastics had been said to shorten the performer's life with its demand on his utter concentration and control. Kiyotsugu did not play the old-man god with wobbly knees and quivering voice. "Heart serene and eyes misty but seeing far" was how he interpreted his Okina. His innate glamour and virility, suppressed under the iron grip of discipline, made the austere ritual dance much more moving and a far better entertainment. The spectators who had seen it danced countless times before by desiccated old men could not believe it was the same dance. After Kiyotsugu's exit, Ogame, with his inimitable good humor, danced the finale, shaking bells, scattering seeds, praying for a bountiful crop.

Even before the stage had emptied, the enthralled audience on the Flat Earth burst into loud clapping, yelling, "Kanze! Kanze!"

"Is the shogun still in his loge?" asked Fujiwaka, the moment Kumao fell on him to remove his costume and hat.

"He is. He took one drink but didn't return the cup for more till *Okina* was over. He *is* still here!"

The first day's program offered three noh plays and two kyogen farces. In the second noh, *Jinen Koji,* Kiyotsugu played the title role of an apprentice Zen preacher in a mask with boyish forelocks, and nobody could have believed that he was not a youth of sixteen. His dramatic repartee in the colloquial language of the day with the slave trader, played to exuberant perfection by Ogame, spellbound the audience. Fujiwaka, unmasked by license of his youth, played the part of a little orphan girl with an enchanting little wig. With only a few spoken lines, he managed to convey so much of the pathos of the poor child who sold herself in order to pay for the prayer for her dead parents' wandering souls that even the warriors, by then half tipsy, dropped their cups to applaud him, whilst the ladies of the shogun's entourage, forgetting their normal decorum, slid forward to have a better look at the child actor.

The kyogen divertissement, thought up by Ogame, with Kogame as an indestructible and ubiquitous mushroom and Ogame himself as a frantic and despairing monk, threw the audience into a fit of hilarious mirth. "How out of place that your kyogen comic should read and write," other sarugaku masters had often derided Kiyotsugu, for kyogens, considered unworthy to be written down, had always been simply transmitted orally from generation to generation; but Kiyotsugu had always defended Ogame by saying, "You can't make good people laugh without intelligence; besides, I don't want just vulgar horselaughs to precede or follow my noh plays." Kiyotsugu and Ogame were both amply rewarded, for the capital's connoisseurs were quick to appreciate the tasteful juxtaposition of the noh plays with the more disciplined yet still excruciatingly funny kyogens which made up the day's program.

As soon as his mask was removed after the last play of the day, Kiyotsugu stole a quick glance through the side of the five-colored curtain and looked out at the shogun's loge. It was empty. He felt his heavy perspiration turn to ice all over him.

Nothing was certain or likely to turn out as expected in his profession, which depended so entirely on chance and the whims of spectators, but during the day there had lurked even in his severely critical mind a timorous hope for a word of appreciation or encouragement from the shogun. . . .

The hubbub of the audience was quickly receding. Kiyotsugu licked his parched lips, and an arrid disappointment spread to the end of his nerve.

"Kiyotsugu-dono." Omina was behind him, her hair straying in the evening breeze over her flushed cheeks. "If you heard what I did on the Flat Earth, you wouldn't be standing here looking like a storm-tossed scarecrow. The love of people lasts longer than the fickle fancy of shoguns, believe me."

"I don't want to sound arrogant or ungrateful," Kiyotsugu said, "but you know as well as I do, I haven't come here looking for an ovation from the Flat Earth. I have enjoyed that elsewhere. . . . Couldn't you find out from Nanami-dono what the shogun really thought of us?"

Omina nodded and hurried off, with Sango in tow holding

his mistress' sandals. But only a few minutes later, a samurai from the daimyo Akamatsu's festival office arrived at the dressing room.

"Kiyotsugu of Kanze, on your knees and listen! Contrary to the original command, you are hereby ordered to perform tomorrow as well."

"Is this change of program by the express wish of the shogun himself, or—"

"I'm not here to answer questions. I suggest you keep your head lower and do what you are told."

On the second day, the shogun arrived with a larger entourage which, Hachi heard from a priest in charge of catering, included a number of high-ranking noblemen from whom the shogun was learning court-style poetry and music. Also conspicuously present was Lady Takahashi, formerly a Kyoto courtesan, whose beauty, *biwa* playing and tact were immortalized by poets and pamphleteers and painters: a true professional of love, who, although more than ten years senior to the shogun, had retained his favor longer than any other woman. The shogun, wrapped in an aloof silence, watched the day's offering, drank moderately and again ignoring the audience's even wilder show of appreciation, left swiftly at the close of the last play.

Kiyotsugu waited, and the same samurai came again.

"You are to play tomorrow, the last day, as well."

Dengaku troupes, originally scheduled for the second and the third days, packed their luggage and declared they could not make head or tail of the shogun's eccentric behavior, but gratefully accepted the generous compensation payment in rice and wine from the shogun's own treasury. By then, the whole of Kyoto was buzzing with curiosity: "If the Great Tree didn't like what he saw, he wouldn't have commanded the Kanze's noh three days running. Must find out for ourselves what they have that so pleases him!"

At the end of the last day's program, during which the Kanze troupe had been instructed by Lord Akamatsu to give *Jinen Koji* for the second time, the shogun did not rise to leave his loge. The Kyotoites were sophisticated enough to also remain seated. They waited and were duly rewarded, for the shogun did indeed summon the Kanze father and son to his loge.

In the incandescent hush that fell over the thousand-strong audience, Fujiwaka could hear his blood thumping against his eardrums as he solemnly lowered his forehead onto the soft red rug imbued with an incense of a quality he had never known before.

"Kiyotsugu of Yuzaki village," a voice pronounced, neither aloof nor intimate, rich with the confident resonance of someone who knew his every utterance was of public interest and importance, "you have amused me well for three days, and frankly, I could have come again willingly."

As Kiyotsugu bowed to the floor with a sibilant indrawn breath, Fujiwaka could not resist lifting his eyes for a second to steal a glimpse of the shogun. He was astonished to find before him a young man—so young, hardly a grown man. Of stern but handsome features and erect as if he had an arrow across his broad shoulders, he was very much a prince of warriors, emanating the power, danger and fascination of his supreme position. Frightened, Fujiwaka dived his head toward the fragrant red rug again.

Lady Takahashi slid down and poured some wine for the shogun. Throwing back his head, he drank up his cup and wrinkled a forehead that had suffered neither embarrassment nor constraint in all his life. He returned the red-lacquered cup to Lady Takahashi with careless speed, sprinkling a few drops of wine on her sleeve.

"Give a cup to the master," he said impatiently, with a slight but noticeable tic running down the left side of his sleek, regular face. With the habit of someone who is seldom not surrounded by a crowd of people, he began his speech by first calling out the name of the person to whom he wished to address himself.

"Kiyotsugu, you're clearly not one to follow the same old rut year in, year out, nor to sit idly by watching other schools prosper. Take this new music: Nanami has told me that you have been through hell to compose it. In my opinion it was worth three, four hells: I have seldom been so enthralled. As Nanami can testify, I don't give praise easily."

In the same bright, impatient tone he continued:

"I'll grant you a retainer worth four hundred koku in rice* a year and a house in the capital, and I'll make you a Companion-in-Arts.

"In your new position, how would you like to name yourself? I have a suggestion. Why not take 'Kan' of Kanze and call yourself Kan-ami? About all the practical details, consult Nanami."

Without taking the slightest notice of the shock and the resultant commotion his series of rapid decisions had produced in

---

* A *koku* of rice in the Middle Ages weighed approximately 265 pounds.

tiptoeing foot just as it was reaching the screens of state that separated the shogun's private room from the antechamber. With no
show of surprise, as if it had been choreographed, the player child
made a high-step jump and alighted on the other side of Yoshimitsu's clumsily outstretched leg, fell lightly on his knee and
bowed, his face flushed to the color of a peach freshly off a branch.

"I only wanted the Great Tree to sleep on."

Yoshimitsu collapsed in a gale of laughter and rolled back on
the chilly wooden floor to the foot of his sleep dais, his gossamer
night kimono trailing behind him in a tousled scatter, hardly any
part of his body under its cover. Moonlight had lost its edge
through the mist: maples and pines cast gently blurred shadows on
the paper screens.

"Sleep on? Idiot! I've been taught to sleep with my ears wide
awake for assassins. I heard your eyelashes flap open. How dare
you desert me this early?"

"I mustn't . . ." Fujiwaka raised his pleading huge eyes.
"Now that we have settled into a new house, I mustn't neglect my
daily lesson."

"Dance and song and drums—I know." Yoshimitsu rolled
back at a wind-causing speed and, bumping against Fujiwaka,
caught the boy's slim hips in his dark hard right arm, which he
boasted was two inches longer than his left arm thanks to his archery training. "Think of another excuse for a change! At this very
moment my famished, footsore, sleepless army is advancing north
to raze to the ground a castle my uncle built, to murder my cousins
I played with as children, to burn alive brave samurais, horses,
women and children, and you dare leave me to scurry back for a
few more dancing steps. A shogun never sleeps alone."

"The Great Tree knows as well as I do that it was Buddha's
design that I was born into this Way; it would not be right for me
to neglect it or abandon it. Father says I must stake my life on each
step I learn as a good samurai would on his sword." Fujiwaka said
this much with great feeling; then, looking embarrassed, he bit his
lip, which Yoshimitsu found irresistibly charming.

"Precocious imp! Has Kanami told you to bring out the
name of Buddha every time I make your life difficult?" He tickled
Fujiwaka under the arm and across his delicate ribs. Conscious as
always of a shogun's personal watch lurking immediately behind a
screen, Fujiwaka endured it, writhing and panting but silent.

"Please don't think ill of my father. He is anxious not to be found unworthy of your patronage. When we were nobody, he tells us, we did our best, folded our fans, went home and slept well, but now he wants us to do more than our best. That is why he's become more severe and demanding with us."

"I can see he has." Yoshimitsu touched Fujiwaka's upper arm where Kanami's grip of violent impatience had left two large bruises, still vividly red like squashed berries.

"Your father is a genius, but a kettle that boils over too quickly. No doubt he is incensed at the sly titter spread about by the dengaku clique that he's been promoted to a Companion thanks entirely to the pretty face of his son. He should rise above such slanders and stop lashing out at an innocent victim such as myself."

Fujiwaka smiled, and over his blushing cheeks and shyly downcast eyelids Yoshimitsu was tempted to believe he had seen a peony open its petals one by one. He sat up and searched the boy with a grave long gaze. An enchantingly beautiful creature, no question about that, he thought. If he were only that and nothing else, things would be simpler: I'd enjoy him as all men do a fragrant young boy; then when his voice changed I'd act his "father" and cut his hair at the ceremony of manhood, release him from the service of the night, find him a wife—perhaps one of my hand-soiled mistresses or a daughter of a rich Kyoto merchant. Neat. No fuss. But, this one, a sarugaku outcast . . .

How many months or seasons ago was it now? Seems an eternity, reflected Yoshimitsu. After the Imakumano performance when he had first brought Fujiwaka back to his palace, he had had the boy scrubbed in steam with a pad of rice bran, rinsed in countless pails of hot water. Then, when he was left alone with the boy, he had bluntly ordered him: "Take everything off. Show me if you are indeed like any of us. I've never known the likes of you, a sarugaku child."

Unbelievable now. Yoshimitsu went on gazing at Fujiwaka, who sat there with the perfect poise and natural dignity of a Chinese cat. Then he placed his large-boned hand on the nape of Fujiwaka's bare back. As always, his own flesh felt warmer against Fujiwaka's. He adored the moon-cold crispness of the boy's skin and was at once reminded of many ecstasies he had savored against this skin. A fresh passion cut him deep.

Yes, the boy was superb in love, infinitely light and pliable, so gentle, patient and selfless that he almost made you unconscious of your own weight as you soared from one height of paradise to another, yet so tough, so unbreakable, the child endured and yielded like a warrior determined to die. The young shogun, although brought up in the fastidiously aristocratized and demurely decadent cocoon of Kyoto, knew in his bones he was a samurai of the eastern land where mounted warriors rode bareback and windblown into and out of the cold sea and dense forests. As a man of war, he was moved more deeply by male sexuality, which, to his mind, seemed always to evoke a voluptuous imminence of death.

"The night before a battle that is certain to end with my head hoisted on an enemy's spear, I'd ask for nothing else but you and strong wine," he often told Fujiwaka.

What could be nobler and more magnanimous than the willing subjugation of one to the other of equal sex and strength or the enduring of the unnatural pain for the pleasure so reckless and sublimating? And in the aftermath, what could a man talk about with a woman, delectable enough in her incomprehensible anatomy and indispensable as she might be in securing the continuity of the house?

Women Yoshimitsu visited in their boudoirs, seldom stayed the whole night with them but returned to his room and slept soundly alone, whereas he generally kept Fujiwaka till his morning toilet and gave him the coveted duty of holding up the ends of his sleeves as he bent forward to wash his face in the gold-inlaid lacquered basin.

In the child entertainer not only did the young tyrant find innate intelligence and strength of character equal to his own, but an exquisite raw material which afforded him the pleasure of educating and molding it to suit his own taste. After a long day in the enervating heat of summer peculiar to the Kyoto basin directing the shogunal administration, or a winter day spent in a deer hunt, Yoshimitsu frequently dismissed everyone except Fujiwaka. With the boy lying supine by his side, Yoshimitsu would talk about his childhood fraught with tribal strifes and treacheries and about his sincere affection for his chancellor, Hosokawa, confidences he had not shared even with his longest-lasting paramour, Lady Takahashi.

Yoshimitsu had been four when in a bitterly cold December

the Southern Court had conspired with the disaffected elements
within the shogunate and made a lightning attack on the capital.
As Kyoto burned, his father, the then shogun, had fled northeast
with the Northern Emperor, whilst his only surviving son, Yoshimitsu, was smuggled out of the besieged capital, hidden inside a
charcoal basket. Seven months later when the shogun's most able
daimyo, Hosokawa, had managed to drive the Southern army back
into the Yoshino Mountains and regain the capital, the shogun
had sent for his son at once.

On his way back to the capital, the child was so taken by the
beauty of the Biwa Hills on the Inland Sea that he had ordered
the escorting samurais: "I like the scenery here. Dig it up and
bring it to my father's house in Kyoto."

This anecdote, probably apocryphal, was much quoted when
he came to succeed his father at the age of eleven. To a great extent
the tale expressed the popular yearning for a shogun with a sweeping broad vision, one who might bring them peace, a lasting peace,
perhaps even putting an end to the unacceptable and accursed
period of carrying two suns in one sky.

On his deathbed, the shogun had put his son's hand into that
of Hosokawa like a pearl into a rough oyster shell.

"I give you a son, Hosokawa," he had said. "Look after him";
and then, with a clinging last look at his young son: "Honor Hosokawa's advice as if it were mine."

Hosokawa, then aged thirty-nine, had intended to abandon
this fleeting world of carnage and sins at forty. Having so loyally
served both the first and the second shoguns, he had earned more
honors, wealth and power than would be good for his soul in
afterlife. But true to his samurai principles, he put aside the salvation of his own soul and vowed he would devote his remaining
years to serving the infant shogun. Ever since, the one thing in
this shifting Terminal World which Yoshimitsu had counted on as
lasting and solid was Hosokawa's total loyalty.

WHEN YOSHIMITSU reached nineteen, with all the great professors
of astrology in the land agreeing that the omens were favorable
and the direction auspicious, the chancellor persuaded his young
shogun to marry Prince Hino's daughter, seven years his senior
but impeccably connected and with a sufficient amount of imperial blood in her veins. But soon rumors were rife in the capital
that early on the very morning after the nuptials, Yoshimitsu had

been seen, one shoulder naked, practicing archery in his palace garden with Fujiwaka kneeling behind him to attend to his arrows.

There were some who ventured that Yoshimitsu slept with his wife and Fujiwaka on either side of him. The rumor was, of course, not entirely factual, but carried great conviction, as by then it was evident to anyone's eye that the young shogun quite recklessly doted on the boy actor.

"If I am as besotted with you as all the scurrilous pamphlets make out," said Yoshimitsu one night, fixing Fujiwaka's profile with his hard, penetrating stare which, many of his mighty daimyos privately confessed, sent cold shivers down their spines, "it's probably because I suspect you'll never give yourself entirely to me. You keep a larger part of yourself to yourself."

"Not to myself!" Fujiwaka protested, trying to face Yoshimitsu, but Yoshimitsu's hard grip held his neck immobile.

"All right—to your Way, your noh, your sliding steps, then! Your gluttonous submission in love, you can't fool me, is a penance and apology for your never really allowing me to come first."

Yoshimitsu turned the boy's face toward him. The boy looked at the shogun with that peculiarly unsettling gaze of a noh mask, the gaze that reflected the beholder's emotion rather than the wearer's. He waited a second for the boy to vigorously insist that of course the shogun came first in his heart as well as in body, even if it was not true. But the wretch said nothing of the sort. An entertainer, a nothing, Yoshimitsu reminded himself, but somehow he felt disconcerted, ill at ease, ridiculous: he so ruthless and wily in politics and wars, so callous with men and women who would gladly die for him. Yoshimitsu, like an agitated horse, flared his prominent Ashikaga nostrils and glared at the boy for a while before, incapable of sorting out his own confusion and thwarted pride, he savagely pressed down his hand on the boy's neck: a scythe mowing down an iris stalk. Fujiwaka fell in a spiral movement and lay on the floor with his eyes shut. Dawn was breaking, and through the latticed shutters many square patches of light like so many enlarged snowflakes fell inside the room. Guards were coughing, and their feet cracked on the fine-pebbled walk.

Yoshimitsu contemplated the boy lying like a forbidden temple, immaculate and impenetrable, and suddenly felt like crying. He threw himself over the cool flesh of the boy for no other reason than perhaps to beg for forgiveness.

8

"EVERY NIGHT I have the same dream: our house with the wattle roof, my silk cloak, a candle for my own use and my box of sweets, they suddenly disappear! I scream and scream and wake up. Till I make sure they are all still there, my heart beats so furiously that I can't breathe," Kogame, now aged twelve, confessed to Fujiwaka and Kumao and Kumaya as they sat in a row against the wall of the corridor outside the stage room, waiting their turns for rehearsal. Kumao, who hardly uttered a word nowadays as his voice was changing, tittered uncomfortably, but his younger brother, Kumaya, stared at Kogame with a look of astonishment and relief.

"You too?" cried Kumaya. "I do too. And often! When I don't do well at my lesson, Father shouts at me, 'If this is the best you can do, I'll send you back to Yuzaki village!' Then at night I dream I'm back there and those village bullies are snatching away my wooden sandals and sweet-bean buns."

"They wouldn't dare—not any longer; not now!" sibilated the greedy Kogame, who had already lost several teeth since his move to the capital from eating too many sweets, although he remained as scrawny as a bean sprout.

"Of course—everything's different now," said Kumaya, carefully straightening the fold of his new kimono sleeve. "Every morning when I arrive here, Master Kanami's servants come out and bow and help me take off my sandals. I get so embarrassed, I don't know what to do."

Fujiwaka blushed, listening to his friends and stroking and stroking the skin of his hand. How grateful I am to possess skin, hair, skull to hide behind; if they only knew what I have seen, heard, done, how favored I have been, and yet how frightened I am.

A prince's favor is seldom pure bliss to one who receives it. Had he never known it, he'd have longed for it and given his right hand for it. Once he has received it and knows what it is, he is horrified by the precariousness, inconstancy, intolerance and inconsiderateness of it; yet he would still do anything, even kill himself, to retain it.

Fujiwaka, who had survived the degrading poverty and hunger, the humiliation of his birth and the barbarities of the Jozen monks, felt like crawling back to his mother's womb and crying whenever he imagined the consequences, to himself, to his parents and to the Kanze's noh, if he should lose the shogun's favor. He had learned by now that there was in Yoshimitsu a streak of savage intolerance toward weakness and failure in others. Like a predatory beast sensing a spot of vulnerability, he was impelled at once to dig his sharpest claw into it. His adventurous and generous nature, given his position of shogun since the age of eleven and his penchant for luxury, pomp and things exotic and original, made him an inspired and committed patron of the arts in all fields—Chinese, vernacular, aristocratic or plebian. But a patron always of the successful and the victorious. If, for instance, Fujiwaka, whom he had deigned to lift from obscurity, failed in any small measure to vicariously flatter his megalomaniacal and omnivorous ego, Yoshimitsu would be resentful that Fujiwaka had diminished his glorious image, and his persecution of the offending artist would be just as overwhelming and prompt as his initial enthusiasm. Fujiwaka was painfully aware of being called "the Great Tree's protégé," for in that possessive article lay the basis of their relationship, and thereby his daily fear. Besides, Fujiwaka could not ignore the fact that the shogun, who disdained the Buddhist vegetarian regimen as enfeebling and ate against all taboos not only fish and fowl but the deer and the wild boar he hunted, had a prodigious vigor: even after his marriage he neither noticeably neglected his mistresses nor shortened the time he spent with Fujiwaka.

Whilst Yoshimitsu's wife, Nariko, née Princess Hino, was too much "above the clouds" for anyone even to guess at her true feelings, her own household, mostly composed of her unemployed or unmarried relatives, counting on their mistress' tacit approval and even gratitude, did not refrain from any base tactics to remove the player boy from the shogun's favor.

"Day and night I think of nothing else but the good of the Ashikaga dynasty, and I embolden myself to . . ." Nariko's remote spinster cousin or her step uncle would come to warn Yoshimitsu or, failing him, his chancellor, Hosokawa, that they had heard from the most reliable source that Fujiwaka was suffering from an insidious fungous disease which, whilst it never harmed the original carrier, once transmitted, proved fatal.

"Surely the Great Tree is aware that the vagabonds, drinking and washing in the river water, carry parasitic worms?" or "As no one of a better class wishes to marry an untouchable, the wretched creatures have been obliged to marry only their own kind, and I am told this inbreeding explains the high incidence amongst them of insanity and deformity . . ."

Yoshimitsu would blankly listen to his noble in-laws, who themselves showed varying degrees of deformity and decrepitude resulting precisely from centuries of intensive inbreeding, and mentally humming to himself a *kusé* music from Kanami's latest work, he would think all the while: Let me risk fungi, worms and insanity in bed with Fujiwaka before I turn into a princely carcass of degeneration and impotence like them!

Once Nariko's Chief Lady-in-Waiting, who was helping Yoshimitsu undress before joining Nariko on her sleep dais, went too far and alluded to Fujiwaka's "river-water stain."

"Madam," Yoshimitsu hissed like a wet log on fire, "let me remind you that I often have the pleasure of washing the boy with my own two hands, and I assure you he has the cleanest, soundest body I am ever likely to find in the realm!" He grabbed back his robe, put it on again and stalked out of his wife's pavilion.

As for Yoshimitsu's mistresses, they demonstrated their disapproval of the shogun's absurd passion for the little vermin with more restraint, as they reckoned that the fluke of a pretty child would monopolize the shogun's favor for only a short time before he grew out of boyhood; still, their malicious tongues wagged without rest, and their applause for Fujiwaka whenever he danced at the shogun's entertainment was a mere gesture, as soundless as clapping two limp lilies. Only Lady Takahashi showed her chic and intelligence by recognizing both the nature of Yoshimitsu's infatuation and Fujiwaka's intrinsic quality: she, a former courtesan and innkeeper's daughter, spoke well of Fujiwaka to everyone and invited him to her games and entertainments. When early one morning, slipping noiselessly out of the shogun's chamber, Fujiwaka found that his clothes had mysteriously disappeared from the antechamber, it was to Lady Takahashi's suite that he ran to ask for some clothes to go home in.

The jealousy against the untouchable cur amongst the page boys, all much better born and educated than Fujiwaka, was understandably intense, and their petty daily harassment made Fujiwaka's life at the palace often unbearable. Given the fickle, perversely cruel side of Yoshimitsu's character, Fujiwaka feared they might one day land him in a serious predicament; and they did.

Kenyasha, fifteen-year-old son of the captain of the shogun's palace guards, was one of the very few who had not suffered a drastic decrease in the shogun's favor since, as the boys put it, the Great Tree had "succumbed to the dancing beggar's sorcery"; for Yoshimitsu had not loved Kenyasha for his beauty or artistic talent. Yoshimitsu often simply called him "Dog!" and indeed the boy resembled the short-legged, short-necked, tough, loyal and fearless dogs indigenous to the northeastern marshland where the Ashikagas had come from; he even had the same ingenuous round-eyed stare with a very little white of the eye showing. Whilst the other boys indulged in such nasty pranks as dropping a snake into Fujiwaka's jug of toilet water or smearing fresh *urushi* lacquer on his comb and undergarment to cause him an agonizing skin rash, Kenyasha alone, like a sleeping but vigilant dog, just watched Fujiwaka but did nothing. Fujiwaka was naive enough to regard the absence of active hostility in his senior colleague as a sign of his uprightness, if not benevolence.

One cold and rainy night in February, this Kenyasha came to the Kanze house. Fujiwaka, who had been laid up with a very bad chest cold, put on his mother's quilted jacket over his night kimono and went out to the entrance hall, his forehead and neck shiny with a heavy film of perspiration and his eyes more be-jeweled than usual.

"Because of the heavy rain, the Great Tree has returned earlier from the wild-boar hunting and sent me to ask if you can come to the palace tonight." Kenyasha said this with his round, black, mindless gaze fixed on top of Fujiwaka's head, apparently taking no heed of Fujiwaka's sickly appearance.

"I am not . . . I feel rather . . ." Fujiwaka licked his parched dry lips. "Is it the Great Tree's wish that I come at once?"

"No," said Kenyasha, his dog-gaze imperturbable. "Not really. It's not that important. He has no guests. He's very tired. I'll tell the Great Tree that you're unwell."

No sooner had Fujiwaka fallen back into a feverish slumber than a couple of the shogun's guards on horseback were at the Kanze gate with the shogun's explicit command that Fujiwaka be brought to the palace at once.

Tamana brewed an infusion and made Fujiwaka drink it as Ogame dressed him. After Fujiwaka had swallowed a sip with a grimace, Tamana took back the cup from his hand and blew at it to cool the hot liquid, keeping her vivid, anxious eyes on him. Fujiwaka returned her gaze with equal trepidation. The mother and the son did not take their eyes from each other as the cup of infusion passed back and forth between them. Tamana and Ogame sibilated their prayers as Fujiwaka, wrapped up like a mummy in Tamana's quilted jacket and a thick straw rain cape, was hoisted onto one of the horses in front of the sodden, ramrod-stiff guard.

Fujiwaka entered the shogun's private suite shivering and perspiring out of control. Had Yoshimitsu been alone in the room, he would have fallen on his knees and begged for forgiveness straightaway; but the presence of several pages lined up in a row against the wall and Kenyasha beside the shogun gave him an un-expected surge of strength to manage a smooth, courtly bow and to reply to Yoshimitsu in a hoarse but audible voice:

"No, I never said 'I don't think it's important enough an occasion.' Nothing of the sort. That is not why I did not come to the palace with Kanyasha-dono. I have been ill with a fever, My Lord."

"Do you mean to say Kenyasha is a liar and I a fool?" screamed Yoshimitsu, sitting coiled up like a snake on his recently acquired ugly square red-lacquered chair from China, his one bare foot planted on the seat, the other hooked like a claw on the edge of his dais. His nostrils flared; anger combined with his facial tic made him stammer; his hair, untied and wild, gleamed wet from a whole day wasted under the downpour in the woods. Kenyasha sat holding one leg of the shogun's chair, staring at Fujiwaka as expressionlessly as though his eyes were two holes.

"Never mind the exact wording; the message is clear enough! You wretched nothing not only dared brush aside—ignore—in fact, defy the shogun's summons, but intimated to his messenger that you have so turned the shogun's head that now *you* can decide when and how to appear at the palace!"

Yoshimitsu jumped off his chair, grabbed a pale green porcelain vase and threw it at Fujiwaka. Water traced a long arc; flowers cascaded on Fujiwaka's head, neck and spine; the vase crashed against the pillar behind him. The irreplaceable value of the Korean vase, the noise, the first camellias from his garden littered around Fujiwaka on the floor did not help Yoshimitsu feel less turgid with anger. No, he felt rabid and randy with rage and utterly miserable. Had he been a snake, he would have eaten himself up from the tail backward and disappeared.

"Fujiwaka! You keep watch on my chamber tonight. Come, Kenyasha, sleep with me." Yoshimitsu simply glared at the row of pages and waved his hand casually at the four guards squatting in the covered corridor outside the room. Everyone withdrew.

Yoshimitsu had often been resentful and even upset by the fact that Fujiwaka would seldom weep or cry aloud in either jealousy or ecstasy; he could never quite understand the player child's inherent pudicity, his inhibition from showing an uncontrolled flight of emotions or senses, not even at the most intimate moments. Kenyasha, a warrior's son, raised battle cries of pleasure and sobbed blissfully in submission, conscious of his two listeners, the shogun and Fujiwaka.

Crouching in the narrow secret space behind the shogun's chamber,* Fujiwaka shook till his teeth rattled from the wheezing effort to suppress a cough, and his chest felt like a honeycomb of

* Night watch on the shogun's private chamber was a task and honor sometimes assigned on a state occasion, such as the shogun's nuptial night, to the highest-ranking officials. When the shogun slept with his legal wife, it was her Chief Lady-in-Waiting who lurked behind a silk screen all night. Normally, however, it was a security measure carried out by palace guards, and never by pages or favorites.

lava. The cruelty of the shogun's punishment did not surprise him. He who had no right to exclusivity or to constancy was not entitled to be jealous, and the prince gave and took as he pleased—Fujiwaka understood that; yet how grateful he was that his physical debilitation helped blunt the full emotional impact of the shogun's outrage. Mercifully, too, his fever-addled brain was not even capable of contemplating the possible repercussions of his gaffe on his father and the future of the Kanze's noh. As to Kenyasha's treachery—his word against mine—Fujiwaka could blame no one else but himself for having so stupidly taken Kenyasha's words at their face value.

As the shogun's and Kenyasha's moans rose to a swooning pitch, Fujiwaka thought of Yuzaki village and his homecoming on that frosty November morning, and he tried, tried desperately to hear Meisho's single-voiced flute again.

—Hold on, Fujiwaka, hold on! You have a Way. Never lose the beginner's awe. Bury your eyes in your hips. Right foot, left turn and—

Quickly regaining his breath, Yoshimitsu, the fresh-air fiend, who was seldom ill and had as little sympathy for infirmity and plaintiveness in others as in himself, yelled, clapping his hands viciously three times, "Give us some fresh air. Open the shutters!" He did not say "Open the shutters, Fujiwaka," although he had drawn most of the night's bitter pleasure from Fujiwaka's immediate presence.

With not a stir coming from behind the screen, Yoshimitsu sat up. Kenyasha lifted his tousled head. How unattractive the way this boy's eyelids and lips bloated after pleasure! Yoshimitsu looked away angrily; *his* face always seemed thinner and paler afterward. . . .

"Fujiwaka?"

Still no response. Yoshimitsu's naked body crashed past the screen. When he found Fujiwaka's inanimate body squashed in the farthest corner in the posture of an escaping animal, Yoshimitsu gathered him up in his arms and sucked his mouth. His long, straight eyelashes, which Yoshimitsu had so often loved pressing between his lips, quivered but went limp again. Panic and voluptuous remorse almost choked Yoshimitsu. He carried the boy to his antechamber, brusquely told Kenyasha to get dressed and to call the shogun's own doctor and attendants, but did not put on clothes himself till he had brought his own eiderdown and sleep mat into the antechamber and put Fujiwaka carefully between them.

THE DOCTOR forbade draft and cold. Yoshimitsu put up with the stifling, overheated airlessness for seven long days, cancelled many of his entertainments and expeditions, and when he was obliged to leave the palace, asked Lady Takahashi to stay with Fujiwaka. That consummate artist of tact, timing and survival, nearing forty but supreme in her allure, magnificently filled the role. When Yoshimitsu returned in the evening and fed the sick child, securing Fujiwaka's half-raised body between his opened thighs, or lay beside Fujiwaka with his head propped up in his hand, Lady Takahashi played her *biwa* guitar and sang soothingly.

The rumors of the shogun's nursing his player boy himself in his private wing made the rounds of the capital, and it was mostly through such rumors that Kanami and Tamana learned of their son's state of health and recovery before he was finally brought home.

Taking one look at Fujiwaka, pale and emaciated, Tamana burst into indignant tears, saying the Great Tree's selfish whim could have cost her only son his life.

"Theater cannot exist without spectators," said Kanami laconically. "Such being our karma, hard as it is, we just have to bear it." He put his hand gently on his son's frail shoulder. Fujiwaka nodded. Not a word more was necessary between them.

Ogame, whom everyone called "the worry-ahead," had prepared a bagful of Confucian homilies against conceit and sloth in case the Great Tree's inordinate favor turned his little master's head silly; but it was not needed. Fujiwaka, even when he came home in the early hours of the morning from the palace, worked with frantic application, fearful of wasting a second of his father's and his elders' tuition. "The horse is willing; let him run." Ogame shrugged his shoulders with a broad grin and went about mixing the precious incense bars that the shogun had the habit of freely giving Fujiwaka. "So potent that my eyes water and my fingers itch from just handling them," Ogame proudly told his wife. He also took immense pleasure in arranging for his little master's new clothes to be made up by the women of the troupe with the rolls of finest silk that Fujiwaka received from the shogun.

It was not only Yoshimitsu who showered the boy actor with gifts; many daimyos and nobles and clergy who wished to curry favor with Yoshimitsu followed an old proverb: To kill a rider, shoot his horse. One wealthy daimyo of the North sent him a magnificent small palanquin. Another, who controlled the largest port on Kyushu Island, gave him a block of sandalwood from India, enough to make a hundred fans. Others sent mother-of-pearl-inlaid saddles, and rare delicacies from faraway provinces, and even a sword and a bow made specially to suit his height. Each time a liveried messenger bearing gifts for the boy arrived at the house, Tamana—who mistrusted and was frightened by the sudden onslaught of affluence and grandeur—pressed her small hands against her lips.

"Oh, no, not again! Not a thing like *that?* He's just a child, an entertainer's child at that. If it goes on like this, the poor boy will be punished in the next world for having lived too far above his station in life."

Servants in the house thought their mistress mad and laughed behind her back.

"We could not but accept, Tamana," Kanami would say, taking a quick, disdainful glance at the opened parcel. "Whether it's priceless incense or a kick into a dunghill, we performers cannot choose but must humbly accept. Take it in, Hachi."

After the move to the capital, Kanami had begun putting aside an hour or two whenever he could, ordering everyone out of the stage room, with Ogame sitting outside in the corridor to turn away any prying ears, and taught his son and heir the *hiden*—literally, "secret transmission." Trying to make his son see the ineffable myth and depth of the art, which had taken him all of his forty-five years to fathom and then still only in his gut rather than in so many explicit words, his teaching was densely personal and intuitive. On rare occasions he chose to explain in words alone, but hating to incarcerate the magic of his art inside the limited scope of language, he would resort to the simplest vocabulary so that Fujiwaka could learn more by surmising what was left unsaid: for example, his *others' eye:*

"Destined to be a shadow and without substance till seen by *others* on stage, we performers must be equipped with what I call others' eye: the detached self watching you constantly from the back and from the side and from afar."

Kanami, who was arrogant enough to believe that the best of his work could outlive many generations of shoguns, warned Fujiwaka all the more severely against complacency: "When you are fourteen, even the most exacting critics would pardon your many failings for the potent charm of your extreme youth and might even call you a prodigy, but that is only a fleeting, treacherous grace, merely the Flower of the Moment, which could also be a cruel trap in an artist's career. What you must strive for is the Flower of Eternity. Even in its autumnal neglect and decay, a tree that once bore the Flower of Eternity will always touch the onlooker's heart. Once that Eternal Flower has taken root in you, no one, nothing, no vicissitude of fortune could ruin you, for then you will stand outside the time and history of ordinary mortals. It is a mighty, wondrous thing, our art; it can give joy and solace to people of many generations. That is why I tell you, Fujiwaka, that you must work—simply and humbly and desperately work!"

At this period in Fujiwaka's life, outside the radius of his father's flying whip, the shogun's cultural influence began to play an important role in his future development as an artist.

Having linked in matrimony the House of Ashikaga with one of the noblest families, the Hino, Chancellor Hosokawa wasted no time in securing from the Emperor for his young shogun the highest court rank that had ever been conferred on a commoner and suggested that in celebration, Yoshimitsu should visit the shrine of Iwashimizu Hachiman, the god of war, in an impeccably aristocratic style—driven in a sumptuously decorated ox carriage with the maximum number of outriders allowed by strict court etiquette befitting his exalted new rank, preceded and followed by six hundred resplendently attired mounted guards and foot soldiers. From this point onward, Hosokawa urged the young shogun to demonstrate to the whole world his mastery of court etiquette and culture.

"The *renga* poems, for instance. No better way to get into the highest circle of the courtiers," said Hosokawa, once a samurai, always a samurai, his words minimal and straight to the point, his elegant clothes and hat sitting on him less congenially than a helmet and armor.

Unlike the traditional poetry of 5-7-5-7-7 syllables, the *renga* chain poetry was created extemporaneously by a group of poets, each participant adding either the 5-7-5 or the 7-7 lines one after another till the chain reached the 100th line. It had long been the custom at the court not to sleep a wink on the night of Koshin, which came around every sixtieth night, as the superstitious courtiers believed that even one minute of sleep on that night would shorten their lives; and for such long nights the *renga* poetry game had become their preferred pastime, for some a veritable passion. It was sociable and entertaining, could be either sarcastic and funny or just as confessional and introspective as traditional poetry composed in solitary seclusion.

Yoshimitsu accordingly hosted many lavish *renga* poetry banquets at his palace, to which celebrated court poets willingly came, first lured by the unsurpassable quality of food and wine and the gifts distributed at the close of the evenings which the upstart shogun alone could afford, then gradually for the sheer joy and excitement of competing against the brilliant plebeian poets the shogun had astutely collected around him in the shape of Companions-in-Arts.

Yoshimitsu was a quick learner, but once in possession of skill and knowledge, he tended to grow bored and, thereafter making little real effort to deepen his art, bluffed his way through quite impressively. He played *shô* guitar, danced court dances before the princes of the blood, competed commendably in the *kemari** game against expert noblemen and attended all the major rituals and festivities held inside the court as if he had been born "above the clouds."

Several great eastern daimyos who could still recall the unspeakable hardship which Yoshimitsu's grandfather had endured to establish the Ashikaga shogunate voiced alarm and disapproval at what seemed to them the third shogun's unwarriorlike and over-cultured conduct, repeating the hackneyed maxim: what the grandfather built up, the son maintains but the grandson will wreck; whilst Fujiwaka, for a totally different reason, was gnawed raw by misgivings.

—Acquiring so much courtly refinement, will not the Great Tree soon find me a clumsy and laughable bumpkin?—

Seizing a suitable opportunity, he pleaded with Yoshimitsu to allow him also to be taught what the shogun was learning at the court. Far from being offended, as was everyone else, by the river-bank beggar's outrageous request, Yoshimitsu took it upon himself to coach the boy in *shô* playing, the game of *kemari* and *gagaku* court dancing, and as for the *renga* chain poetry, he promptly sent Fujiwaka to his own tutor, Prince Nijo.

---

* A gentle type of football, played exclusively within the imperial court.

Then aged sixty, Prince Nijo was a repository of the highest and the best of aristocratic tradition and culture, a living dictionary on court etiquette and a peerless poet in *renga* who had already edited two imperial anthologies. With a shapely bald head elongated like an aubergine, teeth exquisitely blackened and a beautiful lineless face powdered white, he was charm and dignity incarnate and with a tongue capable of both nectar and venom, either of which could flow at will in memorable phrases. The old prince was so enchanted with Fujiwaka that he wrote at once to his friend the chief abbot of the Todai Temple:

"The boy is a marvel, straight out of *The Tale of Genji*.* At my age I consider myself an old plant half-rotted in the cold earth, but when I look at this child something stirs in me that I thought I had long forgotten, causing such a melliferous and vivid sensation, almost a tremor of youth. Where his brows shade his eyes, I swear there linger dreams we ordinary mortals will never know. The child is ingenuous, merry and has indescribably graceful manners, and in my whole life at court I have not known anyone with more tact and perspicacity. Aside from his professional genius, what is quite astounding is the wit and the speed with which he learned chain poetry and can now cope with me as if he had been at it from birth. Had not the Great Tree sent him to me, I'd never have believed such a creature existed."

Prince Nijo, having lived all his life amongst the insipid and stunted offspring of imperial inbreedings within the Forbidden Enclosure, may have been guilty of a slight exaggeration, but his admiration for the untouchable boy was perfectly genuine, for thereafter, he frequently invited Fujiwaka to his own chain-poetry parties, to which the mightiest of the land had to scheme and compete for an invitation. He went even further by introducing Fujiwaka to the art of flower arrangement, to the tea-tasting ceremony and, most significant of all for Fujiwaka's future as playwright, to the great literature of the Heian period.†

* *Genji Monogatari*: A gigantic novel written in the early eleventh century by Lady Murasaki, whose hero in the first forty books is Prince Genji, the Shining Prince. His name has become a byword for male beauty and charm, and he is the personification of the most glorious period in Japanese history.
† The period from the ninth to part of the twelfth century during which the imperial power was still supreme and many of the unsurpassable literary masterpieces were created such as *The Tale of Genji,* the *Pillow Book Kokin* anthology of poems and the *Gossamer Diary*.

9

HAVING AT LAST arrived in the capital and reaping all the éclat, honors and material rewards of success, Kanami, the man who could make the spectators of the quality of a Prince Nijo weep behind their scented sleeves and at the same time hold the illiterate masons' and seaweed merchants' enthralled attention for hours on end, now felt himself pursued.

Kyoto had been the city of emperors centuries before the warriors first came rumbling down from the east, and a large body of Kyotoites tended to consider the shoguns a passing phenomenon. They did not like being told to admire the Kanze's noh just because the shogun of the day fancied it. After nearly a century of predominance, dengaku's roots had spread into every stratum of the capital's society, and the two dengaku leaders, Kiami and Icchu, continued to enjoy tremendous popularity. In addition, a faction of powerful daimyos headed by Yoshimasa Shiba, who opposed Chancellor Hosokawa's policy of concentrating all and every executive and legislative power in the sole hands of the shogun and also resented the chancellor's gruff, uncompromising personality, made a discreet but tenacious show of their support for dengaku.

One day Hachi came home quite demoralized from a visit to an old drum maker, considered to be the best in the country. The old man had flatly refused to make hand drums to meet Kanami's requirements:

"Sorry, boy. I've served dengaku masters all my life, and at my age I can't be bothered to start learning the way your master likes them."

Kumazen and Ogame bristled at the provocative impudence, but Kanami swallowed the insult. "Don't worry, Hachi. Omina is touring the Lake Biwa region. Send word to her; she'll find me an eager young lad with nimble fingers and good ears. I'll train him to make them my way."

Kanami was the type of man who in the face of opposition and adversity felt inspired and invigorated. He wrote, composed and choreographed a prodigious number of plays, rehearsed the troupe from early in the morning, punctually carried out his duty as a Companion-in-Arts at the shogun's palace, found time to set to music many of Nanami's lyrics for Omina and yet never failed to fulfill his traditional duties for the Kofuku Temple in the Yamato province, where his old sarugaku colleagues were busy reaping an indirect benefit from Kanami's undreamed-of success in the capital—borrowing all his work free of charge, advertising their close connection with the nationally renowned Kanze's noh.

And as is so often the case, they repaid Kanami's generosity with a rankling bitter jealousy ill-disguised under their opportunist flattery. They paid regular begging-bowl visits to the Kanze's spacious new house in the capital's quiet residential area. Kanami gave them copies of his new work, offered food and wine, but never sat down with them for more than half an hour. He would then simply stand up and look down at his guests, who had made themselves comfortable with jugs of excellent wine and Kyoto delicacies, and say to them, "You must excuse me. I must work."

Affronted by his hardly veiled request to leave, they would comment ironically:

"More work at this time of night? With the gracious patronage of the Great Tree, can't you afford to relax and sit awhile with your old friends?"

"Their crass naiveté and shortsightedness frighten me," Kanami would tell Toyodayu and Raiden after their guests' reluctant departure. "Today we enchant our protector and critic, but tomorrow he may find us stale without the Flower of Invention. I'd rather forgo sleep today than sleeplessly lament my lost fortune tomorrow."

His determination not to slacken an inch of his discipline was doubled when later the Komparu troupe, by far the oldest and most reputable of the four Yamato sarugaku schools, was at last commanded by the shogun to perform in the capital. With the phenomenal success of the Kanze, naturally the Kyotoites were curious to know the work of another Yamato sarugaku troupe, and the three-day subscription performance on the Kamo river-bank was heavily attended.

The master of Komparu had hardly been on stage for more than ten minutes when the audience began jeering and booing, with the shogun angrily walking out of his loge. The Kanze and Kiami's dengaku troupe were ordered to fill the remaining two days, and the crestfallen Komparus were chased out of the capital the same evening. The following month, the uncouth but good-natured Master Komparu on a begging-bowl visit to the Kanze cut a very sorry figure, gasping now and again with the vivid memory of his reception in the capital:

"It's a veritable lair of demons and witches, Kyoto! And my mind boggles, Kanami-dono, wondering how you managed to conquer it."

Kanami, currently the youngest to carry the title of *ami*, his youthful good looks in surprising contrast to his shaven head, attracted much attention whenever he entered the room assigned to the Companions-in-Arts at the palace. Whilst many faces lit up with a complaisant smile to catch his attention, Kanami did not fail to see that as many faces averted their eyes with the subtlest inclination of their heads. Nor was he fool enough to be unaware that Kiami, although reputed to be of a saintly good nature, was assiduously spreading foul rumors about him and Fujiwaka. Recently Kiami's grandson Zomasu, a year younger than Fujiwaka, had been honored by the ambitious warlord Shiba's favor and patronage. Furthermore, Yamana, Kyogoku, Doki and other daimyos from the top echelon of the shogunate hierarchy had lately banded themselves together with several of the capital's wealthiest temples, which had come to resent Hosokawa's severe handling of their moneylending activities. Together they threw their support behind Kiami and Zomasu. As it was well known in the capital that the upright samurai chancellor was a vociferous admirer of Kanami, their action could only be interpreted as hostile to Hosokawa and as a pledge of political allegiance to Lord Shiba.

The Hosokawas and the Shibas were both blood relatives of the Ashikagas, but since the first shogun had laid down the law that during the reign of each Ashikaga shogun a regent or a chancellor was to be chosen from only three families, Hosokawa, Shiba or Hatakeyama, the rivalry between the two families had intensified, at times to a fratricidal degree.

Yoshimasa Shiba, whose superficial charm and bonhomie hid rampant ambition and ruthlessness, was twenty years junior to Hosokawa, and he waited, impatient but astute, for his rival's fall, which, he reckoned, could not be too far off, judging from how things were going: Hosokawa, an unblinkered pragmatist, indifferent to his personal unpopularity or danger, had recently begun negotiating with the Southern Court to bring about, as the first step to clear the way for uniting the divided courts, the return to the capital of the Three Divine Wares, the very symbol of the imperial authority, spirited out of the Forbidden Enclosure by the Southern sympathizers more than forty years earlier. Despite its material and political superiority due to the support from the shogunate, the Northern Court undoubtedly suffered a psychological disadvantage as long as the Three Divine Wares were in the possession of the Southern Court, and no one was more aware of this weakness than the chancellor.

Naturally, Hosokawa's secret dealings with the Southern generals, involving many dubious intermediary characters, brought much obloquy on him and even suspicion as to where his loyalty lay. Under these circumstances, with the Southern Court and its spies ceaselessly working to split the precarious unity amongst the daimyos close to the young shogun, nothing, not even petty backstage rivalry between dengaku and sarugaku, could be left politically unexploited.

IN THE SUMMER of 1378, nearly four years after the Imakumano performance, Fujiwaka was still the shogun's favorite, so much so that on the day of the Ghion festival Yoshimitsu boldly took the sixteen-year-old actor into his own loge to view the tumultuous procession of floats which each district of the capital had spent the whole preceding year building in intense competition. As in every year, the central loges on the Fourth Avenue were studded with the mightiest, holiest and noblest of the land, and naturally all eyes were fixed on the shogun's loge. But the young autocrat, paying not the slightest heed to many a censorious gaze, had Fujiwaka share his own cup of wine and, carried away more by the dizzying clamor, music and colors of the billowing streets below than by the strong wine on a warm afternoon, allowed himself to be seen dallying with the boy actor as if they were alone behind a screen.

One doyen of the nobility was so scandalized that he dared attack in writing the shogun's appalling behavior in public with an untouchable. If the shogun himself, he fumed, began breaking down class distinctions, who would defend the order and security of the society?

Hosokawa finally decided he must broach the subject with the twenty-two-year-old shogun, to whom his wife had just borne a girl.

"Perhaps it is time for you to give Fujiwaka the ceremony of manhood. He is sixteen, and the criticism at his still wearing a boy's front locks at his age is growing too loud to be ignored. As you may recall, you cut yours at eleven."

"Let the worm-eaten nobles say what they like. I won't make Fujiwaka a man. Not yet!" Yoshimitsu threw back his head, and his boldly chiseled Ashikaga nostrils flared like a thoroughbred horse's. Seated in his bulky Chinese chair two or three heads above Hosokawa, who sat on the floor on his folded knees, the young potentate brimmed with insolent vigor and confidence, his radiant complexion and alert air no doubt resulting from his blasphemous meat-eating diet.

The chancellor gave a quick circular massage to his bristly beard, which had lately turned gray, and grinned with the comfortable knowledge that he had fostered in Yoshimitsu a shogun who could afford to ignore the attacks of a handful of noblemen as if they were mosquito bites on an elephant's back.

Hosokawa thought, not without complacent satisfaction, You're all right, my boy. All things considered, the Ashikaga shogunate has never been more secure.

10

ONE EVENING, returning from a deer hunt through the Muromachi district of Kyoto, Yoshimitsu spotted what must have been a magnificent mansion now gutted by fire. Its extensive grounds, though heavily overgrown from years of neglect, still contained many shapely old trees that reared their noble heads above a tangle of undergrowth. Sharing one of the common traits of despots in time of peace, Yoshimitsu had a mania for building. He was inspired at once. A man of quick decision, if he wanted something he had to have it yesterday; within a matter of a week he became the owner not only of the property—which turned out to be a deserted palace of the old Cloistered Emperor*—but also of an adjoining property belonging to an impoverished noble family, covering all together nearly six acres of land.

Yoshimitsu's wife, Nariko, had recently died, having never recovered from complications following the birth of her baby girl. Was it worth dying for a girl? Yoshimitsu wondered, then promptly dispatched the baby with a wet nurse and a suite of governesses

---

* In those days a reigning emperor often abdicated, regardless of age, and took the tonsure in order to enjoy a less protocol-restricted life.

and attendants befitting her rank to one of the most generously endowed nunneries on the outskirts of the capital with the intention of one day making her its principal.

Yoshimitsu, neither the firstborn nor even of the legitimate womb, had been blessed with the rarest luck in the annals of the shogunal dynasties of Japan,* in that he happened at his father's death to be his only surviving son. His smooth succession, he was keenly aware, had greatly strengthened the otherwise precarious unity of the Ashikaga shogunate. Lacking the absolute feudal authority of the later Tokugawa shogunate, under which its daimyos, however powerful, remained by solemn law and ethics mere vassals, Yoshimitsu's grandfather and father had not managed to bring under complete control the personal and aggressive territorial ambitions of their daimyos and provincial chieftains, and a disputed line of succession would have given a ready excuse for those self-seeking, opportunistic daimyos to install by force of arms their own particular candidate as the next shogun. It was perfectly understandable, therefore, that Yoshimitsu should be determined to send all his children, with the exception only of his eldest son and heir, into religious seclusion.

Having neatly put the fruit of his first marriage out of sight and mind, he took his poor deceased wife's niece, Yasuko, as his second bride and designed for her and her suite and the growing number of his mistresses a sumptuous detached building on the grounds of his new palace. He had no intention of being faithful to his new wife at twenty-two and at the crest of his virility. Apart from Yasuko and Fujiwaka, he flitted from one casual sleep dais to another and went so far as to dare pick one of the proudest flowers kept inside the imperial harem. As a consequence, one night in the depth of the Ninefold Forbidden Enclosure one Lady Azuchi, the favorite of the Emperor, was kicked off the covered gallery by no less than His Imperial Majesty's own foot and was hurriedly banished to a remote nunnery. The Emperor then threatened that he would commit suicide by disembowelment unless the impudent upstart of a shogun wrote His Imperial Majesty vowing that no such illicit liaison as had been widely rumored in the capital had at any time taken place between the shogun and Lady Azuchi.

* There were three shogunates in Japanese history: Minamoto (1192–1333), Ashikaga (1336–1573) and Tokugawa (1603–1868).

Yoshimitsu and the Northern Emperor, Goenyu, were only six months apart in age, and although the two young men nourished an active fraternal rivalry, each perfectly understood the other's usefulness. Without the shogun's military and political and economic backing, His Imperial Majesty would have found it difficult to contend with his indomitable cousin the Southern Emperor, who continued to claim his legitimacy if for no better reason than that he possessed the Three Divine Wares, the tokens of a god-ordained right to rule Japan. And for his part, Yoshimitsu, as the actual ruler of the country, without the Northern Emperor closely on his side would have seemed to the whole nation merely a transient clangor of swords and armor plate; for however cardboard-thin the Northern Emperor's tangible authority might be, he represented the sacred and inviolable continuity of the nation.

"The Divine Person, methinks, is a paranoid child," Yoshimitsu chuckled to himself, greatly amused, but promptly wrote the demanded oath in his thick-stemmed bold brushwork and had it sent to the Imperial Palace with a collection of rare and costly gifts.

Whilst Chancellor Hosokawa cudgeled his brain for a way to raise money to realize the shogun's extravagant conception of his new palace, Yoshimitsu enlisted all the most talented artisans in masonry, woodwork, furniture making, gardening and carving, regardless of their class or cost, and to the dismay of the establishment, imported gangs of riverbank vagabonds to dig a canal from the Kamo River to feed water into a serpentine lake for which he himself designed a floating covered gallery which was to shed its graceful reflection on the clear water.

When all the building work was nearing completion, Yoshimitsu had the nerve to suggest to the Emperor's cousin Prince Konoé that he would be much pleased to receive a gift of some of the famed weeping cherry trees from the Prince's garden. After Prince Konoé acceded to this outrageous request, no outstanding collection of trees, flowering shrubs or statuesque rocks, whoever the owners might have been, was safe from the shogun's covetous eye.

When the new Muromachi Palace was finally completed, it was a far cry from the old shogunal palace, which, purely functional, was more like a military headquarters. What made the new palace so remarkable was not only the splendor of the buildings themselves but the immense garden with its rare and precious specimens of plants so chosen as to have flowers blooming through the four seasons, whose variety, profusion and quality were so breathtaking that soon the shogun's new residence became known as the Flowering Palace.

On the eleventh of the third month, upon which all the eminent professors of astrology agreed as being auspicious, Yoshimitsu moved into the new palace with a great procession whose scale and pomp no Kyoto residents could recall. The shogun's gold-leaf-decorated carriage was harnessed to twelve beauteously dressed oxen, borrowed for the occasion from no other than the beleaguered Konoé family. Several hundred daimyos, officials and retainers of the shogunate in splendid new finery followed the shogun from the old to the new palace. Kanami, as the shogun's Companion-in-Arts, and Fujiwaka, on the shogun's personal insistence, were included in the procession. The route was so densely packed with onlookers from the capital and the surrounding regions that even the great number of guards lining the streets had difficulty in controlling the surging crowds.

A few days later when Prince Konoé asked for his oxen and drivers back, Yoshimitsu sent a perfunctory reply that he liked them so much that with His Highness' kind permission, he would like to keep them. Poor Prince Konoé, who was just then fighting an important case through the shogunate's justice department to recover one of his provincial estates from a usurping bailiff, could do nothing but say he was flattered that the shogun was so pleased with his oxen and drivers.

Yoshimitsu, true to his "split-bamboo" character, as his chroniclers flatteringly put it, in whom no rancor smoldered long to the detriment of his own peace of mind and digestion, blithely asked Emperor Goenyu to visit his new palace as if nothing disagreeable had ever occurred between them over Lady Azuchi.

"The Divine Son of Heaven cannot visit a commoner's house, let alone stay under the same roof!" "Unthinkable!" "Most improper!" the courtiers buzzed, and a team of noble scholars in court etiquette and precedence, headed by Prince Nijo, argued for two years before they finally settled on an acceptable formula: they chose the particular three days on which the Imperial Palace faced a so-called Dark and Pernicious Direction and counseled His Imperial Majesty to displace himself toward an auspicious orientation, which, the wise men pointed out, by sheer coincidence happened to fall in the direction of the shogun's Flowering Palace in the Muromachi district.

Endless negotiations and consultations then ensued between the court and the shogunal office with regard to the appallingly complex details of protocol, while Yoshimitsu and his Companions-in-Arts racked their brains as to how best to organize suitable entertainment to keep His Imperial Majesty amused during his three-day visit. Water music, *gagaku* dances and string concerts, *kemari* games and *renga* chain-poetry competitions were planned; but for the last day Yoshimitsu wished to surprise his imperial guest with something utterly different from the archaic and heavily Chinese-influenced court music and dance. Yoshimitsu, who now believed he had personally transformed the plebeian, hitherto much-scorned entertainment of sarugaku into a fashionable theater for the new ruling class, resolved that Kanami and his troupe should for the first time perform before the Emperor.

The idea was immediately put into operation by Chancellor Hosokawa, but as soon as news of this arrangement leaked out, Lord Shiba stepped in and made strong objections to the presentation of only one school of popular entertainment. The dengaku school must also be represented, he insisted. The Zen high priests, the spiritual guides of all Ashikaga shoguns, who deeply resented Hosokawa's incessant cracking down on their abuse of religious prerogatives, opened their sour lips in support of Lord Shiba's claim—which inevitably impelled the older established sects of Buddhism such as the Kofuku, the Todai and the Enryaku temples to rush to Hosokawa's support.

The dispute, if left unchecked, seemed likely to bring about consequences far beyond its original importance. To resolve the matter, Yoshimitsu sent for both Hosokawa and Shiba.

"It's getting much too noisy. Let us make it a competition performance—Kiami and his grandson Zomasu competing against the Kanze father and son. Three numbers each school. In respect of his age, allow Kiami to open the day's program in *Okina*."

Although having to maintain an ostensible neutrality, Yoshimitsu had chests filled with gossamer silk, linen gauze, Chinese damask and brocade secretly sent to the Kanze house, as his spies had informed him that Lord Shiba was lavishing money and material on his favorite, Zomasu. Kanami put himself on a purifying fast for a week before he began working on two new plays, as Yoshimitsu had confidentially requested that Kanami include in his program *Jinen Koji,* which he said he particularly wished the Emperor to see. When Kanami finished writing and composing *Lady Shizuka in Yoshino* and *Matsukaze-Murasame,* in which he and Fujiwaka would portray two sisters who loved the same man, there were still two months to go before the performance. Kanami at once set out to write a third.

"But, Master," put in Toyodayu diffidently, as usual his question sounding more like an apology in advance, "I thought you'd decided to present two new plays, and—"

"I know," Kanami cut him short impatiently. "But don't forget this is a competition performance. We must be prepared for all adverse eventualities. Suppose it poured with rain on the day and *Matsukaze-Murasame* seemed much too wet and lugubrious. Or suppose our dengaku rivals by coincidence put on a play also about Lady Shizuka; how could I be sure that one of our kitchen maids or our mask carver's apprentice hadn't been bribed to spy on our program? By preparing one or two extra plays, I can confuse our rivals and retain till the last minute a free hand to choose the best plays according to the circumstances."

Kumazen, whom the shogun identified as "that splendid *waki* player with centipede brows," wholeheartedly agreed with Kanami on taking every precaution and ordered his sons:

"Listen, till the imperial performance is over, you two stay on either side of the little master wherever he goes; don't walk too close to the edge of rivers or canals, and if someone unknown sends Fujiwaka-dono fanciful cakes or spicy condiments, try them first on a cat—you understand?"

Kumazen's wife, Suzume, laughed, thinking her husband was going too far.

"Wife, I am not exaggerating." Kumazen lifted, then lowered his infinitely mobile brows. "Put yourself in our rivals' place. No one alive at the moment could write like our Master: his lyrics, his dialogue, the way his plots hold together! As for his music, even a mackerel dead for an hour would revive if Buddha granted it a chance to listen to Master's *kusé* music. I know people say that when Kiami sings, weeping wisteria curls heavenward. That's very nice, very pretty; but tell me, what does he sing, this so-called God of Musicality? Some stodgy, hackneyed lyrics which mean nothing—noodle cooked yesterday. And as to this famous pet of Lord Shiba's, Zomasu: is he anywhere near our young master? If our Fujiwaka-dono is a moon, Zomasu is a turtle. The only way the dengaku fellows could possibly win is to physically prevent either Master or young master from appearing on stage. No other way. So till the performance is over, watch out; keep your eyes peeled, front and back!''

It was Suzume, thus inspired by her husband, who, only a few days before the imperial visit was to start, reported to Kanami that a knife sharpener who regularly called at the Kanze kitchen and was a fanatic theater lover had overheard the dengaku troupe rehearsing a play about Lady Shizuka. Kanami rewarded Suzume for her information with a roll of fine linen, abandoned his *Lady Shizuka in Yoshino* and added extra rehearsals for his latest play, *Sotoba Komachi*.

THE FIRST DAY of the imperial visit was a warm, still spring day with fleecy light clouds melting like handfuls of snow as they drifted slowly nearer the sun. At the Flowering Palace cherry blossoms cascaded in ten, twenty different shades, and the perfumed exultation of flowers and young leaves welcomed the Emperor and his suite, numbering over seventy. Musicians floated on the lake in colorfully painted Chinese-style barges with dragon heads, and the shogun's exquisitely liveried guards and attendants lurked everywhere, averting their eyes from the Sacred Person as they had been strictly ordered to do by the chancellor. The imperial guests so enjoyed the banquet and the *renga* poetry competition that they did not retire till shortly before dawn. The second evening the *gagaku* court dances were offered and the young Emperor himself played a six-string zither, which gave the shogun the opportunity to show off his expertise with a thirteen-pipe flute.

The third day broke with an overcast sky of opalescent gray with irregular gusts of wind that scattered cherry blossoms over the clean-swept white gravel.

"It'll rain, Father," Fujiwaka said as they arrived to prepare themselves for the performance.

"Already spitting," Kanami said as he stretched out his arm from the immaculately white screens of the actors' quarters garlanded with plaited crimson silk ropes.

"Fujiwaka, you feel the weeping willows loosening their shy, soft-green fingers? There's an indescribably gentle caress in spring

rain; it doesn't dampen one's heart as it would in the winter." Kanami did not elaborate further, but Fujiwaka nodded, understanding his father's oblique instructions as to how he should feel in
that day's performance.

At the Hour of Goat* the Emperor arrived, accompanied by
his host. Compared with Yoshimitsu, the Emperor appeared frail
of form, but his movements were unhurried and edgeless, one gesture linked into the next with a dreamlike elaborate slowness. His
expressionless small white oval face looked more like a noble
priest's or an enlightened and resigned quail's egg. He sat down,
and some four hundred guests followed suit to the sibilant rustle
of the best silk in the land.

With the flute solo piercing the tense silence, the day's performance began with Kiami in *Okina*. The energetic, lithe and
saintly-looking septuagenarian sang like an old mellow flute and
danced with a superb elegance of understatement. His grandson,
Zomasu, danced *senzai*, unmasked and clad in an exceptionally
beautiful costume of gold and silver woven into deep moss-green.
Now seventeen and considered Fujiwaka's arch rival, Zomasu
showed outstanding quality as an actor-singer worthy to be Kiami's
successor, but his appearance was nothing beyond common good
looks. Taller than Fujiwaka, he had a high-hipped carriage that
lacked the serenity and the uncanny elasticity with which Fujiwaka's every movement was distinguished. Still, with Kiami's exquisite singing and the moving authority of mature age, *Okina*
drew enthusiastic applause.

The finest of rain continued—not making the slate gravel that
surrounded the protrudent stage visibly wet but adding an unde-
tectable shimmer to the atmosphere. A warm flower-scented breeze
and a mintlike fresh breath of air cooled by rain and wet grass
wafted in alternate streams over the spectators.

Kanami believed the Flower of theatrical experience to be
surprise; accordingly, on this historic occasion he made his first
entrance behind a sunken-eyed and shriveled-mouthed old woman's mask, presented to him for this particular role by his friend
the fabled mask carver Himi, wearing a white hemp wig and a tattered straw cape. This most celebrated actor in his prime tottering
across the stage on a wobbly cane as Ono no Komachi, once the

* Two o'clock in the afternoon.

legendary beauty and gifted poetess, took the spectators' breath away. The Emperor was seen urgently whispering to Prince Nijo behind his sandalwood fan, and the courtiers' powdered white faces appeared even more than usually inscrutable. Kanami held his audience in the palm of his hand with that strange thrill which only a great actor with an overwhelming inner tension can evoke; and the crackling repartee exchanged between the old beggar woman and the traveling priest, played to perfection by Kuma-zen, made the spectators gasp and sigh with sympathy; yet at the same time, as Prince Nijo afterward remarked to Yoshimitsu, Ka-nami's ninety-nine-year-old Komachi had managed to suggest the remains of the arrogant beauty and triumph of her long-lost youth.

Suzume's information obtained through the knife sharpener proved reliable: the dengaku troupe's second play was indeed about Lady Shizuka. Kiami's warrior with a passion-gutted mask was beyond all praise for the pathos he could put into every line he spoke without ever being mawkish; Zomasu, playing his par-amour, Lady Shizuka, was faultless as a sensuous and somewhat coy courtesan; but the play itself was meanderingly slow, and be-fore developing any dramatic interest it came to an abrupt and disappointing end.

Kanami's combative instinct, almost a voluptuous enjoyment of a competitive performance such as this, showed in the clipped, sharp orders he threw rapidly at everyone, stalking up and down the dressing area, his eyes staring up into his forehead. Only when Hachi panted in every so often, reporting on the dengaku's *Lady Shizuka*, did Kanami stand still and listen.

Having heard Hachi a few times, Kanami said with a broad grin: "Let's surprise them. Ram *Jinen Koji* into their dragging heels!"

In *Jinen Koji*, Kanami was as recklessly free as a tightrope dancer who knew he could in fact fly. With the license of truly gi-gantic talent, one surprise and marvel after another, he was a law unto himself, and next to him, Fujiwaka as a pathetic orphan girl was immaculately disciplined in not doing a thing that was not within his role, which impressed the connoisseurs nearly as much as Kanami's flamboyance. The success of the play surpassed even the exaggerated expectation of the shogun: for the first time the Emperor showed some humanly recognizable expressions on his inviolable boiled-egg face, and as Kanami made his exit, Yoshimitsu, to his gloating satisfaction, saw some of the impassive-faced nobles bring out their limp tapering hands from under their heavy sleeves and actually applaud.

"Quick! Quick!" Kanami whispered behind the Jinen Koji mask as soon as he was led into the Kanze dressing area, and the moment his mask was removed, his face drenched in streaming perspiration, he anxiously questioned Toyodayu.

"Now, where's that sluggard, Hachi? Haven't you sent him to the front?"

"Yes, of course he's out there; but Master, the dengaku lot have hardly started. We must wait a few minutes."

At last Hachi scuttled in, hissing, "A comedy, Master; a typical dengaku acrobatic comedy!"

"Couldn't be better!" Kanami leaped to his feet. "We can follow it with *Matsukaze-Murasame.*"

"Master, they're not bad today." Hachi continued his report on what he had seen of the dengaku's last offering as Kanami was being dressed and sewn up. "In fact, I've never seen Zomasu do better. But the dialogue between Zomasu and the drunken monks is a shameless copy of yours straight out of *Jinen Koji.* I gather they were flabbergasted when they saw you'd brought back *Jinen Koji* again, *and* at the shogun's special request! Red faces everywhere, including Lord Shiba's."

The dengaku comedy was over; the enthusiastic applause for Zomasu's bravura dancing exit was tapering off. Meisho began wetting his flute, ready for the "first voice" of *Matsukaze-Murasame,* and other musicians and the chorus nervously stroked their instruments or straightened the folds of their *hakamas* as they awaited their turn.

"Meisho," Kanami said, "take your time. I count on you to wipe out the dengaku comedy left in the air before our entrance. Make it wistful and damp."

Meisho rubbed his wine-sodden red nose with his stodgy hand that held his magical instrument and gave his master a roguish quick grin.

When the dengaku troupe had vacated the entrance-curtain area, the Kanze troupe was allowed into it. Before sinking his face into a young-woman mask, Kanami whispered to Fujiwaka, who was standing behind him holding his mask cords:

"To play Murasame unmasked is hard, I know; but it's the

Great Tree's particular wish that you show your face to His Imperial Majesty. Feel a thousand in your heart, but show not one on your face."

Fujiwaka shut his eyes in response to his father's advice, his face under the wig already an alabaster mask.

The father and the son slid onto the stage as the two sisters Matsukaze and Murasame,* and there began the performance that was to be talked about for generations afterward, every spectator then present passing down to his children and grandchildren the wonder he had seen that afternoon as if it were a piece of precious family treasure.

The plot itself was simple: On the beach of Suma on the Inland Sea a traveling priest is awakened by two beautiful sisters with two pails balanced on a pole over their shoulders, who make their living by scooping up seawater to be evaporated into salt. In cold moonlight they reminisce about the heartless nobleman poet who, when exiled to Suma, had loved them, but then abandoned the lowly-born girls as soon as he was pardoned and allowed to return to the capital.

Kanami's Matsukaze, more tormented by passion and rancor than the younger sister, Murasame, dons the hat and the hunting cloak left behind by the poet and dances like someone possessed by a vengeful demon. The priest prays for her soul to be rescued from purgatory; the chorus joins the priest Kumazen's powerful voice; as the music crescendos on the surging *kusé* rhythm, the sisters, dancing and singing together, disappear.

When the priest, left alone on an empty stage, said that all he could hear was the wind in the pines and the receding sound of a shower, many amongst the audience literally bent their heads to listen to the wind and the rain, so profoundly immersed were they in the spirit and magic of the performance.

The impact of the play took time to lift its spell; a taut silence prevailed before the audience began wildly applauding and cheering. Before the musicians had left the stage, the shogun's cloak was on its way down for the Kanze troupe.

"What happened, Fujiwaka?" Kanami asked urgently as soon as his mask had been removed from his sweat-spangled face. Those in hearing distance, struck by the tone of their master's voice,

* Matsukaze means "Wind in the pines" and Murasame, "Passing shower."

stopped congratulating one another and looked at the father and the son.

"My voice . . ." Fujiwaka applied his palm to his throat, and there was a look of terror on his pallid face. "After 'Forget you must, sister,' it just died! If Meisho hadn't helped me by changing the pitch every time I started singing alone following you or the chorus, even someone tone-deaf would have noticed I was singing out of tune. It just went!" His voice, now a frail falsetto, now a husky croak, was obviously out of his control. Fujiwaka bit his lips, his eyes brimming with tears.

"I remember doing the same when your father's voice cracked," said Meisho. "Nothing new, little master; happens to everyone; nothing to cry about." Meisho blew his red nose, his stocky square fingertips so at odds with the beauty of the music they coaxed.

"Oh, come, come, little master, no tears after such a triumph, please!" Ogame stroked Fujiwaka's back as if he were still the child of Yuzaki village; but Fujiwaka shriveled at his nanny's touch, more wretched still amidst his elders' sympathy.

EVEN DISCOUNTING Fujiwaka's natural reluctance and fear of having to cross the threshold of manhood at seventeen, as performer and shogun's favorite, to have to lose the privileges of extreme youth, what Kanami called the Flower of the Moment, was a cruel disaster.

Since his first memory, one sole advantage which he had never been allowed to forget or contradict had been his physical beauty, the mellifluousness of his voice, his airborne grace. To have just had to hear a harbinger of the death of that conviction, that myth, his only and entire wealth, not only on stage but in front of spectators who included an emperor and a shogun—his shogun! It covered him with cold sweat just to recall how he had managed not to show any of the panic of that catastrophic moment when he first felt a big stiff spider in his throat blocking the flow of his voice. He had been watching with a mixture of horror and pity how Kumao had lost his Flower of the Moment and turned into a gawky, overelongated and gruff brute. The voice first, then the jaws, neck, hands, hair, beard . . . What will the shogun say, do, think when my legs and arms become muscle-bound and covered with hair? And to think that I can no longer play unmasked and in future will have to be purified of my this-worldly stain by the sprinkling of salt before performing in *Okina*.

"Don't fret; hold on; take your time. It's lifelong, the Way of noh," repeated his father. "If you get discouraged or sulk now, you're finished for good. Just go on and on at it as if there were no alternative to the way of noh but death."

He told Fujiwaka to return to the beginning. "When you forget the beginner's awe, you start decaying. Go all the way back to your earliest lessons: breathing, voice production, stance, posture and simple carriage of feet."

To his amazement, after so many years of stage experience Fujiwaka found the beginner's training just as hard and bone-breaking as on the first day of his lesson as a child. With the patience and determination to cut a rock with a silk thread, he attacked every step and every phrase that he had already learned during the last ten years.

Ogame, being a kyogen comic, had no right to meddle with the *shite*'s business; but the dear "Worry Ahead" remembered everything he had watched his little master learn from Kanami at Yuzaki village and helped Fujiwaka go through his old lessons, and Kanami gratefully turned a blind eye.

Tamana, with touching discretion, began leaving a fresh linen loincloth in Fujiwaka's room every other night, took away the soiled one and washed it herself as she did Kanami's, and she would cook an egg yolk in a dry earthenware pot on a slow fire till it turned black and made her son eat it every morning to strengthen his growing bone and muscle.

Kanami told Fujiwaka to stand on the wide bank of the Kamo River every morning and night when he was not at the palace, yelling and singing loudly for at least an hour to fortify and stabilize his vocal cords. Tamana woke before the first blush of the morning touched the rim of the Higashi Mountains and cooked the egg yolk, and Fujiwaka would wake as the greasy burnt odor permeated the house. As he left the house, Tamana came out to the gate and always gave him her gentle good-luck pat on his right shoulder.

11

"HOSOKAWA's been nagging me for years," Yoshimitsu said, "and now that you've turned eighteen and your voice has changed, I can't hold it off any longer: I'll have to act your ceremonial father and cut your front locks. I'll hate it, Fujiwaka!"

A stifling hot night. The attendants busy with the large round Chinese fans had been dismissed. The guards on night duty could be heard on the gravel outside, and their tread was so ponderous that each pause between their steps made listeners feel even hotter with irritation. The gossamer mosquito nets hardly moved in the torpid air, and not even the artificially guided stream trickling into the pond could cool one's ear. Yoshimitsu felt such a tug at parting that with an impetuous groan he threw his head onto Fujiwaka's lap.

Fujiwaka held the fan still for a second, then resumed fanning with a languid steady rhythm. The weight of the Great Tree's warm head on his thigh was as familiar and as dear and indispensable to him by now as the gentle final pat his mother would give him on the right shoulder whenever he left the house. At the beginning of the shogun's favor, it was true, Fujiwaka had been so overwhelmed by a sense of intensest gratitude and terror of Yoshimitsu's power that there was no room to consider his own feelings. "Give pleasure to others; ask none for yourself," his father had always warned him, and he had worked frantically hard to please Yoshimitsu, indeed slogged at it, with no other thought than to retain the shogun's favor, telling himself every hour of the day and night that it was a battle on which not only his own fate but that of Kanze's noh depended.

And now, faced with the time limit of the shogun's carnal favor, Fujiwaka suddenly felt his heart overflow with a molten, clinging tenderness for this leopard of a young man whose hot breath was scorching his knees. Is this a commerce of the heart? Have I allowed myself some selfish, possessive feeling? I, an untouchable, for a shogun? Once released from the service of the night, will I still be quite as special to the Great Tree as before? Without the spur of the infatuated flesh, will he still cherish me, protect me, guide me, teach me as before? But why on earth should he, now that I have overnight become a gawky, raucous, half-boy/half-man with arms and legs too long to nail myself to the stage floor!

Feeling sick with disgust at himself, Fujiwaka went on mechanically fanning.

"You! Smug, hateful, unfeeling you!" Yoshimitsu hissed, but not violently, as it was too hot. He grabbed hold of Fujiwaka's fan and threw it away; then, in the light of the oil lamp, he saw tears well up in Fujiwaka's eyes, then fall one by one. One thing Yoshimitsu had often held against Fujiwaka was that the boy hardly ever wept; Yoshimitsu, in fact, had accused him of having sold his soul and tears in exchange for his talent and unparalleled beauty. Immensely touched, Yoshimitsu drew the young boy into his arms, and the inimitable way Fujiwaka's body went limp and light at his touch rekindled in him such a violent passion and a surge of memories that he was as sincere as a shogun could be, and enjoyed being mawkishly so, when he sighed in a tear-throttled voice:

"I have never loved anyone as I have loved you. Once I make you a man, I'll have to learn to love you in such a way that the two of us can live together with Buddha's blessing in our next lives."

YOSHIMITSU procrastinated further, but after three postponements finally in November ordered a ceremony of adulthood for Fujiwaka at the Flowering Palace, to be attended only by himself, Prince Nijo, Nanami, Kanami and the shogun's own hairdressing attendant.

That morning, Fujiwaka vomited the burnt egg yolk. Tamana stroked and slapped his back, then washed his face clean and could not help blushing, even though he was her own son, as he gazed wistfully at her with those bejeweled dark eyes, so disgracefully, so stunningly beautiful and seductive a young man he had grown into.

Yoshimitsu, acting as the Father of Scissors, and Nanami as the Father of Eboshi Hat, a symbol of manhood, sat facing Fujiwaka, behind whom sat Prince Nijo and Kanami. Six pages assisted at the ceremony, lined up behind the shogun and Nanami, looking exceedingly smug and content that at long last Fujiwaka would be officially out of the shogun's carnal favor.

Yoshimitsu, who knew the ceremonial procedure backward—Buddha knew how many pages he had made men—proceeded briskly and mechanically with his aquiline profile austere and rigid, till a page handed him a pair of scissors. At its cold metallic touch he winced and looked at the scissors; then, raising his eyes to Fujiwaka, he flinched. He showed his hesitation, his repugnance—for a fleeting second, but the shogun did show them.

"Come, Fujiwaka, let's get it over with."

From the way he said it, one would have thought him talking about beheading or suicide. Fujiwaka slid forward, his long eyelashes almost digging into his pale cheeks, and offered his head forward but downward.

"Up, up—lift your head, you clot! How am I to cut . . ."

The heartless page boys bit their lips not to laugh, but Prince Nijo, Nanami and Kanami grimaced as if they had an urge to sneeze: they had never so nakedly witnessed the extent of the shogun's affection for his player boy. Nor had they imagined the shogun capable of such affection.

Fujiwaka lifted his chin, his eyes desperately shut. He choked at the proximity of Yoshimitsu's scent, his rustling sleeve, the heat of his body. Yoshimitsu's fingers scooped up his front locks. The scissors bit into the hair. Fujiwaka heard that dull slippery noise.

—So that we can live together with Buddha's blessing in our next lives— Fujiwaka repeated to himself Yoshimitsu's words, and it was the only time that he ever allowed himself consciously to admit that he, an untouchable, loved the shogun.

Having performed his part, Yoshimitsu looked drained; forgetting to hand the scissors to the hairdressing attendant waiting on his left, he threw them onto a tray on his right, so carelessly that the scissors bounced from the tray and fell to the floor. The poor hairdresser then had to crawl behind the shogun to pick them up before he could dress Fujiwaka's hair in the required adult fashion. As Yoshimitsu watched with petulant impatience, Nanami carefully placed the tall black-lacquered eboshi hat on Fujiwaka's head, and the ceremony was over.

With his high forehead exposed, the bluish haziness above Fujiwaka's eyes was even more accentuated than before and added a smoky sensuousness to his face, which had lately thinned about the jaws. The purple silk cords of the hat pressing tightly into his lean cheeks gave him a brave grown-up air, but his neck seemingly so fragile out of the daffodil-yellow garment loosely worn over white-and-mauve robes and his eyes uncertainly downcast, he looked lost indefinably between man and boy. Prince Nijo, who had chosen for Fujiwaka the adulthood name of Motokiyo, was moved to say to the young man: "Motokiyo, I'll live many years longer for the sheer joy of having seen you grown from a fawn to a deer. Now you run alone, and far. The forest is deep."

THEREAFTER MOTOKIYO spent no more nights at the shogun's palace, nor with his voice still unstable did he perform at private banquets at the Flowering Palace for some time. A rumor soon reached Motokiyo's ears that the shogun was now sharing his pillow with young sons of his palace officials or new page boys at random. Since his very early years, hardship and suffering had meant to him a necessary penance to make him a humbler pilgrim on his Way of noh. The regret and sorrow that he felt at having outgrown the shogun's carnal love were howled and spat out of his system as he stood alone at dawn on the Kamo riverbank and with a voracious concentration began learning from Kanami playwriting, composition and choreography.

Whilst Fujiwaka was fighting a merciless battle of will against his own body, there was another battle gathering momentum within the shogunal hierarchy. The feud that had been smoldering for so long between the Hosokawa and Shiba clans had to explode sometime. When several daimyos, with Shiba's clandestine encouragement, confiscated a number of huge manorial estates belonging to the Kofuku Temple, Hosokawa ordered Shiba, Doki,

Togashi and Akamatsu to send their armed forces to punish the usurpers; whereupon these mighty daimyos raised their standards instead against the chancellor himself and in a blinding dust storm caused by what to horrified Kyotoites' eyes seemed no less than a thousand horsemen, rushed to the Flowering Palace to demand that the shogun purge Chancellor Hosokawa from his office.

Yoshimitsu was spared the agony of a painful decision, for his old-samurai chancellor promptly sent in a letter of resignation. At the same time he summoned a priest friend to perform the ceremony of relinquishment of this turbulent world, shaved his head and set fire to his great mansion. Then, with his magnificent armor bulging out from under his new ink-dyed priestly garments and surrounded by a massive corps of mounted soldiers, he rode out of the capital to sail from Nishinomiya Harbor to his province on Shikoku Island. The shogun forthwith installed Lord Shiba as his new chancellor.

Despite the widespread rumor that those daimyos who had strutted the inner corridor of the palace during Hosokawa's chancellorship would now either be banished or have their estates confiscated, Yoshimitsu showed no sign of raising his hand against them, nor when in the following month he came to reshuffle offices and ranks within the shogunate hierarchy did he drastically eliminate Hosokawa's old allies.

Such impartiality would have been unthinkable during the two earlier shoguns' reigns, even taking into consideration Yoshimitsu's profound gratitude for Hosokawa's long and brilliant stewardship. No wonder people were led to speculate behind their fans that in fact the shrewd old fox Hosokawa had arranged his own departure with Yoshimitsu's full connivance in order to safeguard and further strengthen the shogun's personal position. A farfetched story, but perhaps not completely unfounded, for as months passed, poets and painters from amongst the shogun's Companions were seen traveling down to Hosokawa's island fortress to participate in *renga* poetry competitions or paint his likeness. Famed artisans of the capital traveled the hazardous roads and sea to create armor, helmets and saddles for the Hosokawa clan and often brought back some of the most beautiful works to the shogun with Hosokawa's compliments. Rumor had it that many lengthy letters passed between the Flowering Palace and Shikoku Island by the hand of these artisans.

As for the position of the Kanze troupe, although inevitably the new Chancellor Shiba did everything in his power to help the dengaku companies recover their lost ground in the capital from the Kanze, Yoshimitsu, with his zealous drive to build or repair temples and monasteries and bridges, commanded an increased number of subscription performances to raise funds and made sure the Kanze had a fair share of them; therefore, they did not suffer any noticeable decline in number of performances in the capital or in their income.

As for their popularity in the provinces, Kanami continued to be the most adored of all entertainers, and frequently the old and the ill were carried on wooden stretchers to see him, believing they could be indirectly blessed by Buddha's merciful miracle through Kanami's genius.

The dengaku actors and their patrons eagerly watched out for signs of the shogun's waning favor toward Motokiyo, but they did not seem to find much consolation in this regard, as the following anecdote demonstrates.

The shogun, who could not resist novelty, was then much smitten by the cult of tea-tasting contests, a cult brought back by Zen priests who had recently returned from the Chinese Continent where the tea contest was said to be the height of fashion. Yoshimitsu collected many beautiful miniature tea caddies made of rare materials and made a habit of stringing a favored few onto his saddle or around his armored waist whenever he went on military expeditions or a leisurely progress. When people nearest to the shogun gossiped that one of the shogun's most cherished tea caddies had been given to Motokiyo as an end-of-the-year gift, Kiami of dengaku exclaimed, "But tell me how, how does the sarugaku monkey manage this? Why, he's been a man for more than a year now!"

12

"THE AUTUMN foliage is excuse enough," the young autocrat said, cutting the argument short. "Make my procession to Nara the most majestic that has ever been seen. In Nara itself I'll visit the Todai and the Kofuku temples and the Kasuga Shrine. And on the third day I want the Kanze to offer a program of sarugaku noh plays to the Kasuga deities."

Yoshimitsu scanned the faces in the audience room with a slow grin: the Kanze having been for so long and diligently the Kofuku-Kasuga retainers, no one could criticize the shogun's choice as being partial. The preparation for the first shogunal visit to the ancient capital of Nara was begun at once, and the daimyo vied with one another to secure the service of the best craftsmen in Kyoto to make them new saddles, armor and helmets for what promised to be a particularly magnificent occasion.

Yoshimitsu had in mind to kill two birds with one stone: to ameliorate his somewhat soured relationship with the old established temples in Nara after Hosokawa's banishment and to put indirect pressure on the Southern Court lurking at Yoshino, only a few mountain ranges beyond Nara.

The Kasuga Shrine, bowing to the hint from Yoshimitsu, had ordered its own retainer-artisans to create a superb suit of armor with a tiger and a sparrow in deep relief in gold and bronze on the breastplate. Yoshimitsu was to wear it on his way down to Nara, but on the last day of his visit would offer it back to the shrine to accompany his farewell prayer.

The shogun's procession, from the advance runners to the rear guard, stretched for two and a half miles, and the scale and the sumptuousness of it, as Yoshimitsu intended, dazzled and awed the spectators who jostled along the road, spilling over into the paddy fields and tea plantations. As Yoshimitsu, mounted on a sparkling black stallion, passed, even those Yamato locals traditionally more sympathetic to the Southern Court knelt down on the roadside, often moved to tears by the sheer splendor of the shogun's appearance; and their gratitude for the prolonged absence under his reign of a major war which could have devastated their fields and forests was sincerely felt. When Yoshimitsu entered the ancient capital, he found the Kofuku Temple dignitaries much more hospitable and anxious to please than he had anticipated, showing no sign of their defiantly independent spirit.

At the sarugaku noh performance on the last night of the shogunal visit, Kanami presented his new play, *Kayoi Komachi,* and this, which tragically was to be his last masterpiece, made Yoshimitsu, by now accustomed to expect only the best from Kanami, slap his knee and exclaim, "My heavens, this is superb!"

The shogun's undisguised enthusiasm prompted the Kofuku high priests, amongst whom was the scar-faced chief abbot of the Jozen Monastery, to make exceptionally copious and valuable gifts to the Kanze troupe.

On the return journey, satiated from the banquet that had followed the sarugaku performance and loaded with gifts, Yoshimitsu traveled in an ox-drawn carriage. The weather was fine with a cool scintillation in the air, and the pace of the endlessly winding procession was leisurely, some carriages slowing up the progress still further as their passengers were busy creating poems and having them sent by foot messengers from carriage to carriage.

The procession had left the town of Kizu and was approaching the Kizu River when suddenly four of the outriders surrounding the shogunal carriage dropped to the ground, their necks and helmets pierced through with arrows still violently quivering from the force of the impact. Two ox-carriage attendants, hit in the ribs, lay groaning with pain. Simultaneously, some dozen heavily armored men on horseback darted out of the dense bamboo forest, brandishing long heavy swords with terrifying yells. In anticipation of the possibility of such an ambush the shogun was riding in the second carriage, the first and the third identical ones being filled with armored samurais, who, leaping out of the carriages, overwhelmed the assassins in no time. Seven of them were cut to death on the spot, and the rest were herded into a line, some of them bleeding copiously.

Yoshimitsu, raising the palm-leaf blind of his carriage, surveyed the line of blood-splattered warriors, their hands tied behind them by coarse ropes, and gave orders to behead them all on the Kamo riverbank. Then, leaning forward with his eyes narrowed, he ordered his captain of guards: "The sixth from the left—find out his name."

"You have sharp eyes, all right, accursed usurper of the heavenly throne!" the prisoner singled out by Yoshimitsu yelled before the guard had time to gag him. "I'm the grandson of Masamune Kusunoki!"

THE FOLLOWING morning Kanami and Motokiyo arrived early at the Companions' lobby in the palace, where there was already a larger number of artists than usual: the news that the shogun's procession had been attacked by some Southern Court assassins had spread throughout the capital overnight.

Kiami was seen in the corner, surrounded by painters and caligraphers, sipping tea with his gourd-shaped face even more elongated at each noisy sip. Meeting Kanami's eyes, he held them for a split second before turning away, deliberately failing to return Kanami's bow, which disturbed Kanami, for his senior dengaku rival had always taken meticulous care not to publicly demonstrate his enmity. Motokiyo noticed the exchange and bowed all the more courteously toward Kiami's group, who all chose not to notice him. Kanami felt relieved when he saw Nanami breeze in with his customary affable manner, exchanging small talk with everyone. His face already set in a friendly smile to catch Nanami's attention, Kanami sat up taller, but Nanami went quickly to the other end of the room without seeing Kanami and engaged himself in an animated conversation with an old Zen priest, famous for his landscape painting.

Tea was brought. Motokiyo found a small folded paper under his saucer, and handing Kanami a cup of tea, he looked his father in the eye and slipped the paper into the latter's equally alert hand. Kanami sipped his tea quietly, then opened a book of poetry and inside it read the note. It was in Nanami's hand.

"Go at once to *his* inner rooms. Take M."

Motokiyo left the lobby pretending to ask for more tea. Kanami followed.

At the last turning of the covered corridor before the shogun's private apartment, beyond which no one without special permission was admitted, the guards, who knew the shogun's favorite actors well, inclined their heads in stiff silence and let them pass inside.

"Kanami, explain!" yelled Yoshimitsu, barely giving the attendant time to close the sliding screens behind the Kanze father and son; his brows frowning dangerously, the tic that harassed the right half of his face more noticeable than usual, he seemed for once ill at ease and tried not to meet Motokiyo's eye. Lords Akamatsu, Shiba and Isshiki, below the shogun's dais, scrutinized the actors with an expectant malice.

"Explain what, my lord?"

"Are you a Kusunoki?" Yoshimitsu came straight out, pronouncing the name as if it were a poisoned spittle. Motokiyo's thunderstruck glance shot from the shogun to his father.

"Not in any actual . . ." Kanami shifted from one buttock to the other, and the father's discomfort caused the son to turn white and dry-mouthed.

"Yes or no will do, Kanami," Chancellor Shiba cut in impatiently.

"Yes, but . . ." Kanami, who had never faltered his lines, gyrated with an inarticulate mumble. Motokiyo loudly gulped dry saliva: having lived far more intimately and perilously than his father had ever done in the quicksand of the palace intrigues, Motokiyo understood the hair-raising implication of his father's reluctant "Yes."

"Kanami—" Yoshimitsu lifted his hand; he could not bear watching his favorite artist fumble ignominiously. "The young Kusunoki spoke before he was executed. The Kusunoki blood flows in you; we know it; don't deny it."

"My mother was the youngest sister of Masashige Kusunoki, so I am told," Kanami said simply, his forehead frank and his voice straight. Such a devastating admission so casually delivered produced a visible reaction of amazement amongst the high officials and a friendly grin from Yoshimitsu.

"But," Kanami continued matter-of-factly, "by the time I was born my mother had nothing whatever to do with the Kusunokis. She had been excommunicated by her elder brother for having eloped with a low-ranking samurai retainer."

Chancellor Shiba kept his steely cold gaze on Kanami, as he found no mitigating point in the fact that Kanami's mother had been an excommunicated Kusunoki. A Kusunoki was a Kusunoki: a leper was a leper. Masashige Kusunoki had been one of those perfectly ordinary resident landowners with a large self-defensive army made up of kinsmen and retainers, but by fighting and dying so heroically and selflessly to uphold the legitimacy of the Southern Emperors against the Ashikaga shoguns and their "puppet" Northern Emperors, he had become a national legend, a haloed martyr, a paragon of Confucian virtues. He was now sung and painted and written about all over the country. As a sanctified symbol, it was the name, Kusunoki, that counted; excommunicated or not, it counted far more than an army of a thousand men.

Kanami, pressured by the tense hush in the wide room, continued: "How they kept themselves alive, what was their end, I do not know. All I do know is that they could not afford to keep the baby they had brought into this world and had to give it away to the chief of a sarugaku troupe in Yamato. The fact that they could not do better than give it to someone belonging to the lowest of the seven lowest social castes shows how desperate their situation by then had become.

"I haven't the slightest recollection of my samurai parents, enjoyed neither samurai education nor privilege; as far as I am concerned I am the adopted son of a sarugaku actor. In fact, I would never have known of my samurai roots had not one of the Kusunoki relatives, hunted by the shogunal soldiers, come to ask for shelter in our home. According to him, my existence had been made known to the Kusunoki family by a letter my mother had written just before she died somewhere in the East.

"I could not very well refuse him a roof, but did not encourage him to visit me again either. His contemptuous, high-handed attitude toward the members of my troupe did not make him a welcome guest. He stayed with us only a few days and I have never seen him again.

"I haven't told anyone, not even my own son, about my connection with the Kusunokis. I may be guilty of being too naive, but frankly, being what I am, an entertainer, I never thought it significant or relevant enough to tell anyone. I repeat, aside from that portion of the blood which runs in me, I have nothing whatsoever to do with the Kusunokis."

Yoshimitsu, looking overtly satisfied with Kanami's explanation, finding innocence in Kanami's casual, almost dismissive attitude toward the Kusunoki ties, turned to the grim row of his councilors, but Akamatsu slid quickly forward, his thin slits of eyes disappearing behind his smirking heavy eyelids.

"Whilst we do not wish to soil your name, graced with the title of *ami,* by calling you a spy in the pay of the Southern daimyos or an exceedingly convenient messenger between the Southern court and the former chancellor, Hosokawa, the facts accumulated by reliable offices of the shogunate oblige us to view your case with grave suspicion. What would be your explanation for the fact that you seem to have toured in the South always, as it so happens, at times of intense political tension or armed revolt in the region?"

"I have never taken my troupe on the road, whether to east or west or south, with any consideration other than for the weather, availability of festivals and our local popularity. If our troupe's visits coincided here and there with political unrest it was purely coincidental."

"I am told you know the Way of swords and are a competent horseman as well. Why should you, an actor, excel in such martial arts?"

"I find an immense store of choreographic beauty and discipline in swordsmanship, learn from it and use it in my work. I learned riding as a small child from a traveling trick rider who used to visit my adoptive father in the winter months."

Yoshimitsu suddenly stretched both his arms straight above his head and yawned—not a polite muffled yawn, but a loud and extensive one. Before his appalled daimyos knew how to react, he simply gesticulated for them to leave, his yawn turning into an irritable scowl. As they hurriedly slid backward out of the room on their knees, the mighty lords failed to notice the shogun's little nod signaling the Kanze father and son to stay.

"Kanami, you'd be hounded and driven to the ground if you stayed in the capital," Yoshimitsu began in a whisper. "Today, they were not brilliant; they couldn't bring out a single solid piece of evidence against you; but they won't stop there. They neither are convinced of your innocence nor wish to be. But just think: no one clan has tried harder to annihilate the Ashikaga shogunate than the Kusunokis. You must admit it's a strange karma, eh, Kanami?"

Yoshimitsu laughed, but then, erasing by a stroke all the amusement from his face, he said sternly: "I suggest you go on a long tour, Kanami. I'll let you know when to return to the capital."

"But, my lord, the very fact that I have been so much on the road has aroused such suspicion . . ."

"Choose your way judiciously. Don't slink off southward, whatever you do. Go east. But leave me Motokiyo. Can't be deprived of both of you. And don't forget to teach him *Kayoi Komachi* before you leave."

Kanami fell to the floor, and his bulk shook with a big man's sobs as Motokiyo dropped his forehead onto the trailing end of his father's garment.

13

KANAMI RECKONED that the tour, which was tantamount to a working exile, would last a year, perhaps even two. He ordered new masks and costumes and a portable stage floor of boards larger than the rush mats that Himi, the mask carver, and Tamana had bought for him for the mud road preceding his entry into Kyoto. He also purchased sturdy bamboo canes and long cotton curtains to encircle the area where the paying audience sat, without forgetting to order a new billboard and some bright-colored banners announcing the Kanze troupe.

Kanami then chose the touring company with careful consideration for Motokiyo and those to be left behind in Kyoto, for he hoped, despite Chancellor Shiba's eager patronage of the dengaku groups and the damage done to the Kanze's popularity through his Kusunoki connection, that Motokiyo and the remaining company could manage to retain some of the ground they had so painstakingly gained from the dengaku. He taught Motokiyo the advanced roles in all three categories—gods, the aged and females—as far as Motokiyo, at barely twenty-one, could master. With a late-February departure in mind, Kanami already smelled the restless sharp tang in the air of the touring road, and his training was accordingly urgent, intense and as always punctuated by flying whips and invective.

Through long winter nights, Tamana sewed her husband's clothes and underwear for the long tour. Warming her hands from time to time over a small wooden brazier, she told Kogame and Kumao, who were to be taken on the tour, that they ought to start praying for a cloudless Mount Fuji.

"When my father's troupe toured in Suruga I was thirteen. One October morning, having slept in the dried rice field after the harvest had been taken, I woke up and saw Mount Fuji right above me. The two most wonderful things that have happened in my life were becoming Master Kanami's wife and seeing Mount Fuji without a shroud of mist or cloud on it."

Finally, with the plum and peach blossoms bursting forth in every garden and street corner, the touring company, thirty in number, left the capital for Nara and having dutifully performed at the Festival of Ten Thousand Stone lanterns at the Kasuga Shrine on February the fourth, set out eastward.

When the company reached the province of Suruga in May, Kumao wrote home:

"Rewarded for all those prayers! Saw Mount Fuji without a trace of cloud over it. Before dawn it's dark blue-purple like a young aubergine; then suddenly, literally between two blinkings of my eyes, with the first sunlight breaking on it, it turned fuchsia-red all over. Till you've seen it yourself, you can't possibly understand why people have always said, You cannot go to heaven till you've seen Mount Fuji."

Everywhere they went they had an eager, warm reception, and temples and shrines in the vicinity, hearing of the Kanze's presence in the area, hurried to send their invitations.

"So different from humid and close Kyoto," diligently reported Kumao, who, having learned to write from Motokiyo, acted as company scribe on tour, "here on the slope of Fuji the air is so dry that Fuzen's hand drum has split in the center and Jumon complains that he hasn't enough saliva to keep the colt hide of his small drum sufficiently moist and pliable during a performance. Otherwise, all is well: no cancellation of performance due to bad weather or accident; no theft, no report of bandits in the area and so far no attack of diarrhea from the change of water. Tomorrow is the last day of our performance at the Asama Shrine. We are to be honored with the presence of the great daimyo Imagawa of Suruga, who has particularly requested Master to play *Jinen Koji*. Being the Great Tree's uncle, Lord Imagawa must have heard how his young nephew loves Master Kanze in the play."

In the dry, clement weather of May, Kumao's letter reached Motokiyo in just four days. The same evening, a handyman-cum-ticket-attendant boy from Omina's dance troupe, known to the Kanze members since Omina's first visit to Yuzaki village as Sango, collapsed into the Kanze stable gate, worn out to the point of vomiting the first sip of water. He sobbed and ranted alternately in a most pitiable, incoherent manner, and it was not till moments later that his repeated jabbering became intelligible.

"Master Motokiyo! Let me see the young master!"

It was Suzume, Kumazen's hefty, level-headed wife, whom everyone called "a man in a wig," who took the matter in hand and brought the wretched creature straight to Motokiyo in the stage room. "Something about him told me . . ." Suzume said later.

"Sango, what has happened to you? Calm, calm—I'm here, I'm listening," Motokiyo repeated gently after having asked Suzume and others to leave the stage room, for Sango had gesticulated frantically for him to send everyone away.

"Your father . . ." Sango struggled to bring out the two words, then burst into a tearing wail.

"What? My father what?" Motokiyo slid forward on the polished wooden boards like a snake alerted. Sango lifted his eyes and, meeting Motokiyo's dilated, frightened eyes, covered his stubbly grimy face and shook himself in even fiercer sobs.

"The Master of Kanze is no more!"

Motokiyo blinked and strained his eyes as if he could not quite focus them on Sango; then, inclining his head sidewise like a man hard of hearing, he asked slowly, "My father—no more, you said?"

Sango fell flat, face downward, on the floor, broken by exhaustion, voiceless. After a moment of insensate stupefaction, Motokiyo said aloud, though his tongue and mouth felt like pumice stone, "You are telling me Kanami of Kanze is dead?"

Like the first drops of water on fine dry flour, the meaning would not seep into his comprehension but rolled and rolled in demented circles on its impermeable surface.

"Murdered!" Sango blurted, squirming from the horror of

the memory. "I saw both Master Kanze and Omina-sama killed before my eyes."

"Omina-dono? Was she there?"

"Yes—we joined Master Kanze's troupe from Mino and traveled eastward together; but it must have been straight into a Dark and Pernicious Direction that we marched: how else could you explain that both of them had to be slain from the back in the middle of a dance and burned without a prayer, like rabid dogs?"

"But, Sango, during *what* dance? My father and your mistress do not perform together; besides, who'd murder a shogun's Companion-in-Arts in front of the shrine gods and audience?"

"Not a public performance at the Asama Shrine, Master Motokiyo! After three days of sarugaku noh, your father and my mistress were asked to go and perform at His Lordship's private banquet."

"Which lordship?"

"The old Lord Mizuno." Sango shivered involuntarily as he mentioned the famous warrior of a generation earlier.

"And you too went to Lord Mizuno's mansion?"

"I'm like her dog—I go everywhere my mistress goes. They'd been asked to come alone: a private evening; His Lordship's sons would like to play the music—that was the idea. But I carried my mistress' robes, bells and chest drum, and when dismissed by a samurai who received your father and Omina-sama, I didn't leave but sneaked in through the stable yard. It's an enormous mansion, surrounded by a landscaped garden with a high roofed wall all round it. When the moon rose, I went toward the tea arbor by the lake where the music was coming from and sat on a stone under a weeping maple. I could see Master Kanze's dancing shadow on the sliding screens and could just hear his famous voice. The picture I'm used to, you know: great people drinking, making music and poems, and dancing and me squatting outside on my haunches, sipping cheap wine from my gourd; no worldly cares, just the night breeze and me. Then I heard my mistress scream— a noise like tearing heavy silk. On the sliding screens a jumble of shadows; and suddenly with a furious yell two latticed paper screens were kicked down. Your father leaped from the veranda and ran into the garden, upright but unsteady, cut in the back.

"At first I couldn't see my mistress, but heard her scream. It was terrible, terrible! 'Run, Kanami-dono, run, run!' Another swing of a sword cut short her scream, and all the lamps in the room went out. On the white graveled garden path three samurais were pointing their swords at your father, who also held a long sword like a born samurai. How he'd got the sword I don't know. I was crouching inside a thick azalea bush, chanting the prayer *Namu ami dabutsu, namu ami dabutsu*. The samurais were careful not to raise their voices, and I could tell they were growing impatient, but your father held them off by staring at them like the fire-spitting demon he used to play so awesomely. No one budged for some time. It was in the end your father who hacked at a samurai in front of him. Then, I saw nothing. I covered my eyes. Every sword was down on Master Kanze. *Namu ami dabutsu, namu ami dabutsu . . .* The last thing I saw was two rolls of straw mats being set on fire down by the lane."

Motokiyo lifted both arms in front of his face as if he were drowning in Sango's words, his mouth distorted, out of which escaped a quick succession of harsh, short moans of revulsion. Sango was alarmed, wondering if the young master had difficulty breathing, but as he timorously moved forward, Motokiyo opened his huge dry, clear eyes, stopping Sango dead on one lifted knee, and said in a calm, soft voice:

"Keep what you know to yourself. Confide it to no one. If you have nowhere to go, I'll keep you as a Kanze retainer."

He made Sango sleep in the corridor directly outside his own room in case Sango should rave in his sleep. The moment Sango, behind the paper screens, began breathing regularly through his windy dry throat, Motokiyo put both his fists on the floor, his shoulders squared, his head hanging loose. He ground his teeth together till his head and eyes vibrated with pain, but still an animal-like cry of despair swelled up and escaped. To lose a father was an unmeasurable tragedy, but to lose a Kanami, a creator, a peerless genius, a teacher, a beacon, an illumination! Kanami just a mutilated blood-stiffened lump, wrapped up in a straw mat? Never again to experience that rolling sea of excitement as Kanami surges to the limit of the stage? Never again to feel cold shivers at his hypnotic silence? Never to be slapped by his big hand, never to hear him say, Well done, Motokiyo? And now, at twenty-one, to carry the forty-strong company on my inadequate shoulders! Life has an end, the Way of art is limitless, Kanami said; yet he and all his unknowable future glories had to be butchered to extinction halfway on his Way, leaving me alone, I, who have hardly started. . . .

It was a catastrophe too gigantic and horrendous for Motokiyo to cry. His bloodless white knuckles digging into the cold midnight floorboards, he sat stunned, aware only of the unbearable loss.

The dawn had hardly broken when the shogun's messenger arrived quietly at the Kanze gate to fetch Motokiyo to the Flowering Palace.

Yoshimitsu was having his hair combed, with a tray of breakfast before him.

"Leave us alone. Go!"

He waved the pages and attendants out of the room. Motokiyo avidly inhaled the familiar incense and, suddenly feeling faint, fell prostrate with his forehead on the back of his hands. From the height of his dais, Yoshimitsu's eye caught with rapacious speed the slim, white, sinuous neck gleaming like a wet stalk of leek. In the pit of his stomach an animal jerked and stood up. He had not seen Motokiyo alone since the latter's ceremony of adulthood, and he knew it would not be totally honest to say he had craved for Motokiyo: there had been new discoveries and favorites, male and female, who had satisfied him adequately. But he had had to discipline himself rigorously not to compare them with Fujiwaka; it was in his "split-bamboo" nature not to look back and lament the inevitable change decreed in the law of man. Now, for the first time alone with Motokiyo again, in the voluptuous immediacy of death and tragedy, his entire being, heart and guts and every fiber, reawakened by a flood of memories, yearned for the sarugaku boy. He stayed immobile and speechless for a whole minute or even longer; the harder he fought the forbidden passion inside him, by an aberrant twist in human emotion, the more intense grew his sorrow over Kanami's death. The hot tears that washed his lascivious gaze on Motokiyo were sincere, whatever it was that impelled them to flow so abundantly.

"My fault, Fujiwaka; my inexcusable inattention to details; I cannot blame myself enough. Go east, I told Kanami without properly warning him that the region swarmed with old fanatics. My uncle Imagawa and his veteran general Mizuno fought every battle that helped to keep the shogunal throne for my father, and I believe this Mizuno lost an eye and a few fingers in doing so. Considers me a pipsqueak fledgling, finds my handling of the

Southern Court and its sympathizers too tame. Kanami's Kusu-noki connection must have been adroitly planted in his ear by someone in advance of Kanami's arrival in Suruga. My guess is that Mizuno's son and sons-in-law actually carried out the murder, and if this is any consolation to you, Fujiwaka, Kanami maimed the young Mizuno for life before he himself perished."

"My father . . . maimed Mizuno-sama's son!" What reper-cussions now? Motokiyo felt the floorboards below him open and engulf him.

"No need for panic. The official notification delivered to me from my uncle Imagawa ascribes the sudden disappearance of my renowned Companion-in-Arts to an epidemic. For hygienic rea-sons, says he, the actor's body and all his belongings had to be burned. And you and I know perfectly well no epidemic has been reported in any part of Suruga. Much as I loved Kanami, till I achieve the unification of the North and the South Courts, I can-not afford to lose the Imagawa clan's support. We must maintain it was an epidemic that killed Kanami. As for this *kusé* dancer, the less said the better. Her troupe left quietly on a long tour far-ther northeast in exchange for a continued free pass over the Su-ruga border."

Yoshimitsu moved down from his dais, and placing his palms flat on the floor, he bowed deeply and correctly.

"Fujiwaka, will you forgive me?"

Motokiyo, bowing even lower, protested in bewilderment at the shogun's extraordinary behavior. Yoshimitsu raised himself promptly, pleased and rather moved as well by his own gesture of magnanimous humility, and succumbing to the proximity, im-pulsively laid his hand on the back of Motokiyo's neck.

"Since I freed you from the night duty . . ." Yoshimitsu be-gan in a hoarse voice as compelling tenderness like a turning screw tightened his chest. Their eyes met; and it was Motokiyo who looked away and shut his eyes slowly and heartbrokenly. Yoshi-mitsu retrieved his hand from Motokiyo's neck, hurried back onto his dais and banged on the damask-covered armrest like a mad-man, screaming:

"Don't lose a minute; announce yourself the new master. And a wife. I'll find you a wife. You must think of the continuity of the Kanze!"

He abruptly dismissed Motokiyo and clapped his hands for the pages and attendants to resume the interrupted morning toilet.

14

It HAPPENED in the early spring after Kanami's death during a torchlight performance at the Kofuku Temple, in which all four Yamato sarugaku schools had been commanded to participate. The program opened with *Okina,* presented, in token of his seniority, by Master of Komparu, and Motokiyo followed him in *Hagoromo,* an anonymous old play with a magnificent closing dance in which his father had made many improvements.

The Temple's high priests, hooded and wrapped up as thickly as mummies in layers of holy garments, together with their lay guests, sat above the wide white stone steps beneath the great South Gate which soared massively, blacker than black, against a fine sky disturbed only by a half-moon surrounded by a fleecy, almost transparent wreath of cloud.

The theater-loving Yamato people, so proud and pleased to see the son of their cherished Kanami on his home ground again, filled every space till a pin would have found it hard to drop straight to the ground. Many Kanze faithfuls had been vociferously regretting that as an adult Motokiyo Kanze would now be obliged to hide his face behind a mask, but when Motokiyo made his first entrance the entire audience raised an involuntary sigh of Ah!, so out-of-this-world beautiful was his appearance. In the flickering and undulating light of the torches which always added to this type of performance a special magic and character, Motokiyo's heavenly maiden, a headdress delicately hanging over his mask like a cobweb of light and shadow, appeared all the more haunting. One connoisseur, a shipping magnate from the port of Osaka, was moved to sigh loudly to his entourage, "Now, look at that! The sheen of the pearls I buy in the South Sea!"

Kumazen, in the *waki* role of the fisherman who steals the angel's cloak of wings, found Motokiyo in excellent form that evening: his voice was taut, and the way he balanced moments of utter serenity with swift bravura attacks was masterly. Touched by the maiden's grief, the fisherman returns the robe to her in exchange for a dance. Toyodayu, acting as *koken,* helped Motokiyo put on a gossamer-light cloak with wide sleeves reaching down to the ankles as the chorus, led in this performance by Raiden, sang:

> *"The maiden dons her robe and dances*
> *The rainbow skirt and cloak of wings . . ."*

The angel's dance was building up to a climax when Toyodayu, sitting slightly behind and to the right of the musicians, saw Motokiyo's feet come together like two hands in a prayer, then stop. With his left arm, in the ample feather-light sleeve, held high above his head, he remained motionless: not a stir, not a twitch. Masked, wigged and ornately costumed, except for a thin strip of his skin below the mask there was nothing of Motokiyo visible to enable anyone to hazard a guess as to what was happening behind it.

Toyodayu knew it was the *koken*'s duty to instantly take over from an incapacitated *shité* and bring the performance to a finish, but in front of his very eyes stood Motokiyo so matchlessly a heavenly maiden, only immobile. Toyodayu hesitated till he felt the perspiration dripping from his forehead. With Motokiyo thus petrified, the twenty or thirty seconds that passed in silence and inaction seemed to those on stage like an hour, a dozen hours, an eternity, and for the first time that evening they could hear the huge piles of burning logs hissing and spitting below the solemn rows of the priestly audience.

It was old Meisho who broke the hideous spell of silence:

his flute let spiral a long shrill appeal. He blew and blew till his neck, turning red and turgid, seemed about to explode. Fuzen responded with bullet-sharp beats on his hand drum. Taking the cue from the veteran musicians, Toyodayu nodded to Raiden, who at once led the chorus ahead and sang Motokiyo's lost verses:

> *"I left the moon, and briefly*
> *Descending to the east . . ."*

Toyodayu saw a slight quiver on Motokiyo's sleeve, which was then unhurriedly drawn in a large arc as Motokiyo glided into the rest of the dance with his uncanny airborne serenity as if nothing whatever had gone wrong. Kumazen peered for some indication, some explanation. None. The mask of the young maiden was implacably sealed in all gentleness and celestial dignity.

Motokiyo was the first to come off the stage. As soon as he stepped inside the dressing room, he sat quietly down on the floor, facing the wall. Ogame and Kogame rushed behind him to untie his mask cords, and Kogame noticed how cold and dry the master's skin was as his hand brushed across Motokiyo's nape.

The cords were untied, but Motokiyo would not let go of the mask; he held it an inch away from his face as if he were afraid to face the world outside the mask.

"Master?" whispered Ogame, and very gently removed the valuable mask from Motokiyo's limp hands.

"I don't know how that happened," said Motokiyo at last. Something, either the gasping hoarse voice or the slurring of his words, made Kogame fix his myopic eyes on his master and friend, but as always Motokiyo's perfect features thwarted his prying gaze, like a mirror that flashes back candid sunlight. Kogame could only gawk at Motokiyo's profile, which as always appeared thinner after a masked performance.

Presently, Kumazen and Toyodayu, then the musicians returned from the stage and finding their young master in a stupefied isolation with his face averted to the wall, halted, at a loss as to what to say or do; whereas Meisho, who after so many years of self-imposed abstinence had begun drinking again and hard since Kanami's death, walked straight up to Motokiyo and squatting next to him, patted him on the lap.

"You've frightened me, you've killed me, Little Master. I shan't be able to play for you again. You've put a knife into this old wine bag, you have!"

"Meisho!" Toyodayu pulled the old man aside. "You can't punish Young Master with such a dastardly threat. Of course you'll play again!"

"Punish my master's son? Hold your tongue, Toyo, never! You don't understand. You have no ears. I do. I hear it. I play it the Old Master's way; the Young Master goes his own way. Naturally, something rips on stage. It's like—"

"Don't be ridiculous," snapped Toyodayu, cutting the shriveled old man short as he anxiously gazed at Motokiyo's petrified profile. "There's no old or new way. We have just one Kanze way."

"That's what you think. Oh, you earless idiots drive me to drink!" Meisho wailed, and defiantly he pulled out a small shiny gourd from under his hakama fold.

THANKS TO Motokiyo's hypnotic presence and his veteran performers' tact, the incident had gone unnoticed by the majority of the audience that night; and those who did notice it had ascribed it entirely to the young Kanze's distraught grief over the loss of his great father. But it was manifest to every member of the Kanze troupe that the incident had smashed their young master's mask of composure to smithereens. Soon they had to witness the ignominious scene of their master losing a competition performance, held at the daimyo Hatakeyama's mansion, to Kanze's long-standing rival Zomasu of dengaku; and shortly afterward, at a shrine outside the capital, Motokiyo was heckled and hit by a muddy straw sandal as he was again struck inexplicably dumb halfway through his monologue.

His disarray extended to the company rehearsal as well: more frequently than could have been dismissed as merely a passing phase of disorientation, he would walk to the center of the stage room at the Kanze house, then stand there with a terrified lost look on his face, and those who were close to him would hear him breathe irregularly as if there were not enough air. Musicians and actors alike, their hands idle on their instruments or laps, tried not to watch their twenty-two-year-old master seized by a sort of agoraphobic terror: he who was the idol of the capital and for whose subscription performances the officials in charge had had to take extra security measures to cope with the massive turnout; he who had been believed to have appeared in the dreams of two dying persons and saved their lives.

"Hardly had the poor boy had time to recover from the

dreadful shock of suddenly finding that he had outgrown his Flower of the Moment when his father died," said Tamana in her gentle healing voice to Toyodayu, who had come to express his keen anxiety over the young master's state. Tamana, whose unobtrusive presence when her husband was alive had resembled a dimly lit lamp in strong daylight, surprised everyone with her show of indomitable courage and calm in the face of catastrophe, which sprang from the simplicity and goodness of her soul. The illiterate woman, with Ogame's help alone, not only had coped with everything to do with Kanami's funeral rites and Motokiyo's succession to the Kanze mastership, but, what was most impressive, had at the same time engaged twenty priests to pray for their gallant old friend Omina and her departed soul. She had installed Omina's mortuary tablet on the Kanze family altar and every morning offered the same quantity of candles, fresh flowers and prayer before Omina's mortuary tablet as before her late husband's.

"Remember, Toyo, how often the late Master repeated that the crucial period in an actor's life is at about twenty-four," continued Tamana. "Just think, twenty-two and without his father and master, on top of having to perfect himself he is now expected to look after his forty-odd disciples—both their progress in our art and their material welfare. There's a surprising number of chores and duties required of the head of the troupe, for which the late Master had too little time to prepare him. Nor had he given Motokiyo enough instruction in playwriting, and you know what importance the late Master placed on that branch of the art. The boy realizes that only too well. Put yourself in his place, Toyo: wouldn't you be rattled out of your wits? All we can do is to sit tight and pray for him."

NANAMI, who had suffered a stroke soon after Kanami's death, having stayed up two whole days and nights composing endless *renga* chain poems and drinking heavily, asked for an audience with the shogun as soon as he was well enough again.

"I've been to see the lad," said Nanami, looking twenty years older, noticeably paralyzed in the left arm and leg and with the left corner of his mouth slack, but still exquisitely dressed and scented. "He needs time. He's not one to cry aloud for help when he's beaten. Like a cat he must hide and lick his wound alone. I am convinced he'll one day crown your reign with an eternal glory."

"Never mind the eternal glory; I want him to do me proud now!" Yoshimitsu barked irritably, as he stood upright amidst several attendants who busied themselves in dressing the shogun for a court ceremony. The shogun hated being constrained to immobility, even for a minute. "Surely, you have heard what Shiba and his dengaku protégés are saying? That Motokiyo is finished; that he was just a firework prodigy fizzling out in the blink of time. And can't you see how the dengaku lot are taking vigorous advantage of the vacuum left by Kanami's death and Motokiyo's inexplicable absence from public view? What's he playing at?"

"In short, My Lord, he's come this far and now doesn't know where to go from here."

"Would it help if I made him a Companion? Although I'd loathe to see him taking the tonsure. Aesthetically. Too young."

"With due respect, I advise the Great Tree not to make him a Companion, not now. Instead, may I humbly suggest an alternative scheme to help draw him out of the doldrums?"

Nanami spoke with a heavy, dragging effort, and his once rubicund and fleshy cheeks were gray hollows; only his eyes set on the shogun twinkled with the former mischievous animation. "Bring to the capital Inuo of sarugaku, who's been fighting a lonely and hard battle against the dengaku ascendancy in the Lake Biwa region."

"What? Inuo of Omi? I remember your telling me he's a self-indulgent old bore!" Yoshimitsu gnashed his teeth as two attendants squatting on either side of him tightened the long sash around his waist.

"What I once told the Great Tree stands true today, to a degree; but the Great Tree will also recall how often and with what passion Kanami used to praise Inuo as a lone bright star, a pilgrim, peerless in the roles of celestial maidens and noble women. Too introverted, maybe, but no one could deny that he is a visionary giant who could give inspired help and stimulus to Motokiyo at this crucial stage in his career."

"Another sarugaku troupe in the capital, eh?" Yoshimitsu chuckled to himself. "Not a bad idea. One seems to have a glut of dengaku these days in Kyoto. So be it. I'll appoint Yamana to build a stage on the Kamo riverbank. It won't ruin the old rascal:

another gold mine was found in His Lordship's province last
month. And, Nanami, make it a competition performance; it
might help shake Motokiyo out of his sulk."

Yoshimitsu nodded to Nanami by way of dismissing him,
shoved both his arms into the proffered sleeves of a court-style
cloak, then sat on his monstrous Chinese chair.

Chancellor Shiba was announced. Tapping his fingernails
lightly against the arm of his chair to the rhythm of his favorite
kusé dance from Jinen Koji, his eyes gloating with a malicious curiosity, the shogun watched Lord Shiba slide forward to deliver to
him the latest report on the fate of his cousin in Kamakura whom
he had ordered his chancellor to quietly eliminate.

Yoshimitsu had put into practice with spectacular success the
sly tricks ex-chancellor Hosokawa had taught him of systematically
liquidating potential threats to the shogunate; whenever he judged
that one of his relatives or his vassal daimyos had become too powerful and prosperous for his own security, he would subtly plant
seeds of strife amongst the usually numerous family of his target
victim, often by being seen to be unduly partial to one of them in
a territorial dispute or a race for a coveted shogunal office. Then,
as soon as the aggrieved party rose in arms or openly plotted
against the favored one, with lightning speed he would send out
massive punitive armies, recruited from amongst his minor or me-
dium-ranking daimyos. Once the revolt he himself had provoked
had been put down, he confiscated the rebel's territory and proceeded to divide it into small fiefdoms, which he then distributed
to whomever he fancied, usually keeping the most fertile or strategically valuable portion for himself.

Having thus multiplied his fortune and military might and
without Hosokawa nagging at his extravagance, Yoshimitsu could
now freely indulge in his favorite hobby of building and collecting and sending scholar priests to the Continent to bring back news
of the latest trend in the arts and the new teachings on Zen. As if
to atone for his flagrant sins of killing and philandering, Yoshimitsu had lately taken zealous interest in both the practice of Zen
and building Zen temples and monasteries, which, combined with
the prodigious number of his concubines, did not fail to cause a
wicked tongue to wag: "But of course, the Great Tree must somehow house all those bastards of his somewhere!"

Yoshimitsu had turned twenty-eight, and although his consort, Yasuko, was barren, his concubines had borne him a more than adequate number of sons. He was indisputably in the prime of manhood and having the greatest and best fun in this material and visible and transient world—as Prince Nijo had remarked, "like a salmon leaping upstream with the richest spread of fat under its skin." It was not at all surprising, therefore, that Motokiyo's solitary inner struggle to find his own footing on the Way of art seemed to him a mere "sulk."

THE MOTOKIYO versus Inuo competition performance in aid of restoration of the Second Avenue bridge damaged by the last autumn's typhoon took place in late May on that part of the Kamo riverbank known as Tadasu field.*

Although he was twenty-six years senior to Motokiyo, it was Inuo who paid the courtesy visit on the young Kanze master before the first performance. Inuo was a tall, emaciated, unremarkable-looking man with a long gourd-shaped head made to appear even longer by his long dimpled chin. Only his eyes were extraordinary, like patches of melted snow in a granite rock, shining with startling brilliance and purity.

"Moth-eaten and dust-covered as I am in a provincial town like Omi," said Inuo, lowering his head with a conventional self-deprecating opening phrase, "I worshiped your father as an incomparable genius and creator and seldom failed to catch his performance whenever he toured near the Lake. As a fellow sarugaku performer, I gratefully and vicariously basked in the Kanze's success and national renown, but never did I dream that one day I'd be invited to the capital to perform in a competition performance against a Kanze master. I gather from Nanami-dono that it was your father's disinterested recommendation which greatly helped move the Great Tree to have a look at me. All I hope is that you'll find me worthy of sharing a stage for the next three days."

Motokiyo noted at once that the man, unlike any other rival actor he had come across, meant what he said. He felt his back loosen and his eyes focus on his visitor without strain or mistrust. —But why does this man so disarm me? Is it not a bad omen that I cannot bring myself to feel combative against him?— Motokiyo was again assailed by a crippling fear of the stage.

* For centuries the name Tadasu field conjured up awe and the stench of blood, as it was here that many public executions took place.

From the very start it was obvious that Kanami had left his troupe polished to the tautest ensemble perfection, so that in comparison, Inuo's company, competent and dourly earnest as they were, could not help appearing dull and untidy; further, this fiendishly well-drilled company was fighting the performance on the strength of Kanami's masterpieces, which gripped and would not let go of the audience' enthralled attention throughout, whilst Inuo's plays seemed even to his confirmed fans who had traveled up to the capital from Omi a somewhat feeble excuse for Inuo to dance and go on dancing.

The Kanze elders had been gnawed sore by misgivings that their young master might lose his nerve against Inuo, for whom his late father had not stinted superlative praise. Tamana had put herself on a ten-day vegetarian diet prior to this important performance. The entire Kumazen family offered the hundred-step prayers every morning at the Kiyomizu Shrine, and there was not one Kanze disciple who in one way or another did not pray for Motokiyo to regain confidence in himself. But Motokiyo, becoming morbidly superstitious, would not agree to appear in any of the roles in which he either had dried up or felt insecure, and confined his appearance during the three-day event to only four *shité* parts.

Once on stage, however, his truly exceptional and indestructible beauty and bearing, aided by the audience' own eagerness to be convinced of his legendary spell, did more than his actual performance, which struck his elders as tentative and uneven, to win a huge ovation. And there was no question that Inuo himself helped make Motokiyo's triumph so easy: Inuo made not the slightest attempt to ingratiate himself with his spectators, no extra effort at all to entertain or to excite the wide and diverse range of the capital's public. Not the smallest concession. He remained inaccessibly elusive and ingrown; he would not turn his fan or tilt his neck even five degrees unless such a move had been a part of his trancelike interior design.

More than half the audience could not fathom him; only an initiated few, mostly amongst the shogun's guests and Companions-in-Arts, realized that there was before them a performance the like of which they had not experienced before. Those same few also understood that the stark simplicity and serenity of his art could have been attained only after he had exhausted an ocean of extrovert emotions and gymnastics. Like a pearl that grows inside a closed shell, his art was not gregarious, not obvious: it was for those who could peer into the jewel hidden behind the austere hard shell.

The Flat Earth, understandably, found Inuo monotonous at his best and excruciatingly tedious in large doses, and it was no wonder that at the end of the three-day event they gave unanimous approval when the Kanze troupe was declared the winner. They howled Motokiyo's and even Kanami's names as the young man was called to the shogun's loge for a congratulatory cup of wine; but when the shogun proceeded to invite Inuo as well, they stopped cheering and applauded politely but reluctantly. The Kyotoites were notorious for being vain and appearance-conscious; that Inuo, placed next to the legendary beauty of a young actor, looked more like a provincial clerk or a herbal medicine man not only failed to thrill them but positively offended them.

"You've grown thinner, Motokiyo. Tough at the top, eh?" said Yoshimitsu mildly, holding out a cup toward Motokiyo. His eagle-bright eyes narrowed as he tried to assess Motokiyo, whom he had not seen face to face for many months now; and immediately the young actor's extraordinary beauty—or rather, the potency of its particular appeal to his senses—struck Yoshimitsu with an undiminished force. Damn, he tutted mentally, and with a studied friendly sarcasm, he added:

"I *have* seen Kanami do better in *Matsukaze,* though; eh, what do you say, Motokiyo? Still, I'm glad you've stopped moping."

Turning to Inuo, Yoshimitsu scanned the middle-aged ascetic with an unsparing rude gaze as if he were a scroll of landscape painting that a shipwrecked Chinese monk might have solicited him to buy. "Inuo, you're a singularly arrogant performer. You don't give a damn about what your customers think. You float miles above their heads, wrapped up in your own lofty mirage of an ideal. Kanami brought the fire and the devil of *kusé* music into sarugaku, and you must admit his plays at their best are a sorcery—so theatrical, so entertaining. But you, Inuo, if I had to put into one word your way of art, I'd use the word *yugen*. Know what that means?"

"No, My Lord," replied Inuo with a childlike candid smile. "I'm just an entertainer."

Yoshimitsu laughed at this and turned on Motokiyo, anticipating and certainly not overlooking Motokiyo's pale-lipped agitation at the mention of *yugen*. "Explain to Inuo what *yugen* is, Motokiyo."

"*Yugen,* literally meaning mystical and somber, is often used in the art of poetry," Motokiyo began docilely but with his eyes downcast and his voice uncertain. "It connotes a supreme rank in the beauty of poetry, like a bird that has stopped beating its wings but planes suspended in midair with no outward show of effort. The ultimate of serenity and elegance."

"There, Inuo, so much for *yugen*. But don't flatter yourself, I didn't say you've got it. I merely said you're on the way to *yugen*, like a water diviner after a deep-buried spring."

Inuo dropped his forehead onto the red flannel carpet by way of submission to Yoshimitsu's assessment and from this position replied:

"The Great Tree has hit the nail on the head. I've worked with no other thought in my mind than this ideal beauty which defies time and men, but have never even known how to describe it till now. Indeed, I'm like a tortoise climbing Mount Fuji, inching forward to the impossible height and sometimes not even knowing where he is."

"Will you ever get there?" Yoshimitsu asked.

"I don't know, My Lord."

"You don't much care if you don't—that's what you mean? You're perfectly happy as you are in your pursuit; you neglect your disciples, don't even notice that your drummer is a drunk and your costumes and props are eccentric rubbish, to put it kindly. I gather from Nanami that without the retainer from the Hiei Shrine your troupe would starve tomorrow, because you give no time to actively soliciting patronage elsewhere. You're a dreamer, a visionary, foolhardy to the point of being self-destructive. Yet I confess you have something that moves me—a peculiar genius if ever I saw one."

Yoshimitsu turned on Lord Shiba and, drawing much pleasure from the expression of choked astonishment on his chancellor's face, told him to make Inuo his new Companion-in-Arts. He went further by giving Inuo one Chinese character out of his own Buddhistic name and named his new Companion Do-ami—the *ami* of the Way.

A couple of days later, Nanami's elegant palanquin entered the Kanze's small gate. Tamana hurried to the entrance hall to welcome the old friend and benefactor, but after one look at him she involuntarily raised a short cry of pain.

"Ah, yes, as you see, I've paid for the gluttonous dissipated life I've led all these years. With so many of my dear friends gone, I confess, Tamana-dono, I'm sorry that the stroke didn't finish me on the spot."

He asked Kanami's widow if he might offer a prayer to his old friend. When he noticed Omina's mortuary tablet placed on the Kanze family altar, his eyes quickly brimmed with tears, and he said with difficulty, 'Ah, Madam, you have a true Buddha's nature in you!"

After kneeling for a long while before the altar, he asked to see Motokiyo alone in his small room.

Motokiyo, clad in a simple indigo-blue linen kimono, looked touchingly like a sick child; the bluish haze of veins above his large flame-shaped eyes accentuated the pallor and vulnerability of his face, now bereft of its boyish fleshiness.

As soon as the protocol exchange of greetings was over, Motokiyo stole his visitor's thunder by simply stating:

"Doami should have won the competition performance. I wouldn't be worthy of being Kanami's son if I didn't realize that. After watching him in one dance I knew he was my master, he a noble elephant and I a lame rabbit far behind his colossal tread on the way to *yugen*. You can imagine how I felt having to receive the shogun's cloak, knowing I was not the true winner. Nanami-dono, would you believe me if I told you I am terrified to go on stage? Meisho said I was not comfortable in my father's Way, and he was right. I am not. Without Kanami's immense, fascinating presence his plays now often seem to me depleted and false."

"I understand perfectly what you say and what Meisho must have meant. Kanami was a realist on *this* side of the world. He was that rarest of geniuses, perhaps a once-in-a-thousand-years phenomenon, who could enthrall everyone from a prince to a woodcutter in one huge sweep. He measured his success against the love of his spectators, masses and masses of them, not just a handful of the capital's elite connoisseurs. His appeal was therefore immediate, physical and potent. Take the protagonists of his plays: a courtesan, a street dancer, a preacher, a minor samurai;

not the exalted personages you have come across reading the classics in Prince Nijo's library. Kanami was happiest when he put his big feet—remember what big feet your father had, Motokiyo?—those big worldly feet on a makeshift traveling stage in the middle of a dusty swarming marketplace and, above all, fighting a competition performance. His dramaturgy was "in order to win." Nothing more, nothing less. His Flower was youth and surprise. His reward was acclaim and adoration. He knew and was reconciled to the fact that a performer cannot exist without spectators, many, many spectators.

"But you, Motokiyo—I have a feeling you are tempted to climb the same rainbow-shrouded height as Doami is attempting. Your spectators are not the mob from a shrine's festivity ground. Since you were twelve, you've been steeped in a culture totally different from your father's. Through Prince Nijo and his coterie in high places, you've absorbed the quintessence of the Heian court culture with all its elitist prejudices and sophistication; furthermore, the Great Tree has left on you unmistakable fingerprints of his own, himself the embodiment of samurai and aristocratic culture at their highest attainable level. Naturally, you cannot go in the same Way as your father. Take this idea of *yugen*. Kanami would have found *yugen* much too untheatrical a notion in *his* theater, whereas you and Doami are clearly oriented in that direction. That was one of the reasons why the Great Tree made Inuo a Companion there and then, hoping that he might be able to help you and work with you. The Great Tree has unshakable confidence in you. He's asked me to give you this message: 'Tell Motokiyo to come and see me whenever he likes, but only if he wants to and when he is ready. I shan't force him. I'll wait.' Those were his actual words. For myself, I hope I'll still be alive to see you on stage again in your own creations. Soon, Motokiyo."

15

IN MARCH the following year, Hotan, aged eighteen, who as a child actor used to dream of one day understudying Fujiwaka and stepping into his roles, won an ovation in *Shizuka,* on the strength of which the Kanze troupe won their first competition performance, without Motokiyo's taking part, over the dengaku troupe. And Meisho died on stage immediately after the performance. A quick, merciful death, slumped over his old flute, having magnificently accompanied Hotan in the final dance.

In early April, Nanami suffered another stroke, and this one killed him. Two months later, in the rainy month, Prince Nijo died of a swollen liver. Motokiyo had daily offered the hundred-step prayer up and down the Kiyomizu Shrine's famous cascade of stone steps for his old mentor's recovery and was prostrate with grief from the quick succession of deaths of three men who had done so much for him and his father.

—The end of an era, perhaps?— the unvoiced thought communicated itself amongst the disciples: Kanami gone, Nanami and Meisho too, and now the Prince, and their young master just a ghost, scarcely seen or heard in daylight, shutting himself up in a small low closet of a room originally intended for a couple of scullery maids, eating little of what Tamana brought him on a tray, reading Buddhist litanies and innumerable books in Japanese and Chinese. The only time he went out was when he visited Doami at his new fine house in the same district. This last, quite understandably, upset the elders of the company, for although of the same sarugaku camp, Doami was now a formidable rival: his patronage amongst the nobles and daimyos of discerning taste was quietly but steadily growing; besides, the Kanze elders, who were far from wholeheartedly enthusiastic about Doami's style, feared his undue influence on their young and impressionable master. This time again, it was Tamana who pleaded with the anxious elders for tolerance and without uttering a word about it to anyone sent Doami the first-of-the-season fruits and flowers by way of thanking him for the help he was giving her son.

What their enemies now derisively called "the headless Kanze" went on winning a laudable number of competition performances over their sarugaku and dengaku rivals, mainly on the strength of their peerless ensemble playing, although the mutely struggling shadow of their young master was there to constantly darken their thoughts. With Chancellor Shiba's continued backing of the dengaku and without Motokiyo participating in any of their performances, the Kanze troupe were now more or less completely denied the opportunity to perform at the grand palaces and the major subscription performances of the capital, except when the shogun himself insisted on having the headless Kanze make up a program with Doami and his Hiei troupe for his private entertainment at the Flowering Palace; but thanks to following Kanami's farsighted policy of never neglecting the rural customers, they were in constant and heavy demand in the provinces and particularly in Yamato, where they often joined forces with one of their sarugaku colleagues on important occasions at the Kofuku Temple or the Kasuga Shrine.

Motokiyo's aberrant behavior, hibernating in his north-facing hole of a room, immersed in books and seemingly fruitless meditation, naturally dealt his mother a cruel blow, for she was the one who saw him most frequently and closely and yet was not allowed to come anywhere near his suffering. Motokiyo made it abundantly clear that he did not wish to talk, let alone be questioned, about himself. If Tama but drew a purposeful breath, still undecided whether she could risk asking such an innocuous question as "Wouldn't you perhaps like to go out for a change and see the autumnal foliage at the Nanzen Temple?" Motokiyo would shoot her between the eyes with an intimidating glance of supplication not to. So she would hold her breath with the look of a surprised pigeon, then exhale, trying hard not to make it sound like a reproachful mother's sigh, and with a diffident smile pick up his tray or his soiled linen and leave the room.

Aware of his inactivity, Motokiyo also refused to eat anything costly—or even much of anything—and to wear anything new or silk. One night, Tamana offered her son, who appeared to weigh even less than when he had been a young boy, a grilled mackerel in season. He would not touch it.

"I am not earning a penny toward my keep," he insisted. "Please give it to Ogame, who is. To Hachi, to Sango, but not to me, Mother."

"But, Motokiyo, the storehouse is packed to the ceiling with the invaluable treasures you have earned; and the Great Tree meticulously pays us the same Companion's retainer in grain and money as when Father was alive."

"Mother, please." The way he said "please," so sweet, so agonized and obdurate, she would do just as Motokiyo wished without ever questioning or contradicting him; and whenever Toyodayu urged her to confront her son and draw out the truth behind his prolonged seclusion, she would shake her head with self-deprecating cheerful laughter.

"He's suffering," she would say, "and I feel for him. But, Toyo, I'm just his mother. Like a toothache, it's his pain; he'll have to suffer it till the rotten tooth is out. And this *truth!* What can I or you or anyone do with it when it obviously does my poor boy no good?"

So she went on bringing and taking away Motokiyo's trays and darned clothes and linen, seen but seldom heard, with a sad, hopeless elation in her heart.

THE FOURTH anniversary of Kanami's death was approaching, and every Kanze disciple in his own fashion began reliving the old master's memory with the sense of loss undiminished by the passage of time. An unknown traveler from Yamato came to the house and asked the widow to place before the great actor's altar some peonies picked in his garden two days earlier and kept fresh during his journey in a long bamboo vase. As the only elder disciple to live with the master's family, Ogame spent much more time praying before the altar during the days before the anniversary rite, and one day during the lunch break, as the sliding screens were opened between the altar room and the adjacent stage room, he had a long moment after his prayers to gaze wistfully at the stage room which still seemed to echo with Kanami's yells and cracking whip.

It was then that it suddenly struck him how like a freshly lacquered tray the stage floor shone. Being of an inquisitive nature, the old comic inspected the stage surface, squinting at its proud sheen, feeling the unctuous grain of the wood here and there; then, his arms folded, his face squashed in a searching grimace, he stood immobile at the center of the stage till the others returned for the afternoon rehearsal.

The same evening, after eating some rice-and-millet gruel with roasted sesame in the kitchen, he returned to the altar room. When the temple bells sounded midnight and the whole household had long been asleep, he slid open the sliding screens just about the width of his goldfish-protrudent eye. The dogs were barking far off; the wind was rising; a lone fire watchman was meandering the streets crying, "Beware of fire!"

He saw a blurred disk of light looming behind the paper screens, which flickered its way down to the floor level, and the sliding screens opened noiselessly, revealing Motokiyo kneeling on the corridor floor. After a deep bow to the stage room, he slid inside, brought in the rapeseed-oil lamp and a few white parcels, and shut the screens behind him with the discipline and economy of movement that came natural to him. He moved to the far corner of the room and set down his lamp a little distance away from him; then, taking what Ogame now recognized as a piece of cloth filled with bean-curd refuse,* shutting his eyes and with his head slightly inclined like a dog waiting for his master's whistle, he began scrubbing the floor on his knees.

It would have been far easier for Ogame to bear the pain of intestinal rupture than it was to stifle the urge to howl and cry then. He understood—Buddha have mercy, how he understood—

---

* The refuse from bean-curd making is to this day used to polish and grease the noh stage surface.

the extent of his little master's ordeal, the depth of his hell. When at seventeen his voice and physique had changed, Kanami had told his son to return to the beginner's awe and start all over again; but now the twenty-four-year-old artist was going even further back to offer penance on the sacred altar of his art.

Ogame's head must have touched the frame of the sliding screens as he buried his face in the cup of his hands.

"Ogame?" whispered Motokiyo, continuing to scrub the floor. "Is that you, Ogame?"

Ogame, wiping both his face and his bald head with his sleeve, crossed the stage room till he came inside the circle of the meager oil-lamp light. When he lifted his head and faced Motokiyo at such a close range, he was taken aback: in that livid light Motokiyo looked not exactly haggard or drawn, but diminished, chiseled down by the dimensions of his doubt, his disorientation, his loss of vision and confidence. All his flawless features were still there, but who would have imagined it possible that the loss of inner cohesion could so alter that loveliest of faces to an unfocused, obtuse, dead mask?

"I knew you'd catch me one night," Motokiyo mumbled, like a child, petulant and relieved at the same time, admitting he had wetted his sleep mat.

Ogame had a nanny's horse sense: his little master wanted to talk, a child talk. "Eh!" he said. "I see you enjoy polishing the floor more than being the Kanze master."

Motokiyo visibly tensed at the sally, but immediately his face broke loose in an inadvertent laugh, which, with his mouth warping downward and his nostrils pinched, crumbled at once to a whine.

"If you want to know, Ogame . . . I feel like a wasp, turned upside down, wings wetted. The harder I struggle, the quicker I drown. It's the sense of obligation, nothing else—my duty to Mother, to you and to everyone—that keeps me here, when I know in my heart of hearts I ought to be a hermit, totally alone, unfettered, selfish, utterly and single-mindedly on the Way of noh. The Kanze's noh was Father's noh, not mine. Not yet. I haven't written a single line, haven't choreographed one dance, haven't invented a single plot or a character. Buddha knows how I have tried. But here, Ogame, I can't! Father's everywhere and I'm just his residue. To find mine, I must . . ."

"Go away, be free?" Ogame offered the words as one would a cup of gruel to the starved.

Motokiyo, suddenly alert, even shrewd, scanned his old nanny's moon face, and seeing there only true compassion and understanding, he sighed.

"Want to!"

"Go, then, little master, go! Go, on the condition you'll never quit the Way of your art and end up being one of those precious dried-up hermits or lazy beggar monks in the marketplace."

"Ogame!" Flushed with fury till his eyelids glowed red, Motokiyo violently grabbed Ogame's wrists, and the clammy bean-curd refuse spread on their laps. "Me, quit? If you say that again in the hearing shadow of my father, I'll kill you! If I *could* quit the Way of noh, would I be writhing in this agony so long? I'll show you and the fickle world what it is like to possess a Way, what it is like to be possessed by it. I'll show you!"

Ogame wanted to make his celebrated triple somersault and scream with joy; but the master kyogen comic groaned, looking glum and unconvinced. "All right, then—you'll show me, eh, little master? I'll wait till my neck is as long as a crane's for your own *Jinen Koji* and *Sotoba Komachi*." He was delighted with the murderous gleam that flashed in Motokiyo's eyes at the mention of Kanami's masterpieces.

"Frankly, little master, I'd much rather lose sight of you awhile and have you back with us fine and strong than see you go mildewy day after day. Well, then, now that you've started, I'll help you finish polishing the floor."

Ogame collected the spilt bean-curd refuse inside a cloth and began scrubbing the floor from the opposite corner of the stage and did not see Motokiyo press his palms together and pray for Ogame's longevity.

THE NIGHT after the religious rites for the anniversary of Kanami's death, Motokiyo came into his mother's room, where she was already sitting on her sleep mat in her old night kimono. By now so conditioned not to ask questions, she welcomed him with a somewhat perplexed but delighted smile and watched him come behind her and kneel down. When Motokiyo began gently massaging her shoulder and neck, now and again carefully lifting a stray strand of her hair, she raised a cooing little giggle of surprise; but soon her eyes shut and with her head loose, she showed her appreciation by relaxing her muscles as only someone who had never suffered a bad conscience could. She thoroughly enjoyed the massage, and when he removed his hands, she turned back and looked up at him with a frank smile.

"Thank you, Motokiyo. That was a lovely farewell."

Motokiyo stood speechless, but Tamana was already up, busily collecting the underwear and clothes she had recently washed and darned.

"Will you tell me where you'll be?"

Motokiyo shook his head without looking at her. "I can't. I don't even know where I'll be going."

"I'll pray for you. Don't worry about us—we'll manage; we always have."

"How did you guess, Mother?"

"Ah, I have no brain, can't read or write, but I do have antennae like a little insect."

Quickly, almost brusquely, she turned him around and ushered him out of her room, without, however, forgetting that gentle pat on his right shoulder for good luck.

THROUGH ALL seasons and weathers, just as the dawn was breaking in the woods surrounding a dilapidated small Zen monastery in the foothills of the Takao Mountains, woodcutters and charcoal burners would come upon a slender upright figure singing and dancing like a madman on a narrow flat strip of earth. They would never have suspected that this strange apparition was Motokiyo of Kanze, the son of the famed Kanami and once the cherished favorite of the great shogun Yoshimitsu and the darling of the capital.

16

A GUSTY bright December afternoon, 1392.

A teenage apprentice monk came to Motokiyo's cell and told him there was a visitor asking for him at the monastery gate, a samurai in hunting attire.

Hardly had Motokiyo had time to step outside the crumbling thatch-roofed gate when he heard Yoshimitsu's voice, petulant like a spoiled child's: "Hosokawa died!"

They had not seen or corresponded with each other for more than five years. If Motokiyo had to steady himself against the weather-roughened wooden pillar of the monastery gate, it was not due only to the spare diet and rigors of his monastic life. He was flabbergasted: the shogun seeking out an entertainer left forgotten on the edge of a turbulent great world! Patronage, yes; protection and favor, certainly; but Motokiyo, conscious of his lowest-of-the-lowliest birth, had never allowed himself the presumption to hope, let alone ask, for friendship from the shogun.

Still, as unthinkable and improbable as it was, there stood before his very eye the shogun Yoshimitsu, now thirty-five years old, his neck and jawline somewhat thickened, but taut, alert, vital, his profile more dignified and inscrutable with the accumulation of power and years, and the tetchy facial tic of his early youth no longer evident.

"Too windy and cold to stand still. Let's walk, Motokiyo." Yoshimitsu began walking at a quick pace down a lane narrowed by pervasive weeds and dense bamboo forest, heedless of the fact that Motokiyo, unexpectedly summoned out, was not dressed or shod for walking in the bitter-cold wind. In a recess of the monastery wall, about a dozen shogunal guards holding their nervously stamping horses leaped to stand at attention. Yoshimitsu casually signaled them to stay where they were.

"I tell you, Motokiyo, Hosokawa's death cut me up more cruelly than my own father's. I've done everything to come to serene terms with his death, but all to little avail. I carried a corner of his coffin myself; I fasted for two whole days praying for his next life, copied sutras and litanies till my eyes blurred and did what he'd told me to do on his deathbed: unite the Northern and Southern Courts."

Motokiyo, who had purposely avoided knowing what went on outside the monastery walls, halted in his tracks, disbelieving his ears.

"Ah, yes! You didn't know? Promise anything; get the Three Divine Wares back to Kyoto, Hosokawa had told me. When the wretched Southern Emperor Gokameyama was left with only seventeen nobles and twenty-odd samurais in the Yoshino Mountain hideout, he consented to talk. After the most trying negotiations, we signed the unification agreement. The Three Divine Wares were safely returned to the Imperial Palace in Kyoto in exchange for a clause in the agreement that the future emperors of Japan will be chosen alternatively from the Northern and the Southern imperial lines—which, of course, we have no intention of honoring. The old Southern Emperor is not too unhappy living at the Daikaku Temple in comfortable retirement. So, all is well; only now there is no Hosokawa to tell me, Well done, my boy! After the thanksgiving service to celebrate the unification, I told Chancellor Shiba: 'If I continue to feel as black as I do now in a year's time, I have a mind to take the tonsure.'" Yoshimitsu stopped abruptly and struck off a desiccated branch of bamboo with his riding whip. "And told him to find out where you were."

Yoshimitsu had not said, I wanted to see you. It was not a

shogun's wont to make such an admission. But the unmistakable implication was there: the shogun had sought out his untouchable entertainer. Motokiyo turned quite pale, went down slowly on one knee in the middle of the path and picked up the severed bamboo stalk. Yoshimitsu put his fist wrapped in a quilted hunting glove on Motokiyo's shoulder, which came level with the scabbard of his sword.

"Took damn long. In the end it wasn't the chancellor's office but one of my overpaid spies who tracked down a shop in a small town near here where you had bought paper, ink and brush. Does this mean you have started writing?"

Motokiyo bowed humbly by way of confirmation. Yoshimitsu's eyes devoured the extended back of Motokiyo's neck, its slenderness, its pallor and the threadbare edge of his coarse linen collar.

Inexplicably touched, almost to tears, Yoshimitsu rapped out irritably, beating the air with his whip: "But, why, why this reclusion and self-abnegation, Motokiyo, when you could have been leading the enviable life of a celebrated actor in the capital?"

"I have a madness in me," said Motokiyo simply as if he could actually see it before him as he stared at the dry caked earth, one knee still on the hard ground and the dead branch in his hand. "Madness to presume that ultimately my Way of noh is no different from Buddha's Way." He lifted his eyes to Yoshimitsu, and his emaciated pale face glowed from the heat of his conviction. "Hit me, kick me, My Lord, if this strikes you as unpardonable arrogance, but I do believe I have created a handful of noh plays which could survive my perishable flesh and live their own lives outside the time and the world you and I know. It's been a long and merciless struggle since my father's death, but, Great Tree, I think at long last I have found my own noh!"

"Arrogance? Outside time and the world as we know it?" Yoshimitsu snorted. "Sounds more like damned insolence to me. But never mind, no one knows his place anymore; such is the Terminal World we live in. Go on: so you bought paper and ink, started writing your eternal masterpieces, eh?" Yoshimitsu felt himself eighteen again, as if it were only yesterday that he was teasing the player boy and tickling him in the armpit.

"I have written many of my own and also begun rewriting some of my father's. Awestruck admirer of the great Kanami though I am, I found that without repudiating certain features of his work I could not go further. For this filial impiety I know I deserve every torture and fire in hell."

"Did you touch *Jinen Koji* and *Sotoba* too?" Yoshimitsu asked, half-admiring and half-detesting the new strength he spied in each word Motokiyo spoke.

"Hardly. There's in them such vigor and spirit as to break any meddling brush. Not my own ideal of a noh, but indestructible masterpieces when interpreted by someone like my father."

"I listen with indulgence as you dare insinuate that what you now pretentiously choose to call noh will survive me and the Ashikaga and Buddha knows what other dynasties of transient glory"—he nudged Motokiyo in the cheek with his gloved fist, his eagle eyes narrowed with a dangerous smirk—"because I believe it was *I* and *my* reign that made someone like you possible in the first place and also because I know you are as fettered to time and men as I am. Have there been great kings or great entertainers without the approval of their public? Answer me that! I feel infinitely better having listened to your highfalutin twaddle. Get up, Motokiyo. You've neglected me long enough. You're coming back to the capital with me. What? *Now,* of course! In March next I am scheduled to visit Nara and have to entertain the Kofuku armed monks at Ichijo-In. Show them your new noh plays, Master Kanze!"

MOTOKIYO knelt on the cold wooden floor outside his mother's room and slid open the screens. Tamana, busy blowing at the charcoal fire, lifted her smoke-blurred eyes, stared at Motokiyo incredulously for at least ten counts. Although nearing fifty and suddenly gray-haired in recent years, with her demure small features and slender frame she looked in the dim light of a rainy morning like a pretty girl flustered out of a deep sleep. With a loud gulp of air, she swung her arm straight at the altar room behind her and pleaded urgently in her caressing voice:

"Tell your father you're back! Tell him! I'll make tea."

She jerked to her feet, but her heart, giddy with such joy, was racing far ahead of her knees. She faltered, and Motokiyo, already devastated by his mother's gray hair, caught her in his arms and buried his face and tears in her sleeve.

By then, all who were in the house at that early hour massed outside the opened sliding screens, having been alerted by Sango, who had opened the gate for Motokiyo. The elders, Toyodayu, Raiden, Kumazen, Ogame and veteran musicians—all variously showing the mark of the years they had lived without either Kanami or Motokiyo—inched their way forward into the room, their eyes and souls devouring the apparition, their long-missing young master. Ogame had to literally crawl up to Motokiyo on all fours; his proud springy knees, famous for double and triple somersaults on stage, had collapsed at the sight of his own little master. While Toyodayu went gently limp like a salted cucumber with lachrymose rejoicing, Kumazen bristled with loud sneezing and coughing and cursing of his cold, all in a futile effort to hide a torrent of tears that kept pouring down his cheeks.

Those young disciples recruited during Motokiyo's absence were more struck by the eerie bright calm that emanated from the twenty-nine-year-old actor's person than by the remarkable beauty of his face which, having heard so much about it, they took for granted. This famous actor and son of a legend seemed to them to move within a shaft of strange light, recognizable as an area somewhat clearer and cleaner than its environment. This uncanny quality, coupled with the implacable composure he seemed to have gained in monastic seclusion, was potent; even those few who had been accusing Motokiyo of cowardly evasion of responsibility meekly and at once accepted his regaining absolute authority over their lives.

When all of the disciples had gathered in the stage room, Motokiyo simply but sincerely apologized for his long absence and said, "All I would like to say now is Thank you; forgive me; read these." He unwrapped a large scarf and placed four unbound volumes in front of his knees.

"The plays I'd like to present at Ichijo-In in March."

The excitement, the curiosity and at the same time the dread of possibly having to read something unworthy of Kanami's son, their hearts throbbing with trepidation, the players all stared at the slim volumes on which their future depended.

Motokiyo read aloud all four plays, one after another, without halting, without adding one extraneous comment. The hushed attention amongst his men was so voracious and alive that Motokiyo felt his each word being sucked out of his mouth before he had finished pronouncing it. When all four plays had been read, the silence in the stage room vibrated as if with an inaudibly high-pitched clangor. Toyodayu broke it, tears oozing out of his old eyes and slowly spreading into a web of deep wrinkles.

"What you must have gone through, Master, to write these . . ."

Toyodayu could not finish the sentence. He sprang to his feet and disappeared into the next room, and kneeling in front of Kanami's altar, almost hysterical from relief and gratitude, he blubbered again and again, "Kanze's noh is saved. Young Master has done you proud, Master Kanami!"

NEARLY TEN YEARS since Kanami's death, the company was ten years older: Toyodayu with his skeletal shoulders sagging like a smashed-up paper umbrella, yet in the roles of gods and old men, he was still superb—if anything, singing better than before with that quaky dark timbre of old age. He modestly told Motokiyo: "Your father used to tell me, 'Cheer up; in our art you can go on improving till you drop dead.' Ah, I am lucky indeed to be an actor. If I were a stone carver or a boatman, I'd have been put out to grass long ago."

His adopted son, Toyojiro, had been admirably filling the gap left by Homan, who had died prematurely at fifty, crushed in sleep under a fallen beam during an earthquake two years after Motokiyo's disappearance. Bulky and square in build, with a correspondingly powerful vocal projection, Toyojiro made a thrilling warrior and demon and was a superb leader of the chorus, although he was sheer embarrassment in female roles.

Kumazen, the *waki* player, now sixty-two and still the hardest drinker of the troupe, had gained weight and with it an air of authority; with his centipede brows frosted white but just as expressive, he could now look suitably dignified in such roles as holy priests or highborn princes.

"Young Master, remember how your father used to despair of me?" Kumazen chuckled wistfully. " 'Kuma, you're stamped with a look of the gutter. Change your face, change your neck. What else can I do with you? You can't even hide behind a mask!' Getting old and gouty has one advantage: I've lost the look of the gutter."

Ogame, on the other hand, who had been bald at thirty, showed very little outward change. Only his full rubicund cheeks had dropped and now hung level with his chin. At sixty-four, he could still manage his trademark somersaulting entrance onto the stage just for the fun of hearing his audience break into a delighted uproar and having his son frantically beseech him afterward not to do it again. Considered beyond any argument the best comedian of the day, Ogame had become the first and only kyogen comic to be invited, independent of noh performances, to perform at the shogun's palace.

Yoshimitsu told Motokiyo the anecdote which he found so delightful that he never tired of repeating it to everyone, from his masseur to the Emperor: in a smart street of Kyoto, Ogame had chanced upon a nobleman who had been present at many of the shogun's banquets at which Ogame had performed. Recognizing that it was merely the kyogen comic, the nobleman hid his face behind his fan and walked on faster, whereupon Ogame, with an innocent look of curiosity, caught up with him, stole a good sidelong glance at the man, then, horrifiedly hiding his face behind his own fan, tiptoed away to the other side of the street.

"For the life of me I can't see why the Great Tree finds that so funny. Do you, Master?" asked Ogame, scratching his bald head as perfectly polished as a kettle.

Ten years older too were Motokiyo's contemporaries. Hotan, now twenty-three, had made remarkable progress, especially after his father, Homan's, brutal death. Aside from his talent and application, he had a style and innate elegance which Motokiyo now exploited to potent effect in the roles he had written of tragic young warriors or highborn ladies in torments of love. Besides Hotan, as a young *shité* player, there was Raido, some years junior to Motokiyo, the fourth son of a principal actor in the Hosho school whom Raiden had adopted when Ogame had made it clear to the troupe that Motokiyo's disappearance would be of long duration. Bright, ambitious and personable, the young man was blessed with a resonant strong voice and an enviable plasticity of body. With a view to quickly training a young *shité* who could somehow fill the Motokiyo's place, the Kanze elders had worked assiduously and successfully to eradicate certain repugnant traits of the Hosho school in Raido, and up till Motokiyo's reappearance the young man had been given almost as many leading roles as Hotan, and understandably, he was not as wholeheartedly overjoyed by Motokiyo's return as the rest of the company. But Motokiyo coped with Raido's tacit disgruntlement with exemplary patience and worked hard on his obvious talent.

Motokiyo's old friends Kumao and Kumaya, thirty-five and twenty-eight respectively, with their manly good looks which in *waki* players are not wasted behind masks, had won such popularity amongst the women audience that Motokiyo was told by their proud father that no fewer than two most sought-after courtesans of the capital's gay quarters had tried to commit suicide to prove their love for the brothers and that in fact the gentle-hearted Kumao had ended up marrying one of them. What Kumazen would not tell Motokiyo was that, good *waki* players being so few and far between, countless propositions had been made to Kumazen and his two brilliant sons to leave the headless Kanze, to which none of the three, nor even Kumazen's pragmatic and shrewd wife, Suzume, would lend an ear. In fact, when Master Hosho, Kanami's foster-brother, persisted in urging them to desert what he called "the sinking ship," Kumazen gathered his bushy brows in a thunder of indignation and lectured the Hosho master on company loyalty.

Kogame, a year younger than Motokiyo, seemed not to have grown in any direction since the age of fourteen. Five feet two and as skinny and alert as a mosquito, he was the complete opposite of his extroverted and gregarious father. A reserved, intent and unsociable young man, he exploded his jealously saved-up energy and hilarity only on stage.

Of the minor members of the troupe, the one who had been most marked by the absence of his master was Sango, whom on Omina's death Motokiyo had brought into the comparative security and comfort of the Kanze troupe from his former life of street entertainment; he had grown somewhat dim in the head and stood every morning outside the gate, sniffing the air with a pathetic cooing sound in his nostrils like an abandoned dog. Motokiyo's return seemed veritably to reinject life and sense into him.

Hachi, shrewd and fiercely loyal, had run the entrance-fee collection with exemplary efficiency and honesty during the long years when the troupe without Motokiyo had been obliged to "beat the mud road." Several times he had courageously resisted thugs who had tried to snatch the day's takings.

•

As REHEARSALS began, it was evident to Motokiyo that the elder Kanze members' almost religious idolatry of Kanami was a mixed blessing: the slightest difference between the father and the son did not go unnoticed.

"Why doesn't Young Master kick us, spit and yell at us as his father used to do, eh? Doesn't he care? He didn't scream at me once today, and I don't feel I've really worked," Kumazen would wail, he who during Kanami's lifetime had complained about the master's whip and invective more defiantly than anyone; but now he was flummoxed, even upset, by Motokiyo's style of working. Motokiyo with neither a whip nor outbursts of temper but just a frayed old fan in his hand explained, coaxed patiently, corrected and if he could not get what he wanted just looked miserable and defeated but said nothing more, which in a way stung the offending actors more than Kanami's hissing whip.

At every turn and on every level Motokiyo had to fight against the colossal shadow of his father to convince the actors that, although continuing on the path left so fertile by Kanami, they must now bend to the will of a creating, innovating, advancing and perhaps iconoclastic new master.

One morning, Motokiyo assembled the entire company in the stage room.

"During the years I spent at the monastery, I learned to listen to what I call 'the reflection of the rhythm in Heaven's Time,' which may sound ponderous, but like all Buddha's designs in nature it is simple and grand. You can feel it in the way buds open, bloom and drop or when you watch a frog leap. It's a rhythmic and kinetic order that governs our universe. I call it *jo-ha-kyu*—literally meaning 'begin, break and hurry' or, if you like, 'cause, relation and effect.' As everything in nature has its own *jo-ha-kyu*, so should everything on stage: every step we take, every word we utter. Even your entire performing career. As to how to program a day's performance, I have fashioned an order based on the *jo-ha-kyu* rhythm and would like in future to stick to this order without fail. For *jo*, a noh of god; for *ha*, three nohs of warriors, women and madness; for *kyu*, a noh of demons.

"Next, I come to something that I am afraid may shock some of you, but perhaps is the only way to explain to you why I call my work a noh and not sarugaku noh anymore. I have entirely rewritten my father's sarugaku masterpiece *Matsukaze-Murasame*."

In the horrified and barbed silence that followed, Motokiyo faced his men, his beautiful luminous eyes planing across the room from one face to the next with the stillness of a top that sleeps. No one stirred, everyone was hardly breathing. Motokiyo picked up an unbound pile of papers and began reading aloud his new *Matsukaze-Murasame*.

When he finished, from every lung escaped a groan of amazement, bordering on disbelief. Toyodayu and Raiden, their mouths agape, stroked their jaws pensively, while Kumao, Kumaya and Kogame, beaming elatedly, nodded at their wonder-struck fathers. There was no denying: like it or not, the son had gone beyond his great father and crystallized a form of theater worthy of a new name.

Motokiyo bowed his head by way of apology.

"We have all grown up worshiping Father's *Matsukaze*. It's painful for you and for me to see it tampered with, but Father wrote the play in the present tense, its characters real people of his time; and nothing fades faster than the present and the realistic, especially in a play like this which depends so much on the truth of human emotion.

"As you will have gathered, I made only the *waki* role, the traveling priest, of our world and time, and what we see on stage takes place in his dream. By this means I was able to eliminate all that is inessential, with a freedom to travel backward and forward in the expanse of time and to focus exclusively on the landscape of human emotions. When we dream, you agree, we are not afraid of extremes, contradictions or taboos; thereby we may perhaps go much nearer to Buddha's truth than when we are awake.

"The two lowly-born sisters in my *Matsukaze* are not played with sarugaku realism as sluttish girls, barefoot and sunburnt, dipping their pails into seawater, for they are the images dreamed of by a venerable priest, reflecting *his* culture and *his* sensibility. In the noh of distanced time and space you must not portray the sisters' grudge against the faithless lover as virulently as you did in the sarugaku present tense. Even when they dance in a frenzy of thwarted passion, in a timeless nowhere of a haunted dream, the accent is not on vengeance but more on the pathos of their helpless love and regret. I remember the late Homan playing the scene where Matsukaze mistakes the pine tree for her departed lover and caresses it with a pulsating sensuality and receiving tremendous applause from the audience. In my *Matsukaze* such crude realism would seem sickening and out of place. In the heatless moonlight of a dream, even the rancor of the flesh should be portrayed with a befitting reserve and lyricism."

Motokiyo slapped his palm with his fan. "I've spoken long enough. Father would have yawned and said, 'Shut up; get on your feet and show me!' Let us begin."

THE SHOGUN's March visit to Nara was scheduled to begin with the solemn annual rites to mourn the death of Buddha at the Kofuku Temple and to end with the shogun lavishly entertaining the temple's mighty corps of armed monks with a banquet and noh performance by the Kanze at the Ichijo-In.

The Yamato region and its capital, Nara, having long been the proud cradle of the Kanze and the sarugaku noh, the expectations aroused by Motokiyo's return to the stage in his own creation mounted to such a pitch that the Kanze elders, pondering how much was at stake on this single performance, fell prostrate before Kanami's altar whenever they had a moment free from the grueling rehearsals that Motokiyo was putting them through. Ogame, the Worry-Ahead, was positively ill from sleeplessness and loss of appetite. Doami, to whom Motokiyo had been scrupulously sending each of his new plays for his senior colleague's comments, had been laid up in his hometown of Omi with a kidney ailment, but hurried to Nara with some of his senior disciples a couple of days in advance of the performance.

"No exaggeration, my friends," he said, looking yellow and shriveled from his recent illness, "the entire theatrical profession will be here, and I hear the shogun's suite on this visit is to be double its usual number as so many courtiers, daimyos and Companions want to see what really amounts to a second debut for Motokiyo-dono. I confess I am as nervous and excited as if it were my own performance."

EARLY on the morning of the performance, Hachi in his overeager, panting-dog manner came into the Ichijo-In monks' mess hall assigned to the Kanze actors for the day and told how there had been a nasty incident started by a teahouse owner, a fanatic Kanze admirer, outside the Kofuku gate. The enraged man had emptied a large bamboo sieve full of old wet tea leaves over the

head of a dengaku actor who had been loudly telling his street bar-
ber some malicious gossip about the shogun and the Kanze master.

Kogame, who suffered the same vicarious stage fright for his
master as did his father, Ogame, kicked Hachi out of the room:
"Get out, and don't you bring any more news from the town that
might upset the Master!"

Motokiyo himself, however, seemed little affected by the
strain of the occasion. Having now been for years on a strictly
vegetarian regimen, he had not felt the necessity to observe the
traditional abstinence prior to a performance of such importance.
Calm, cheerful, having examined the stage floor and pillars, he
sat on the edge of the stage, gazing at the overcast sky, which was
exactly the color of half-opened cherry blossoms, till Sango timorously came up to him.

"Isn't it time for Master to dress?"

"Why, Sango, you do look worried! Don't. It's I, not you,
who's on trial."

Trial it would certainly be, and in no fewer than three dis-
tinct capacities: as an actor, as a playwright-lyricist-composer and
as a choreographer-director. In whichever role, Motokiyo was
doomed to be compared with his father. With the public equipped
with disastrously short and slippery memory, after his prolonged
absence nothing less than a thundering triumph would suffice to
reestablish his former reputation. He knew it; everyone knew it.
As he passed under the raised entrance curtain onto the bridge,
everyone behind him shut his eyes with sibilant words of prayer.

Atsumori was one of the rare noh plays in which the *shité*
player makes his first appearance unmasked. As Motokiyo slid
onto center stage, turned and faced the central loge kept empty
for the gods, the entire public gasped: such was his undiminished
physical beauty; so hypnotic was his stage presence. From that
moment onward even Yoshimitsu, usually a restless spectator, remained as immobile as a tombstone.

Atsumori became a classic overnight and set the tone of all
warrior plays not only in the noh but in the bunraku and the kabuki for centuries to come and in no small measure contributed
to the emergence of the Japanese inclination to worship defeated
heroes, rather than the triumphant. Further, unlike the play-
wrights before him, Motokiyo did not refrain from emphasizing
the accursed futility and inhumanity of wars and did so in a lan-

guage hitherto unspoken in popular entertainment, a language of uncompromising literary felicity and of a texture richly interwoven and complex. Whilst Kanami's plays came straight at the public, seized their interest immediately, then heaped on every device and surprise to keep it, Motokiyo drew them into a world of introspection, a private world as vulnerable and profound as each spectator's own sensibility would allow.

Motokiyo had Atsumori, the beauteously attired teenage general, absorbed in playing his flute on the eve of battle against the background of a desolate army encampment. His youth struck the audience as all the more tragic, the serenity of his flute music all the more heartrending with the near-certainty of his defeat and death the following morning. As the ghost of the young general recounted the event of his own death, even the Flat Earth spectators, normally insatiable for bloodthirsty, bombastic warriors, sat quietly weeping. Motokiyo's exit, therefore, was not accompanied by a torrent of acclamation; hearts were too sore, eyes too wet.

As soon as his ghost-Atsumori mask was removed, Motokiyo proceeded to sit with Hotan and Raido, who were to play the two sisters in his new version of *Matsukaze-Murasame,* and until the first-voice flute announced the start of the play he was seen whispering his last-minute instructions to them, whilst Kumao, also making his first appearance in the *waki* role of the traveling priest, listened to his father, Kumazen, with the same voracious attention as the two young *shités.*

The young cast went on stage. Motokiyo sat behind the entrance curtain and listened with such concentrated sympathy that his soul, if colored, would have been visible hovering over his friends and disciples on stage. Halfway through the play, he broke into a large grin and nodded to Sango, who lurked behind him.

"It works; they are fine. Come, Sango, help me. It's *Hanjo* next."

In *Hanjo* again, Motokiyo declared a leaping departure from his predecessors in the category called "the possessed" or "the madness," in which the protagonists had always been persons actually possessed by an evil or violent spirit so as to justify ranting, flamboyant acting or a frenzied dance, to which the audience unfailingly responded with enthusiasm. But in Motokiyo's plays in this category, the leading characters were possessed not by external elements but by their own inner impulses, were it a betrayed lover's vengeance, regret at one's lost glory or youth, or simply too keen an empathy with nature's ineffable beauty or its inconstancy.

In *Hanjo,* a courtesan in a provincial town goes mad from pining after the lover who deserted her for the attraction of the capital. For her possessed dance, Motokiyo had devised a music that breathed the heartbeat of her lacerated emotion: the erratic tempi were highly calculated; the frantic crescendo of three drums was punctuated by jagged and excruciatingly intense pauses. The audience felt themselves physically assaulted by the daggers and suspense packed in the music, and as Motokiyo made his fast dancing exit on the bridge, they emitted to a man a sigh of relief. Yoshimitsu slapped at his chest with a throttled groan:

"After that, I badly need a kyogen and a cup of strong wine."

And no one better understood the public's thirst for lighthearted relief than old Ogame. Having reverently bowed to Motokiyo as he had always done to Kanami before his each entrance to the stage, Ogame darted onto the bridge, followed by Kogame dressed up in a droll costume as a monkey. Instantly the five-colored silk curtain billowed inward from the storm of laughter and mirth their entrance had provoked.

After his two grueling roles Motokiyo's face was drained and white, but he put on yet another mask for his last appearance of the day, this time that of a white-haired old man with a tortured expression, the *shité* in *Burden of Love.*

For a few moments the audience was uncertain who was playing the pitiable old janitor who has fallen helplessly in love with one of the Emperor's concubines; but as she puts him through a taunting test of his love by having him lift a large parcel wrapped in damask, looking deceptively light but in fact containing a rock, it became obvious that only an actor of Motokiyo's caliber could bring out the moving Flower of a decaying gaunt tree of an old man. In the second part of the play, returning as a demon of vengeance, Motokiyo added a new dimension to the so-called "demon act" of which his father and other Yamato colleagues had made a specialty, for here was a dramatization of a demon that lurked in every ordinary heart and psyche, of unexorcised human malice and wounded pride. As Motokiyo's demon stormed the stage, tormenting the imperial concubine whose heartless little amusement had driven the old man to suicide, the audience was not only pleasurably horrified but moved to unexpected depths of pity.

At the end of the performance, the accumulation of excite-

ment, admiration and gratitude of a thousand spectators fulmi-
nated in deafening acclamation. Even the burly, rocklike armed
monks were seen clapping their hands like children. Yoshimitsu
flared his nostrils and chewed his lips, his eyes fixed and his fists
clenched; he could hardly speak. In his loge, no one dared move
a muscle. Suddenly, he took off his bat-winged crêpe cloak, put his
short sword on it, opened his fan and impatiently shook his right
hand toward his pages.

"Brush! Brush!"

One of his pages fortunately had with him a portable set of
inkwell and brush. With a ferocious grimace, Yoshimitsu scrawled
on the gold-powdered face of his fan:

"Words fail. Tears blind me. Long ago at Imakumano and
here today, you've conquered me twice. Yoshimitsu."

Motokiyo's spectacular return to the stage at the helm of the
Kanze troupe, carrying with him the awesome wealth of new
plays, affected many people in various ways. All sarugaku troupes
in the land began assiduously copying Motokiyo's new plays and
advertised them simply as noh. Soon the public too dropped the
word "sarugaku" from their theater vocabulary.

Doami, back in the capital, regaled everyone he encountered
with a glowing account of Motokiyo's second debut at Ichijo-In
till pearls of tear rose in the corner of his eyes, adding invariably:

"Motokiyo-dono is a magician of the theater, which hard as I
may try, I shall never be."

Such meek generosity on the part of Doami vis-à-vis his young
rival made Yoshimitsu and other highly placed sponsors of Doami
cherish the ageing lone genius all the more. "As long as I can go
on dancing till I crumble in a heap of ashes, I shall be a happy
man," he would say, and indeed he was.

Motokiyo's renown reached the point at which people began
seeing some supernatural potency in his art. A wealthy pawnbroker in Fushimi had been gravely injured, and one night in
his kitchen maid's dream a god appeared, saying if her master
asked Motokiyo of Kanze to offer ten noh plays before the Fushimi
Shrine, his life would be saved. Motokiyo performed according to
the oracle, and the pawnbroker duly recovered. As a reward, he
gave Motokiyo many rolls of magnificent silk and precious Sung
Dynasty coins.

17

ONE WINTER evening toward the end of that year, Yoshimitsu
asked Motokiyo alone to his chamber. Having dismissed his pages
and attendants, Yoshimitsu himself poured Motokiyo a large cup
of wine; munched his favorite snack, peas boiled in their hairy
pods, and throwing the emptied pods one by one inaccurately in
the direction of an orange-lacquered bowl, remained silent for a
long while. In the long-forgotten but familiar scent of the shogun's
apartment, Motokiyo felt memories rekindle a gentle warmth under his skin. He could not recall when he had last been so happy
and at peace as he picked up and put into the lacquered bowl the
pea pods discarded by the shogun.

"I'll be soon thirty-seven," said Yoshimitsu at last. "At forty,
Hosokawa used to say, a man is to go beyond all worldly tempta-
tions. I've been at it for thirty years now, Motokiyo. I've brought
peace to the land—precarious and incomplete, I'm the first to admit, but every class of the population has had time to fatten and
to grow a few morning glories outside the windows. With my private army larger, better trained and equipped than ever before
and the shogunal succession secure, you could say I might have
done much worse."

He poured more wine for himself and for Motokiyo.

"You don't know yet, but Emperor Goenyu died this morning. We were the same age. He was only twenty-six when he abdicated and was cloistered, remember?" Yoshimitsu curled his sensuous wide mouth in a half-smile, half-grimace, remembering the Emperor who had been his arch rival, ally and finally good friend. "With his last breath he told his seventeen-year-old son, Emperor Gokomatsu, to honor my advice as if it were his own."

Yoshimitsu brought the rapeseed-oil lamp closer between them and, peering at Motokiyo with a blunt, friendly solemnity, passed his right hand, hardly touching, from Motokiyo's forehead, temple and high cheekbone down to his chin as if to draw his likeness. Motokiyo inhaled the green, waterlogged smell of the boiled peas from the shogun's fingertips and his heart could have burst from so much tenderness.

"I have some advice for you too. You must marry, Motokiyo. Have sons, three at least. A house is not a house unless it continues: that's what Kanami used to say. Look at Doami: he has no continuity. He doesn't care, the fool! But you must. *I* care for the continuity of your line and art. Remember, it's half *my* continuity. I have a wife for you."

Yukina had been brought up by nuns outside Kyoto. Her mother, daughter of an impoverished but noble family, had died giving birth to Yukina, and the father's identity had never been disclosed. It was surmised that he had been of a more humble origin, but the truth had died with Yukina's mother. When Yukina grew up to be a quiet, well-behaved pretty girl of twelve, the head nun sent her to serve in the household of Nariko, Yoshimitsu's first wife; like most nunneries, it had become overcrowded with well-connected but destitute orphans, and at an appropriate age as many girls as possible had to be "weeded out" to lessen the number of hungry mouths to be fed.

Yukina, taciturn and lovely to look at, although perhaps too withdrawn for a seemingly healthy young girl, was after Nariko's early death handed down to Yasuko, Yoshimitsu's second wife, amongst other possessions that were passed from the aunt to the niece, such as clothes, furniture, palanquins, cages of rare birds and musical instruments. As Motokiyo, then called Fujiwaka, also became a part of Yoshimitsu's household, Yukina had opportunities to come into contact with Fujiwaka, and this retiring, silent girl fell desperately in love with the shogun's favorite. In so confined and watchful a female society, this could not fail to be noticed. It became for a while a mildly amusing topic of conversation amongst Yasuko's entourage; but as year after year Fujiwaka remained either totally unaware of or indifferent to the poor girl's infatuation, everyone lost interest, and soon no one bothered even to tease her. Fujiwaka was then sixteen and Yukina, fourteen.

Many years later, when Motokiyo disappeared like a dying elephant leaving no trace behind him, Yukina surprised the fickle ladies around her with a show of intense grief and for at least a year thereafter did not once fail to offer the hundred-step prayer for Motokiyo's safety and eventual return. The others giggled nervously and looked away as if they had seen something bizarre or unseemly when, at the remotest mention of the young actor who had once so enchanted the capital, Yukina's pupils seemed to come closer together, as in the eyes of one possessed by a fox demon.

Yet for all this, she had probably exchanged not more than a few dozen words of customary courtesy with Motokiyo in her entire life. In fact, when the shogun mentioned Yukina's name, Motokiyo had some difficulty in recalling her. Motokiyo was not a sensual man in the normal context of the word. As with wine, which he could drink to excess without showing the slightest sign of intoxication, yet could do without for years on end, so it was with carnal pleasure. After being released from the shogun's service of the night, he had received countless amorous approaches from women of all classes, but he was a voluptuary or an ascetic at will. Yoshimitsu's spies reported that since leaving the shogun's pillow, Motokiyo had not shared another with anyone.

"She's now twenty-seven—an old maid—but I assure you she's still quite good to look at; besides, she's loved you all of thirteen years. Think, Motokiyo, that's half her life! Tenacious, proud, loyal, I reckon she's someone who'll be able to last as your wife. The noh comes first in your life, so you'll need to marry someone who'll tolerate being always second to the noh." Yoshimitsu spoke without irony or unkindness, then continued with the efficiency of a good administrator: "I've already consulted the professors at the imperial astrology office and they have chosen the date. The Lady of the North-Facing Palace"—Yoshimitsu called Yasuko by the exalted female court rank he had recently cajoled out of the Emperor for his wife—"will give the woman a decent dowry. Don't waste time. I want you to concentrate on the noh and ensure its continuity. If this one proves slim-hipped and barren, I have others in mind."

Motokiyo, like Tamana and the members of the troupe, did not meet his wife till the day of his wedding.

"A bride from the heaven above!" cried Ogame with joy and much pride, for even as the shogun's old favorite, Motokiyo would have had to consider himself exceedingly honored had the shogun chosen for him one of his hand-soiled mistresses or, to save himself the expense of a seemly dowry, the daughter of a wealthy money-lender or a Continental trader whose fortunes depended on obtaining a favorable license from the shogunate; whereas now the shogun had arranged a marriage for his noh master with someone he had not even touched, and what was more, from within the coveted and closed circle of women serving his own wife, the Lady of the North-Facing Palace, which manifested to all more eloquently than anything else the shogun's profound esteem and favor for the artist and added dignity to the future house of Kanze. What the bride was really like as a person, how the bridegroom and the bride would find each other, let alone the bridegroom's family and troupe, all that was quite immaterial in the blazing light of the shogun's unprecedented favor.

The bride's name, Yukina, meant "grass under snow," and it snowed on the night before the wedding. Despite the intense cold of the following morning, Tamana greeted her daughter-in-law-to-be outside the gate as the latter descended from her palanquin. An elaborately dressed and coiffed bridal attendant, one of Yukina's senior colleagues from the North-Facing Palace, led Yukina by her powdered white hand to a small room, screened off from the banqueting area, where the bridegroom alone waited.

The bride was dressed in traditional bridal fashion, with a trailing robe of luminous white silk over a white crêpe kimono and a large white shawl draped over her head and face: no part of her was visible, as she knelt down and bowed deeply before Motokiyo and Tamana, but her icicle-slim fingers.

The bride's attendant cautiously removed the shawl from the bride's head so that she could drink the scented wine from a red-lacquered cup in three-three-and-three small sips with her husband—the essential, binding part of the wedding ceremony. As the bride's face was revealed, Tamana could not help raising a bird-

like little noise in her throat: her daughter-in-law was more beautiful, more dignified and perhaps older-looking for her age than
she had imagined.

As the couple exchanged the red wine cup with ceremoni-
ous deliberation, Motokiyo's eyes met Yukina's once. She neither
flinched nor blushed; she held her heatless burning gaze squarely
on him. Her long, tapering eyes shaded with thick-hanging lashes
were lovely, but somewhat disconcerting with an all-devouring,
unblinking intensity.

Having changed from her white ceremonial garments to a
set of sumptuously colorful robes, the bride was led into the improvised banqueting room, the stage room and the three smaller
rooms having been made into one large space by removal of the
sliding screens between them. There, Doami, the masters of Hosho,
Komparu and Kongo with their elders and all male members of
the Kanze troupe held their wine-scented breath in admiration of
the exquisite picture the bride and bridegroom presented. The
wives of the Kanze members in their best finery, carrying and
serving drinks and food, stopped to stare at their young mistress—
slower than men, perhaps, to make up their minds.

With the large number of additional cooks in the kitchen and
the barrels of excellent wine presented by Motokiyo's admirers,
the wedding feast was endless, copious, noisy and full of jocose
good humor, during which the bride and the bridegroom hardly
had the opportunity for a personal conversation.

Shortly after the midnight bells of the neighboring temples,
Motokiyo and Yukina went to their room. In the precious little
space left free by the bride's dressing mirror, writing box, brow-
painting box, comb box, good-luck dolls and painted animals sent
in advance from the North-Facing Palace there had been laid a
wide sleeping mat with a white-satin-covered eiderdown.

Tamana accompanied the bridal couple as far as the sliding
screens of their room. She had been worried till she could hardly
sleep by the fact that Yukina was at least partly descended from a
class of people whom Tamana had been brought up to look up to
as "those who live above the clouds." She had been gloomily pre-
dicting to herself, "When you marry above your own class, nothing good will come of the union. I tremble for my grandchildren. . . ."

"Yukina-dono," Tamana said as she was about to close the

screens, unable to call her own daughter-in-law without the ponderous honorific: "I hope you'll find much happiness in my son's
house."

"Please love me and trust me as your own daughter," Yukina
said as she fell to her knees, bowing decorously in front of Tamana's
feet. "I know little of the life outside a nunnery and my patron's
palace, but if you will teach me, I'll learn anything to please you."

Tamana, simple and gullible, was moved to warm tears, closed
the screens and went away hopeful and happy.

When Motokiyo held Yukina in his arms, he was indescribably moved. She was not only his wife and a total stranger but the
first woman he had made love to. He had played women, he had
written women, he had been praised that he expressed and understood women far better than women themselves. But he had never
known a woman's body, had never experienced her deep caressing
interior, her serpentine clinging limbs, her convoluted sinuosity;
and most mind-boggling of all, he had not realized in all his
twenty-nine years how natural it was for a man to give pleasure
to a woman, without force, nor violence, nor pain, nor artifice,
and he understood why in the union between man and woman
there was a god-blessed fecundity, for it seemed to him to be in total harmony with the Way of things as designed by Buddha, two
individual but complementary bodies fitting together in a natural
perfection.

An entertainer, disciplined beyond his subconscious to serve
and please others, Motokiyo loved the unknown woman once, and
twice, assiduously exploring the unfamiliar terrain and crevices
with as much rapture of discovery as stoic endurance till she, his
wife, subsided, tremulous and satiated, like a creature of sweet
thick liquid.

The following morning, the fatigue of her nuptial night dark
under her eyes, Yukina was as closed and unforthcoming as she
had been eloquent and assertive in the dark chamber of love. Her
voluptuous abandon of the night before was nowhere to be detected, perhaps except in the way her eyes devoured Motokiyo
whenever he came into her sight.

With the air of a brave doll, she began learning from Tamana
the working of the house, the house of the untouchable entertainers, with neither contempt nor condescension, nor manifest joy or
interest. She was polite and patient with the servants and wives of

the actors, and with Tamana she could not be accused of lacking in the respect and attention due from a daughter-in-law. She even offered to rub Tamana's shoulders and legs on the nights when Motokiyo was summoned to perform at the shogun's palace. During the day whenever she was not needed by Tamana she would be found either sitting on the hard corridor floor outside the stage room watching Motokiyo rehearse through a narrow gap between the sliding screens or copying his new work. It was obvious she lived entirely and solely for Motokiyo and the nights with him.

In the presence of such suffocatingly dense devotion of someone whom he neither fully understood nor felt strong sympathy with, Motokiyo could not help feeling vaguely inadequate, guilty and even disloyal; perhaps for this reason he strove all the harder to give her satisfaction in their physical union, in fact just as sedulously as he had been taught since his infancy to perform his night duty, whether with an abbot or with a shogun.

What will they do and talk to each other about when they are old and left to themselves? Tamana often wondered to herself.

"WHEN YOU have your son, Master, please, will you let me be his tutor and nanny as my father was to you? I count on you for that!" Kogame, who had married the late Meisho's youngest daughter but had not been blessed with children, missed no opportunity to pester Motokiyo with his quaint request, and his customary expression of intense gloom somehow never failed to make Motokiyo burst into incongruous laughter.

"Of course, Kogame; I'll be delighted. But whether I'll be blessed with a son or not and how soon, that'll have to be decided up there." Motokiyo raised his smiling eyes to the heaven.

The heaven decided to bless him with two sons within the space of three years. The firstborn was named Juro and the second, Goro. It was perfectly understandable that Tamana should dote on her grandsons and that Kogame should at once begin taking a touchingly proprietary interest in the older baby, but the surprise was that Motokiyo too turned out to be the most adoring and infatuated of fathers.

Small children, dogs and cats had always shown a remarkable lack of resistance toward Motokiyo; and Ogame used to explain, "That's because Little Master has no needles of tension in his perfectly trained muscles. He's like a sleeping cat, thrown off a window ledge, that drops to the ground on his four calm paws." The wet nurse was surprised to find that the Master, after hours of concentrated work either in the stage room or in his study, would slip into the babies' room and by simply giving Juro his forefinger to chew could stop the baby from crying. The babies made it quite clear that they preferred being bathed by the men rather than by nurses or maids or even Tamana, who never tired of watching Motokiyo and Kogame wash the little things with as much care and attention as if they were handling the masks by Miroku or Himi. Frequently in the dead of night Motokiyo and Kogame would collide as they tiptoed to the babies' room, where Juro was crying, with the maid and Goro fast asleep.

Having watched Yukina being quite uninvolved and even mildly resentful of the inconvenience of a closely repeated pregnancy, no one was surprised to see her abandon the care and thereby the natural enjoyment of a mother of her babies to Tamana and the wet nurses. Looking fresher and younger, with a new sensuous sheen under her skin, she lived in fact more like an honored guest in her own house, and after two childbirths she no longer even tried to stifle her cries of passion at night, which spilled like a crawling mist into the corridor, and Tamana wondered if it was normal for a highborn lady, used to living in a vast house and surrounded closely by ubiquitous servants, not to develop a common people's sense of modesty and shame.

FOUR MONTHS after Goro's birth, in the persistent heat and rainlessness of September, an epidemic of dysentery broke out in the overcrowded lower-class district of the capital, which then spread with rampaging speed through the rest of the city. October came, but the heat did not abate. The weather turned airless and humid. In the face of the hourly worsening situation and with the mistress of the house, Yukina, drifting through the day like an innocuous ghost, Tamana decided to take the matter in hand. First, she sent Yukina and the two infants with the more experienced older servants to Omi, where Doami, with his characteristic generosity, had offered them the shelter of his own house; then she taught the remaining young domestics to boil everything they ate from and to brew disinfectant infusion all day and saw to it that no outsiders and nothing contaminated should pass the Kanze threshold.

After the notoriously debilitating summer of Kyoto, it was

the elderly members of the troupe who were struck down. Toyodayu and Ippen died within ten days of each other in mid-October.
Toyodayu was seventy-two and Ippen, the recalcitrant drummer,
was sixty-four. It was in December, soon after the epidemic was declared over, with Yukina and the babies still cautiously kept in
Omi and the capital greeting without mirth the most festive month
of the year, that Tamana went down with dysentery and a chill
which, neglected, developed into acute pneumonia.

When she realized that death would soon follow her appalling dehydration and racking chest pains, she asked to see Motokiyo alone. Her breath smelled of death, and her eyes, sunken to
the bottom of the gutted sockets, had little light, but with a determination painful to watch she whispered, raucously and intermit-
tently, her parched white lips hardly moving:

"Ask Ogame if I cannot finish . . . telling you everything.
Father and Omina-san had a child. You may not have known this.
I knew and was happy. I wanted and offered to bring up the boy
as a Kanze son, but you know Omina-san, such a decent, meticulous woman, she wouldn't hear of it. She wanted no possible cloud
over you, the legitimate son and heir. She brought him up as best
she could under the difficult conditions—constantly on tour, surrounded by dancing girls and gallant men. After Omina-san's
death he kept the *kusé* dance troupe going for a while, but bungled
it badly, and taking what remained in the kitty, he eloped with
the leading dancer. We'd never heard of him again till just at the
outbreak of the epidemic, he came here. He left a baby, hardly a
year old, and disappeared. . . .

"Motokiyo, listen: the baby carries your father's and Omina-
san's blood. I loved them both. They and you were the light of my
life. Please, bring up their grandson as your own. I asked Ogame
to evacuate the baby to his relatives in Yamato. Now that it is
safe . . . please, bring him here. . . . The rest, Ogame will . . .
I pray for you . . ."

Thinking she was dead, blinded and choked with tears, Motokiyo gripped his mother's arm, a desiccated twig of an arm. Tamana
half-opened her eyes.

"You're so alone, Motokiyo, always. I can still see you coming
home from the Jozen Monastery at dawn. . . . So alone, so strong.
Poor child, you love nothing else. Just noh."

These were her last words.

A simple funeral service was held three days later at the house. What surprised and profoundly touched Motokiyo was not only the amazingly large number of people connected with the profession who had come a long way to pay their last respects but the very considerable number of itinerant street entertainers who used to seek shelter at Yuzaki village. After the meteoric elevation of Kanami and the Kanze troupe in the capital those "vagrant scum of the earth" had not dared come asking for shelter at the spruce Kanze gate, yet here they were, weeping, clapping hands in prayer, offering wildflowers from the riverbank, as if it were their own mother whom they had lost.

It was long past midnight in the cold, drafty stage room when Motokiyo had his first chance to speak to Ogame alone. Having had to attend no fewer than six funerals of his disciples and now his own mother in the space of a mere three months, Motokiyo felt like crying at the sight of old Ogame looking as perky and benign as a big scrubbed persimmon.

"Thank Buddha, Ogame, you're still with us!" Motokiyo sighed. "Well, tell me about this baby—*my half-nephew.*"

By adding these words he saved Ogame much embarrassment. With a whistling sigh of relief Ogame slapped at his own chest.

"Master, I stopped judging what goes on between a man and a woman as soon as I could recognize the difference between them. Your mother was a great lady. And Omina-dono! Who could not have loved her? She was a good woman. Did you ever see her treat your mother without true affection and deference?"

"Ogame, I agree with you completely. I loved Omina-dono just as much as my parents did. Tell me about her son."

"Frankly, Master, a wastrel, not worthy of your father's blood. Did he have his parents' talent? That, yes—in a way, he did. Built as tall and handsome as your father—ah, yes, a very good-looking lad, all right; and that was his ruin. Brought up and disciplined here, he'd probably have become a fabulous actor, but he wasted all his promise and talent in debauchery and is now most likely either dead in a double suicide with some rotten woman or a kept man somewhere."

"Who's the mother of this baby, do you know?"

"The girl Omina-dono counted on as her successor. Not a bad dancer. She wasn't young anymore when she eloped with the lad. That's probably why she died giving birth to this baby. The

child is in Yamato with my niece's family. No problem, Master—
I told them it's an epidemic orphan. Bless her departed soul, your
mother saw to it all. Paid generously for the wet nurse, food, clothes
and everything else."

"Before I bring my wife and children back to the capital,"
Motokiyo said, "I would like you to send the child to Omi so that
they can all return together. With things as chaotic as they are in
the capital, no one will notice or care why we suddenly have three
babies rather than two. Now, what about his name? And what
about his age?"

"I've been thinking about that, Master. Children are fussy
and quick to notice the slightest difference and take offense. We
must be careful to give him a name that rhymes well with the
other two boys'. I thought Saburo might do very well, Master;
what do you think? As to his age, I would guess there is a difference of only a few months between Goro-dono and him. Make
him the youngest, eh?"

"Saburo? Juro, Goro and Saburo. Sounds right. Three little
brothers. The Great Tree said to me before I married that a house
remains a house so long as it has continuity. In our profession,
continuity must also mean quality. The ablest of the three shall
carry on the noh and the name of the Kanze."

Ogame was an emotional man. Turning red to the top of his
bald skull, clasping his plump hands, he prayed for Buddha's
blessing on the three little Kanze futures. Neither Motokiyo nor
Ogame could possibly have suspected then what potent seeds of
conflict and tragedy would germinate from the three babies' warm
cradles. . . .

Motokiyo, who since his earliest days had always felt a certain uneasiness and misgiving whenever normal human happiness,
marriage and children, riches and honors were extolled, took a
deep breath and gazed far beyond his sight. Ogame knew the look.
The look of the loneliest yet the strongest of men.

YOSHIMITSU took the tonsure in his thirty-seventh spring. Although
taken by surprise, many of his sycophantic entourage, including a
number of highest-ranking courtiers and shogunal officials, quickly
followed suit, as it had been the established custom to follow their
master into the cloistered world, very much like widows forced
to enter nunneries after the untimely death of their husbands.

Soon the streets of Kyoto were littered with satiric pamphlets and cartoons mocking the rows of newly shaven glossy heads.

As in everything else Yoshimitsu had done, behind the seeming "split-bamboo" rashness of his decision to forsake the fleeting world at thirty-seven, there had been long and meticulous preparation. A year earlier, Yoshimitsu had made his eldest son, Yoshimochi, aged nine, take the adulthood ceremony and declared the child the fourth Ashikaga shogun, with himself as regent. Simultaneously, he had obtained for himself the highest existing court rank, that of Imperial Prime Minister, the post once so graciously held by Prince Nijo, only to renounce it now in order to assume the ink-dyed robes and the simple priestly name of Dogi. Everyone who knew the former shogun could well imagine how he must have enjoyed the theatrical effect of returning to the Emperor the supreme court rank as if it were a piece of chipped porcelain.

Those who had watched the undeterred rise in fortune of Yoshimitsu for the last thirty years were also quick to point out that for a man who had done and possessed everything, it would be the most sensible thing to take leave of the sordid world, yet keep the reins of power intact in his grip in the guise of regent to his young son, and thus continue to enjoy life, art and nature unfettered by much of the protocol of his former position.

His youthful, alert figure in disconcerting contrast to his bluish shaven head and somber attire and beads, he energetically undertook long and stately journeys, taking with him a huge train of people including his wife or mistresses, a selected number of his numerous offspring and favorite artists and scholars. On the rare occasions when the new chancellor, son of the old Lord Shiba, dared to present the complaints voiced by some of the daimyos who had had the misfortune of having to host the cloistered former shogun's progress, which, with Yoshimitsu's love of pomp and luxury, was bound to involve on each visit a stupendous cost, Yoshimitsu would scowl with an unpriestly passion:

"Ungrateful pigs! Don't they realize my travels are the best political maneuver to avoid insurrections and peasant uprisings in the provinces? Without the peace and security I have brought them, they couldn't have grown as fat as they have—tell them that!"

As for his building mania, in keeping with his new status he now fancied a retreat of meditative peace and calm: no more flowers and dragon-headed boats loaded with musicians on a serpentine lake, but a landscape of aged rocks and serene pines with a hermitage and a tea arbor reflected on winding water. His daimyos waited in trepidation for Yoshimitsu's new labor levies and demands for contributions as he began negotiating the purchase of land in the Kitayama district of the capital, reputed for its wooded calm with Mount Kinugasa as its background.

Neither his collector's mania for rare and beautiful objects nor his love of theater, music, dance, tea and incense and *renga* poetry competitions appeared to lose its healthy appetite. His interest in noh also became more committed—or to put it ungratefully, more interfering—as he grew to see himself more and more as erudite critic and creative patron. It seemed to give the autocrat a childlike pleasure, for example, to advise Motokiyo: "Master Kanze, your opening verse for that play is far too gruff and masculine. Perhaps you ought to adopt a more lyrical and gentler voice, eh?" and to find that the noh master in a rage of creative inspiration promptly rewrote the verse in question for the following performance.

On Motokiyo's side, although he never allowed himself for a second to ignore the streak of predatory cruelty hidden inside the priestly former shogun's curled paws or to forget that he was but a mere entertainer, he knew he could now as the great Yoshimitsu's noh master count on having the means to create work of an uncompromisingly high quality and the occasions to have these creations appraised by men of the best taste and culture of the day. Whether this was an unqualified blessing or a curse that would, under changed circumstances, condemn him and his work into isolation from the larger, less cultured general public remained to be seen.

18

It was Lady Takahashi who warned Motokiyo first.

The fifty-five-year-old former courtesan was still very much in Yoshimitsu's favor and probably the only woman he trusted. As Yoshimitsu's philandering now had to be carried on more discreetly and his partners more judiciously selected than before, Lady Takahashi's impeccable tact, judgment of character and wide range of acquaintance proved essential in making the forty-two-year-old cloistered former shogun's life, as she herself put it, "not without a tremor of pleasure."

She procured for him but did not herself sleep with Yoshimitsu any longer, although there was a persistent rumor that she did. Judging by her young-girl's fine skin and just an intimation of plumpness, no one quite knew what to believe; and apparently the way she taught and disciplined girls and women before they shared Yoshimitsu's pillow was so brilliant that Yoshimitsu was said to have lamented, "What a pity you're not one of my generals to train my soldiers to the same perfection!"

And as she remained, despite her intimate friendship with Yoshimitsu, irreproachably correct and self-abasing toward Yasuko, the Lady of the North-Facing Palace praised Lady Takahashi as one who knew her place and regretted that Yoshimitsu's other mistresses were not as well brought up as the old courtesan.

Lady Takahashi had asked Motokiyo to come to her suite in an annex of the North-Facing Palace to teach her the guitar accompaniment to Kanami's famous "Songs from the Western Isles." Halfway through the lesson, she gave Motokiyo a long radiant smile and removed the ivory protective pieces from her fingernails.

"Now no one could say you didn't come to teach me your father's music. I'll come to the point quickly. Yesterday, the Great Tree asked the young shogun and a few *renga* poets and me to come to his apartment with a view to interesting Yoshimochi-sama in something other than falconry and archery. A charming and far-seeing thought of a father, for, as you well know, in order to be accepted into the best court circles even a shogun must excel in *renga* poetry.

"Yoshimochi-sama, I am afraid, is lamentably deficient in outgoing charm and spirit, and physically too—maybe it is due to his weak kidneys—he has a sallow, dull, puffy look, with a corresponding humor. Although people tell me he is a good horseman and archer, I find his deportment sluggish and graceless. I wish to Buddha he tried to redeem his lack of outward charm with the solid affection and loyalty of a good son; but no—he never misses a chance to criticize and belittle every decision of his father's behind his back, yet face to face, he cringes and tenses with visible fright. As you can imagine, this only further exasperates the Great Tree, who, I gather, told the shogun's mother, 'The son you bore me is truly remarkable: he's already a geriatric and not yet seventeen!' Of course remarks like this get promptly reported back to the shogun by one of Chancellor Shiba's competent but humorless spies.

"In a situation like this both are to blame, each bringing out the worst in the other. Poor Great Tree, so youthful and overflowing with curiosity and enthusiasm for everything, finds it an uphill task to tolerate an inert, negative sixteen-year-old who is busy striking a posture of callow defiance. Poor Yoshimochi-sama, too: he is constantly made to feel so inadequate and unappreciated that he has reached the point where he no longer even tries. At this *renga* party, as a sort of cowardly challenge to his father, he seemed to me to be trying hard to be even duller than he really is. After one insipid line of poetry after another from the young shogun, the Great Tree was irked beyond endurance. Patience, we well know, is not among the Great Tree's virtues. He began comparing Yoshimochi-sama with you when you were the shogun's age, and with only a few of his intimates present the Great Tree let himself go so far as to add: 'Oh, what a dismal bore trying to teach *renga* to a toad with no sense of the ridiculous; and when I think what joy and thrill it gave me to teach raw material as rich and inspired as Fujiwaka!'

"The shogun did not react; he seldom does, not in front of his father. He just looked sallower and broodier.

"We stopped the *renga,* wine was served and I played the *biwa* guitar and sang and hoped that the unhappy business would be forgotten.

"This morning, one of the Great Tree's spies came to tell me that Yoshimochi-sama later last night supped with his entourage, including the chancellor and other high shogunal officials, and gave them a lurid account of the incident and concluded—which made everyone *guffaw:*

" 'It seems to me that in order to be loved and appreciated by the Great Tree all that I, his son and heir, will have to do is become a catamite and be reborn untouchable.'

"Motokiyo-dono, I beseech you, take care. A weak man does not bear an insult lightly and has a greater tenacity of malice than a strong man."

Motokiyo was keenly reminded of Lady Takahashi's warning when several months later he and Doami with their respective troupes were commanded to perform at the Daigo Temple under the canopy of the famous weeping cherry blossoms, to which all the elite of the capital swarmed. On the first day, from the moment of Motokiyo's entrance, the young shogun in the loge next to his father's paid no further attention to the stage but, drinking and petting his long-haired Chinese dogs, could be seen chatting and sniggering not only with his chancellor, the young Lord Shiba, but worse still, with Zomasu of dengaku, the longtime favorite and protégé of the old Lord Shiba, the former chancellor.

Yoshimitsu, whose own theatergoing manners were at times far from irreproachable, lost his temper and as soon as Motokiyo made a change-of-costume exit ordered the shogun and his entourage to either leave the theater at once or keep their mouths shut. The shogun flew out of the loge, followed by his excited, yapping dogs and his suite in noisy disarray.

The incident publicly confirmed what had long been observed by high shogunal officials: that the son, possessing little of the father's character or quality and knowing this, bore a festering grudge against him. A common enough reaction of a great man's son, perhaps, but given the positions they occupied, the slightest gesture of irritation or the softest utterance of disloyalty by one or the other became a matter involving the state and its future.

To cite an example of even international importance, there were Yoshimitsu's Ming ships. Yoshimitsu, with his love of the novel and the exotic, had for years been sponsoring trading ships mandated by him to and from the Chinese Continent and had reaped huge profits from the trade, as had his fellow investors such as powerful temples, wealthy daimyos and Osaka and Sakai millionaire merchants. One of his favorite excursions was to the port of Hyogo whenever one of his ships safely returned from China. On these visits Yoshimitsu would select only the favorite few from amongst his mistresses, children, vassals and Companions-in-Arts, together with a handful of bilingual Zen priests who acted as interpreters and scribes, to greet the Ming Emperor's envoys, who brought him some astounding gifts. He would then invite the envoys to stay at one or another of the newly constructed or refurbished temples in the vicinity and entertain them sumptuously, always having Motokiyo perform at the banquets.

Yoshimochi was conspicuously never included in his suite on these occasions, for, encouraged by his chancellor, who sought to make a political issue of the cloistered former shogun's being personally involved in the lucrative trade with the Ming Dynasty, Yoshimochi had been openly critical of his father's "xenophilia and sycophantic attitude toward the Ming Emperor." But Yoshimitsu was having too good a time and making too large a financial gain to be seriously provoked by his son's attack.

"The boy must grow up. How does he think I'm able to finance the construction of my Kitayama domain without the money I make from my Ming ships?"

He was not being entirely truthful, for a large proportion of the cost was being borne by his vassal daimyos through their contributions of labor and materials. The construction—or rather, creation—of his final home on this earth would take all of three years, and Lord Hosokawa, the son of the late chancellor, alone was said to have supplied three thousand laborers from his province, and Lord Akamatsu, two thousand eight hundred.

In the northwest of Kyoto, on a thirteen-hectare site—an unheard-of size in the capital—Yoshimitsu had built, one after another, temples, pavilions, tea arbors and hermitages. Of all his creations, the most superb and literally dazzling was Kinkaku-ji, the so-called Golden Pavilion, built on the edge of a lake dotted with islets of often no more than a few pines and some magnificent rocks. Reflecting Yoshimitsu's expansive and cosmopolitan taste, it contained three architectural styles in one building: the ground floor, unpainted and uncluttered, was of the pure Heian court style, whilst the second floor was in the Zen-samurai style and the third floor in a pronounced Chinese style, with the upper two stories plated with pure gold leaf. In the rising and setting sun a heavenly golden heron, placed on top of the gracefully curved roof, sparkled with iridescent vigor, and its owner and creator could not help imagining himself soaring on its proud wings.

Yoshimitsu still firmly held the reins of government in his grip; peace and prosperity, marred only seasonally by the inevitable and more or less containable epidemics, earthquakes, typhoons and famines, seemed durable. Neither the peasants nor the dispossessed Southern Court sympathizers had lately risen in armed revolt against the shogunate; and to Yoshimitsu's delight, the twenty-four-year-old Emperor Gokomatsu, who had succeeded Emperor Goenyu, was being perfectly amenable, so much so that when the dowager empress died, His Imperial Majesty meekly accepted Yasuko as His "Vice Mother."

"What—a commoner woman calling herself a *mother* to the Son of the Sun God?" Private horror and indignation mutely reverberated amongst the courtiers; but the cloistered former shogun's authority now being so absolute, even the most inflexible nobleman scholar on court etiquette bowed before the aberrant imperial decision.

And all Yoshimitsu's numerous children, excepting only the shogun Yoshimochi, had been neatly kept out of the dynastic struggle for earthly power: eight daughters had been settled at the head of richly endowed nunneries and seven sons at various important religious institutions. As he surveyed the world from the height of Kitayama, surrounded by carpenters and masons vigorously hammering and chiseling away, Yoshimitsu was, not without justification, pleased with himself.

A month after the Daigo Temple event, the Kanze put on three subscription performances of their own on a site on the Kamo River. The fact that they could sell out all three performances independently of a mighty temple or a shrine's sponsorship eloquently illustrated the extensive support Motokiyo then enjoyed in the capital; and Yoshimitsu's presence at the first and the last performances added much prestige to the occasion.

Motokiyo presented six new plays, all of his own creation, plus three of his father's works, rethought and molded to suit his style and conception. The public was drunk with rapture by the end of the three-day program. Yoshimitsu, who brought Yasuko, together with his priestly sons and three of his daughters residing in the capital, was unable to control his joy and pride.

"I cannot go on *not* making you a Companion-in-Arts any longer, Motokiyo. Not after this! Pity to cut your hair now. Take the tonsure later, but today let me make you my Companion by naming you Ze-ami, taking the *ze* of Kan-ze."

Yoshimitsu in fact had another good reason to hurry to make Motokiyo a Companion: after Kiami's death at a Buddha-blessed age, presumed to be somewhere between ninety-two and ninety-seven, his grandson Zomasu had continued to enjoy the patronage of the old Lord Shiba, father of the current chancellor, and the young shogun Yoshimochi, at Lord Shiba's prompting, had recently made Zomasu, as his position now entitled him to, his new Companion, naming him Zo-ami. At the same time he nominated Zoami's eleven-year-old son, Eio, to be one of his pages.

No ONE, not even Yukina, knew that Zeami had been writing down his innermost thoughts and secrets on the Way of noh, let alone that this now-fabled artist at the zenith of his career was doing so driven by an unnamable fear. Even as he was laughing irrepressibly with his three small boys crawling all over him, a disquieting premonition never stopped breathing down his back. He watched his young sons and thought of Kanami; between the growing life around him and the memory of the death, he felt himself pursued and was even more urgently impelled to record and leave for the future Kanze all that he had learned from his father and had himself discovered on the Way of noh.

By the time he had finished the seven chapters of what was

to be called *On Transmission of the Flower,* Juro was nine, Goro seven and Saburo, who had been officially registered as Goro's younger brother by a year although his actual date of birth was thought to be only a month or two later than Goro's, was six.

Five years after delivering Goro, Yukina had given birth to a mettlesome pretty girl who was named Tama after her grandmother Tamana. The arrival of the baby girl delighted the boys and made them feel important and grown up. The three boys each had a markedly different personality but got on well and worked with ardor under the close guidance of Zeami, with Kogame, for Juro and Goro, and Hotan, for Saburo, assisting as their respective tutors-cum-nannies.

In looks Juro, the eldest, was the most privileged of the three: the way his lower eyelids slanted upward to form a pair of large flame-shaped eyes and the delightfully haughty uprightness with which he carried his small head, no one, even at the first glance, could fail to see his father in him. But with closer scrutiny, one could also perceive a certain friableness and melancholy that Fujiwaka, despite his small frame and wretched childhood, had never given way to. Maybe it was just the childish way he pursed his lips and thrust forward his small pointed chin, but that coupled with his tendency to sit alone gazing at the end of the horizon or the back of his hand with an intensely absorbed air attracted the grown-ups' attention. Comes from his mother, thought Kogame.

Like his mother, Juro was not physically robust either: his feet and hands were icy even in warm weather; he caught cold easily, and with the slightest of fever his eyes glowed with an alarming intensity. Kogame, who cosseted and worshiped the boy, swore that his little master was a vessel of genius, and when Zeami was teaching him the famous double dance from Kanami's *Shizuka,* Kogame had his ailing father, Ogame, carried on a sedan chair to the Kanze house. Ogame had been suffering for nearly two years from cruel spasmodic pains in the intestines, on which repeated thermal cures and Chinese medicine had had little effect.

Diminished in size by half and greenish in color after so prolonged an illness, Ogame watched Juro dance with the irresistible charm of extreme youth the dance he had witnessed being created by the boy's grandfather so long ago. Having watched as if his eyes had teeth and claws to devour and record every detail as a keepsake for his next life, Ogame had to lie down awhile before he could whisper to Zeami:

"The little master has everything my son tells me he has, and more—oh, more! He has class, he has pathos, he *is* noble. Now that I have seen three generations of the Kanze, I am ready to die."

Zeami, beaming at Ogame's enthusiasm and gently stroking the back of his beloved old nanny, shook his head as if to refute such exaggerated flattery, but he understood what Ogame meant. Since the time of the Jozen Monastery he had had to fight tooth and nail to obtain nobility of bearing, but his son had been born with it.

Goro, the second son, was the baby who cried the least and laughed the most. He had so greedily chewed his wet nurse's nipple that she begged to be dismissed. When his teeth were scarcely visible in his gums, he had eaten a whole steamed cake stuffed with sweet-bean paste and shown no ill effects afterward. By the time Goro was two, he was already heavier and taller than his brother Juro. The big-boned, tall boy with convulsive loud laughter had dexterous strong hands with which he could climb any tree and make excellent catapults, bamboo flutes and birdcages, and during his first lesson he declared he liked playing the big drum better than practicing "those sissy sliding slow steps." Overflowing with physical well-being himself, he considered his mother and Juro sickly and weak, for otherwise, he argued, how could they possibly spend hours on end just sitting and gazing at a dot in the sky?

As Saburo was being brought up as Zeami and Yukina's own son, those very few who knew that he was in fact the old master's and the famous *kusé* dancer's grandson had been strictly bidden to hide the truth at least until the child was grown up. As the baby had been brought back to Kyoto by Yukina herself with her own two sons when the epidemic chaos was over—after an absence of ten months—everyone just thought: How very lucky that the mistress had her third son in the safety of Omi.

When Zeami had his first opportunity to talk with Yukina about Saburo, he was dismayed to catch a scornful little smirk on her lovely regular features.

"Whatever you may think of his mother," Zeami pleaded, "Omina-dono was not only a great artist but one of the best friends of our family. Please, till the boy can stand on his own feet as an artist worthy of his grandparents, love and care for him as your own. You will try, won't you?"

Zeami looked at his wife and knew he might as well have

spoken to a stone effigy. He took her cold hand in his. At this one touch her entire being was awakened and glowed. As he collected her into his arms, he could not help asking himself if there was no means to communicate with his wife other than physically; and with a quick shudder his mind leaped back to the nights spent at the Jozen Monastery, to the memories of serving hungering flesh and flesh alone.

Yukina, who was tepid and lazy in showing maternal affection toward her own children to the point of appearing dismissive and indifferent, could not be expected to be otherwise toward Saburo. Still, with Hotan diligently tending him and teaching him to write and to read and Kogame's wife and Kumazen's unmarried daughter, Sazami, coming to the Kanze house every day to cook and sew and pamper the boys, Saburo had a perfectly normal and agreeable childhood.

He did not very much resemble either of his brothers, but a very good-looking and attractive boy he certainly was. To crown a tall, well-proportioned body he carried a head of feline interest—an impression perhaps reinforced by his large and superbly elongated ears and the color of his pupils, which varied from bluish gray to dark amber, and the curious way his long, slim red lips were contorted when he smiled or sulked.

As he sulked frequently, the young disciples living with the Master's family, whose duties included playing with the children and taking them for walks, knew Saburo's scimitar grin only too well and called it "the little master Saburo's cat face." Hotan too was well acquainted with it, for Saburo would sulk and even refuse to eat till Hotan allowed him to learn lessons at the same level as Goro. Finally having got his way and being given a difficult dance sequence or a tricky passage in singing, he would then grapple with it like a fiend and not let go till he had mastered it. Sometimes when a general rehearsal had been scheduled to follow an individual lesson in the stage room, Hotan had to carry him out of the room with the boy struggling and hitting Hotan's back with his flying fists and legs, screaming, "I can do it. Let me try again. I can do it!"

Zeami praised Saburo's tenacity in generous words with the intention of stimulating Goro to harder, more committed work as a *shité* rather than spending so much time practicing with the big drum. On such occasions Saburo would turn bright red in the face and flare his nostrils, his chest visibly expanding with pride. It was a touching sight, but at the same time it warned Zeami of the boy's jealous and emulous nature. Whenever he returned from a journey accompanying Yoshimitsu, Zeami had to be extremely careful to hand out to his three sons gifts of almost equal size and value, for Saburo would immediately scrutinize his brothers' gifts and compare them with his own.

With the uncompromising eye of a professional, Zeami knew that his eldest alone possessed the magic of stage presence, which cannot be taught or learned, and with the house and its art always in the forefront of his mind, it would have been hypocritical of him to think that he loved all his three sons impartially; in his gaze that surveyed and took pride in Juro there was a prayer far more intense than a mere father's. But with the extreme caution of hiding from the head the heart's design, once outside the stage room, Zeami disciplined himself never to differentiate between Saburo, who was not his own, and Juro, who by birth and talent was his rightful heir. In return, Saburo worshiped Zeami with an enslaved passion.

Goro teased him, saying, "Whenever Father comes into your sight, your jaws drop, your eyes goggle and your tongue hangs out a foot long."

Whenever the little boys were permitted to watch the adults rehearse, Zeami could feel Saburo's eyes focused on his back like the point of a sword and the child's bated breath follow him like an ensnaring mesh around his dancing ankles.

The first time the household had a serious warning of the degree of Saburo's possessiveness was when Zeami completed *On Transmission of the Flower*. The innermost secrets of a house and its craft in any art, whether martial, cultural, industrial or even culinary, had by custom been transmitted from a father to his heir—one transmission only in each succeeding generation.

During the first secret lesson, Zeami showed Juro the treatise he himself had painstakingly bound and decorated which was to be the exclusive property of Juro when he became the third master of Kanze. The boy could not help proudly telling the others how impressive the volume was.

"I am to honor it and keep its secrets as if it were made of Father's and Grandfather's hearts and blood."

Saburo was missing at supper. As Zeami had to perform at

the recently completed West Palace on the Kitayama domain that night, Kogame, Hotan and the Kumao and Kumaya brothers took three or four young disciples each and systematically searched various districts of Kyoto. It was not till early next morning that Kumaya's group found the boy fast asleep on the Kamo riverbank. He had gone there to drown himself, but extensive work on the dikes against flooding of the river had prevented him from descending to the water. Famished and exhausted, he had cried himself into a deep sleep curled up on a patch of soft new grass.

When the boy was brought home, his face smeared with dust and dried tears and eyes swollen red, Yukina scolded him with hysterical virulence, keeping all the while a disdainful distance from the dirty child:

"You shameless little brat! Is this the way to repay the love and affection your father has shown you? Juro is the eldest and has certain rights which you will not have, and the sooner you accept that, the better for us all."

Hotan swore he would never forget how the child had drawn himself up taller under his mother's cantankerous outburst and stared unflinchingly back at her. "It was not the little master Saburo's usual cat face. It frightened me," confided Hotan when he later paid a bedside visit to Ogame.

As soon as Zeami came home, he went to find Saburo in the room that he shared with the other boys. He squatted to come level with the child and asked gently what had made him want to kill himself.

"Because you gave your heart and blood and secrets all to Brother Juro!"

Smiling and rather touched, Zeami put his hand on the boy's head. Saburo slapped away Zeami's arm with an unexpected ferocity and ran away. Zeami licked his lips slowly and stayed in the empty room for some time, feeling troubled and frightened. When he finally rose, he went to find Juro and told him that as the eldest and next master of Kanze he had to be scrupulously kind and humble and cautious with his younger brothers so as not to arouse their jealousy.

Juro selected some of the most attractive toys he possessed and gave them to Saburo, explaining as best he could:

"I'm the eldest and I am taught and given more than you or Goro. It's like this in a house like ours—no one can change it. So don't be angry with me; you're my dear brother."

Saburo was pleased to have the toys and went around the house showing them to everyone who had the time to admire them. But it was not Hotan alone who noticed that Saburo put on his cat face whenever Yukina spoke to him and that with his eyes hovering somewhere about her white throat, he always replied with a minimum of words and expression.

Adopting a son was a practice so common as to be banal in a profession where the continuity of an individual artistic style was of cardinal importance, and in most cases the affection and loyalty that grew between a father and his adopted son were true and binding. No logical reason, therefore, why Zeami should not now inform Saburo of his adoption even at his young age, especially as he was closely related to Zeami and his children through Kanami. Had the boy's possessive adoration of his father and master been less intense, Zeami would have done so earlier; had Yukina been a woman capable of motherly love that could have alleviated the pain the disclosure would be bound to cause Saburo, perhaps he would have found it easier; but as it was, with four rapidly growing children in the house, months and seasons seemed to fly like an arrow, and the longer Zeami procrastinated, the more intimidated he became.

Then came Ogame's death from intestinal ulcers, which threw Zeami into a pit of inconsolable grief. For days all he could do was whimper like a sick dog in front of Ogame's mortuary tablet. And no sooner had the forty-ninth-day rite of the incomparable kyogen comic's death been observed than Kumazen, so boastful of his indomitable health and hard drinking, collapsed like a felled tree, face down, just after he had made an exit in the middle of a performance at the Kofuku Temple's spring festival. Zeami's heart lost a beat with ominous intuition when through the tiny eyeholes of his mask he observed Kumao making the next entrance in the role which till only several minutes earlier had been played by the father. A heart seizure. Yoshimitsu deeply mourned the deaths of his long-familiar artists and sent unusually generous amounts of condolence money to the two almost consecutive funerals.

With the demise of the two veterans who had personally known Kanami, Omina and Saburo's father, Zeami felt even less inspired to confront the boy with the secret of his birth. It was soon already December 1407 when the master of Yoshimitsu's household sent Zeami a message informing him that he and Doami of the Hiei troupe were to offer a performance of noh plays in front of the young Emperor Gokomatsu, who was to be Yoshimitsu's personal guest at his Kitayama domain, now finally completed.

"The Heaven's Son *asking* to see a noh performance!" It showed how the popular entertainment had risen in stature since the days when Kanami would not have been allowed to speak to even a provincial shrine clerk in the same room but only from the other side of a sliding screen. Yoshimitsu had proposed to the Emperor only Doami and Zeami, once again blithely ignoring the inevitable cry of indignation from the dengaku camp and their patrons, notable amongst whom was his son shogun Yoshimochi.

Everyone at the Kanze dropped preparations for the New Year family feasts and plunged into work. Zeami took his frugal meal on a tray in the stage room, which he seldom left during the day, and slept on average no more than five hours a night. On the New Year's eve when all the temples of the capital began sounding their bells the traditional one hundred and five times, Zeami put down his writing brush and prayed that the New Year would bring no more bereavement among those close to him.

On the third day of the New Year, the old master of Komparu paid Zeami his annual courtesy visit, bringing with him a shy little boy strapped to the back of one of the Komparu disciples.

"My fatherless grandson, Yashao, only four," the old man said between loud, sizzling sips of the warm spiced wine. He looked ruddier and burlier, despite the catastrophe that had struck the Komparu family only a few months earlier when his son and heir had been murdered by a gang of mountain bandits on his way to perform at the Izumo Shrine.

When, many years earlier, Master Komparu had been jeered off the stage by an appalled Kyoto audience, the first and last time he had ever set his foot on the capital's stage, Kanami had said, "The poor man should not have attempted to play an angel. Look at him—he's built exactly like a bear standing on its hind legs." But in his old age Komparu had abandoned all female roles, and his very bearlike physique and gravelly old voice gave his demons and warriors such moving substance that in the Yamato province he had actually enhanced his popularity.

"An enchanting little parcel, your grandson," said Zeami, taking note that fortunately for the child, he did not take after his bearlike grandfather but after his erect and regular-featured father, and he offered Yashao a New Year cake. His small red lips open in a perfect circle, Yashao stared unblinkingly at Zeami before he lifted his right hand with grave caution. With both Zeami and his grandfather watching encouragingly, the child's little hand took almost twenty full counts to reach the cake held out by Zeami. As Yashao began to nibble the cake, chuckling and purring to himself, Master Komparu straightened his collar and the folds of his best kimono, then bowed his bristly white head low before Zeami.

"Today I have come to ask you the greatest favor of my life. As you can see, I'm old and becoming decrepit, and with my son gone, on this boy's shoulders rests the future of the Komparu. I may be able to hold out another seven or eight years—during which time, please, Zeami-dono, would you train him and let him learn by example from yourself?"

Zeami looked at Yashao, who, meeting Zeami's eyes, raised an exultant bell-like laugh, showing Zeami his empty cake-encrusted hand.

Zeami nodded, still watching and smiling at the boy.

"Of course. I'll be delighted to." He clapped hands three times to call a servant to fetch his daughter.

Tama was a precocious, bossy six-year-old, very pretty with her father's eyes and her mother's fairness. She idolized her father, and while her brothers were incarcerated in the stage room or learning a musical instrument or singing in any available room in the house, she went to the kitchen and chirped away, reciting everything her father had done or said within her hearing. Without the master-and-pupil relationship coming between them, Zeami felt at his most relaxed and intimate with Tama, and there was a fond complicity between them.

"Tama, this is Yashao. He's coming to live with us."

Tama was delighted to have a friend near her own age. She begged Zeami to let the boy sleep in her room, urgently adding, "No, no, I shan't bully the little boy. I shan't talk all night to him either."

They became inseparable, and Yukina, for some reason which no one quite understood, took a particular liking to the little orphan and taught the two of them together in calligraphy and composition.

ONE NIGHT, Zeami was alone in the windowless closet of a room where he could work best, rubbing the bar of charcoal ink in drops of water, when Juro came and sat quietly outside in the chilly corridor, asking permission to speak with Zeami. As Yukina frequently mentioned with a proud half-smile to whoever would listen, Juro did have the manners of a born aristocrat, not of an entertainer; as he entered his father's confined study and shut the sliding screens behind him, people would have thought his movement a part of a courtly dance. He did not speak at once. His downcast eyes under their long lashes took on a dense, humid-looking shade which accentuated his grave, preoccupied look.

"What is worrying you, Juro?"

"At supper, Tama said something which . . ." Juro swallowed the rest. "I am worried that Saburo might go to the Kamo riverbank to try to kill himself again."

"What did Tama say?"

"She heard it from Yashao. He was very much surprised we didn't know. His grandfather had told him that though Saburo is a grandson of our grandfather Kanami, he is not our real brother. I think it's practically the same thing, and so do Goro and Tama, but Saburo is so very quiet and closed up, just as he was when I told him about the secret transmission, that I'm worried he might disappear again. I know the three of us sleep in the same room, but I can't keep awake all night watching him, and you know how soundly Goro sleeps. Would you talk to Saburo, Father, and tell him even if he's only your adopted son, it doesn't change anything, makes no difference at all?"

Zeami immediately went to the boys' room. A maid had just finished laying three sleep mats on the floor, and Goro, already in his night kimono, seeing his father, scurried out of the room, his face red and his eyes swollen with tears. Saburo, not yet undressed, sat in the corner with his face to the wall, shunning the light from the rapeseed-oil lamp. Pity scorched Zeami's guts. He respected the boy's immense suffering too much to utter a word or even to go near him. By one careless word Saburo's kingdom of games and pranks and insouciance had been laid in ruins, and he sat there in a stupor, crushed under the enormous weight of his loss. The extent of his catastrophe was in proportion to the extravagance of his own adoration of the greatest artist and master, who he now knew was not his father.

Sensing Zeami's presence, Saburo tautened his spine and lifted his head imperceptibly. Zeami understood the boy's refusal of sympathy or any kind of explanation. The withering memories of his own childhood convinced Zeami that Saburo would have to find the strength to withstand the blow in his own solitude and virulent pride, perhaps even in hatred against the one whom he had loved the most. Leaving the boy alone in his mute wretchedness, Zeami noiselessly backed out of the room.

19

THE EIGHTH day of March was a windless warm day with the sun just a humid halo behind a silvery screen of cloud. Any indignity in visiting a commoner having been alleviated by the excuse of "avoiding the evil direction," the Emperor with a large train of courtiers, numbering nearly a hundred including his own household staff, left the Ninefold Forbidden Enclosure for the Kitayama Palace.

Double-petaled cherry trees in full bloom formed a massive flowering and perfumed wall along the entire stretch of the entrance drive, and to the incredulous joy of the imperial guests, the surface of the drive on which their palanquins and carriages progressed had been decorated with pebbles of five different colors, laid out in a pattern of waves. At the end of the drive in front of his magnificent palace, Yoshimitsu, attired in his priestly robe adorned for the occasion with a gold-threaded ceremonial *kesa* surplice and with strings of crystal beads around his wrist, perfectly at ease and beaming, greeted the Emperor and his court. The seventy-strong orchestra struck up the first note of music as His Imperial Majesty alighted from his palanquin and his twenty-day visit began with all the effulgent blessings of springtime and the sumptuous hospitality made possible by Yoshimitsu's colossal personal wealth and power. Each banquet offered the rarest early-season delicacies and the best wine from Hyogo; each entertainment ended with a distribution of gifts of breathtaking value and loveliness.

The absence of Shogun Yoshimochi from the festivities day after day was conspicuous, so that when on the thirteenth afternoon of the imperial visit Yoshimitsu formally invited the young shogun together with his other sons and several of his daughters to a noh performance, with Yoshimochi's dislike of noh by now well known, his very presence aroused even more curiosity and malicious gossip than if he had stayed away.

Now past seventy, Doami, by token of his seniority, opened the performance in the ritual *Okina* and followed it with a new play, *Kinuta,* that Zeami had written specially for his senior colleague for the great occasion. Doami played the ghost of a woman who has died from lamenting too passionately the absence of her husband, evoking their conjugal love with a haunting intensity but never making her sexual longing strident or odorous of vulgarity. Even those insular and anachronistic noblemen, predetermined to execrate the plebeian theater, found themselves fascinated, and at last the young Emperor's smooth round face, a quail's egg with three tiny dots for eyes and mouth, showed some surprise and confusion.

"I don't know how to explain what I feel," he sighed.

"I broke a cherry tree but found no flower,
For the flower was nowhere else but in the spring sky,"

replied his host, quoting a two-hundred-year-old poem, and the all-purpose inscrutability of such a reply seemed to relieve His Imperial Majesty of all mental discomfort. He smiled gratefully and added what he knew would please Yoshimitsu:

"If you knew how impatiently I wait for the legendary Zeami to appear!"

Yoshimitsu inclined his head to acknowledge His Imperial Majesty's gracious remark.

Zeami was forty-five this spring and showed not the slightest sign of change or decay in his looks, vigor or technique; so much was this the case that when he occasionally performed unmasked, his longtime faithfuls asked incredulously: "Is he wearing a mask carved in his likeness of twenty years ago?" Yet when Yoshimitsu had wanted him to appear in at least two, possibly three plays before the Emperor, Zeami would not agree to make more than one appearance, saying:

"An actor reaches the pinnacle of his career at about thirty-five, and after he passes the gate of forty-five he had better know the grace of *not to do*."

"You sly weasel!" Yoshimitsu had slapped his lap with his string of beads, trying to show anger but instead bursting out laughing. "To know *not to do!* When you get to that stage, you've arrived at the heightless height, and you know it, damn you!"

"Instead, Great Tree, I have broken bones to write *Kiyotsune* and *A Flower Basket* expressly to show off my sons."

"A risky gamble. I admit they are your sons and Kanami's grandsons, but they are no more than kids."

"But in *my* plays, in roles specially tailored for them, Great Tree."

In the end, Zeami had won Yoshimitsu's reluctant approval. The former shogun had been far from convinced or pleased. But when Juro appeared, unmasked, in the title role of *Kiyotsune* with a white military headband tied above his huge slanted eyes, his frail long neck rising like smoke from what on him appeared a massive burden of costume, Yoshimitsu felt a hot lump in his throat at once, and as the boy proceeded to speak in the keen, bell-like voice of a fourteen-year-old, he had to swallow hard to hold back his tears. Zeami's verses and music were superb, of course; irresistible, even. But then, Yoshimitsu had come to expect that; the singular phenomenon was his son Juro. Whatever the boy did, sing or dance or speak, he did it with such pathos and intensity that Yoshimitsu was convinced he was seeing the boy actor for the last and final time. The impression Juro gave of the urgent transiency of youth, of life and of this world was staggering. Listening to Juro as the ghost of a young warrior prince singing to his inconsolable wife, Yoshimitsu found himself already regretting Juro like an old friend doomed to drop dead the moment his song was over, and he was not the only spectator who could not help comparing Juro's performance to Fujiwaka's no less remarkable debut at Imakumano thirty-three years earlier.

It was not surprising that following Juro's Kiyotsune, even

Kogame, in a howlingly absurd costume as an octopus, had a few difficult moments before he could disperse the audience' melancholy mood.

In *A Flower Basket* Zeami had set out to entertain, cramming it with one lilting melody and colorful dance after another, and with Hotan in the prime of his career and Goro and Saburo with the privilege of their Flower of extreme youth, Yoshimitsu was convinced that far from being just "a bunch of inexperienced kids," the Kanze's younger generation was capable of bringing out every theatrical enchantment that Zeami had promised.

During Kogame's second kyogen farce, Yoshimitsu gloated as he observed His Imperial Majesty in agonized contortions trying not to join the rest of the audience in guffawing at Kogame's performance as an umbrella maker in a tantrum over his thieving servants. And surely, Yoshimitsu reflected, the proof of the Kanze's astounding wealth of talent was the fact that the master of the company himself had not yet put one foot on stage.

"Once you possess a legendary fame, the public's expectation paves your way," said Zoami tartly, sitting behind his patron, the old Lord Shiba, in the loge next to the young shogun's. "You do nothing, *they* do the work and you walk away with a triumph."

Indeed, just before Zeami's entrance there was such a palpitating excitement in the air that even His Imperial Majesty could not help feeling his throat uncomfortably tightened and dry; he had to nibble a few crystallized cherry blossoms, minding his bad teeth, a hereditary imperial debility.

Zeami called the play *Lady Aoi*, but the *shité* role was Princess Rokujo, no longer young, whose lover, Prince Genji, has left her to marry Lady Aoi. Her jealousy and rancor against the illustrious newlyweds erupt like molten lava. In the first part of the play Zeami, as the rejected Princess, came on behind a mask called "a woman of deep affection." So noble, so proud and pathetic was his portrayal that he glided easily over and above the already heightened expectation of the public, and no one thereafter could remain outside her suffering.

After a quick costume change Zeami reappeared behind a horned demon mask, mouth slit wide open and metal-studded eyes bulging and flashing with vengeance, and many courtiers gasped and covered their eyes, while the imperial household attendants became momentarily transfixed with terror. Kumao as the holy priest, called upon to lift the evil spell that Princess Rokujo had put on Lady Aoi, rose magnificently to the occasion. He challenged the horrific fury of Zeami's demon with a towering force of conviction in the mercy of Buddha. Everyone, agape and aghast, thought he could actually see sparks flying between the two combatants of evil and good. Finally, to the physical and emotional relief of the spectators, Zeami made his exit.

"Oh, I have never been so frightened!" squealed His Imperial Majesty, and Yoshimitsu struck his own thigh with the string of jangling crystal beads, conduct quite unbecoming someone cloistered, and laughed as contentedly as if he had just won an empire, which naturally gave much satisfaction to his daimyos who had been coerced into contributing hugely to finance the imperial visit.

Yoshimitsu was in fact so overjoyed with the success his noh master had wrung from his exacting noble guests that he sent word for Zeami's three sons to entertain them further at the succeeding banquet to be held in the immense hall of the West Palace.

A thousand paper and stone lanterns were alight, hung from the endless stretch of the palace eaves, extending along the winding covered galleries and scattered outside over the garden and the lake. As the guests were seated and cups of wine were being passed around, Goro and Saburo danced a lively dance that Zeami had taught them in judicious anticipation of a command such as this. When they finished, they bowed deeply in the direction of the Emperor till their smartly swaying front locks scraped the floor, stood up and turned to go. Just then, Ghien, a swarthy, willful-looking priest, elegantly attired as befitted the head of the Seiren-In monastery and one of Yoshimitsu's younger sons, raised his forefinger with a commanding authority and beckoned Saburo to come and sit beside him, while Goro, hot and bothered and dazed by so much light, was happy to retire at once behind the gold-and-silver screen.

For Juro's dances, Zeami played the flute and Goro, the hand drum. Clad in the most attractive combination of spring colors, Juro entranced everyone with that hypnotic placidity of movement inherited from his father, his slender hips drawing a line perpetually parallel to the ground, regardless of his leaping and spinning feet. Zeami, the proud father, did not overlook the sur-

reptitious lifting of the screen at the back of the banqueting hall
behind which sat Yasuko, the Lady of the North-Facing Palace,
and her ladies-in-waiting. After two dances Juro had not only the
honor of receiving a fan from Yoshimitsu's own hand but the exceptional honor to be invited up to Yasuko's screen to receive her
warm congratulations and the gift of a splendid gossamer silk
kimono.

Nor was Zeami unaware of what was taking place between
Ghien and Saburo. Despite the fact that Ghien was placed near
the young shogun Yoshimochi, his own brother, the head of the
Seiren-In monastery, looking much older than his actual age of
sixteen, did not refrain from holding the boy actor by the waist,
touching his cheek or even feeding Saburo with his own chopsticks. Zeami was not a little taken aback to see Saburo cope with
the lecherous young priest with the subtle coquetry of an experienced courtesan, his cat face now blushingly inviting, now primly
protesting, and he could not help being reminded of Saburo's real
father, said to have ruined himself in debauchery.

By the time Zeami, Juro and Goro, aided by Sango, had col-
lected the costumes and instruments and were ready to leave,
Saburo had gone. The entertainer father said nothing, nor did
Juro or Goro ask how and why.

Saburo came home shortly before his lesson with Hotan was
due the following morning. Hachi reported that the little master
had been accompanied home by an apprentice monk from the
Seiren-In. The boy was perfectly at ease, and from the way he kept
yawning unabashedly, stretching his arms like a tree, the family
surmised that he was even proud of having been singled out by
Yoshimitsu's son and the reigning shogun's brother to share the
night with him.

Zeami's former relationship with Yoshimitsu being so widely
known, he was not in a position to object to Saburo's repeated
absence from the room he shared with his brothers; besides, Saburo never once missed or returned late for a lesson. In fact, after
being taken into Ghien's adult world, he began working with a
keener awareness of the wordly power and glory of his profession
and soon was treating his elder brothers with a mixture of mild
scorn and condescending overfriendliness. Hotan, who was still
Saburo's tutor-cum-nanny, kept to himself what Saburo told him
with his cat face wreathed in a grin: "If you can't get shogun

Yoshimochi himself, you could say that with his brother I've got the second-best!" It was well known that out of hostile rejection of anything his father, Yoshimitsu, had appreciated, the young shogun strictly denied himself the pleasure of boys.

Ghien was entitled to a comfortable revenue from many provincial estates, patents and privileges held by the Seiren-In, and although nowhere near as rich as his father or his eldest brother, he could afford some attractive gifts which Saburo, after all only a boy of twelve, could not help flaunting before his brothers and the troupe members.

HARDLY A MONTH had passed since the imperial visit to the Kitayama domain when one evening Yoshimitsu, who had seldom been known to be seriously ill and looked far younger than his age of fifty-one, complained of feverishness. Before his personal physician, a Chinese Zen priest, could arrive, he had lost consciousness. His temperature remained alarmingly high despite all the infusions, moxibustion and needles the doctor administered to him.

Every potent sutra was read and chants were sung everywhere for his recovery; the Emperor himself offered a three-day music supplication at the Kitayama Shrine, and the entire population held its breath as the intonation of prayers continued without pause throughout the capital. Zeami, unlike other Companions, who came and went, spent the days and the nights of Yoshimitsu's illness in the Companions' lobby at the palace, sitting up and unremittingly impressing into his string of beads all the inexpressible ardor of his prayers, oblivious of the sidelong glances of his rivals and enemies inwardly gloating over the prospect that the days of his supremacy might now be numbered. For Zeami, the fact that Yoshimitsu, who had always pooh-poohed the curative effect of prayers and chants, had himself agreed to have them publicly offered at temples and shrines across the country and his personal knowledge of the excesses in which Yoshimitsu had continually indulged himself made him view the abruptness of Yoshimitsu's collapse with ominous dread.

On his third morning at the palace, Zeami made his toilet early and was slowly walking back from the ablutions area tucked away in an evergreen grove when one of Yoshimitsu's old attendants whom Zeami knew well came up to him.

"The Great Tree regained consciousness and seems a little

better this morning, though the doctor says . . ." He wrung his unshaven gray face in a tortured grimace, incapable of finishing the sentence. "Would you come with me? The Great Tree kept murmuring your name, and it is the Lady of the North-Facing Palace who sent me to fetch you. . . ."

Even the outer rooms of Yoshimitsu's private wing were filled with silent, dull-eyed crowds; courtiers, daimyos, high shogunal officials, innumerable priests and doctors who, seeing Zeami, with no more show of contempt or resentment resignedly made way for the one whose name the Great Tree had uttered in and out of his comatose sleep. In the first anteroom to Yoshimitsu's chamber were his mistresses, huddled together like so many shipwrecked bodies, and as Zeami passed through the room, one of Yasuko's ladies-in-waiting silently opened the sliding doors to Yoshimitsu's sickroom.

Yasuko, sitting by her husband's pillow, her head wrapped in white silk and clad in nun's attire, raised her head, and she too for the first time looked Zeami in the eye, almost as if he were her equal. Neither her kindly heavy-lidded eyes nor her prudish small mouth and nose betrayed any emotion or thought, as befitted her "above the clouds" status; she just so slightly lifted her right sleeve that her string of beads, but not any part of her hand, protruded from it in response to Zeami's humble deep bow.

With one glance at Yoshimitsu, all Zeami's hopes were dashed: the warrior prince from the gusty East who so loved fresh air lay there in festering stale incense smoke which had accompanied endless prayers and combat of medicine and human will, so futile, futile against death. The certainty of losing Yoshimitsu quite mutilated Zeami. Had he been standing, he would have collapsed against the sliding screens; bent as he was on his knees, his broken shoulders dropped to the floor, his face buried in his palms.

"Zeami is here," he heard Yasuko say.

After a mind-boggling silence there came a whisper, vaporous but lucid:

"Fujiwaka."

Yasuko, on the other side of Yoshimitsu and facing Zeami, swayed her folded knees just a few inches away from Yoshimitsu's pillow, making it easier for Zeami to come closer to her husband's head. From the rampant fever, Yoshimitsu had shed in so short a time much of his bulk, and the abnormal stirring of blood made his fleshless face glow like an oiled-paper lantern painted unevenly in blood, in stinging contrast to the white of his sick robe, his pillow cover and the cold compress on his head.

"I'm scorched. So hot. Seem to just sleep and sleep. And no one tells me the truth, just when I need it."

Careful not to waste his thin burning breath, Yoshimitsu panted in a tone of an intermittent rave, but far from raving.

"That play, *Autumn Voice,* Fujiwaka—it doesn't quite work, does it? A beautiful *kusé* dance, superb chorus, yet still something is missing. I love it, though. Two friends walking the autumn field; one wanders off, haunted by the music of autumn insects; the other friend finds him dead. 'Wind and moon, friends of old. Madness in heart, he went beyond, to return no more.' You must go on working on it till you find your usual perfection."

With a tremendous effort which instantly made the Chinese doctor sitting at Yoshimitsu's feet react with reproachful agitation, Yoshimitsu turned his head toward Zeami, his gutted avid eyes open for the first time. His gaze, lit from the root of his remaining life, was opaque like a thick gelatin.

"What will happen to you and your noh when I'm gone?"

Zeami wasn't to know that it was the very first time Yoshimitsu had admitted aloud the certainty of his own death; he was too beside himself to notice the sudden immobility that struck Yasuko. Before Zeami could draw a breath, Yoshimitsu continued in short, chopped phrases.

"Damn silly, though, to worry, about you, who live, in the eternal, world of noh, but, frail, aberrant human heart, give me, an illusion, you needed me, you still, need me . . ."

Suddenly, Yoshimitsu's shaking hands began feeling and clutching at his white linen cover.

Zeami swiftly slid closer.

"Great Tree, what are you looking for?"

"My beads, from the Ming Emperor—my beads."

Yasuko found them and put them into Yoshimitsu's hand. With a surprising fit of energy, Yoshimitsu flung the strings of beads toward Zeami.

"Fujiwaka, keep them, but sell them, if you need money."

Then he sighed an all-emptying sigh which deflated him of strength. Despite the presence of Yasuko, Zeami could not refrain from clinging to Yoshimitsu's hot hand, which stuck to his as if soldered. Yoshimitsu gave Zeami's hand a short, convulsive grip.

"Your cold hand, Fujiwaka. Don't go yet. A shogun . . . doesn't sleep . . . alone. . . ."

His hand went limp. The doctor quickly moved up along the sleep mat and, wanting to come near his patient's head, whispered something to Zeami, but with his heavy foreign accent Zeami could not understand him, whereupon with that peculiarly Chinese unoffending brusqueness the doctor removed Yoshimitsu's hand from Zeami's, shoved Zeami aside and peered at Yoshimitsu, now obliterated by an insensate sleep.

Yasuko regained her authority as Yoshimitsu sank back into a coma. Neither hostile to nor hurt by the bondage she had just witnessed between her husband and the entertainer, the imminence of death erasing many tormenting considerations of this fleeting world, she gently nodded to Zeami, You may leave.

Zeami bowed to Yoshimitsu and to Yasuko and slid backward out of the room; each yard of distance he came away on his knees made both Yoshimitsu's death and his love for the dying man that much more real.

For three further days Yoshimitsu remained in a coma, and when his temperature suddenly dropped, he was dead.

Zeami did not come home till after the death of the third Ashikaga shogun had been made public. After a long solitary prayer before the altar, he ordered his family and troupe to gather in the stage room.

"Yesterday we were standing on the crest of our fortune," he began. His bloodshot eyes, sunken in his haggard face, were dry of tears and bore the dead calm of grief beyond all griefs. "And today we begin plummeting downhill. I do not offer you any false comfort, saying one day we might yet see another turn in our fortunes and rejoice in a new glory and prosperity and might meet another patron and spectator with the eye and heart of the Great Tree. No, I would not count on that. I shan't count on anything any longer, except on you. If you don't lose faith in the Kanze's noh and in me, the noh will not perish from external threats and will survive many shogunates and many more generations. The integrity of our Way is our lifeline. Remember what my father used to say: Never forget the beginner's awe. We are forever beginners."

Zeami smiled at every face that sought strength from him. He felt elated, like a martyr, already.

20

As soon as Yoshimitsu's funeral and the religious formalities of the customary forty-nine days were duly over, Shogun Yoshimochi vacated the Flowering Palace in the Muromachi district and moved into his father's Kitayama Palace. When Emperor Goko-matsu, sincerely fond of and grateful to Yoshimitsu, informed Yoshimochi of his unprecedented decision to give Yoshimitsu the posthumous courtesy title of "the Cloistered Emperor Father," the shogun curtly declined it.

"My father, all said and done, was still only a mere subject and commoner. As shogun whose duty it is to uphold the celestial dignity of His Imperial Majesty I could not possibly accept such an unmerited honor, which might embarrass court history."

Yoshimochi simultaneously announced his intention to move away from the elitism dear to his father and promote the militaristic character of the shogunate, to which a group of daimyos who had not shone brilliantly under Yoshimitsu's overcultured reign gave enthusiastic support.

Of an insular and suspicious nature, Yoshimochi also wasted no time in declaring an end to all official trading activities between China and Japan and unceremoniously asked the Ming Emperor's envoy to leave.

With the new shogun's obsessive hatred of everything his father had loved, it was not surprising that months and seasons passed without a single command for a performance at the Kitayama Palace reaching the Kanze or the Hiei troupe. All the great palaces, daimyo mansions, temples and shrines in the capital also shut their gates to the noh troupes, and as had been expected, the dengaku troupes revived spectacularly. Every subscription performance after that fateful year of 1408 flaunted the dengaku banners high over the Kamo riverbank. Zeami was obliged to fall back on the suburbs and provinces; Doami sold his house in Kyoto and returned for good to his native town of Omi on Lake Biwa.

The younger generation in the troupe, who had not known extensive provincial touring, were thrilled with the bustling activities of repairing the portable stage floor and packing costumes and props, but this sentiment was not shared by the elders, who knew what life had been like at Yuzaki village and roaming endlessly on the mud road. They had been the fortunate witnesses of the dramatic encounter between Yoshimitsu and the Kanze father and son at the Imakumano Shrine and had seen how overnight it had transformed the troupe from the Kofuku Temple's mere chattel to the peerless theatrical company of the capital; but now that both their hard-won independence from the religious power and Yoshimitsu's patronage were lost, all the glories the Kanze had known in the capital seemed to them like something one only reads about in a fairy tale.

Zeami, taking with him Toyojiro, who like his late father, Toyodayu, had the most emollient and ingratiating manners, began paying begging-bowl visits to their old Yamato sponsors. Fortunately, the popularity of the Kanze, nurtured since the days of Kanami, had not lost its firm grip on the people of Yamato, and although the other three Yamato noh troupes were far from pleased with the Kanze's now more frequent appearances in the area, they did not dare dispute the legitimate right of the Kanze to ask for a certain number of seasonal performances at the Kofuku Temple and the Kasuga Shrine.

Although their income was more than halved by the loss of lucrative performances in the capital and the generous gifts they used to receive from Yoshimitsu, the number of performances actually increased under the touring regime, giving the younger generation a heaven-sent opportunity to learn and try out important roles before a live audience, which would not have been advisable or possible in the capital with its hawk-eyed, exacting audience.

Regardless—or rather, in defiance—of the inadequate, uncivilized and sometimes downright humiliating conditions on the road, Zeami insisted on maintaining the highest artistic standards and professional discipline, telling his troupe, "The only way to survive a storm of misfortune is to turn into granite-hard rock and sink deeper and deeper into yourself and your art." He would take the company's daily lesson in dancing and singing and miming himself wherever they happened to be, rehearse old and new plays, often outdoors for lack of suitable covered space—in a corner of a shrine precinct or even on a flat vacant piece of earth outside a town—watched and laughed at by curious children, and after the rest of the troupe had collapsed into sorely needed sleep, he would still have the energy to go on working on *Mirror of the Flower,* which was the continuation of *On Transmission of the Flower.* Even when the troupe was obliged to spend the night in a deserted temple for lack of an inn or a hospitable patron in the locality, as long as he had a lamp, a brush and paper at his disposal, he would continue with his writing. In the dreadful void both artistic and moral into which Yoshimitsu's untimely death had plunged him, writing was the only way left for him to avert his horrified gaze from the present and to look back in infinite gratitude on the years between meeting Yoshimitsu and losing him and to crystallize all the inmost reflections that had come to him during those happy fertile years.

When Yashao, aged eleven, was taken for the first time on the road, he wrote to his dearly missed friend Tama:

"Uncle Zeami is everywhere, busier and tougher than any of us, without seeming to need much food or sleep. He never complains and is always calm and joyful. He sleeps on a handful of straw on the beaten dirt ground just like any of us when that is all we've got, he who was the most pampered and adored artist of the capital! He has even started giving playwriting lessons to Juro, which as you can well imagine makes me so envious. I do so long to write plays like Uncle one day! In Obama, where I saw the dark, angry Northern Sea for the first time, Jippen and Toyojiro both fell ill from eating stale crab. So Goro had to play the big drum and Juro took Toyo's part, and all of us from Uncle down to me gave one of the best performances we'd yet given on the road—though rather wasted, I'm afraid, as the audience was small and then mostly fishermen and silk-mill workers coming for the first time to a noh."

WHEN JURO's voice changed, Zeami had him take his coming-of-age ceremony. As the Kanze no longer had any powerful patron in the capital, Zeami gratefully accepted Lord Mitsumasa Kitabatake's offer to hold the ceremony in his fortified castle in Ise when the Kanze troupe performed in a nearby town. The highly cultured warlord not only acted as the Father of the Scissors but gave Juro his adult name of Motomasa by granting one Chinese character of his own name.

"Is it judicious for our future master to be so conspicuously identified with one of the most prominent Southern daimyos?" "The Kitabatakes have been quiet as long as the Great Tree was alive, but now . . . ?" Kogame and Toyojiro whispered anxiously to each other; but the troupe had had so little chance for celebration and merriment that neither of the veteran actors had the heart to utter depressing words of warning. . . .

So Juro was renamed Motomasa, an adult of seventeen, whose progress in playwriting gave Zeami particular satisfaction as he was convinced that a master of a troupe, however gifted as a performer, unless he was capable also of creative writing, could not lead his troupe far on the Way of noh.

Goro too had his front locks cut at seventeen and was renamed Motoyoshi. Saburo, on the other hand, under pressure from Ghien, kept asking for his coming-of-age ceremony to be postponed, and in fact he did not have his and the adult name of Motoshige till he was nearly twenty, by which time his boyish front locks looked incongruous with his strikingly handsome and well-developed physique.

Even after Saburo Motoshige's ceremony of manhood had taken place, Ghien did not honor the normally observed custom of entirely releasing his favorite from night service. Although much less openly, Saburo Motoshige still frequently came home at an early hour of the morning whenever the troupe was in town preparing for the next tour; and as Saburo Motoshige had ceased sharing a room with his brothers in the main house and occupied a room by the stables, made vacant by the departure of the grooms when Zeami had had to sell the carriages and most of the horses as too costly to keep, no one knew very much what he did outside his working hours. In fact, aside from being an ambitious and assiduous member of the troupe, he had become more or less an outsider, as his relationship with Ghien became something more deep-biting and committed than the casual fancy of a superior for an inferior.

Hotan had for some time noted an increasing quantity of clothing, footwear and accessories in Saburo Motoshige's wardrobe, more luxurious and of a flashier fashion than those Zeami could now afford for Juro Motomasa and Goro Motoyoshi. Since he was now frequently fed and housed as well at Ghien's expense, it would not be an exaggeration to say that Saburo Motoshige had won a sort of privileged independence, whose awareness seemed to give the young man a gloating sense of superiority, especially over Yukina, whom he began treating as if she were an innkeeper's wife on the infrequent occasions when he came face to face with her in the house.

On the other hand, as he matured as man and artist Saburo Motoshige became more respectful, tractable and even in profounder awe of Zeami as his teacher. He worked with the tenacity of an animal that hooks its long claws deep into the flesh of its prey. He sulked less and, with his feline sensuous mouth screwed up and perspiration streaming down his forehead, went at it and at it till Zeami nodded, saying, "That's it, Motoshige. Well done."

As fellow artists treading the same Way, Zeami and Saburo Motoshige outwardly seemed to get along in viable harmony; but as to their father-and-son relationship, those few who knew how to read Saburo Motoshige's cat eyes could tell with what active rancor he continued to regret and resent not being Zeami's own son and illogically to blame Zeami for it.

IN 1418, exactly ten years since Yoshimitsu's death, his widow, Yasuko, died at the Kitayama Palace. Proving that the intervening decade had not taught him the virtues of filial piety and mercy, the shogun Yoshimochi moved out of the palace and ordered the immediate dismantling of the entire estate save the Golden Pavilion and a few other buildings. Precious timbers, roofs, architectural decorations and stones were piecemeal given away to various temples, shrines and vassals currently in his favor. Soon the once-glorious Kitayama domain was literally wiped out of sight; only the Golden Pavilion continued to dazzle in the sun and glow heatlessly under the cold moon.

The dengaku's monopoly of the capital continued unabated, to the total exclusion of the noh troupes, obliging the devoted noh fans in the capital to make an expedition to catch a glimpse of Zeami and his sons whenever the troupe was given a chance to perform in towns not too far outside the gates of Kyoto.

In the same year, Yashao, now sixteen, had his coming-of-age ceremony. As the young man, now renamed Ujinobu, was to return home the following day to Yamato, where he would be officially declared the thirtieth master of Komparu,* the betrothal of Ujinobu and Tama was announced on the same evening.

Ujinobu was loved by everyone. Even Yukina could not conceal her fondness for the gentle dreamer of a boy, who, behind his Prince Genji beauty—narrow slanted eyes under calm, puffy eyelids and small shapely nose and mouth all so unobtrusively placed on a perfect oval face—hid a keenly inquisitive and imaginative intelligence.

"A know-all who can't tell a duck from a goose!" Tama teased him, she who was two years older than her doll-faced fiancé and as practical, bossy and decisive as she rightly said Ujinobu's wife ought to be. "Can't have two poets in the house; otherwise we'll end up having cobwebs and books but no rice for our children."

How much Zeami adored Ujinobu was obvious from the fact that he himself had suggested giving his cherished only daughter to the rival house of Komparu, for Tama, who mended and washed all her father's underwear, combed his hair, packed for him, mediated between her parents whenever there was a thorny problem to be settled, copied out all his plays and was the only person in the house who somehow managed to bully Yukina out of her melancholy, was to be most sorely missed by her father.

Tama without doubt would make a splendid wife for Ujinobu, combining her grandmother Tamana's heart and industry

* The Komparu family is said to descend directly from the naturalized Chinese entertainer who performed the famous sixty-six dances to accompany prayers for peace and the end of famine and plague in the early seventh century.

with all the sophistication and culture her parents had imbued in her. The old Master Komparu had been besotted with Tama ever since she had spluttered her baby saliva all over his ear and screeched at him, "Bear, big, big bear!" He was beside himself with joy as though he himself were the lucky fiancé.

"I remember Tama wetting my lap, and that seems like only yesterday. Oh, how time flies!" He went on rhapsodically. "Each year nearer the grave, heavier with memories. Remember, Zeami-dono, your own coming-of-age ceremony? Kanami-dono still alive and the Great Tree himself acting the Father of Scissors!"

As tactful as grit in boiled rice, the old Komparu seemed totally unaware of the pained hush his reminiscence was producing amongst his listeners. Squinting his eyes blurred by age and wine, he looked about perfectly good-naturedly.

"Saburo Motoshige, where are you? Before I die I must tell you about your grandmother Omina-dono. What a dancer, what a woman she was!"

"He isn't here," Goro Motoyoshi blurted. "He asked me, in fact, to apologize to you and to Ujinobu . . ."

"Brother Motoshige had good news from the Seiren-In this morning," piped up Tama. "Ghien-sama has been appointed the new head of the Tendai Sect."

"The Tendai Sect!" Innocently overacting as usual, Master Komparu jubilantly lifted his wine cup toward Zeami. "A glad news indeed! Let's hope with the increased riches and power of his new position, Ghien-sama will help you get a command from above to perform in the capital again, eh?"

"It would be nice. . . ." Zeami sipped the wine that had gone cold. He had no illusions about getting help from Ghien, for he knew Saburo Motoshige only too well.

Ujinobu's letter from Yamato, giving all the details of his first visit to the Kofuku Temple office as the new head of the Komparu school, coincided with the unexpected arrival of a flute player of the Hiei troupe carrying with him the news of Doami's death. Doami had died on stage, masked and costumed; and for years and generations afterward people on the Lake spoke of the night of Doami's death, when purple and red clouds had raced low over the lake and although it was October, flowers had seemed to rain down. Most probably a rainbow or a halo reflecting the setting sun, but to the people of Omi who had long been haunted by Doami's artistry, they had to be purple clouds and raining flowers.

Doami—a solitary genius and the most loyal of friends, who had not once failed to have prayers chanted by two priests on every anniversary of Kanami's death; the only artist aside from Kanami whom Zeami had looked up to as a mentor. Now there had disappeared another great rock on whose help Zeami had counted so much for the survival of noh. Zeami prayed all night long; then as the dawn broke, his lean jaws set in a battlefield severity, he returned to his writing, Kanami's dictum sizzling in his ears:

"Desperately and single-mindedly, work, work, work! Never forget the beginner's awe. Life has an end; our Way is infinite. You are forever a beginner."

"So LONG AGO that I cannot remember exactly when I first went on stage, but say I was eight, then I have been on stage for fifty years now," said Zeami to no one in particular as he turned from the family altar at which he had just offered a long prayer for a safe journey on the road. Breaking from his recent custom of giving Juro Motomasa as much experience as possible of leading the troupe on tour, Zeami had decided to head the Kanze's tour to the Lake Biwa region himself in order to visit Doami's grave and to offer a performance in his memory at the Hiei Shrine.

Yukina, sitting behind Zeami, remained silent and expressionless; only her long, beautiful eyes stretched their focus farther like spilt water, no doubt chasing memories of better days as the wife of the then most celebrated actor, or perhaps wondering to what bitter end she was to share the actor's dwindling fortunes.

Juro Motomasa was too sensitive a son not to see and suffer for his father's sake the cruel irony in that Zeami's career, after fifty years of superhuman dedication and innumerable glories, had brought him right back to where it had started: the mud road. He hung his head and fixed his eyes on his traveling gloves and leg covers, which lay neatly on his lap.

"Fifty years!" Goro Motoyoshi raised an innocent cry of amazement. "More than twice my whole life!"

"Indeed." Zeami smiled affectionately at his younger son. "Your grandfather said, 'Never lose the beginner's awe.' By the erosion of time I may have lost much of my youthful zest, but even now I am still as excited and frightened by the stage, though it is now on a stony riverbank rather than on a shogun's sumptuous stage. The road we entertainers tread is like a ring of life, an endless chain of cause and effect. Kanami always maintained that he couldn't have understood life and men half as much and wouldn't have become the artist he was, had it not been for all the encounters he had had on the road."

Kogame appeared outside the altar room to announce that bullocks had been harnessed and that everyone was ready. Zeami nodded; then, turning around to the altar again, he mumbled his last quick prayer, rubbing the crystal beads Yoshimitsu had given him; and the image of the Slug Maiden with her eyelids glowing like twin fireflies, praying for him to reach the flowering capital of Kyoto nearly half a century before, flashed through his mind, as it invariably did when he was about to set out on the road.

ZEAMI had walked past the beggar at least six steps before he suddenly stopped. Kogame looked back and said something, but Zeami did not hear him. Just as frightened and fascinated as he had been at eleven, Zeami cautiously turned only his head. The tub was there, with two worn small wheels. Of course, not the same one, painted in red and white stripes, that he had seen before, but a resin-blackened low round tub, containing a wizened, bent old woman in filthy rags with her receding thin white hair matted in grimy strands hanging in uneven lengths. Her shriveled thin, torn thighs were uncovered to arouse the pity of pilgrims and passersby. The unseeing eyes had sunk deeper inside their sockets, and with all the teeth fallen out, the lower half of her face from cheekbones to chin was skeletally gutted. On a wooden plate before the tub was one persimmon, but no sign of coins or rice.

"Master, we mustn't be late." Kogame walked back to hurry Zeami. They were on their way to the temple office to receive money and grain for the two-day performances they had finished giving. "Buddha have mercy!" Kogame clasped at Zeami's arm, his jaw dropping. "It's that Slug monster!"

"Wait here. I shan't be a second," said Zeami firmly, and walked back. Squatting in front of the old beggar woman, he said gently, "Remember the sarugaku child who asked you to pray so that he and his father with the troupe could get to the capital? Many years ago. I gave you my Kasuga Shrine talisman."

"I have it right here."

The tiny hands with deep black wrinkles fumbled inside her collars and pulled out the wooden piece tied on a soiled string around her neck. The holy words on the talisman had been completely worn off. "Hope you got to the capital?"

"We did. Thank you."

"Come back and see me after sunset, please. Right here. Will you?" she whispered. Her voice was made all the gentler and more pathetic by lisping due to her toothlessness.

"Of course."

Kogame was not pleased. All the way to the temple office he did not stop scolding his master.

"Sentimental I call it, Master. I bet you she is covered with lice and fleas, carries Buddha knows what incurable diseases and stinks atrociously. You really shouldn't have gone as near as you did. Think what evil omen she could bring on you too! Tonight give me all that you are wearing; I'd better see if there are any lice."

Zeami said nothing; he looked grave and determined.

Having finished his own packing and made sure all the masks had been properly wrapped and put back in the right boxes, Zeami took an oiled-paper lantern, in case he should return after it became night, and was quickly on his way.

The temple and its many auxiliary buildings were built atop a densely wooded mountain. The pilgrims who came flocking here for the promised longevity and prosperity had long since begun climbing back down the steep winding path in order to return before dark to the town at the foot of the mountain and soak their weary bones in its famous sulfurous hot water. As Zeami crossed the wide, white-graveled court before the temple's main hall, it was already drained of the festive bustle and animation of the day; a thin rim of the setting sun cast ghostly elongated shadows of stupas, stone lanterns, passing monks and a lone peddler carrying his load of wares twice as large as himself.

In the long-stretching shadow of the temple's great gate, the Slug Maiden sat like a squat mushroom that had sprung up unseasonably and had rotted. Even with a considerable distance between them the blind woman seemed to have sensed Zeami's approach; she began swaying her head impatiently.

"There are two ropes attached to my tub," she said without any preamble or effort to first make sure the steps that lightly crushed the gravel belonged to Zeami. "Pull them and take me where I direct you to. Will you? Please?"

There was urgency in the way she entreated him, as if she had something of supreme importance to attend to. Zeami picked up the frayed dirty ropes that lay on the ground behind the tub, which was an old barrel crudely sawed off, more like a shallow plate.

"First, let us get off the gravel," she lisped. "The wheels are so small; it's hard for you to pull and hard for my sore bones. Take the dirt path along the cedars. Straight north. Past the bell tower, take the lane through the pines till it comes to the stony end. There, that's where I want you to take me. I know every square inch of this place. I've been stuck here ever since Father died. Father! He was no more my father than you my brother, but still, I didn't have to just sit and beg whilst he lived. Oh, smell the tree-black scent?"

She raised her miserable old face and slowly rotated it with an expression akin to ecstasy, her toothless mouth cavernously open; the sun had set, and indeed the trees seemed to exude a more pungent, darker-green perfume.

"You pull my tub as no one's ever done, beautiful man. It's as though we were crossing a moss garden; smooth, soundless; you never kick up dust or turn a stone or flip-flap your sandals as you go. Bet you dance well. Very well. Why you haven't stayed on in the capital, covered with adulation, I simply don't understand. But here you are, back on the mud road! Unfortunate for you; but for me, you are Buddha's last grace—you are, you are." She chuckled to herself. Revolting to look at though she was, like a chewed, then spat-out piece of animal meat, she was infectiously merry, alert, and her voice, despite her lisping, had little changed since Zeami had last heard it.

"Is this the spot you wanted? We can't go any farther. There is a ravine in front of us," said Zeami.

The path through the pines ended abruptly over a stony apron of land which sloped down to a sudden precipice, at whose foot Zeami could hear rushing water. In the little light that remained he could not see how deep the ravine was, but the water seemed to stir at an unfathomably great depth. The cliff on the opposite side of the ravine, densely covered with needle-sharp fir trees, soared almost perpendicularly, convincing Zeami of the equally sheer angle of the cliff on this side. Holding the ropes of the tub tighter in his hands, he peered at the old beggar woman uneasily, not so much from fear as from a certain foreboding.

She was silent for a long while, immobile like a moss-covered stone, and Zeami had an uncanny feeling that she was too moved, too exultant to speak.

"The moon, you know, will be full tonight, my old friend," she said at last. Whether her old friend was the moon or himself Zeami was not certain.

"I know you will understand. I am ashamed of myself even to be looked at by the moon. I am. I am," she mumbled matter-of-factly, which choked Zeami with far greater pity and despair than if she had wept and beaten her breast; so he was not in the slightest shocked when she went on to ask in a sober, calm breath: "Will you help me to die?"

Zeami raised his helpless eyes to the sky. The huge moon had risen behind a black mesh of pine needles.

"I've been praying for death from starvation or exposure for many years now, but people are kind—they have given me food and all sorts of help. Now Buddha has sent you to me. Think what a blissful relief it will be for me to be rid of this, my carcass! Think of my next life. Imagine what sparkling eyes and strong legs I'll be given then." She spoke with pure exhilaration. Zeami could not help smiling.

"What do I do?"

"Make sure I drop fast and clear of stones and thickets. If there are any in my way, would you remove them? But be careful—the ground slopes down; don't go too near the edge."

Zeami crawled on his knees and in the moonlight managed to throw many stones aside from the straight line he reckoned as the smoothest down the slope. No sooner had he done this than the old woman was lisping cheerily again.

"Get me stones—about ten, the size of a baby's head."

No longer repelled by the odor of the old beggar woman, Zeami handed her, all together, seven stones.

"Five . . . six . . . seven!" She counted them like a child at a play. "Oh, this is a big one. I'll hold on to this when I drop."

She then handed Zeami an old straw cord about three feet long.

"The best I could get. Tie this cord onto the ropes of my tub so that you don't have to stand too near the edge yourself. Just hold on to it till I say 'Goodbye'; then let go."

The moon sailed higher and disengaged itself from the summits of the pine trees. Zeami did as he was told in the clearest of moonlight, heatless and still, which made everything easier. When Zeami had finished positioning the old woman's tub on a slope about four feet from the very edge of the cliff and all was ready, the Slug Maiden looked straight in front of her; she seemed to Zeami to be either enjoying the moonlight that bathed her forehead or measuring the depth of the void into which she was to fly from the far murmuring of the water. Zeami, standing directly behind her, was watching the back of her tiny round head in a suitably somber mood, though far from feeling funereal, when she startled him, saying, without turning her head, in a friendly loud voice:

"But tell me, beautiful man, I still don't understand. Didn't you have any success at all in the capital when you finally got there?"

"I did."

"Immense? Or middling?"

"Immense."

"I thought so!" She laughed, extremely pleased, and went on lisping buoyantly:

"Of course, such a thing as fame, wealth, favor never lasts, not in this fleeting world. But, old friend, if this is of any consolation to you, let me tell you a Buddha's truth—a dying woman has no need to lie or to flatter anyone: you are a great man. You have gained an eternal life since I last saw you, that I can tell. In you I feel the calm and the cheer and the humility of someone who's suffered a lot to attain it.

"My father, so called, used to sing, on rare occasions when he wasn't drunk, 'Saints and beggars are dipped in heaven's same eternal water. Hey-ho! Hey-ho! Tee-tee-tee!' And I tell you, you're the only man I have met who has both the saint and the beggar in him, dipped in heaven's eternal water. You'll live again and again. I'll go with the talisman you gave me and will pray for you from the other side of the world so that we shall meet again."

She rowed her tub vigorously forward, and the cord in Zeami's hands tautened. Zeami saw her small head in silhouette rise stark into the moonlit void over the ravine. She cried with voluptuous joy:

"Goodbye!"

Zeami shut his eyes, let go of the cord and prayed for the falling beggar woman, wringing the crystal beads that had once belonged to the third Ashikaga shogun.

"Namu ami dabutsu, namu ami dabutsu,
Namu ami dabutsu, namu ami dabutsu . . ."

On his way back, he did not light his lantern: the moon followed him with ample light, like an old friend.

21

FIFTEEN YEARS from Yoshimitsu's death, the state of stability and affluence he had left behind was showing signs of rapid disintegration. When Emperor Gokomatsu of the Northern line abdicated, becoming the Cloistered Emperor, he disregarded the famous and bitterly disputed clause in the 1392 unification agreement which stipulated that the imperial succession was to be alternated between the Northern and the Southern lines and nominated his own baby son to succeed him.

Had Yoshimochi been a vessel of leadership brimming with his father's political foresight, sense of timing and above all personality, the inevitable discontent amongst the remnant Southern sympathizers would not have been allowed to deteriorate into open hostility.

Yoshimitsu, with his assiduously cultivated and almost genuine friendship with Emperor Gokomatsu and his court, would have also succeeded in persuading His Imperial Majesty to placate his unhappy Southern cousin with some tangible concession. Furthermore, when disaffected elements within the shogunate itself deserted to the Southern rebels, Yoshimitsu would immediately have

mobilized a massive shogunal army. Yoshimochi hesitated and did
nothing, and when he did belatedly make up his mind, his ill-
prepared army was ignominiously beaten despite its superiority in
numbers, and the rebellion in the South dragged on indecisively,
with periods of truce during which both sides went home to take
in their crops, to repair their arms and morale or even to change
sides.

Piqued by the ghastly muddle and his kidney complaint growing progressively worse, Yoshimochi suddenly took the tonsure
and made his only son, Yoshikado, the fifth Ashikaga shogun;
whereupon the teenage shogun promptly threw himself into a
whirlpool of debauchery—boys and women, hard drinking and
gambling—and his constitution having always been a worry to his
nurses and doctors, he died of liver infection and other unspeakable diseases at the age of nineteen.

Having had no other son, Yoshimochi, reluctant and thoroughly demoralized, returned to assume the shogunship, keeping
the priestly tonsure and attire; but his heart was no longer in it.
He hardly went out of the Muromachi Palace, no longer as flowering as it had been during his father's time, seldom commanded
dengaku performances and hardly ever organized the archery contests, falconry or other outdoor pageantries he had used to indulge
in with so much pleasure.

"When the Great Tree was alive, I felt inspiration pulsating
in the air and smelled fresh-cut bamboo shoots. Now I sense decay
and smell mildew," sighed Kogame, and resumed painstakingly
arranging ready-threaded needles in a neat row inside his old sewing bag in preparation for another long tour. He, who sewed up
both his young masters, Juro Motomasa and Goro Motoyoshi, before every performance and mended all their costumes and clothes,
boasted that he got through silk thread the length of the road from
Kyoto to Nara in less than a month.

Zeami raised his eyes from the latest volume of his secret-
transmission treatise, *On Music and Voice*, which for reasons of
secrecy he was binding himself with strong silk thread. Kogame
stole a quick glance at his sixty-year-old master and friend, and he
regretted having mentioned the late Great Tree. After Yoshimitsu's
death Zeami's hair had rapidly turned white, although it remained
abundant and strong, and his face, framed by the lustrous mass of
white, had with the years lost its haze of bluish veins above the

eyes and with it perhaps some of the hard, bejeweled brilliance of his eyes, but had gained a tranquil strength which struck people as both forbidding and heartbreakingly beautiful.

"Ture, the Time of Female, seems to have firmly taken over our fortunes. I am beginning to doubt if there will be a Time of Male again in my lifetime, and that is why I work as hard as I do on the secret transmission for Juro Motomasa. I must prepare him for the grimmest eventuality."

"Grimmest? Oh, Master, before you talk gloom and despondency, you ought to see how the people in the South, from great daimyos and landlords to the humblest tea pickers—the whole lot of them—welcome us with open arms and refuse to let us go home without loading us with gifts and produce from the fertile South. Honestly, Master, put down your writing brush from time to time and tour with us. You'll see what I mean."

"No, no, I want Juro Motomasa to lead the troupe himself—except, of course, when we are carrying out our traditional duties at the Kofuku and the Kasuga. The boy must establish his position with the disciples and the public as future master. Besides, I am more and more tempted to take the tonsure and gradually separate myself from this fleeting world."

"Are you thinking of handing over the mastership soon, then, Master?"

Kogame shoved his knee forward with such vehemence that he pushed the small charcoal brazier they were sharing between them right into Zeami's kneecap. Zeami winced but with a friendly grin quickly forgave Kogame.

"I'd like to, very much. But I must wait till Juro Motomasa has written such a play that his grandfather would have slapped it between his two big palms and said, 'Let's rehearse this!' "

"Ah, but he has!" blurted Kogame—then, immediately wrapping his head with both his arms with an exaggerated kyogen gesture of abject horror: "Oh, Motomasa-dono would kill me for telling you this! I shouldn't have opened my big mouth. Mother always said my mouth would be my ruin."

"Come, come, Kogame, you've made me breathless with curiosity. Go on, tell me. Motomasa wrote a play?"

"Would you be kind with my little master if I told you? You promise, Master?"

"Of course. Now go on."

"Motomasa-dono had tried writing many plays, but he was not satisfied with any of them, but since our last harvest-time touring in the South he'd been working on a *possessed* play, by no means the easiest of categories; worked on it like a fiend; and when he finished it, he was like a kitten dancing on a ball, so excited, so relieved to have got it out of his system. Well, it was like this, Master—all my fault, my fault! I, who copied the play and was so proud of it, incited both Motomasa-dono and the troupe to rehearse it whenever we were stormbound touring the Ise region last spring, and we finally put it on in Ochi."

"How did it go?"

"Well. Not what I'd call an immediate popular success . . ." Kogame's furtive eye met Zeami's. Kogame swallowed hard, then spat out: "A disaster! People hated it. That's why Motomasa-dono hasn't shown the play to you and we are to keep quiet about it. It haunts me, this play, though. I can't stop thinking about it. Kumao weeps just talking about it. It has neither a happy ending nor any kind of religious salvation to send a provincial audience home happy. Some actually asked for their money back, complaining that noh plays ought to spread joy and peace even in the possessed or mad categories."

Naturally, at the first opportunity Zeami asked Juro Motomasa to show him the play, *The Sumida River.* * Juro Motomasa hardly moved a muscle as he waited for his father to finish reading the play. As Zeami's eye left the last word of the play and settled on his son's face, Juro Motomasa took a deep breath.

"Motomasa . . ." Zeami could not speak. He quickly left the room, laid Juro Motomasa's manuscript before Kanami's mortuary tablet and knelt at the foot of the altar. When Juro Motomasa sheepishly followed his father into the altar room, Zeami was still praying, and when he at last turned to face his son, he said simply: "It's a masterpiece, your play. This is one of the happiest moments of my life, and I thank you and I thank my father for it."

The play that had had to be taken off after only one performance in Ochi! Juro Motomasa was too stunned to react in any way to his father's verdict.

"Now I can make you the third Kanze master. And as soon as possible. I don't want you to go through what I had to. I want you

* *Sumida Gawa*: One of the most popular plays in the current noh repertory. Benjamin Britten's opera *The Curlew River* is based on this noh play.

to become master whilst I am still alive and sound and can help."

Juro Motomasa's face tautened at once with a solemn awareness of his inheritance; intuitively, he looked up at the incense-
blackened mortuary tablet of his grandfather Kanami. Zeami gazed
at both the altar and his son, overcome less by family pride than
by a huge sense of mission.

THE AILING shogun Yoshimochi's waned interest in dengaku sapped
its hitherto preponderant sway in the capital; besides, Zoami, who
had been a pleasure-loving and hearty eater and drinker all his
life, was now crippled by gout and suffering from what his herbal
doctors diagnosed as "sugared-urine disease." As a consequence,
there soon emerged signs of renewed interest and patronage for
the long-neglected Kanze amongst the prelates and daimyos, who,
with the odor of the shogun's sickroom thickening in the air, no
longer feared his displeasure.

Shortly after Zeami had handed down the Kanze leadership
to Juro Motomasa, the Daigo Temple—where Kanami and Zeami,
still a child, had made their very first appearance in the capital—
offered the new Kanze master the honor of becoming the Temple's music master. Although poorly remunerated, it was a post of
some prestige, and more important still, it secured for the Kanze
a few performances each year to be appraised by the capital's connoisseurs.

When Zeami decided to include in the new music master's
inaugural performance *The Sumida River,* which had proved so
dismally unpopular on the road, and to act in it himself, the
young author was understandably worried.

"Father, we haven't been seen in the capital for ages now; can
we really afford to take a risk with my *Sumida River?* Surely not
on this important occasion."

"Motomasa"—Zeami put his hand on his son's shoulder; a
physical contact was so rare between father and son that Motomasa looked up at Zeami with startled attention—"your grandfather taught us: once out of favor with the great and cultivated people of the capital, cater to the far and barbarian provinces; lurk
and survive there, for so long as the house remains, there will be
another day of glory back in the capital. But I no longer share his
view. Of course it is true that our art exists only when we are seen;
we are slaves to our audiences. But at the same time, we must al-

ways be a step ahead of them. We must tantalize, not bore them. You've told the story of a mother whose child is kidnapped without the conventional happy ending: the son dies, the mother goes mad. Too bleak and unrelieved, yes, but then, truth often is; besides, you've told it with such theatrical lyricism that I find myself exhilarated. To shock, Motomasa, is a Flower of our art, like a sting of a certain bee that is said to revive the dead. Without it, our ungrateful and changeable public will discard us like an overfamiliar street song, without respect or mercy. I may be guilty of arrogance and pride, and we may one day starve for that reason. Well, let us starve. Better than to sink into mediocrity under the vulgarians' sway. We must take the risk. We'll show your play to the capital."

To JURO MOTOMASA's inaugural performance flocked not only many of the confirmed Kanze faithfuls but also those who were too young to know Zeami other than by reputation. Elegant carriages blocked the Temple gates, and palanquin carriers vied with one another to set down their masters as close to the temple stage as possible and were soon climbing the surrounding trees to have a peep: "So that I can say I too have seen Zeami."

Zeami was to act as a *koken* attendant to his son in all plays except the fifth and last, which was to be *The Sumida River* with himself in the role of the deranged mother.

After several steps onto the entrance bridge, Zeami paused, and at once that sensitive instrument inside the entertainer who had spent his lifetime on stage caught the gasp of sympathy deep inside his audience, and he could have wept for bliss. He knew he was back in the capital; he knew he was in front of an audience sentient enough to respond, gut to gut, to a performer's savage interior tension. From that moment on, he took the spectacular risk—a far greater risk perhaps than presenting the play itself—of trusting his audience to come inside his performance.

The Sumida River has a simple plot: A Kyoto woman's son has been kidnapped by a slave trader. Distraught with grief, the mother travels eastward in search of her young son. A boatman on the river Sumida takes pity on her and carries her across the river, only to find on the opposite bank a small crowd of villagers praying where a sick child, abandoned by his kidnapper, has died exactly a year ago that day. As the mother joins them, she sees her son as in a dream, and his voice mingles with her prayers; but a moment later, the boy is nowhere to be seen or heard. Only grass sways on the mound of earth where she knows her son was buried.

Ujinobu, who had come all the way from Yamato to attend the performance, later told Tama about one moment in the play which he said he would never be able to forget so long as he lived:

"The mother collapses and wails. The boatman tries to persuade her to strike the bell and pray for her dead son. At that moment, Uncle Zeami should have replied, 'If you tell me it is for my son . . .'; but contrary to what had been rehearsed, he remained totally immobile and silent, one minute, two minutes, Buddha knows how long! Kumao waits; the chorus, the musicians, the *koken*, everyone is staring straight into the air, waiting, waiting. But not a sound. Not a flicker of movement.

"And I swear, Tama, during the excruciating tension of this long pause, Uncle's sad-woman mask changed its expression before our eyes. The possessed woman became a woman broken; I saw the outrage of her grief being tamed to a deep, incurable pain without Uncle's moving a muscle or saying a single word. What he can do by doing is stupendous, we all know that; but what he achieved then by not doing was beyond belief!

"Meiroku says he can't recall for the love of Buddha why just then he felt compelled to start playing his flute, but he did, and he did so as he had never done before, such a sound, such a plea poured out of his flute, which at last cajoled Uncle into saying, 'If you tell me it is for my son . . .' And when he did say it, eight hundred hearts broke and melted like salt in water."

For some days after this performance, everyone found Saburo Motoshige more than usually sullen and wrapped up in speculation, his gaze constantly scrutinizing Zeami and Juro Motomasa at work.

Then, one sweltering rainless afternoon in June, he handed Zeami a letter with an irrepressible wide grin on his face. He must have been clutching it all the way from the Seiren-In: the letter was steamy and limp. It was Ghien's in his own hand, laconically asking Zeami to lend him four musicians, a chorus of eight and Hotan, Goro Motoyoshi, Kumao, Kumaya and Kogame for a one-day subscription performance, in aid of the construction of a shrine for dead children, which Ghien was sponsoring for Saburo Motoshige.

Zeami was prepared for the omission from the list of re-quested artists of himself and Juro Motomasa. After a small bow to the letter, held reverently in both his hands, Zeami smiled at his youngest son.

"I am pleased, Motoshige! Wait and take my reply to Ghien-sama at once. Have you thought about the program?"

"*Jinen Koji*," Saburo Motoshige answered instantly, as if the title of his grandfather's masterpiece had been waiting impatiently behind his scimitar-curled lips. "And I'd like to try *Kayoi Komachi* and *Shizuka*."

Both also by Kanami. The implication there was no longer latent: Saburo Motoshige was denying not only Zeami the per-former but Zeami the playwright as well. Zeami averted his eyes from Saburo Motoshige's triumphant cat face and did not argue, as he might well have done: "But, Motoshige, you're not ready for *Kayoi Komachi* yet. Wait at least five, six years." What would have been the point of telling him that? Such advice from Zeami would have made Saburo Motoshige want to do it all the more urgently, and at once.

Zeami rehearsed Saburo Motoshige, Goro Motoyoshi and oth-ers for the performance, which included, aside from *Jinen Koji* and *Shizuka*, three old anonymous plays adapted by Kanami and Zeami—but not *Kayoi Komachi*, as in the middle of the first re-hearsal Saburo Motoshige himself admitted that he could not yet quite manage the play.

On the day of Saburo Motoshige's performance, in a house emptied of most of the men and the usual bustle, Juro Motomasa showed his father the manuscript of his first warrior play and watched Zeami read it, with his long slim neck slightly inclined to one shoulder with an air that could only have been likened to "a swan with a lily in its mouth," and when Zeami pointed out a passage and commented, "Here, you're trying to catch a fish by climbing a tree," Juro Motomasa laughed and accepted this and other criticism with the most endearing meekness. Neither of them uttered a word about the performance that was taking place without them.

Saburo Motoshige's first subscription performance was well attended by those who had been starved for the Kanze's noh, and although disappointed not to see Zeami and Juro Motomasa, they gave the younger Kanze brothers, Saburo Motoshige and Goro

Motoyoshi, a warm and generous reception. Ghien was reported to be exceedingly satisfied. The following day Hotan was summoned to the Seiren-In to receive from Ghien a gift and a few words of appreciation for the Kanze family's unsparing cooperation.

"It was the first time I had seen Ghien-sama at such close quarters," said Hotan, stroking his prematurely bald skull, apprehensive and preoccupied. "There is something quite terrifying about him, Master. His violent temper and the cruelty with which he treats his underlings, I hear, are appalling. Only a few months ago Motoshige-dono told me, laughing as if it were amusing, that a young apprentice monk, hardly fourteen, had forgotten to feed Ghien-sama's pet Chinese cat and the poor boy had a nail hammered into his right hand. I gather when he's had a little too much to drink, no one can control him. He is said to be loyal and compulsively generous with the very few he takes a fancy to, but Buddha have mercy on those against whom he happens to take a dislike! I keep praying that my young master won't be the next to have his cheek branded by red-hot tongs—the kind of punishment Ghien-sama metes out to his inferiors when the whim takes him.

"I've looked after Motoshige-dono since he was a baby. I know him better than anyone, and I don't much like what I see between them. It seems so sultry, so exclusive, as though the two of them bore a grudge against the rest of the world, and I see little joy and fun there—not at all like a pair of young lads. This morning as I watched Ghien-sama's snakelike thin eyes and that muddy unaired complexion, I kept thinking, I wouldn't like to be in his service, let alone his enemy!"

Zeami had not forgotten Hotan's words when Shogun Yoshimochi's death was announced. Yoshimochi's indifference toward politics and the world in general had become almost repulsion as his health deteriorated. Probably to spite the high shogunal officials who had been pressing him to decide which of his brothers was to be his successor, Shogun Yoshimochi kept his mouth shut and died leaving the question of succession unsettled.

22

"WHAT? Ghien-sama?"

Yukina's hand shook with such violence that a pair of slim tongs slipped from it and fell inside the brazier onto the glowing charcoal. She stared at them with a horrified look but was too stunned by what she had heard to quickly retrieve them.

"Yes, the new shogun is Ghien-sama," continued Zeami, his voice colorless. "The late shogun's surviving brother and half-brothers—Hōson-sama of the Ninna Temple, Yoshiaki-sama of the Daikaku Temple, Eiryo-sama of the Sotoku Temple and Ghien-sama—drew lots at the Iwashimizu Shrine. The sixth Ashikaga shogunate fell into the hands of Ghien-sama."

Zeami had just learned the news from Kakuami, the late shogun's Companion tea-master, who had dropped in. "I am certainly finished," Kakuami had wailed. "Once, that sinister young priest was so drunk and lewd at my tea game that I asked him to leave. How could I have possibly imagined then . . ."

With Kakuami's words ringing in his ears, Zeami too helplessly watched the iron tongs turn from rough black to crimson and visualized Ghien laughingly placing them on the rosy cheek of an adolescent page who had perhaps forgotten to feed one of his nightingales.

"Buddha have mercy on us!" Yukina's cry quivered with the intensity of someone pursued.

There had never been much conversation between husband and wife, and even less since Zeami had taken the tonsure after handing over the Kanze mastership to Juro Motomasa. Yukina had followed suit without protest or enthusiasm, cutting her long hair and wrapping her narrow, dry-skinned but still handsome face in white silk. But tonight, with Juro Motomasa and the troupe away in Osaka to perform for a salt merchants' guild, sitting as they did face to face over the meager warmth of the charcoal brazier with the pervasive damp cold of Kyoto gnawing at their backs, he was grateful that she was with him so that he could at least voice an inane question to a fellow human being, if only to confirm his worst fears.

"Why are we in particular need of Buddha's mercy?"

"You know perfectly well why: Motoshige hates us. He hates you because you aren't his real father. He has a congenital hatred of me because I am the mother of your two sons who stand between him and the right to be the Kanze master."

"But, Yukina, whatever you may say, I have accepted him as my son, a Kanze son."

"A Kanze son, yes—your son in name and as a means to perpetuate the Kanze's noh! With you it's only and forever the noh that counts, nothing else. But mark my words, he'll soon hate you even as teacher and fellow artist. He is vindictive; he'll egg his patron on to ruin us all. You'll see. You'll see!"

"I admit the boy has a jealous nature; but it might have helped if you'd been more affectionate to him yourself, Yukina." Zeami tried his best not to sound reproachful, but Yukina's face contracted and turned into a mask of pale sand. Zeami added quickly: "But let us not assume the worst. What is auspicious for Motoshige must eventually spread its benefit onto us. I am sure . . ."

No, Zeami was not at all sure. He knew better than anyone alive what it meant to be a reigning shogun's favorite; what staggering reflected power and glory one enjoyed in that position and how desperately one endeavored to keep such favor entirely for oneself. Zeami was convinced that Saburo Motoshige would use his privileged status hermetically for his personal benefit.

Whilst the Kanze troupe was in Osaka, Saburo Motoshige stayed away altogether from the Kanze house, as, according to Sango, who collected rumors in town, he was actively assisting the removal of his patron's and his own belongings from the Seiren-In to the Muromachi Palace, where Ghien had given him a room in the shogun's private quarters. Not only Sango but every professional acquaintance or tradesman who crossed the Kanze threshold had some gossip concerning the now-famous young actor who had long been in the new shogun's favor and retailed it with an ingratiating and congratulatory gush.

The day after the troupe's return from Osaka, Saburo Motoshige came punctually as always; but it was no longer the son of the family coming home after a night at the monastery; it was now a proud young artist attending his teacher's lesson, having awakened and breakfasted at the shogun's palace. Every little nod or glance or greeting exchanged with Saburo Motoshige could no longer be innocent of the shogun's shadow behind the handsome, expensively dressed tall young man with a feline smirk.

How delighted he was to learn of Ghien's accession, Zeami told him at the first opportunity, then continued with a fatherly concern.

"Your gracious patron would be flattered and pleased, I'm sure, if you wrote your own plays, Motoshige. What if you now seriously—"

"He is flattered and pleased enough," retorted Saburo Motoshige, cutting Zeami short. "I don't have to go around ranting his praises in poems and plays. Where is Motoyoshi, Father? Tonight we are having a snow-viewing banquet and I want Motoyoshi to play the big drum for me."

Zeami had never cut Kanami's words short. Every utterance from his father had been gratefully absorbed and treasured. Zeami felt his teeth cringe in cold distaste as he shut his mouth. The overfamiliar insolence with which the young entertainer spoke of his shogun and protector also struck Zeami as most unattractive. As to Saburo Motoshige's patronizing exploitation of his easygoing and obliging brother, it was nothing new, and Zeami did not bother to take offense.

On the same afternoon, as it was the first of February and the new shogun had just been installed at the Muromachi Palace, Zeami dressed in an exquisite assortment of clothing, all Yoshimitsu's gift, of which Tamana and Ogame in the past and now

Sango had taken such good care that they remained as fresh as new. Zeami had not attended the first-of-the-month reunion of the Companions for the entire fifteen-year reign of Shogun Yoshimochi. Entering the wide, low-ceilinged artists' lobby, he could not help feeling morose and apprehensive—as indeed did many of the Companions who had survived from the time of Yoshimitsu. Those made Companions by Yoshimochi, the new shogun's blood brother, looked noticeably hopeful and expectant, as they felt they could count on continued patronage or at least some commands for service; but those who had gloried under Shogun Yoshimitsu, who had had his son incarcerated in the incense-smoked obscurity of the Seiren-In, had to be prepared for anything between neglect and positive persecution.

"Ah, Zeami-dono, you must be the only exception amongst us, ghosts of the past, who can for certain expect a change for the better in your fortunes. Lucky, lucky you to have a son who is so loved by the new shogun!" sighed Hatoami, who had throughout Yoshimochi's reign lurked as far as possible from the capital, working for wealthy, independent-spirited daimyos on the Kyushu and Shikoku islands.

Zeami said nothing, forcing a smile which felt parchment-stiff. He was far from sure whether to rejoice in or deplore the new shogun's favor for his son; but at least one thing reassured him: for the moment, the rift between him and Saburo Motoshige had apparently gone undetected even by the Companions, always the quickest ears to pick up such gossip in the capital.

Hours passed agreeably enough listening to many of Yoshimitsu's old Companions as they compared notes on how they had managed to survive the last fifteen years on the strength of their craft and knowledge; but Zeami was aware, like everyone else, that all the while pages were entering and approaching certain Companions, who then in twos and threes or sometimes singly, with expressions of grave joy and trepidation, slipped out of the lobby. Neither Zeami nor any of Yoshimitsu's old Companions were sent for. As the artists' lobby became bare of its earlier bustle and congestion, Zeami took leave of his old acquaintances, signed his name and turned to leave. Just then, an ashen-faced, frail old man spoke to him. The voice was unmistakable. It was Zoami of the dengaku.

"Like the sounds of the Kiyomizu Shrine bells, nothing remains constant in this world—power and glory least of all, eh, Zeami-dono? You look incredibly young, ageless! Me? I'm paying dearly for the too good a life I've led. And my feet and knees—if you knew how they hurt: a cloud of wasps stinging me day and night! But merciful Buddha, my hands are all right and I can still carve. Before I die, let me carve for you a not-so-young-woman mask."

Zoami, whose urbane catty garrulity had for so long amused so many, could not have been friendlier. Zeami was charmed and realized that the Kanze's longtime rival, whose patron, Lord Shiba, had been the first to lose office under the new shogun, had also not been summoned out of the lobby.

"We have, you and I, seen a better world," continued Zoami. "Impeccable taste, creative curiosity and such encouragement; an era that produced my grandfather, your father, you and me and Doami! Later generations will be bound to ask in awe: how could that have been possible? And as I lower my eyes onto the present generation, I see only your eldest son and heir. Zeami-dono, frankly, my son Eio is a competent reproducer, and I am afraid there ends my fatherly boasting, whilst I am convinced that your Juro Motomasa will one day attain your height and depth and mystery. For my taste, I find in your youngest too much surface effect and glitter. Still, good luck to him. We'll be seeing much of him and his glitter-glitter style. But then, such is the way life flows—half talent and hard work, half luck and timeliness. Landing a reigning shogun is not like hatching an egg every dawn. Don't we know it, eh, Zeami-dono?"

Exhausted by his little speech, the wheezing raconteur gave Zeami an elegant deep bow and went away in gingerly measured steps. Remembering many an immeasurably moving and dynamic exit he had seen Zoami make in his heyday, Zeami, neither a rancorous nor a proud man, who had so often praised his rival's genius in words both spoken and written, watched Zoami go with his eyes filled with tears, reflecting: sworn enemies at the crest of our careers and now comrades in front of an executioner . . .

When he came home, no one dared ask him if he had been seen by Ghien. Zeami shook the dust from his feet, prayed before his ancestors' altar and began impatiently writing down his ideas for a new play about a legendary beauty and darling of the highest society now ravaged by time and at once forgot the humiliating visit to the Muromachi Palace, the last visit he was likely to make. . . .

GHIEN HAD the return-to-the-world rites, shed his ink-dyed priestly robes, changed his name to Yoshinori and as his hair would take some time to grow, began his reign with his head wrapped in gray silk.

For Zeami, the month of May never returned without reminding him of his first encounter with Yoshimitsu at Imakumano. Narrowing his eyes at the incandescent young green that was bursting forth in his modest garden, Zeami, seated on the veranda, was mumbling some music he had composed that morning when Sango hurried in to announce the arrival of Saburo Motoshige, who was not with Juro Motomasa's troupe on tour in the Ise region, as the shogun had required him to remain in Kyoto.

"Here you are, Father," said Saburo Motoshige as he breezed in, his voice sounding a little too cheerful and jaunty in the silent empty house. "I hear Mother's not at all well?" His cat-face grin reminded Zeami of the little boy who used to ask "Broken his legs?" if someone had only said "Hachi's tripped on a stone."

"Just a change-of-season cold," replied Zeami mildly. "Take a cushion, Motoshige."

Saburo Motoshige sat on one, having turned it back and front to see which side was less frayed.

"Can you and Mother come to my simple marriage ceremony on the tenth?"

"Your marriage?" Zeami was flabbergasted. "You mean in three days' time? But to whom? And where?"

"To reply to your questions in the order in which you've put them"—Saburo Motoshige smiled indulgently, and Zeami was struck by how charming and seductive under different circumstances his son's smile could have been—"yes, in three days' time, on the tenth. A day of Heavenly Peace. I should have told you about it earlier, of course, but you know, what with the shogun's change of residence, his complete new wardrobe for the lay world and his trip to the port of Sakai . . . The shogun, in fact, is the matchmaker of this union. You see, he had a wet nurse who was married to a wine merchant and they had a daughter, called Kikyo. And this Kikyo, the shogun's milk sister as it were, now has the honor to become my wife and with your blessing, your daughter-in-law. Her father is quite well off; he is also a moneylender, and he's bought us a house, where the wedding ceremony, a very simple affair—just the closest family members—will take place."

Sango, who never announced a visitor to Zeami without then staying on to eavesdrop, smacked his mental tongue as he crouched cumbersomely behind the sliding screens. —Naturally! Now that he's become shogun, the lecherous priest is in a hurry to marry off his favorite—

Yukina greeted the news with much the same reaction as Sango's, her expression only even more vitriolic, but Zeami neither reprimanded nor hushed her, for his mind was harassed by the imminent threat to the unity of the Kanze. It was perfectly natural for younger sons of the house to go outside and start a new house but remain always auxiliary to the main house. Zeami knew of many such examples in other professions which succeeded in staying enviably harmonious and cooperative. But not often did a new house enjoy the favoritism of a fanatic and ruthless shogun. When the family beam is split into two rival parts, out flow innumerable splinters of discord and jealousy, which can weaken, even wreck, the house.

THE BRIDE was a year senior to Saburo Motoshige; plain, good-natured, competent, down-to-earth; a typical merchant-district Kyotoite. Landing such a handsome and distinguished young husband, she was beside herself with joy and gratitude, which to some degree compensated for her bad teeth and downtown stridency of voice and manner. That her father was a wine merchant cum astute and expanding moneylender explained the considerable luxury of the home of the newlyweds: a town house once belonging to a provincial governor now in exile had been bought cheaply. What most impressed Yukina, who despite mild fever and persistent coughing attended the wedding, was the ubiquitous use of straw mats, called tatami, on the floors. Such a new and fashionable luxury and the warm comfort it afforded were unknown in her own rambling house.

As the Kanze troupe was still on tour, the wedding feast that followed the short ceremony was attended by only a very few people—from the bridegroom's side, only Zeami and Yukina; the rest were the family or close friends of the bride, all simple, loquacious townspeople whose conversation centered on money, changes of personnel under the new shogun and rumors of famine and peasant unrest in the rice-producing provinces, all of which in some way affected their trade. No dancing or music was offered, but the food and wine were copious and of the best quality.

Throughout the evening Saburo Motoshige, somewhat pale and tired-looking, showed impeccable good manners and courtesy toward his parents, in-laws and wife, and at the end of the feast, bowing low to Zeami and Yukina, he expressed his filial gratitude for all that they had done for him and his regret that, being the third son, he was now obliged to live under a different roof, to which Zeami in beautifully chosen words conveyed his fatherly joy to see his youngest son marry such a worthy wife, adding, his voice grave with emotion:

"As is customary in our profession, I make you a so-called dividing-the-root gift: I give you Hotan and the eight young disciples under him, who shall become a part of your household, forming a wing to the Kanze troupe. I do so hope and pray that we shall all work together in harmony on the Way of noh like children before Buddha."

He then asked a servant to fetch the parcels he had left at the entrance hall. When the two boxes of light paulownia wood tied decorously with deep-purple silk cords were brought in, Zeami caressed the pearly surface of the wood and said:

"My father, Kanami, was a loyal and generous friend to many master carvers of his time, whom he inspired to create many of their best works, and our house is blessed with a splendid collection of them. So, Motoshige, to celebrate your new life, I would like to give you an old-man mask by Miroku and a tormented-woman mask with gold-dusted eyes by Himi. Masks are living things; listen to their souls."

Saburo Motoshige flushed as if red dye had exploded inside his skull. Incredulous and almost suspicious, he stared at Zeami, then at the mask boxes which contained irreplaceable historic masterpieces.

Even Yukina, whose own emotional impulses were as torpid as a hibernating worm under snow, could not help shutting her eyes in prayer for the littlest sign of filial affection and generosity, one final aberration, to surface from Saburo Motoshige. But the color of emotion quickly subsided from Saburo Motoshige's face as he formally bowed and thanked Zeami *and* the Kanze troupe for *their* gracious gift. Yukina opened her beautiful sunken eyes and stared at Saburo Motoshige with renewed odium.

Poor boy, Zeami thought: you have for too long and too far mortified your vulnerability; now you don't know how to sing and reach out with it. For an artist to have his well of vulnerability dry up is a loss far more tragic than losing his father.

YOSHINORI/GHIEN's reign was soon put to the first serious test when the traditionally militant groups of transporters and post-horse keepers in Omi led the local peasants in a fierce uprising. Screaming "Burn our letters of debt!" or "Give us back our mort-gaged chattels!" they looted and vandalized wine merchants' ware-houses and set fire to shrines and temples—invariably the harshest, most grasping of moneylenders, backed up as they were by the bullying might of their armed monks.

The peasant unrest spread like a forest fire to Yamashina, Harima, Tamba, Settsu and some even more distant provinces. Yoshinori would not be persuaded by his three leading advisers—Shiba, Hosokawa and Hatakeyama, who during his reign were to alternate as chancellor—to act with understanding and clemency and to partly grant the peasants' demands. Instead, with fiendish obstinacy he sent out armies to quell the troubled areas. If the sho-gun's armies acted brutally, the peasants retaliated with matching ferocity: thousands of them, driven out of their senses by hunger and despair and often drunk on looted wine, finally stormed into the capital and fought the shogunal soldiers hand to hand in the streets of Kyoto. When the carnage in the capital was completed, the loss of life on the shogunal side was just as great as it was amongst the rebels.

But as later events were to prove with a hair-raising accuracy, the new shogun was not a man capable of reasonable political com-promise, nor was there any sign of human consideration in his character. Yoshinori promptly ordered his commanders to butcher as many as possible of the retreating hordes of famished and bare-foot peasants.

And just then, to pour oil on the flames, Emperor Shoko died suddenly, at the premature age of twenty-eight, leaving no direct heir. When his weary fifty-three-year-old father, Cloistered Em-peror Gokomatsu, proceeded to nominate the ten-year-old nephew of the deceased to the imperial throne, the expected ensued with a

nightmarish speed: the Imperial Prince Ogura of the Southern
line, who had hoped that on this occasion at last the alternate-
succession clause in the 1392 agreement would be honored, was so
infuriated that he swiftly raised his standard and enrolled an impressively large force composed of soldiers who had been demo-
bilized after the 1392 unification, groups of armed monks dis-
gruntled with the Ashikaga shogunate and mere mercenaries in
search of money and battle fame.

Prince Ogura and his men marched south to join forces with
the daimyo Kitabatake of Ise, the very same Lord Mitsumasa Kitabatake who had acted as the Father of Scissors to Juro Motomasa
at his adulthood ceremony. At once other recalcitrant Southern
daimyos and landlords with militias of their own rallied to the
cause with supplies of arms and food and as many men as they
could spare.

Shogun Yoshinori ordered the immensely wealthy and powerful Doki clan to wipe out the insurgents. Even with substantial
reinforcements from the shogunal army, it took the Doki clan a
six-month-long battle before they were able to break into the
rebels' stronghold. Mitsumasa Kitabatake committed disembowelment as his fortified castle fell. His and his generals' heads were
brought to Kyoto, where, skewered atop tall lances, they were ex-
hibited at the Fourth Avenue main crossing. The result of the
fighting, however, was far short of the decisive victory that Yoshinori had sought, for Prince Ogura himself had succeeded in escaping, and other Southern daimyos, massively aided by a rabble of
peasants, continued to harass the shogunal armies stationed in the
area. Yoshinori raged, and his suspicion and hatred of anyone even
remotely connected or in sympathy with the Southern cause began
to reach paranoid proportions.

Hachi, the old man-of-all-work of the troupe who admitted he
was now somewhere between seventy-five and death, went to the
Fourth Avenue crossroads to pray for the departed soul of Lord
Kitabatake; but he came home in a state of panic.

"Whom do you think I saw in the crowd there, Master?" he
panted as he crawled inside Zeami's study. "Master Motomasa
praying underneath the skewered head of Lord Kitabatake! I'm
just a decrepit old nothing, but the young master stands out
wherever he is, and his face is well known all over the capital, and
there were curious people around us. 'He gave me my adulthood
name,' he argued with me, 'and helped me on innumerable occa-

sions. I'd be less than a dog if I didn't come here and mourn my brave old benefactor.' It was quite a job persuading him to leave the spot. For heaven's sake, Master, please ask him to be more careful."

That evening for the first time Zeami explained to Juro Motomasa the exact circumstances under which Kanami had been murdered.

"If our blood connection with the legendary hero of the Southern cause, Masashige Kusunoki, should be exploited by our enemies under *this* shogun, the consequence to the Kanze and the noh would be catastrophic. You must be on your guard, Motomasa, and I suggest you stop touring the Southern provinces for the time being. I'm sure you have taken note that Motoshige has not joined you on any of your tours into those regions lately. He is right. One cannot be too careful."

Juro Motomasa bowed correctly in acknowledgment of his father's counsel; but as always, his infectious sweet smile barred Zeami from further strictures.

Only a couple of days after Zeami's inconclusive talk with Juro Motomasa, Hotan, an emotional, simple good Osakaite, sincerely devoted to both Zeami and his young master Saburo Motoshige, came to see Zeami alone at an exceptionally early hour. As Saburo Motoshige's divided-house troupe grew in number, Hotan, with his art, experience and infinite patience, was indispensable to his new master, particularly in selecting and training many talented and ambitious young actors from the provincial troupes who came asking for admission; and to Zeami too he was an invaluable link of communication between the main and the divided houses, as Saburo Motoshige, who came to lessons and rehearsals of new plays whenever the main-house troupe was in town, was becoming, aware of his new position of strength, so silken-smoothly courteous with his father and brothers, so impenetrably formal, that it was now virtually impossible to know what he really thought or planned for the future.

"I've come to apologize in advance that my young master won't be able to come to your lesson this morning, Master."

After a reverent bow, Hotan wiped his bald skull energetically with an indigo-blue cloth, although it was a nipping cold morning, typical of November, Month of Frost; then he gasped, throwing the formality aside:

"Master! Motoshige-dono came home only a short while ago

with a black eye and bruises on his neck. You know my young master: he never says a word to us about what goes on at the palace; but from what I overheard him say to Kikyo-sama, it was the shogun himself who had interrogated Motoshige-dono last night about the Kanze's connection with the Kusunokis. As the interrogation took place in the exclusive intimacy of the shogun's private chamber, one cannot be sure whether it was the shogun's particular way of heightening his pleasure or his natural suspiciousness gone out of control that prompted the violence, but either way, I thought I'd better warn you and Master Motomasa."

After Hotan left, having begged Zeami not to mention his visit to Saburo Motoshige, Zeami peered for a long while into the rainy morning. —Why did Hotan go out of his way to add "and Master Motomasa"? Have they found something against my unwary young son? What has the silly boy been up to in the South?— Alerted for the first time to the proximity of danger, Zeami could not blame himself more bitterly for having neglected to warn his son earlier.

As it turned out, the shogun's physical violence against Saburo Motoshige had been one of his kinky ways to express his possessive passion rather than an outburst of any well-founded suspicion. Saburo Motoshige laughed and joked about his black eye, and it gave Kikyo, now four months into pregnancy, a delectable excuse to cosset her adored husband. She had been spoken to before the marriage, both by her mother and by Saburo Motoshige himself, about her husband's relationship with the shogun, which, they both had emphasized, should neither be expected to end nor be interfered with after he married her, and Kikyo had willingly acquiesced. And Saburo Motoshige, not unappreciative of his wife's rich dowry and her uncomplicated acceptance of the situation, turned out to be an irreproachably kind and thoughtful husband, who, moreover never looked at other women. As the news of Kikyo's pregnancy spread through downtown Kyoto, no one had reason to doubt that Saburo Motoshige and Kikyo would have a perfectly happy conjugal and family life together.

23

"MASTER, it's highly confidential. May I come in?"

It was Kogame who whispered outside Zeami's study, some time after the bells of the Hour of Rat.*

"You mustn't walk the streets alone at this hour in December. It's asking for trouble. . . . *What is it?*" Zeami dropped his writing brush and stared at Kogame, who had never looked gloomier and more fearful.

"It's my young master!" Kogame sighed such an exhaustive sigh that he literally shrank in size. Zeami shut his eyes.

"What my father was to you, I am to Master Motomasa; so when I say my young master is recklessly emotional and as irresponsible, unrealistic and self-destructive as a big ball of snow that's perched on a single bamboo branch, it isn't criticism: no, I say it with all the affection and devotion of which this humble servant is capable."

Kogame looked desperate as he drawled out, "Young Master came to my house just a few hours ago, with Akiko-sama."

* Midnight.

247

"Akiko? Who is she?"

"Master, they've pledged themselves to each other!" Kogame impulsively shielded his face with his raised hands as if he thought Zeami was going to hit him.

"Kogame, answer me! Who is she?"

"Akiko-sama, the third and only surviving daughter of Ro-kuemon Ochi, the head of the Ochi clan in Ise." Kogame hung his head.

Zeami clenched his teeth as the news sank in. His fault, his negligence; all those protracted and frequent tours in the South! And hadn't *The Sumida River* first been performed at Ochi? The Ochi clan had possessed a fortified village and its surrounding fertile fields for many generations and had fought valiantly for the Southern cause, although the current head of the clan had not been recently involved with the Kitabatakes or other declared enemies of the shogunate.

"The young lady," Kogame continued, "accompanied only by her nurse and the nurse's two sons, with very little luggage, suddenly turned up in Kyoto this evening. We never toured the South without stopping at Ochi, and we've been honored many times with performances at the castle. Master Ochi was particu-larly well disposed toward Motomasa-dono and often invited him to join the family for supper or flower- or autumn-foliage-viewing picnics, and I could tell how exhilarated and happy my young master always was at Ochi, but never have I—"

"Tell me the truth, Kogame," Zeami interrupted. "Has Moto-masa ever acted as a spy for either the Kitabatakes or the Ochis? You can tell from his plays that his artistic sensitivity glories in noble defeat, his sympathy always on the side of the loser. With his muddled childish idealism, he may have volunteered to pass certain information between the capital and the Southern Em-peror's supporters."

"No, no, no! I'm sure such a . . . such a . . ." Kogame shook his head and arms in frantic denial, but quickly deflated, sank to a mumbling perplexity. "But how could I possibly know what he was up to when I wasn't with him?—and I do know there are rumors to that effect. In fact, Motoshige-dono questioned me on this very matter . . ."

"What, Motoshige did?"

"He did. I had the feeling he had some inside information about my young master."

After a prolonged silence Zeami said, as dry and detached as someone prepared for the worst and beyond:

"The girl has left her home to be with Motomasa and you say they love each other; things have gone that far. I know Motomasa. I shan't be able to stop him."

WHEN JURO MOTOMASA brought Akiko to Zeami, he found himself reminded of Lady Takahashi, Yoshimitsu's great favorite, the legendary Kyoto courtesan and the only mistress of Yoshimitsu's who, after his death, had continued to enjoy full respect and favor from nearly everyone till her death at the age of sixty-six.

Akiko, the twenty-two-year-old daughter of a provincial samurai landowner, was naturally far less sophisticated than Yoshimitsu's brilliant mistress, but she had the same innate uprightness which gave her poise, cheerfulness and strength of character. Zeami saw Juro Motomasa visibly glow and lose his timidity in her presence and understood how the adulated young noh master had had his heart stolen by this young woman; and as a father, he could not help being grateful for the most welcome influence Akiko obviously wielded on his introverted son.

"Young lady, you have committed the crime of disgracing your parents and your birth; but since there is no way of undoing what you have done, let us at least protect your maiden's honor. Get married at once," said Zeami.

The two lovers held their hands together and shed tears of mad joy. Akiko showed the mettle of a samurai's daughter by telling Zeami that in order to safeguard the Kanze from possible trouble with the shogunate and to save her family embarrassment, she would immediately send back the elder son of her nurse to Ochi to ask her father to excommunicate her.

Rokuemon Ochi lost no time in sending a courier bearing a letter disowning his daughter on account of the dishonor she had brought on the family by eloping with an actor. Rokuemon Ochi did not throw such expected pejoratives as "untouchable," "renegate" or "riverbank beggar" at the young entertainer who had repaid the Ochi family's kindness by stealing their only daughter; nor did the couple's unpardonable behavior prevent Akiko's mother from sending her a large parcel of clothes, mirror, combs and a new talisman from a shrine in Ochi.

Zeami was so touched by the tacit proof of their unbroken affection for both Akiko and Juro Motomasa, an attitude toward entertainers unheard of under such a circumstance amongst the landed gentry, that he prayed till his palms scorched from rubbing his beads for the union to bring happiness to the young lovers and not too many problems for their respective families.

Zeami broke the news to his wife, and Yukina listened with her hands clasped tightly to her chest, trying to suppress a fit of cough from erupting; but the moment Zeami mentioned who and what Juro Motomasa's fiancée was, Yukina dropped both her hands to her lap, the spasm of coughing gone.

"Not a wine merchant's daughter—I *am* glad!"

Her triumphant grin, in contrast to the pure white silk that wrapped her head, was so earthy, so vindictive that Zeami had to look away, embarrassed for her. Nowadays, the only thing that could stir Yukina out of her languor seemed to be the mention of her adopted son. Indeed, her loathing of Saburo Motoshige had become so unreasonably intense in her semi-invalid solitude that she would have welcomed as her daughter-in-law anyone of the samurai class, who would afford her the chance to spite Saburo Motoshige by humiliating his wife, Kikyo, by comparison of their birth. In any case, Yukina, who looked every inch an immaculate nun yet who now spent her days recumbent reading insidiously erotic illustrated stories she ordered Sazami to buy and sell again in town—about a daimyo's wife eloping with her husband's assassin or a princess kidnapped by an amorous snake—was not a possessive mother, for she had long since given up her sons as lost to the all-devouring noh; moreover, she knew she would get on well with Akiko, if for no better reason than that the girl too was marrying beneath her class.

WHEN HIS HAIR had regrown to a normal length, Yoshinori paid his first formal call on the Emperor and officially became in name as well as substance the head of the Ashikaga shogunate.

Celebration of his formal accession went on nightly at the Muromachi Palace, and Yoshinori ordered a noh performance for the third of May to be given at the horse-game field inside the palace grounds. Reflecting the new shogun's taste, actors were ordered to ride ornately saddled and decorated horses and wear precious armor and arms lent by the shogun, and the performance was to be treated as a competition between the Kanze and the Hosho troupes. For the Kanze, it was the first shogunal command performance in twenty-one years.

Yoshimitsu in his whole life had not once ordered a so-called horse-and-armor performance, which the earlier Ashikaga shoguns and their generals used to find irresistibly exciting, and Zeami ruefully reflected on the rapid turns and returns of taste in patrons of art.

Blessed with fine May weather, and everyone of any substance and importance anxious to get near the new shogun who had so far been little known in the lay world, the Muromachi Palace's horse-game field was thronged with a brilliant crowd. Zeami had chosen *The Battle of Ichino Valley* as a suitable vehicle in which his three sons would play the major roles, with himself appearing briefly toward the end.

With horses restless and neighing at awkward moments, armor too heavy and bulky to permit nuanced movements, the conditions were far from ideal to show off the troupe to its best advantage; besides, as Zeami was the first to perceive, the new shogun's entourage was not the cultivated, discerning elite who had used to surround Yoshimitsu. Yoshinori, who could not tolerate intellectually and culturally superior aides around him, had collected kowtowing men of mediocre quality and talent, who naturally preferred the obvious and the spectacular to the implied and the deeply felt. On them the beauty of *yugen* would have been wasted like seeds falling on a rock.

Still, thanks to the grandeur of the setting and the excitement of seeing actors enter and exit the scene on horseback, both the Kanze and the Hosho received loud applause, and taking into consideration the congratulatory nature of the occasion, the competition performance was declared a draw.

One performer, however, stood out and received an unstinted ovation. That was Juro Motomasa, whose particular brand of pathos and lyricism was in fact even more intensely accentuated than usual by the surrounding din and pomposity, horses and armor and banners and all.

Little did the enraptured audience know, though, how speedily and unfailingly they were applauding the beautiful actor to martyrdom. Zeami had taken pains to give Saburo Motoshige an equally important role precisely in order to avoid offending Saburo Motoshige's patron, and he felt so uneasy at Juro Motomasa's personal triumph, in contrast to the polite but unexceptional reception accorded to Saburo Motoshige, that after the performance he went out of his way to praise all his three sons equally. An actor, however, has a pathologically sensitive perception when it comes to the comparative volume of the public's response. There was very little he could do to mend the broken porcelain of Saburo Motoshige's pride.

Neither Zeami, Juro Motomasa nor Master Hosho, but Saburo Motoshige alone was invited to the shogun's loge after the performance, and Zeami, standing amongst actors and palace attendants, watched his youngest son receive the shogun's cup of wine. Since Zeami had last seen him as Ghien, the priest, Shogun Yoshinori had put on weight and a labored defiant posture of someone fighting the magnitude of an office he had been called by mere luck of the draw to fill. Zeami also noted with some disquiet how Yoshinori's thin lips had a tendency to curve downward whenever he forced something akin to a smile, which gave his expression neither mirth nor kindliness but reptilian cruelty.

Exactly ten days later, on the thirteenth of May, a shogunal messenger delivered at the Kanze gate an order from the shogun himself tersely forbidding both Zeami and Juro Motomasa to enter the Cloistered Emperor's Sento Palace. As mere entertainers, it would have been unthinkable for Zeami or Juro Motomasa to enter the Sento Palace at will; it was simply out of the question. Zeami was at a loss as to how to interpret this inapplicable command. Wondering why it had suddenly become necessary, Zeami told no one about it, not even Juro Motomasa, but waited for some explanation to emerge.

For two days following the shogun's notice, neither Saburo Motomasa nor anyone of his troupe showed up at the Kanze house; but on the morning of the third day Hotan came, literally squirming in embarrassment, hardly able to look in Zeami's direction.

Zeami's misgivings over Juro Motomasa's singular success at the horse-and-armor performance were proved correct. Shogun Yoshinori had not been at all pleased to see Juro Motomasa overshadow his favorite, especially in light of the latest report from his spies that the impudent young actor had chosen to marry an Ochi woman in secret; but his displeasure had turned to positive rage when the Cloistered Emperor Gokomatsu, delighted to hear that the Kanze troupe, after twenty-one years of banishment from shogunal entertainment, had been allowed back to the Muromachi Palace, sent an emissary to intimate to the shogun that His Cloistered Imperial Majesty would be much pleased to have the Kanze perform at his own Sento Palace. Yoshinori immediately replied that Saburo Motoshige of Kanze would gratefully accept the Cloistered Emperor's invitation; whereupon Gokomatsu, with the delicacy of an elephant stepping on a sand castle, corrected Yoshinori, saying, Oh, no, I meant the *real* Kanze—you know, Zeami and Juro Motomasa, whom I once so enjoyed watching at your late father's Kitayama Palace.

Shogun Yoshinori's determination to push his own favorite into the Sento Palace was now as hysterical as if his own prestige were at stake. Having prohibited Zeami and his eldest son from entering the Sento Palace and notified his head of police to that effect, he simultaneously dispatched an envoy there to bid the Cloistered Emperor not to receive the main-house Kanze troupe, then went even further by formally announcing an annual noh performance at the Sento Palace, to be sponsored by the shogunal treasury, by Saburo Motoshige and his divided-house Kanze.

Even Zeami was appalled at how far the shogun had gone: he not only had overridden and denied the Cloistered Emperor's express wish but had jammed down His Cloistered Imperial Majesty's throat his own favorite and protégé.

"On this occasion I could not sit still. I confronted my young master," said Hotan, distraught at the turn of events which threatened to make his loyalty to both masters untenable. " 'You could not,' I pleaded, 'just could not supplant your own father and elder brother, the actual master of the Kanze, and perform at the Sento Palace. Please consider asking the shogun to let your father and brothers as well as yourself perform for the Cloistered Emperor.' And my young master's reply was 'No, I'm afraid I can't. I dare not. You don't know the shogun as well as I do. If I did, I'd be risking the future of the entire Kanze troupe, both Motomasa's and mine. Leave it, Hotan. There's nothing I or you or anyone can do.' That's what Motomasa-dono told me. Master, believe me, I haven't slept nor eaten since. . . ." Hotan fell on his face and cried into the old wooden floor.

"Hotan," Zeami said gently, but his face was a mask set in bronze, "on the whole, I tend to agree with Motoshige myself. Who are we to question a shogun's taste and whims? Besides, as master of a troupe Motomasa has been foolhardy and selfish in his conduct, and I cannot but deplore his lack of judgment. But it's too late now—he's married an Ochi daughter and she is expecting a baby. I am not vain to such a degree that I care more for my or my own sons' personal glory than for the good of the Kanze's noh as a whole. As long as Motoshige and his divided-house troupe enjoy the shogun's favor and put on performances that bring honor to the name of Kanze, we must not complain."

On the second day of the following New Year, Saburo Motoshige's divided-house troupe, strengthened by *waki* players borrowed for the occasion from the Kongo school, duly performed in front of the Cloistered Emperor. It was a sunny but unsettled cold day, with large flakes of snow occasionally gusting across the air.

Ujinobu and Tama came as in every year to pay Zeami their New Year courtesy visit. They were dismayed to sense the atmosphere of broken morale and restlessness amongst the younger disciples and to hear from Yukina that Juro Motomasa had lately lost eleven members, mostly to the divided-house troupe, which now counted twenty-three as opposed to the main house's twenty-nine. And the death of Hachi, that most serviceable man of all trades, was a sorely regretted loss to the already diminished company.

"We used to have nearly fifty—remember, Tama?—when the Great Tree was still alive," said Yukina to her daughter. "But could you blame the young ones for leaving us? Motoshige is going from strength to strength. You've heard that that creature Kikyo has given birth to a son? The rumor has it that she is pregnant again. I shan't be at all surprised if she breeds a son every four months like a wildcat!"

Yukina coughed painfully, and Tama stroked her mother's back, repeating gently: "Now, Mother, please let us not talk about Brother Motoshige. It only makes your chest worse."

Whilst the older disciples, who had more or less grown up with Zeami, showed no sign whatever of wavering, those who had known nothing but ceaseless provincial tours had been understandably lured by the immense political and economic advantages Saburo Motoshige's troupe could now offer. Till recently, the Kanze had meant the main house, but as the divided house could now afford the more expensive materials and pay instantly for services rendered, even the long-patronized costumiers or musical-instrument makers began offering preference to the divided-house troupe.

Tama, with the license of the youngest of the family, jocularly reprimanded her parents, her brothers and the elders of the troupe for looking so funereal on a New Year's day, but behind every word and gesture of forced gaiety there lurked an unspoken thought that at that very moment Saburo Motoshige's troupe was performing, instead of themselves, in front of the Cloistered Emperor.

Since the incident of the black eye, Saburo Motoshige had stopped coming to the Kanze house altogether. Even when Kikyo gave birth to a big lively boy, it was Kikyo and her mother alone who brought the baby for the grandparents to see. Saburo Motoshige, however, continued to send Hotan to clarify various problems of direction or choreography, to ask advice on interpretation and above all to obtain details of any new plays. The grave disadvantage the divided house suffered was that Saburo Motoshige was not a creative head: he could not write or compose and had little talent for choreography. As a result, the majority of the plays his troupe performed were those by Kanami and Zeami, which Saburo Motoshige had had the incomparable privilege of learning personally from Zeami. Taking convenient advantage of the Kanze blood that unquestionably flowed in his veins, he never bothered to ask Zeami or Juro Motomasa, the official head of the House of Kanze, for permission to perform them, as indeed all other noh troupes in Yamato, Settsu, the Lake Biwa district and elsewhere meticulously did; nor did he pay in any manner for the right to do so, although he could not have been ignorant of the increasing financial difficulties the main house was facing.

One young disciple had gone over to Saburo Motoshige taking with him a number of Zeami's and Juro Motomasa's recent plays which he had stolen, together with some vocal and dance notations he had taken down during rehearsals. Saburo Motoshige engaged the decamper, but sent Hotan to Zeami to apologize for the young man's behavior and to return all the stolen scripts—but only after having copies of them made. Saburo Motoshige then proceeded to perform these plays without notifying Zeami or Juro Motomasa at the great palaces and mansions of the capital to which he and his troupe were now frequently invited.

Tama and Yukina were disgusted by Saburo Motoshige's conduct and often nagged at Zeami and Juro Motomasa to take firm steps to prevent Saburo Motoshige from stealing their new works; but they both laughed and dismissed the women's indignation as being female and shortsighted. Zeami, who at so young an age had been so abruptly raised from extreme penury to extreme luxury, seemed never to have developed a sense or taste for material possessions and often surprised people with his total indifference to what he earned or spent or gave away, and this quality was most manifestly inherited by Juro Motomasa.

HARDLY A MONTH had passed since Saburo Motoshige's New Year performance at the Sento Palace, and Juro Motomasa had still not entirely wiped from his mind the sense of forlorn isolation he had suffered that day, sitting at home and watching the flurry of snow all afternoon, when a Kofuku Temple officer in charge of the torchlight performance sent a courier with a message: he had the honor to inform the main-house Kanze that as it was the shogun's express wish to have the divided-house Kanze give the torchlight performance at the Kofuku Temple in the future, the main-house Kanze's presence would not be required this February, nor in subsequent years.

Juro Motomasa felt sick. It was all he could manage to write a short acknowledgment and to hand it to the Kofuku courier without too unseemly a show of dismay. He hid the letter inside the folds of his sash before returning to the stage room, where Zeami was rehearsing his latest play, written specially for this torchlight performance. Juro Motomasa could not bring himself to look at his father, seated on a small old stool, so alert, cheerful and eager to be surprised like a little boy allowed for the first time to watch magicians.

Juro Motomasa, cursed with so vulnerable a heart, could not help suffering the agonies of a guilty conscience: —Am I not the cause of all the humiliation and cruel persecution that fall on my father and the troupe?— He loved his wife and the new life she carried more than his own, but this serene and lively old man in front of him, his father, the master and unique genius, Zeami—was he not more than just one life, more than one generation and one world?

After the rehearsal broke, Juro Motomasa showed the letter secretly to Goro Motoyoshi, and seeing his young brother's face, so congenial to laughter and gaiety, contract and lose color, he knew that he must not delay showing the letter to Zeami, the last person in the world to whom he would have wished to convey such ill tidings.

Zeami read the letter twice. Then, his eyes unfocused, he said to himself incredulously, "The Kofuku Temple too!"

For him, born and brought up as the temple's chattel, the Kofuku's innumerable roofs and spires had in good times and bad been his heaven that brought the sunshine and the rain of beneficence. How glad he was that Kanami and Tamana were no longer alive to suffer this cruelest severance. He had not expected this; not in such a manner, even on the shogun's order; *not* from the Kofuku! The abruptness, the offhandedness of the dismissal after three generations of devoted service rankled with far deeper pain in him than in his young sons; but as he raised his devastated eyes and saw the two brothers beside themselves with chagrin for their father's sake, Zeami loosened his chest to let in fresh air and gave them a militant bright smile.

"Well, Motomasa; well, Motoyoshi! Let us count our blessings. We are together, with a roof over our heads, in good health, every day learning more; and don't forget, Motomasa, you still have the Daigo music mastership."

Exactly three months later, Shogun Yoshinori stripped Juro Motomasa of the Daigo music mastership and gave it to Saburo Motoshige.

As soon as the Daigo Temple priest left, having expressed in whispers behind his dusty straw traveling hat his private shock and regret at losing the Kanze main house's service at the temple, Juro Motomasa's knees failed him. His shaking fingers chafed against the clay-and-straw wall as his weight descended, and he felt his head reverberate confusedly like a gong struck with too brutal a force. Just the acutest sense of catastrophe, nothing else.

A pair of cold soft hands wrapped themselves around his head. He saw his wife's sober, kind eyes looking straight into his. He clasped her wildly in his arms, the Daigo Temple's letter of dismissal crushed between them.

"I'm . . . s-s-sacked . . . from . . ."

"I guessed." Akiko held him firmly as the horror of the fact, once verbalized, struck Juro Motomasa with renewed violence, and the warrior's daughter felt a dragon of strength in her as her artist husband whimpered, "What are we going to do? How can I possibly tell this to Father? And the troupe? What have I done to—"

"Sh, sh! Husband, listen: there is nothing anymore to hold you here, is there? Why don't we go to Ochi, settle there, have children, work and tour from there? What do you lose by leaving the capital that doesn't want you? Your parents and Motoyoshi, they'll be much happier there too." Akiko spoke each word out of the impetuous goodness of her heart and love.

That being stripped of his last official position in the capital did not in his wife's mind mean an ignominious end to his career or happy family life but could actually mean an escape from the shogun's malignance, even a new start, gave Juro Motomasa the courage to face his father.

Zeami and Goro Motoyoshi were feeding their carp in the small pond in the garden. The priceless colorful carp had been Yoshimitsu's gift to Zeami with the joking remark "Look after them well, Motokiyo. Your art may or may not survive the test of time, but the carp I give you will live five hundred years or more."

To the profoundest distress of Juro Motomasa, his sixty-nine-year-old father lost his usual sang-froid, not so much from reading the letter of dismissal from the Daigo Temple as from hearing Juro Motomasa's intention to take his family and troupe to Ochi.

"No, no, no!" Zeami sobbed, his fist weakly beating the sun-struck veranda floor. Juro Motomasa had never before seen his father break down like this. White-faced and -lipped, shivering like a wet dog, Juro Motomasa could not remove his horrified gaze from his father sobbing like a cracked flute. Juro Motomasa, born in Kyoto as the petted first son of the then most glorified actor alive, could not have known what it meant to his father *to quit the capital;* he would never be able to know with what passionate longing and unspeakable struggles his grandfather and father had reached the capital fifty years earlier, as if digging their nails inch by inch into the earth that separated Yuzaki village from the glory of Kyoto. For Zeami, a live performing artist, not to be seen by the capital's audience meant a shriveling slow death, for what he was on stage was to a great degree the creation of his audience, and it mattered to him gravely *who* saw him.

"I will not come to Ochi," he forcefully whispered as soon as he had his breath back. "I will not be hounded out of the capital; I will not have a doting wife tell me what to do, where to go. In your place I would prefer to live on water and salt, prostrate myself on a bed of horse dung outside great daimyo mansions and beg for a chance to perform. I am not proud, I am not important; the noh is. Without being seen by the capital's eye you'll never be as good as you can be."

"But, Father," groaned Juro Motomasa, finding his father's argument unrealistic and overemotional. "Aside from a few old survivors from the Great Tree's time, which daimyo would risk commanding a performance from us in the capital today? I am responsible for the survival of nearly forty men, women and children."

"What about the survival of the quality of your men's work? Besides, no power lasts forever. Sitting out the Time of Female, you can tour as before and return here as frequently as possible so that all of you can be whipped into form again, rehearse new plays with me, study our rivals and keep in touch with what goes on in Kyoto, without all of which moss will grow on your noh. Motomasa, can't you see the simple good sense of what your father is saying to you?"

Zeami's question touched his son to the quick. For a moment he stared idiotically at Zeami's sad, suppliant eyes; then he slowly crumpled in a heap at Zeami's feet, his hands on the warm sand beneath the veranda.

"Please, Father, let me leave! I cannot endure any longer this shogun's capital. Call me weak, call me a traitor, a deserter, a despicable son who loves his wife as much as his Buddha-granted vocation; but I cannot live, let alone work, being the target of such brutal hatred and incessant persecution. No, I am not strong enough for that. Forgive me; I simply cannot cope anymore . . ." Juro Motomasa cried pitiably, so relieved that he had at last spoken the truth, yet so racked by guilt.

"Brother, you go; I'll stay!" It was Goro Motoyoshi who suddenly intervened, his boyish round face crumpled in anguish. "Yes, I want to stay here, look after Father and Mother, guard the house, help Father with his writing and wait for your return till one day perhaps our fortunes change again . . ."

After Goro Motoyoshi's voice tapered off, there followed a long silence during which Zeami slowly regained his upright posture and the usual slow beat of his heart. When he had dried his eyes and blown his nose, he was calm and resigned to accept the worst.

"Motomasa," he began hoarsely, "you copy all the secret-transmission treaties meant only for your eyes and pack them carefully to take with you. And Motoyoshi, you'll help me sort out which Chinese vases and incense bars we can sell so that Motomasa

and the troupe will be provided for on their journey and especially for the birth of his child. Now, Motomasa, you must talk to
the troupe."

Juro Motomasa sat slightly in front of his father and his
younger brother, facing the members of his troupe. At least four
times he raised his face, drawing a breath in readiness to speak,
but each time, meeting his men's eyes, he slowly dropped his head.
In the end, it was Zeami who told them.

Those splendid old fighters, loyal and selfless to the last drop
of blood in them—Toyojiro, Kogame, Kumaya, Kumao, Meiroku,
Jippen and others—listened to the disastrous news but showed not
a tremor of a muscle, not a flutter of an eyelid. They wanted their
masters to know that come what might, they would go anywhere,
do anything, give up anything; they also wanted the young disciples, some already furtively calculating the alternatives that lay
open to them, to know that Way of noh was also Way of faith.

Zeami smiled and, nodding to himself, said gently, "That is
all. Thank you."

ROKUEMON OCHI proved himself a man of heart and true samurai
chivalry: the moment he received his daughter's plea, he dispatched
eight men on horseback and four ox-drawn carts to the capital to
assist in the journey, totally ignoring the fact that more than a
year earlier he had excommunicated his daughter. He also wrote
a kind note to Zeami and Yukina, telling them that they were welcome to visit Ochi when his and their grandchild was born.

Bitterly disappointing, on the other hand, was the departure
of some old members of the troupe: Raido, who had joined the
Kanze troupe from the Hosho troupe as Raiden's adopted son at
the advanced age of sixteen and had since been transformed into
a superb *shité* player under the Kanze elders' guidance, declared
he wished to join the divided-house troupe, taking with him his
sons, Raiman and Raizen, on whom both Zeami and Juro Motomasa had spent an immense amount of devoted tuition. The two
young boys came to take their leave of Zeami and Juro Motomasa and wept miserably, apologizing for what could not but appear, even to themselves, as a base desertion.

Mercifully, neither Zeami nor Juro Motomasa was yet aware
of the tragic circumstance that had prompted Raido to desert just
at this juncture: Hotan had died only a few days earlier of a sim-

ple cold aggravated by neglect and overwork, and Saburo Moto-shige had solicited Raido to join him at once.

Also, two *waki* disciples of Kumao left, and five of the younger members. But the rest, all nineteen of them and their families, began immediately preparing for the move, assiduously helped by Kumazen's widowed daughter, Sazami, who chose to stay on at the Kanze house "to look after my father's and brothers' master till I drop dead like a kitchen fly."

Kogame was in a pitiable dilemma: for him life without either Zeami or Juro Motomasa was incomplete. In the end, Zeami put an end to his dear old friend's agony by firmly saying: "I still have Motoyoshi with me. Tama and Ujinobu come up from Yamato frequently enough. I think you should go with Motomasa."

He did not mention his wife, Yukina, whose strength had been failing since the long Kyoto winter. The poor woman had to suffer the Kanze's adversity with neither a strong interior conviction nor artistic recompense; in order not to upset her too much, Zeami had to lie to her that Juro Motomasa had gone on a long tour taking Akiko with him.

After Juro Motomasa and his troupe left for Ochi, Sango and Sazami tended to whisper and to tiptoe from room to room, intimidated by the cavernous silence that filled the empty large house.

24

In August, the month when one's ancestors returned to the world of the living, Ujinobu and Tama dutifully traveled to the capital to offer some Yamato specialty cakes on the family altar.

As they removed their dust-caked sandals and leg covers, Tama winced to notice so much less footwear on the entrance floor than in the old days; but Ujinobu sighed gratefully, "What a relief—so cool in the house. Isn't it like being inside a deep well?"

To her husband's surprise, Tama glared at him with her lovely dark eyes blown large with tear bubbles and ran inside the house, where, steeped in semidarkness, the unstirred air felt dank and wet. Dressed in white linen and her head neatly covered in white silk, Yukina lay on a sleep mat, looking like a statue carved out of friable old bone. With a wheezy cry of joy she tried to sit up to greet her daughter, but could only frantically stir the air with her fleshless arms. Sazami, till then invisible in a dark corner, darted forward and carefully helped her mistress to sit up, as Tama knelt before her mother speechlessly taking in all the symptoms of Yukina's decline. Clutching at Tama's arm with her trembling fingers, Yukina spoke in a breathless hurry in order to outstrip the cough that seemed to lurk constantly in her chest:

"Motoshige wants to be the fourth Kanze master. He's stealing everything from Motomasa. But look at him: the heinous boy already has everything in abundance. I'm sure you've heard that Kikyo has given him another son. Another son! I hear the shogun has sent silk, linen and Chinese medicine to congratulate the slut whom he calls his 'milk sister.' And to think our poor Akiko lost hers in the sixth month! Yet she was so careful; unlike you, she did not fall from a tree or go on a pilgrimage in a snowstorm. There is no justice in this world, and slowly but surely we are being demolished by Motoshige's evil curse."

"Mother, please! As long as we are here, please don't mention or even think about Brother Motoshige. It only upsets you."

"*Brother* Motoshige!" Yukina's emaciated face, a beautiful white wreckage, wrung a hideous grimace.

"Please, dear Mother, do let us talk about something else." Tama made Yukina lie down again and gently rubbed her legs, which even in the August heat seemed cold and brittle dry. Sazami sneezed and wiped her nose and tearful eyes with crackling rough paper in the dark corner of the room, where the shutters were permanently drawn against the sun and the haranguing of the cicadas.

In the stage room, Ujinobu was listening to Zeami.

"I wouldn't have said it was a courteous letter—no, far from it; but someone in the position of a shogun could have made it an imperative order. He hasn't, not yet. . . ."

"But, Father!" Ujinobu, who had called Zeami "Father" since his marriage to Tama, flushed crimson with indignation. "It is outrageous that the shogun should meddle with a decision of purely artistic merit such as this!"

"When Motomasa decamped with his troupe to the welcoming bosom of his wife's family, I knew this would happen. Motomasa *invited* the shogun to interfere."

Intimidated by Zeami's undiminished bitterness against Juro Motomasa's flight to Ochi, Ujinobu remained silent.

"I have replied in the politest, humblest terms that while Motomasa, my legitimate heir, is actively creating, performing and teaching, I could not possibly consider handing over the Kanze mastership to someone else to whom so far no house secret has been transmitted by myself."

"Do you suppose he'll swallow the logic of it, Father?" the young man asked with an ardent prayer in his voice.

"I'm afraid not. There will almost certainly be another letter amounting to an ultimatum." Zeami, erect and looking cool in a worn, soft and faded indigo-blue kimono, smiled encouragingly at Ujinobu as if it were the young man who was in a dire predicament. "Never mind, Ujinobu; let us talk about our work—so much more important and pleasant. Motoyoshi has been heroic: I cannot find a better word. He's being a great solace to Yukina and is of invaluable help to me. Look, here are the copies he made for you of my two new demon plays, which I know will be to the taste of your Yamato audiences. And these two treatises, Ujinobu, are for your eyes only."

Zeami put two slim volumes before his son-in-law whose honest, kind, generous nature glowed so visibly on his face.

"*Six Principles in Playwriting* and *Pearl and Flower*. I have written them with the particular need and traditions of your school in mind."

For some moments Ujinobu just stared incredulously at the two secret-transmission treatises that Zeami had for the first time written for and given to someone other than Juro Motomasa; then with an impatient jolt he pounced on them and, hugging them against his chest, slid back several yards on his knees and, knocking the floorboards with his forehead, thanked Zeami again and again till he was choked with delirious sobbing. Seeing that he could make the dear boy so happy with so little, Zeami, for his part, was touched to silence.

The young Komparus' four-day visit, which had given every member of the diminished household so much joy and rare laughter, was all too quickly over. Everyone, even Yukina, leaning on Sazami's arm, saw them off at the gate, and Zeami and Goro Motoyoshi walked several streets with the young couple. Ujinobu had been bound by strict tradition and the code of ethics of the profession not to disclose even to his own wife the gift of the secret-transmission treatises. But Tama was no fool, nor new to the world of the noh: from her husband's uncontrollable excitement, the irrepressible grin on his face and the hours on end her father had spent teaching Ujinobu, with old Sango guarding the stage room, she had guessed what had passed from Zeami to her husband.

As she took her leave of Zeami she whispered with a conniving intimacy, "You *are* so good to us, Father. For your sake I'll behave myself and try not to lose a baby next time."

"Yes, wiser not to climb a loquat tree or make a pilgrimage to the Hase Temple in a snowstorm."

"Oh, but that pilgrimage: I did it for you and Mother!"

"I'd much rather you stayed quietly at home and gave me my first grandson—although strictly speaking, it'll be a Komparu grandson."

"Father, if I can, I'll give you not just one, but two, three, even four grandsons, I promise!"

Tama laughed as she waved goodbye, holding up her hand with four fingers stretched out, but as they walked on with Goro Motoyoshi, who insisted on accompanying them farther to the southern gate of the capital, tears were streaming down her cheeks. She turned around again and again to wave to Zeami. As soon as Zeami disappeared from sight, Ujinobu gasped, as if he had not been thinking of anything else:

"How incredible he really is! Motoyoshi, do you realize at his age Father is still changing, growing and advancing further and faster than anyone of our age? In terms of *yugen* his new plays surpass everything he has ever written. After showing me *Izutsu*, he said—rather sadly, I thought: 'Will anyone in twenty or fifty years' time understand a play such as this?' Father is of course much too modest and self-critical. Who could possibly fail to see an eternal truth in a play like *Izutsu*—eh, Motoyoshi?"

"Many will, I'm afraid," replied Goro Motoyoshi with an apologetic smile for spoiling the enthusiasm of the young Komparu master, whom he loved as if he were his own brother. "Unbelievable as it may strike you, Ujinobu, there are many to whom Father's masterpieces have become too demanding, too highfalutin, almost incomprehensible. There is no question whatever that since the Great Tree's death the critical standard of the majority of the capital's theater-going public has sunk very low. Nowadays, they flock to see noh plays performed by pretty young girls who haven't the slightest idea what they are ranting and stamping their feet about. How can you expect the people who swoon over such garish vulgarity to appreciate, say, the dulled-silver refinement of *Izutsu*? There is a vast difference between the moon and a turtle, and the heartbreaking fact is that we live in the age of turtles. . . . Now that I am alone and at such close quarters with Father, I am discovering what it must be like to be the moon amongst turtles, and I confess that day by day I am finding it difficult to live up to the rigorous demands and standards of such a demonic genius."

Tama, who had been keeping her frank, searching gaze on her brother, cut him short with her customary youngest-of-the-family impudence:

"You've changed, Brother Motoyoshi. Is that because you've found acting as nanny to Father and Mother much tougher than you bargained for? Does time hang heavy on your hands without performing? Do you find that Father's genius—the demonic obsession, as you put it—prevents you from being yourself? Is that it?"

Goro Motoyoshi laughed at Tama's savage forthrightness, but in contrast to the old days, his laughter tapered off lamely.

"No, no, it's not like that at all." He chewed his lips and walked silently on before deciding to speak again.

"I've been seeing the Zen hermit Ikkyu for some time now."

"Aha—I thought something was afoot! And what does that notorious eccentric do for you?" Tama did not approve of the combination of her gullible good brother and the freak Zen mystic, rumored to be an illegitimate son of the Cloistered Emperor Gokomatsu.

"Nothing in particular; he just helps me to look at conventional ethics with a new freedom and to get nearer to Buddha's truth."

The way he then incongruously burst into loud hollow laughter inhibited even Tama, with her ferretlike curiosity, from probing further.

Tama had missed her monthly impurity in October, and with November coming to an end without any sign of it, she began to feel some of the other signs of pregnancy. Ujinobu was overjoyed, but anxious that his coltish wife not miscarry again from imprudence. He offered special prayers accompanied with autumnal fruits and grains at the shrines in Nara known for the protection of mothers-to-be; and the silent smiles the husband and the wife exchanged glowed with the deeper, calmer complicity of love.

Tama was having her belly firmly wrapped with a long wide cotton sash by an old midwife who lived nearby when unexpectedly Sango arrived at the Komparu house with a hurriedly scribbled note from her father. On the eleventh of November, wrote Zeami, Goro Motoyoshi had left his parents' roof, abandoning this world to become a wandering Zen monk.

Zeami had not added, Come at once; but in Sango's clinging

long glances the plea was eloquent enough. Ujinobu had to perform in Otsu, on Lake Biwa, in three days' time, which meant Tama would have to make the journey to the capital alone with Sango, who, although still robust in constitution, was now blind in one eye and alarmingly forgetful; and the journey on foot in her present condition would mean spending a night and two days on the road.

"I have married into the Komparu family. It is a Komparu baby I am carrying. If I lost the baby by whatever accident or carelessness on the journey, how am I to apologize to your ancestors? Once married, I must stop being the daughter of the Kanze. Really, it is not fair to you . . ." Tama cried in short shallow sobs as her tummy inside the pregnancy sash felt so strangely constricted and precious.

"Of course you *must* go!" Ujinobu said at once. "Since I lost my parents so young, your father has been just as much my father as yours, and Motoyoshi has been like my own brother. Besides, now that you're with my child, I can't help putting myself in your father's place. . . ." Ujinobu swallowed back his tears and with his delicately extended fingers stroked the surface of Tama's stiff pregnancy obi under which beat the heart of his child and the grandchild Tama had promised her father in August.

Ujinobu walked with Tama and Sango as far as where the main road to the capital left the Nara city limits and watched the two travelers disappear into the morning mist of November, the Frost Month.

"Master's in your old room, where I've already laid your sleep mat. I knew you'd come, little miss," Sazami, who helped Tama remove her footwear and leg and hand covers at the entrance hall, whispered as if the house, now peopled with only the old master and the invalid mistress, could not tolerate a full voice.

Tama went straight to her old room. Zeami was seated on the far side of the sleep mat, which left hardly any margin of space in the tiny room, and was facing the closed paper sliding screens as if he could see the night garden beyond them. An oil lamp burned unsteadily. Zeami turned his head but not his shoulders to Tama.

"Haven't told your mother yet," said Zeami without raising his eyes. He turned to face the screens again. Tama sat down on the near side of the sleep mat.

"Father, are you . . ."

"Thinking you might come, I cut a camellia branch for your room, then realized what an unlucky flower it was and couldn't make up my mind what to do with it. The Great Tree used to love the camellia and in its flowering season had special attendants pick up dead flowers all day long so that he wouldn't see them lying on the ground. The camellia dies in full bloom. Without any sign of decay, not even petal by petal, the whole head drops in an inexplicable hurry."

Slowly, he turned on his knees and faced Tama, who was taken aback by a face so haggard and pale and eyes so tired from sleepless nights. Tama hated her brother: a coward, an ingrate, a despicable son, unworthy—oh, so unworthy—of this, my father!

"I knew no good would come of it when he told me he'd been visiting that bizarre Zen hermit Ikkyu! A child is put on earth to look after his parents in their old age, not to quit them to suit his own convenience. A dog wouldn't do that. I can't believe he's done what he has; I can't!" Tama burst into wild sobs. "I did so count on Brother Motoyoshi, so stalwart, so jolly and uncomplicated. Who'd ever have thought he'd be so easily discouraged and chuck it all away?" Tama whimpered before blowing her nose loudly.

"He left me this. Extremely well written and thought out."

His voice raucous from having swallowed so many uncried tears, Zeami handed her a thick pile of papers crudely sewn together in green silk thread. *What My Father Told Me*. Tama recognized her brother's free, square-shouldered brushwork.

"You'd never have suspected that he would have so meticulously and painstakingly recorded every little comment and reminiscence I have made through the years, would you? The history of our art; our house rules; the etiquette and conventions observed in the great temples and palaces; anecdotes about the famous actors of my father's and my generations; accurate documentation of costumes, masks and musical instruments. In thirty-one chapters he's captured all the essential aspects of our profession. An admirable feat. Since his childhood, his remarkable musical gifts had fooled his teachers and Motoyoshi himself, but as Ogame and I often remarked, he already had the volume and the breadth reminiscent of his grandfather. With years he would have matured into a moving, large-scale actor. All the more inexcusable, therefore, is his desertion of the Way of noh. All the more tragic that the boy didn't realize his own great potential."

As he spoke, a raw anger burned in his eyes which he had not succeeded in taming despite days of hard effort to forgive and accept.

His daughter, who in many ways had more mettle than either of her brothers, slapped shut Goro Motoyoshi's book and threw it on the floor.

"Those three farewell poems Brother Motoyoshi has dedicated to you and Mother on the last page: very touching, very nicely rhymed; but, Father, if he loved you as much as he says he does, why, then, did he leave you and Brother Motomasa to struggle on alone, himself flying off as light and carefree as a migrating bird? Poor dear Mother, having suffered the pain of giving him life, now has to suffer this inhuman ingratitude!"

"Tama, I admit this to you: your brother was a charming boy, but weak—so weak!"

Zeami's already speaking of his son in the past tense gave Tama a chill.

"So unimaginative as well. Look how he sought help in a readily available religion. The Way of Buddha is no different from the Way of noh. Ultimately they come to the same destination. He could have arrived at the final enlightenment by doggedly continuing on his Way of art; but no, he's opted for the easier, conventional well-paved path of Zen. If I failed to instill in him the ineffable value of our Way, even a tenth of the ecstasy and love I have for it, well, Tama, then I suppose I deserve to be deserted by my son and to worry sleeplessly about the future of our Way."

Zeami glared into the night outside, fingering Goro Motoyoshi's favorite drumsticks which had been left with *What My Father Told Me*. The silence that fell between the father and daughter was dense, almost suffocating.

25

FOLLOWING his brutal suppression of the peasant uprising at the very start of his reign, the shogun Yoshinori maintained a policy of maniacal repression. When there was a severe famine in the eastern region, Yoshinori heard a rumor that the powerful guild of rice merchants in the area was blocking the land and sea routes from other provinces in order to raise the price of rice in their warehouse. It was merely a rumor, but he flared up in a characteristic blind rage and had all the leading rice merchants in the region arrested, regardless of the veracity of the accusation thrown at them, and had them immediately beheaded without any lawful trial.

When, on a similar occasion, a number of diamyos pleaded for more leniency and a fair trial, the shogun retaliated by revising the shogunate's legal procedures and regulations to an unheard-of severity and at the same time issued a law prohibiting shogunal officials or daimyos from interfering with or criticizing the shogunate's legal judgments under penalty of instant dismissal or confiscation of their property.

The absolute power of the office of shogun aggravated not

only Yoshinori's congenital inability to take criticism but also his suspiciousness and irascibility to such a degree that he gave the impression of someone suffering from a highly advanced case of paranoia. He had little trust in the officials inside the shogunate but trusted even less the daimyos whose territories were situated beyond the immediate neighborhood of the capital. The richer and mightier these daimyos were, the more dubious their loyalty seemed to Yoshinori. Building his accusations on mere hearsay, he demolished such long-serving vassal daimyos as the Doki or the Isshiki clans and constantly harassed the great temples in the southern provinces on the charge that their armed monks usurped the power of the shogunal army.

His punitive zeal did not stop at economic, legal and military matters: seeing how low moral standards had fallen amongst the nobles, Yoshinori was suddenly inspired to purge the stench of debauchery from the Ninefold Forbidden Enclosure. He exiled or sent to monasteries nearly forty of "those who lived above the clouds" who had been reported to him to be immoral or lascivious or often simply fun-loving. Eventually, his fanatic antihedonist drive extended itself to other levels of society, and the number of those imprisoned or put under house arrest reached staggering proportions, ranging from the highest-placed shogunal officials down to a page boy aged hardly thirteen.

What struck everyone as quite incongruous, although no one any longer dared speak his thoughts in public, was that whilst Yoshinori rampaged as a righteous moral crusader, his own conduct was far from exemplary: having abandoned his priesthood in his prime of manhood, he had since given free rein to his own carnal appetite; and aside from his continued and close intimacy with Saburo Motoshige, he kept a considerable number of mistresses and page boys, yet was commendably assiduous in his attentions to his legal wife, the daughter of Prince Hino, whom he had married soon after arranging a marriage for Saburo Motoshige. It was nobody's secret, for instance, that when Yoshinori treacherously goaded his loyal and hardworking daimyo Yoshitsugu Isshiki to suicide, he did so simply because he had taken a sudden and violent fancy to Isshiki's wife, who after her husband's death unwillingly became one of the shogun's mistresses and committed suicide a few years later.

Zeami was fully aware of Yoshinori's unbalanced character

when a letter from the master of the shogun's household was delivered to him, inquiring if Zeami was now prepared to reconsider the shogun's earlier suggestion that he offer the fourth Kanze mastership to his third son, Saburo Motoshige. But this time again Zeami replied, although in even more roundabout and subservient terms, that the house of noh would perish unless its head was in full possession of both the arcana of his art and the highest attainable rank of *yugen* and that in his humble, purely professional opinion his heir, Juro Motomasa, was the only one equipped with such qualification.

After Goro Motoyoshi's desertion, with no one to talk to about the noh, nor a chance to see his new work performed on stage now that Juro Motomasa and his troupe were self-exiled in Ochi, Zeami worked with an even stronger sense of mission and doom on yet another secret-transmission treatise, entitled *The Beyond-and-Again Flower,* which he intended to hand down to his son-in-law, Ujinobu, who had shown more than ample proof of his sangfroid and unshakable loyalty toward his father-in-law through closely repeated disasters, for Zeami was now tragically aware of the friableness of Juro Motomasa's character.

As the wall of isolation grew denser around him, awake or asleep, a thousand thoughts on the art of noh haunted him; so much so that when rare visitors to the house brought him news of the current state of affairs in the theater, Zeami was distressed to the point of not being able to eat or sleep, lamenting: "Am I punished for my longevity?"

Iwato, for example, the actor who had succeeded Doami at the head of the Hiei troupe, was reported to Zeami as having wrapped the handles of the oars with gold-threaded brocade when he played a simple boatman. This piece of vulgarity had so shocked the connoisseurs amongst his audience that they went home at once. Another visitor told Zeami that the same Iwato had made a laughingstock of himself when he had played a princess wearing her obi in a loose, asymmetrical fashion, which his old master, Doami, used to do with an exquisite effect. Without Doami's art and rank, Iwato had managed only to look slovenly and ridiculous.

It was also about this time that Zeami heard that the shogun, accompanied by his entourage including Saburo Motoshige, not only attended but immensely enjoyed a performance of what had lately become a rage in the capital: female noh plays—mostly plagiarized from Kanami's and Zeami's works—performed entirely by young women, generally recruited from itinerant storytellers or dancing priestesses who were in many ways hardly distinguishable from prostitutes.

When Zeami learned this, he could not sit still. He at once wrote *The Disciplines of the Way,* an impassioned plea and exhortation to each present and future Kanze disciple. He sent it to Juro Motomasa in Ochi together with two new demon plays, which he would certainly not have considered writing for the capital's connoisseurs nor at the height of the Kanze's fortune. But touring had become increasingly hazardous and less profitable, owing to sporadic but widespread peasant uprisings in the South. Although Juro Motomasa was exceedingly careful not to worry his father, by reading between the lines of his letters and from other reports, Zeami surmised that the Kanze actors had been often engaged in farm labor in order to supplement their meager income from performances. Zeami felt it his duty to write for the struggling troupe these potboiler demon plays. . . .

THROUGHOUT June the tollgates between the Southern provinces and the capital were closed by riotous post-horse keepers, so that Kumaya's youngest son, Kumaji, whom Juro Motomasa had sent to Zeami on the last day of May, did not reach the capital till late in June, bringing news that threw the dank, dispirited house into rapture: Akiko had given birth to a healthy baby boy.

Zeami hurried to the family altar to report the glad news, his joy-crazed feet nearly causing him to fall. A boy. A grandson. An heir to extend the Way of noh! The proud grandfather took one Chinese character from his boyhood name, Fujiwaka, and named the newborn baby Fujimaru.

Yukina, who had managed to survive another Kyoto winter, was now rapidly fading. She asked to have a handful of her white hair cut and sent to the baby whom, she feared, she was not likely to meet on this side of the world.

The following evening, Ujinobu's disciple arrived with the same news, which Ujinobu had learned from an itinerant storyteller. It was so like him that, not knowing whether in these troubled times Juro Motomasa had the means of communicating the news to Zeami, Ujinobu had immediately dispatched a messenger of his own to Kyoto. With it came a blissful note from Tama, now in the last month of her pregnancy: she was feeling exceedingly well, obeying her husband and staying quietly at home.

On the day of the Star Festival, the seventh day of July, the same messenger from Ujinobu, who had been to the house only ten days earlier, burst into the kitchen, where Sazami was cooling arrowroot jelly for her mistress, whose shrunken stomach could no longer accept solid food.

"A boy and a girl!" the young man yelled. Tama had given birth to twins, whom the exultant Ujinobu described as "two perfect monkeys, crying like firefighters' bells; without much hair as yet, but blessed with their mother's large, sparkling eyes." Tama, her husband reported, was exhausted and flabbergasted at becoming mother to two babies at a stroke, but otherwise in splendid form.

With the gift of a grandson from Akiko and now twins from Tama, even Zeami, in whom in recent years "Expect the worst" had become a necessary mental attitude, had moments in which he hoped that the Time of Male was perhaps at long last returning for the Kanze.

ON THE second of August, just before the bells of the Hour of Tiger,* a mounted messenger, an Ochi vassal, banged at the Kanze's gate. He carried a message, scribbled by Rokuemon Ochi himself, which annihilated all Zeami's hopes.

Juro Motomasa had died at an inn in the fishing town of Anotsu in Ise the night before. After a performance at a local temple, he had suddenly begun vomiting and within a matter of a few hours died in unspeakable agony without seeing Akiko or his baby son again. He was aged thirty-seven.

Was it suicide, or, as others maintained, had he been poisoned by a minion of one of the shogun's generals stationed in the area who had not forgiven Juro Motomasa for having reputedly spied for the Kitabatakes and of having married into the Ochi clan? Rokuemon Ochi, prudent not to introduce a politically contentious note, had restricted himself to saying as little as possible as to the circumstances of Juro Motomasa's inexplicably sudden death and begged Zeami and Yukina to allow his daughter,

* Four o'clock in the morning.

Akiko, devastated by the tragedy to a state of numb stupor, and her son to stay on in Ochi. He also gave his word of honor that he would do everything in his power to support and protect Toyo-jiro, Jippen and a few others who had chosen to stay and teach the Kanze's noh in Ochi.

It was the last week of August, the nights already sounding with autumnal insects, when the rest of the troupe and their families arrived back from Ochi, too stunned by the accelerating blows of misfortune to take in the full impact of the situation. Kogame in particular cut a pathetically changed figure: his eyes dulled like a stale fish's, he hugged the small urn that contained Juro Moto-masa's ashes. It was wrapped in a black cloth grubby from his hands' constantly caressing it during the long journey from Ochi.

When Zeami asked for it, Kogame, with an agonized look on his face, hugged the urn even tighter against his hollow chest. Zeami's extended arm fell on his old friend's back; then, together, they cried, two old men quivering with the same bitter question: If Buddha has mercy, why didn't he take my life instead?

But this was, mercifully, the only occasion when the troupe had to witness Zeami lose control over himself. By the time the young Komparus managed to reach Kyoto, they found Zeami without any outward show of his mourning. The one startling change Tama saw in her father was that he had stopped shaving his head, and now strong, straight white hair framed his face, chiseled by the greatest loss of his life into a mask implacable in its refusal to be pried into or provoked to tears.

Outwardly, his most pressing preoccupation seemed to be how to cope with the dispossessed members of the troupe and their families, totaling twenty-three. The house was more than large enough for Zeami, Yukina and the two remaining servants, but was not large enough for all the refugees from Ochi for a prolonged period of time; moreover, with no source of income other than what some of the wives were able to earn from occasional sewing and cooking for the wealthier families in the district, they were almost completely dependent on Zeami, who could not go on clothing and feeding them all indefinitely. Zeami asked Uji-nobu to take some of the actors into his troupe. Fortunately, the Komparu troupe, with young Ujinobu at its head, was doing far better than in his bearlike grandfather's time. Ujinobu agreed at once, not only because he was delighted to help Zeami but because the Kanze actors were unquestionably the best trained and disciplined to be found in the profession.

Zeami also asked his son-in-law to help him to inventory the great quantity of precious gifts that Yoshimitsu and other admirers used to shower on Zeami, with a view to deciding which should be sold to support the remainder of the troupe till at least by degrees he might find alternative employment for them.

"I hope things will improve for them before I have to start selling my collection of masks and costumes," Zeami said with a wan smile. "But now that the main-house Kanze has no heir left, I ask myself of what practical use they'll be. . . ."

"But, Father, you still have Fujimaru in Ochi. Surely he is your heir."

"Ujinobu"—Zeami opened his eyes wide, uncompromisingly aware—"do you honestly believe that a boy, even with Motomasa's blood in him, brought up amongst provincial warriors and farmers, taught at best by competent but uninspired teachers, could be the vessel to carry on the Kanze? No, now that Akiko is to keep the boy in Ochi, I have no direct heir left. The Kanze line of Kanami, Zeami and Motomasa is finished."

Zeami looked sternly before him, sinking into a silence. It would have needed a far harder heart than Ujinobu's not to avert his eyes from the bereaved father.

THE NIGHT before the forty-ninth-night memorial service for Juro Motomasa, Yukina, who had been fading into and out of consciousness for some time, followed him to the world beyond ours, unaware of her eldest son's death. Zeami sat by her all night and watched death lift one by one the traces of her worldly sufferings of pain, cruel solitude, pride and unrequited love. It was a beautiful face that was left behind. She was the only woman he had known, the mother of his children and his wife, but whom he knew he had singularly failed to make happy. He had been wedded by the will of Buddha to the noh and its demands, which made no concessions to human happiness.

The double funeral, conducted by two priests and attended only by the three members of the family, the troupe and a very few outsiders, was the most desolating occasion. Saburo Motoshige, his family and his troupe were conspicuous by their absence. For the rest, the present shogun's capital, after four years of his atrocious reign, did not dare to come and mourn the death of an actor who had so openly defied the tyrant.

"Brother Motoshige could have at least sent Raido," said Tama when she, Zeami and Ujinobu sat down for a frugal supper after the funeral. Neither Zeami nor Ujinobu reacted to her remark; both continued without speaking to masticate the pickled aubergine, wondering why each bite reverberated so loudly in their skulls.

"If the wall had ears, I'd most certainly be arrested and sent to Sado Island for asking *this* question," Tama began in a menacing tone.

"Don't, Tama—please don't ask the question." Ujinobu quickly put down his bowl of wheat on his tray.

"In Yamato no one believes that Brother Motosama's death was due to ordinary food poisoning." Tama's face was strangely rigid, and her white lips quivered as if she were ready to vomit.

"Tama, in Yamato people would think it was a demon who killed him; nothing ever happens there without demons." Zeami laughed a short throttled laugh; then, with a piercing hard gaze on her, he added, "Say it was a demon, Tama. The Great Tree taught me many things, and one of them was that truth, like lies, must be used with discretion. He told me to quote this poem whenever I was short of a reply or it was best not to give a straight answer:

'I broke a cherry tree and found no flower;
For the flower was nowhere else but in the spring sky.'

"Ujinobu is right. What's the use? Motomasa is dead."

"Do you think my father is utterly heartless?" asked Tama when she lay next to Ujinobu that night. "I haven't seen him shed a tear since we got here."

"There is a sorrow that crying has nothing to do with, Tama," replied Ujinobu, lifting a strand of Tama's hair that clung damply on her forehead, but refrained from voicing the continuation of his thought: And there is a loss that is synonymous with "to perish."

Although the house was filled with the refugees from Ochi, the house of mourning, with its bleak future, was hushed; children seldom laughed, and the vacant, wondering stares of the adults crisscrossed the darkness like invisible gnats, each mind asking the same questions: Can Master sleep? Does he eat? Will he ever get over this?

On the morning of their departure for Yamato, even the plucky Tama broke down:

"Please, Father, cry or kick or curse or do something! Or at least, tell me how I can help, what I can do!"

Zeami watched his daughter weep, open-faced like a child, her eyes fastened on his.

"No, Tama, there's nothing more you can do for me. Young or old, death strikes us at random. Having reached seventy, I ought to have learned to accept such a banal fact by now. It'll be months before I can crawl out of this impotent senile stupor. Only then will I be able to wash myself in the luxury of tears."

He smiled and patted on the shoulder the only child now left to him. Tamana wiped away her tears, smiled miserably and promised to return to the capital as soon as possible to show her father his Komparu grandchildren.

As Ujinobu took his leave, Zeami whispered with a ferocity he would not show to anyone except to one dedicated to the same art:

"I have already begun work on a new volume, in which I shall leave my final, most haunted thoughts so that people a hundred generations after me will know what it is like to possess a Way, to be possessed by a Way!"

Those words came out of Zeami's mouth like a ball of fire breathed out by a street entertainer. Scorched by the heat in them, Ujinobu remained petrified.

26

ONLY A FEW months after Juro Motomasa's funeral, peasants on the Kofuku Temple properties, following a poor crop, refused to pay an extra levy which the temple had demanded over and above the already crushing annual taxes. Two armed landlords who had for many generations enjoyed both the privileges and duties to exploit and to protect the Kofuku properties and their tenants rallied their forces behind the riotous peasants: the two were none other than the Ochi and the Hashio clans.

Their well-trained soldiers, with effective support from the web of local peasantry, ubiquitous yet invisible in the dense southern forests, defeated the temple's armed monks in every encounter and stripped them of their weapons, their footwear and even their strings of beads. Yoshinori at once dispatched some of his elite troops, but the rebels, fighting on their own familiar ground, taunted and harassed his generals with audacious ambushes and ceaseless night attacks, then, to add injury to insult, won a resounding triumph over the shogunate's forces by gravely wounding no less than its Commander-in-Chief, Lord Akamatsu, and killing more than four hundred of the shogun's army, which was then forced to beat an unseemly retreat back to the capital.

Yoshinori's rage was virulent, lashing out in all directions, and it did not spare a seventy-year-old artist related to the Ochis only by a short-lived marriage. Yoshinori ordered Zeami exiled at once to the island of Sado, lost far out in the North Sea between the mainland and oblivion.

Flaunting his policy of doing everything possible to depreciate his father's favorite entertainer, Yoshinori had his samurai messenger read aloud Zeami's exile order, standing akimbo at the entrance hall of the house, where, abruptly called out of a lesson, Zeami was obliged to prostrate himself on the floor and listen to what amounted at his age to a life sentence in front of his horror-struck disciples and their wives and children.

Just as the samurai finished reading the order and began rolling up the paper, Kumao, six years senior to Zeami and so gallant and devoted a friend through good and bad times of their lives together in the noh, lurched to his feet and started to go at the shogun's emissary, his big white head lowered, his hard drinker's ruddy complexion for once as pallid as a spring onion. Kogame and Kumaya, ejaculating an incoherent cry, tried but were too late to seize the *waki* player; and it was Zeami who, realizing what was happening, said in a loud, rapier-sharp voice: "Yes, Kumao, thank you; do get me the brush and ink!"

The samurai jolted back a step, his right hand on his sword, but in the confined space of the entrance hall, with his elbow already scraping the wall, he had not drawn his sword when Kumao suddenly halted in his tracks, swayed from left to right with his closed fist raised at the samurai in angular rigidity, then collapsed heavily to the floor, right in front of Zeami.

Those who witnessed the scene were not responsible for the rumor which later made the rounds in the capital that the seventy-six-year-old *waki* player had attacked the shogun's messenger and had been cut down by his sword. Kumao died of apoplexy, to which, like his father, Kumazen, he had been prone; by the time the samurai was ready with his sword, Kumao lay inanimate with his wrathful eyes thrusting out of their sockets.

It was Kumaji, the alert and levelheaded nephew of the dead man, who brought the brush and ink with which Zeami quickly signed the receipt of his exile order. Bowing very low, his forehead almost touching Kumao's rapidly cooling hand, as if nothing were out of place, only his trembling lips as white as chalk, Zeami said reverently: "I shall now begin preparing for the journey to Sado Island and await your further instructions."

The samurai, a middle-aged, honest-looking man, nervously cleared his throat and, putting his sword back in its sheath, left precipitately. Everyone present, even children, took the cue from their master and bowed to the departing back of the shogun's emissary.

Zeami closed his old friend's eyelids as gently as if he were catching butterflies; then, breaking down completely, he wailed with his face on Kumao's corpse.

When what was now left of the Kanze main-house troupe returned from Kumao's cremation, Zeami, aided by Kogame, began preparing for his exile by sorting out his papers.

His disciples, squatting here and there in the stage room, furtively muttered and muttered again:

"Buddha would surely never allow this?"

"Master Kanami, then Master Motomasa; and now . . ."

The spitting light rain which had dampened their walk home from the cremation field turned into a steady downpour, and the algae-green dark in the unlit room grew so murky that when someone hissed, "No, I won't take this lying down!" no one at first could be sure who it was.

"I'll go and see Motoshige-dono!" It was Kumaya. "He must plead with the shogun to save his father. Surely, he must have a drop of human blood in him!"

Kumaya leaped up and, turning on his heel, shouted to his elder son, Kumabei, to fetch a straw rain cape and a lantern.

Zeami did not learn of Kumaya's visit to Saburo Motoshige's house till Kogame brought him a tray of wheat-and-millet gruel with a pinch of seaweed for supper.

"What? Gone to see Motoshige? Has he quite lost his senses?"

Zeami was on his feet and would have gone straight out of the house if Kogame had not insisted on combing and tying his master's by now shoulder-length white hair and rubbing on it drops of camellia oil spread on his palms. As he passed through the house, already wrapped in a heavy straw rain cape, followed by Kogame, everyone jumped to his feet; but intimidated by the look on Zeami's face, no one dared ask a question. Complete silence reigned till the two figures strode out of sight.

Zeami walked down the three avenues and the few side streets

that separated his house from Motoshige's at a speed which forced
Kogame with the oiled-paper lantern to trot to keep up with his
old master. Zeami's and Kogame's appearance on Saburo Motoshige's doorstep produced an immediate hush and much scurrying
about inside the house. Zeami quickly removed his sodden muddy
footwear and put on a pair of *tabis* Kogame had been keeping dry
inside his sleeves. He stood up to face Saburo Motoshige, who had
just at that moment hurried out to the entrance hall, closely followed by Raido. Kumaya, too, appeared on their heels, dumbfounded to see his master.

"Hope you haven't taken Kumaya's idiotic plea seriously,
Motoshige. It's the last thing I would ask you to do. Let us go
inside. One cannot talk here."

What took Saburo Motoshige and his men aback and made
them bow their heads in docile subjugation to Zeami was the sheer
elegance and strength of a man who knew he had nothing to gain
and nothing more to lose. Kumaya, who had been embroiled in a
humiliating and unproductive argument with Saburo Motoshige,
was far from being vexed by his master's castigating him in public; he was so appreciative of Zeami's arrival and its magical effect
on Saburo Motoshige and his men that forgetting the place and
circumstances, he smiled brightly at Kogame, who, virtually glued
to Zeami's side, was surveying the divided-house troupe with the
growling mistrustfulness of a watchdog.

Saburo Motoshige led the way to a large tatami-matted room,
lit with many tall-legged oil lamps; and Raido, who had taken
over all responsibilities as the veteran of the troupe from the late
Hotan and gained Saburo Motoshige's confidence by assiduously
disparaging both Zeami and Juro Motomasa, was furious that the
entire troupe of divided-house actors followed them into the room,
gawking at Zeami like a herd of spellbound cattle.

Zeami sat matter-of-factly at the host's position with his back
to the north wall, with Kogame and Kumaya on his right and left,
which obliged all the others, even Saburo Motoshige, to sit closely
huddled together facing Zeami.

"I forbid anyone from the Kanze, whether the main house or
the divided house, to try to gain remission for me, both now and
when I am in exile. Especially you, Motoshige. I know the shogun's character probably as well as you do, having suffered his
persecution as much as you have enjoyed his favor. Any attempt

at reversing his publicly made decision will provoke from him a reprisal far more detrimental to the house of Kanze than if I end my days alone with only sea gulls and wind-torn pines to mourn me. I appreciate Kumaya's generous impulse to ask you to plead for my liberty, but I entreat you and everyone else, save the noh; think only of the survival of the noh."

He then studied Saburo Motoshige attentively for a while, with very little expression on his calm, tired, beautiful face.

"Before I go into exile, I am willing to coach you and make you the fourth master of Kanze."

Ignoring the noiseless thud of reaction that hit everyone in the gut, his eyes firmly fixed on Saburo Motoshige, Zeami slowly licked his lips, and there was not an eye in the room that did not follow the tip of his tongue.

"Only, I'll need time, you'll need time, Motoshige. I'll need at least six months with you and the entire troupe, ideally eight. And at your inaugural performance I'll act as your *koken* attendant. Ask the shogun to postpone my exile date. The shogun has twice requested that I hand over the Kanze mastership to you, and twice I have refused, as my eldest son and heir was then still alive, and he was, my fatherly indulgence quite apart, born with a genius the like of which not many generations in our history are blessed with.

"Saburo Motoshige, I have always regretted that there is very little poetry in you. You have a mean, closed heart which no music or lyrics can easily possess, with none of that vulnerability which, in contact with nature and man, yearns to express their beauty and pain and love. But you are blessed with other of Buddha's wondrous gifts: you have immense physical allure, virtuosity and stamina. You are a good leader; you can imitate, digest and conserve. What I value in you above anything else is your total commitment to your profession and to your personal success.

"Risking the sin of arrogance, I permit myself to say that the noh has today reached the point where there exists no further need for creation and innovation. That has been done. If I can obtain an eight-month postponement, before I am put in a criminal's carriage bound for Sado, I'll have finished putting on paper all my final instructions as to how to perform the hundred-odd noh plays currently in our repertory, with every single detail specified, from the stage direction or position of each single prop

down to the color and fabric of a wig band for a secondary character in the least-performed play. In other words, Motoshige, your
talent to perpetuate and succeed is what we need, and you'll succeed in every sense of the word: you shall be the root of the long
line of the future Kanze."

Saburo Motoshige uttered no word, no noise in reply to
Zeami's proposal, but abruptly dropped his head to his chest, his
hands pressing down the tatami floor with trembling force. He resented with ferocity much of what Zeami had said: that tone of
condescension, the lucid analysis of his limitations, the humiliating comparison of himself with Juro Motomasa, now sanctified by
death; yet, and yet transcending all such squeals of wounded ego
was the mind-boggling fact that no one else but Saburo Motoshige,
the little orphan smuggled into the Kanze family through the back
door, was to be publicly proclaimed by Zeami himself, Zeami acting as his *koken* attendant, as the fourth Kanze master and to possess the entire treasurehouse of Zeami's secret transmissions!

Recalling how as a boy he had wished he were dead on the
bottom of the Kamo River rather than having to listen to Juro
Motomasa boast of receiving from Zeami "the heart and blood of
Grandfather and Father," he had an urge, unfamiliar to him, to
cry. The unhappy boy Saburo had grown up into Motoshige the
man incapable of tears; but on this occasion he came nearest to
shedding dry tears for having at last achieved a certain bitter peace
with Zeami and a triumph, raw and voluptuous, over Juro Motomasa.

To Shogun Yoshinori too it was a personal triumph over his
father, for by having wiped out for good the direct bloodline of
Kanami and Zeami, sullied intolerably by their intimate relationship with Yoshimitsu's great reign and person, Yoshinori had succeeded in securing a Kanze noh master of his own choice and taste,
who would be identified with his own reign down the long path of
history.

He was determined to heap on Saburo Motoshige's inaugural
performance all the luster of distinction and advantage. He himself chose the most flower-redolent dates of April twenty-first,
twenty-second and twenty-third and commanded the chancellor
Hosokawa to personally organize the three-day subscription performance under the aegis of the Ghion Shrine on the Tadasu field
of the Kamo riverbank; he specified that no fewer than sixty-two

loges be constructed of the finest materials to seat the great number of dignitaries expected to attend. The shogun then perfunctorily added an instruction to his head of police that Zeami must be out of the capital, come what might, by the last day of April, which gave Zeami barely five months to complete the handover to Saburo Motoshige of his lifetime work.

At once Zeami started persuading the remaining main-house actors to join Saburo Motoshige, arguing that to remain without work and hostile to Saburo Motoshige out of a misguided loyalty to him and their late master Juro Motomasa served neither themselves nor the Kanze's noh. It was not an easy task; Kumaya, to start with, remained unshakable in his refusal to work for or with Saburo Motoshige.

"Remember, Master, I had that unfortunate interview with Motoshige-dono, and I'll never, but never be able to forget his flinty silence, his white eyes, his curled lips. Call me a sentimental ass, Master, but there *is* a thing called the Way of master and disciples. If I went against it now and chose a richer, securer life under a master I hold in horror and contempt, I shouldn't be able to respect myself. I want to return to Yamato and ask your son-in-law to take me and my family and disciples."

"I understand, Kumaya. Ujinobu is an honorable young man with an immense creative talent, and your joining him will strengthen his troupe immeasurably. As to Motoshige, no doubt he hates me, and to me he is an enemy who indirectly destroyed both my own sons. But think of him as my only viable successor, the only child who has managed to stay on the Way of noh and answered my cry; a house remains a house only so long as it continues. I adored my two boys; they adored me. Then, tell me, Kumaya, what did they do? Motoyoshi deserted his Way and left his old father to what he called 'the demonic obsession.' Motomasa broke like an eggshell under the hostile pressure from the shogun, abandoned the capital and me, then left this world. I am neither rock nor iron; as father I weep till I am dry at the loss of my sons; but as head of the house of Kanze, I can never, never forgive them. Till the day I am a handful of cold ashes I'll curse their betrayal and cowardice! Therefore, if I say to you, I cherish Motoshige more than my own beloved sons, do you understand me?"

"I do, Master, I do," gasped Kumaya, his face a pool of anguish beyond his own comprehension. "I do, but I don't know whether I ought to feel sorry for you or be horrified. . . ."

Kogame was another who for the first time in his life went contrary to his master's order.

"I'm no good any longer as a kyogen comic. I can't laugh, I can't make anyone laugh, I don't want to. I'm sixty-nine. What little use is left in me, please, Master, let me give it to you. Take me to Sado. I'll cut wood to warm you in winter. I'll fish and braid straw into sandals and tell mosquitoes to let you alone."

Zeami laughed, with a noise like a handful of dry leaves being harassed by a sudden gust. Kogame had that bizarre genius of his father, Ogame, who used to be able to make Fujiwaka forget hunger, pain, fear, anything by simply making him laugh.

With a surly sidewise glance at Zeami, Kogame concluded:

"All right, then: I'm coming with you to Sado."

ZEAMI invited Saburo Motoshige and his troupe to come to the main house every morning at the Hour of Dragon,* as in December the sun still rose late. On the first day of the work, Saburo Motoshige arrived before anyone else, followed by a young servant whose sole duty, it seemed to Sazami, who spied on them, was to pick up Saburo Motoshige's carelessly discarded sandals and rearrange them neatly on the entrance-hall floor, then await his master's coming and going for the rest of the day. Saburo Motoshige prayed for a long time before the family altar and lit many fresh incense sticks he had brought with him before the mortuary tablets of Kanami, Omina, Tamana and Juro Motomasa, and when the troupe had entered the stage room, he put both his hands on the floor and lowered his head toward them.

"Many of you worshiped my eldest brother, Motomasa, as your master and hoped to end your days working for him. I understand, therefore, how you must feel today with me sitting here as the next Kanze master. But as my father wishes it to be so, please bear the unbearable and for the sake of Kanze's noh, help me and work with me."

Then began the work that was to be Zeami's fond yet rigorous farewell to every Kanze disciple. The shortage of time was his cardinal preoccupation. Seeing that since he had last taught him,

* Eight o'clock in the morning.

Saburo Motoshige had made little progress outside his favorite warrior and demon roles in which his august patron and other supporters enthusiastically appreciated him, Zeami said point-blank:

"Whether you are afraid to exteriorize your deep hidden emotions or you simply don't have any, let us not waste time try-ing to find out. Relying unabashedly on your physical magnetism and technical virtuosity, you have managed very well in warrior and demon roles. But in order to be a Kanze master you must be able to play the female, the possessed and the aged, for in these parts breathes the eternal soul of my noh of *yugen*. Don't worry—I can and I will train you so that you will come to effectively play the roles that do not come naturally to you. How? By imitating the infallible, fatefully pure outer forms that great artists before you have perfected. You copy me, my every move and pose, with utter exactitude—and I mean exact!"

Indeed, the lesson proved maniacally exacting and repetitious. Departing by an infinitesimal fraction from what Zeami knew or felt or decided was the one and only correct form, Saburo Moto-shige would have Zeami flying at him like a bat, a folded fan in hand, with a speed that made his sleeves flutter.

"Here, not there—feel the difference?"

Saburo Motoshige would wince at the lightest touch of Zeami's fan, as if a nail had been hammered into him, and won-der why on earth Zeami was correcting him in the small of his back in order to achieve a certain effect between the tilt of his neck and his right shoulder.

"Once more! With me still alive in front of you, why don't you watch me, measure me, record me till your eyes suck my liv-ing blood? Don't waste time. Quick, do it again!"

Zeami would quickly leave center stage to Saburo Motoshige and, forgetting that he had earlier kicked away his battered cord cushion, would sit down on the bare stage floor. His eyes never straying from Saburo Motoshige, all the emotions and the quintes-sence of the movements that his pupil was struggling to enact were mirrored on Zeami's face as vividly as breeze-stirred ripples on still water.

While he was coaching Saburo Motoshige alone, Zeami had the elders train the younger members, and after a hurried midday meal taken alone, he would call the entire company day by day to rehearse every play in the Kanze repertory in order of the four seasons, always starting with Saburo Motoshige in the *shité* role, then with other *shité* players repeating the same role.

His capacity for concentration was phenomenal and never flagged throughout the long hours of rehearsal. One perishingly cold evening in January, Zeami complained that the rhythmically repeated noise of Raiman's stamping feet was not producing the desired sonority and precision. No one else found the sound in any way unsatisfactory, but Zeami insisted that the floorboards of the stage room be removed at once. It was nearly midnight when they finally discovered that two of the four huge earthen urns hung by rope for amplification purposes beneath the stage floor had been made ineffective, one by a frozen dead rat inside it and the other by an extensive crack.

Saburo Motoshige rapidly lost weight despite a voracious appetite and being shamelessly pampered by Kikyo, who to the great annoyance of Sazami brought special lunch and tea boxes for him every day; and as Yoshinori was not one to tolerate any nonsense for his favorite on account of mere theatrical lessons, Saburo Motoshige did not dare neglect his attendance at the shogun's entertainments and continued to spend some nights at the Muromachi Palace; but to his credit, he never once missed or was late for his lesson the following morning. The stain of the night before with little sleep showing under his eyes, he surrendered himself totally to Zeami and worked with a kind of palpable glandular intensity which made Kogame remark under his breath: "Like a dog that's smelled a bitch in heat."

As the inaugural performance and Zeami's exile date loomed nearer, Zeami exacted more and more from everyone, and naturally the most from Saburo Motoshige. Now and again, Zeami would demand of him something patently and outrageously beyond Saburo Motoshige's present capacity, but Saburo Motoshige would not demur; he would try and try and try again, visibly withering from exhaustion and frustration, till Zeami would interrupt him with cruel finality:

"Enough. Now you know you can't do it. That's what I wanted you to learn today."

At times, Zeami's method of coaching appeared indistinguishable from torture: rehearsing a climactic sequence danced by a demon-possessed woman to the solo accompaniment of a big drum,

Zeami was not satisfied with the tension between Saburo Moto-shige and Roppen, the thirty-one-year-old drummer whose father, Jippen, had decided to remain in Ochi.

"I want here a life-or-death duel between the two of you, and what do I get? A lullaby! If I had paid for *this,* I'd be demanding my money back!"

He had a screen put up between Saburo Motoshige and Rop-pen and told them to play as if each drumbeat and dance step were a thrown dagger. "Feel Roppen's aggression building up behind the screen," Zeami told Saburo Motoshige. "Just as you feel he's attacking you with his next drumbeat, leap, turn, fall, beat your sleeve, do everything to the limits of the choreography, but by do-ing so, outwit him and save your life. Now try."

After only a short while, the dancer and the drummer, sepa-rated by the screen, were sweating copiously and gasping for air from sheer tension, but they did produce a performance which was dramatically and musically so riveting that when as a final as-sault Roppen let out a tearing yell and blasted a thunder of beats, making Saburo Motoshige fly zigzagging in the air, then swoop down on his knees to the floor, everyone present gasped, except Zeami, who merely told Saburo Motoshige:

"We'll see if we can't build on that tomorrow."

Zeami's penetrating eye did not spare other players either: during one rehearsal Zeami stopped the whole proceedings purely because he judged that Raiden as *koken* attendant at the back of the stage did not sit there "invisibly" enough. And even with *waki* and kyogen players, who had traditionally enjoyed a certain au-tonomy in their acting and direction, Zeami did not refrain from correcting, although he made a point of giving his often scathing criticism through their respective chiefs. So terrified were they of the old master's eye that the poor *waki* or kyogen actors were seen mumbling prayers and clutching at the talismen, hung around their necks before they made their entrances.

27

Since the time when Ogame had so plausibly depicted to Fujiwaka the Terminal World, the world had become more than sixty years older and nearer the *very* End of the World, and as people looked about them they were horrified to find their world so devastated by natural and man-made disasters, which seemed to recur more frequently and more violently each year, with less scope for remedy or even hope of remedy.

Amongst the Kyotoites, who traditionally venerated old age and its godlike powers and sympathized with defeated heroes, the fact that Zeami, bereft of shogunal favor, vanished from public view for so long and believed by some to have long been dead, could be seen again, even if only as his youngest son's *koken* attendant, was guaranteed to arouse a tremendous nostalgic and superstitious yearning.

Sweet-dumpling shops along the Kamo River began selling dumplings named after Zeami and Saburo Motoshige; streamers and banners announcing the fourth Kanze master's inaugural performance flapped in the gusty spring air, which sent the fallen cherry blossoms rushing down the streets in rivulets. A great num-

ber of actors not only of the capital but from the provinces paid
bribes just to secure a place on the Flat Earth; many of Yoshimitsu's Companions-in-Arts, long out of favor and widely dispersed
and old, somehow managed to reappear in the capital to see their
old colleague for the last time; the affluent theater-mad merchants
from Osaka, Omi and even Shikoku took rooms for all three days
at the best inns near Tadasu field; courtesans flirtatiously begged
their rich customers to take them to see Zeami and his handsome
son; and even amongst the nobles, prelates and high-ranking samurais who were obliged to be seen to be applauding the shogun's
favorite in their exorbitantly priced loges, there were many who
in fact were coming to the performance primarily to catch a last
glimpse of the legend and symbol of the halcyon days of the Ashikaga shogunate and to have their eyes blessed by the Buddha-given
divinity of Zeami's genius.

The performance for which the entire capital had been waiting opened on the twenty-first of April, crackling crisp and sunny,
more like a perfect day in mid-May.

With the shogun's committed support behind him and as the
central figure of the three-day event, Saburo Motoshige, in breath-
takingly beautiful new costumes and the best of masks and fans
from Zeami's collection, naturally received a resounding, highly
stage-managed ovation of congratulation from the spectators. He
also had the unheard-of honor of receiving *before* the performance
the shogun's own cloak, brought down to the stage by a page.
However, what caused clapping hands to halt and cheering mouths
to gape in silence was Zeami's modest entrance dressed in simple
black kimono and *hakama* with a plain fan in his waist sash. All
he did was unobtrusively follow the four musicians down the entrance bridge, sit at the back of the stage and remain "invisible"
for the duration of the performance till and in case his interven-
tion was needed.

Only this—yet with his white hair cut and tied in the manner
of a mountain monk, giving a halolike frame to his indestructibly
beautiful face, every spectator who could recall his Fujiwaka or
Motokiyo days had a hot lump in his throat. His so-called "invisible" presence seemed to infuse the actors, chorus and musicians with a scintillating tension, especially amongst the younger
generation of the troupe, who had zealously responded to and
reaped a miracle harvest from his five-month coaching. Zeami,

sitting behind them, felt his heart reach out to them in rays of affection and prayer, and soon a certain intoxication between the master and his disciples permeated the stage, which naturally could not leave the spectators unaffected.

The new master of the Kanze surprised the discerning members of the public with the gigantic progress he had made in so short a while, and Zeami was particularly gratified to see that Saburo Motoshige did not slide back into his old tricks and excesses in response to the rapturous reception his supporters gave him.

Ujinobu, who had come up for the performance without Tama, as her twins were both just recovering from chicken pox, was dumbfounded by the change he saw in Saburo Motoshige.

"I was always impressed but at the same time slightly sickened by his coy surface grease that caught too much light," he told Zeami as they walked home together after the first day's performance. "But today I saw a different beast altogether. His animal magic is still there, but held back, therefore all the more exciting. I doubt if inside himself he really feels that much, but certainly he gives that impression on stage. What have you done to him, Father? I am speechless!"

Zeami smiled indulgently at Ujinobu's youthful hyperbole, knowing there was much truth in what he said.

For the third and last day, Saburo Motoshige had asked the shogun's permission to let Zeami perform in at least one short play of his choice, but Yoshinori had been most reluctant to give it.

"I haven't arranged this costly performance for *his* sake, you understand. He's only given you what you rightly deserve, taught you bits and pieces, and now he can go to Sado Island. Why do you suddenly want to do him a favor? What's behind this, eh?"

Yoshinori's thin bluish lips curled downward, unsmiling; but Saburo Motoshige knew how to cope with this kind of question from the shogun.

"For my own curiosity," replied Saburo Motoshige with a casual sardonic laugh inside his throat. "He's been yelling and lashing out at me all these months, and I am curious to see for myself how much he can really do himself. After all, he hasn't been seen on the capital's stage now for nearly thirty years, and I'd like to see if he is still as good as he seems to think he is. That's all."

Shogun Yoshinori's own curiosity was aroused. In any case, the old man had been stripped of everything and was about to be left to rot on some salt-encrusted rocks.

"All right, let him," he said. "In a few days' time it won't make any difference."

On the first two days, the Flat Earth had seemed full to bursting, and even the loges had been crowded to the point of becoming uncomfortable for nobles and ladies in their trailing wide garments and bulky sleeves; but on the third day, with the rumor that Zeami himself might actually perform, what had seemed impossible was achieved: a few hundred more people, by ruse and by sheer physical contortion, somehow managed to slip themselves in.

Zeami chose *Obasute*.

As Yoshinori's permission had not been obtained till only a couple of days before the actual performance, and with so much to be attended to for the plays already scheduled, Zeami could not spare any rehearsal time for *Obasute,* a play with only two principal roles, neither with Kumatoyo, Kumao's best disciple, in the role of the traveler nor with the musicians and chorus. All he could manage was an often-interrupted and hurried consultation here and there.

"Kumatoyo, after I turn at the Eye-Catching Pillar, the way your master Kumao did on the Kofuku stage . . . remember that?"

"I do, Master. I can still see it; he was superb."

"Raiman, when I am left all alone at the end, make sure you don't lead the chorus in too promptly. I'm so old that I can do fuller justice to 'the moon above, the old woman alone' than when I last played the role."

"Understood, Master."

Then they went on stage.

In not too distant a past, in the barren mountainous eastern region, to reduce the number of mouths to feed, poor men with large families would carry their useless old mothers to the mountain and leave them there to wither and die or to be eaten by beasts or birds. The mountain was therefore called the Obasute-Yama—the Discard-Grandmother Mountain. A Kyotoite visits the mountain of cruel notoriety on the night of a full moon and there encounters an old woman dressed entirely in white: no doubt, the spirit of one of the discarded old mothers. Without rancor or bitterness she talks to the traveler about her utter solitude, but in a little while, so grateful and pleased with the punctual return of her old friend the moon, she dances and recites Buddha's words. As the night pales into dawn, the traveler is gone; so is the moon. Only the old woman remains atop the Obasute Mountain.

One could not learn, or teach, a noh such as this. Far past the level at which one argues technique or musicality or stage presence, the player must have within himself the capacity to gaze unflinchingly into the depth of his own solitude and the ravages done to him by time and to examine his readiness to die. What distinguished Zeami's last performance in *Obasute* from a performance in any role by any of his great predecessors was what could best be described as its fatal purity.

Ujinobu, being of a rival troupe, had discreetly refrained from entering the dressing area during the performance and watched from the Flat Earth. What a stupendous impression Zeami in *Obasute* had made on him could only partly be gauged from what he said several decades later when he himself was revered by the nation as a great playwright and poet and one of the most celebrated actors of his time:

"After seeing Zeami in *Obasute,* no one alive and sentient could remain the same. I certainly couldn't. There was in it a line spoken by the old woman: 'Too ashamed to be looked at by the moon, my constant friend.' The way Zeami's old woman almost but not quite lifted her fan toward the moon above her before she cowered in utter misery makes my spine freeze by just recalling it today. It was no longer a performance; it was how he understood life and the human heart. It was the only time in my whole life when I experienced the fatal purity of a so-called rankless rank, made as vividly visible as a beacon on the next hill. Ever since, I have humbly and elatedly inched my way toward it, but, of course, with no hope whatever of reaching it."

As the old woman's solitary image froze and the chorus' last sustained note was absorbed into the deathly silence, Saburo Motoshige, watching from between the entrance curtain and the pillar, found himself soaked in perspiration, although it was not a warm day and he had not moved a muscle.

However tortuous and murky his personal feelings might have been, his professional judgment had always been lucid: he

had never once wavered from the belief that Zeami was the greatest, most phenomenal genius of the theater.

But pitiably, there ended his sanity. His sincere and prostrate
admiration for Zeami as artist, even after the impact of *Obasute,*
could not find an honest straight entry into his heart, inside which,
if only he had had the courage and humility to admit it, lurked a
love of a kind: certainly not that whole and ardent love the child
Saburo had so long ago offered his supposed father, but something
just as overwhelming, a tragically deformed extension of it. As his
ungenerous soul fought the ravished sensibility of Saburo Motoshige the artist, he sweated oily sweat as "a toad surrounded by
mirrors" was popularly believed to do.

Shogun Yoshinori was appalled. He tried not to admit it to
himself, but he had been moved. Throughout the performance,
the man who was sending Zeami to *his* Obasute Mountain in a few
days' time sat there immobile, his whalelike thin eyes startled, for
once forgetting his father Yoshimitsu's shadow behind the actor.
For a long while after Zeami's exit the shogun stared and stared
at the empty stage where there had stood the old woman bathed
in cold moonlight.

He came to himself when the spectators began hysterically
clapping and yelling Zeami's name. Then he thought of Yoshimitsu
and was glad that he had already signed and sealed Zeami's exile
order. He extended his right hand and growled angrily when it
took a page more than a few seconds to hand him a cup of wine.

Zeami walked through the five-colored curtain, breathing as
slowly as if he had been reading. Just as Kogame squatted behind
him to help remove his old-woman mask, outside beyond the thin
partition a clamor broke out, starting low but rapidly reaching a
shrieking, concussive insistence. The Flat Earth, with a customary
overfamiliarity as if they were long-lost relatives of the actors they
loved, not only screamed and ululated all his three names—Fujiwaka! Motokiyo! Zeami!—but did the same with Kanami, Juro
Motomasa and Saburo Motoshige; then, carried away by their own
deafening eloquence, they began demanding of Zeami to give
them more.

"We've waited for you so long, Zeami! Give us more; give us
more!"

Zeami listened, and on his face bloomed a smile. No, nothing
so tame and decent as a smile; rather, the voluptuous grin of a

beast scenting the kill. Kogame, alerted, watched his master closely.

Zeami had been born and would die an entertainer, to whom the public's pleasure and approbation was as warm blood to a leech. His old performer's bones and sinews, so long deprived of it, swelled up with dizzying ecstasy, whilst out there the uproar from the Flat Earth was becoming urgent. The recurrent famines, plagues, fires, riots, looting and wars had made people's life a continual struggle. They wanted to dream, to be taken elsewhere; they wanted Zeami to reassure them that there *was* a Buddha, there *was* more than this life, this pitiless confinement.

Zeami inclined his head, listening with his eyes shut. His grin became hardier. Kogame inched nearer Zeami, his myopic eyes hardly blinking for fear he might fail to catch a glance from his master, and now the whole roomful of disciples, including Saburo Motoshige, intently watched Zeami.

"The heron?" Zeami said with an imperceptible wink at Kogame.

"Master!"

Kogame spun around and, yelling short, cryptic instructions to his disciples, gesticulated to the frightened young attendants to lift the curtain. His sprinting entrance produced an incisive cut into the earsplitting cacophony of the audience, followed by a hush that throbbed with expectation.

Kogame bowed, scraping the stage floor in theatrical reverence, then in a piercing kyogen voice announced that his master would offer his gracious audience a farewell dance.

" 'The White Heron!' "

With his inimitable sense of timing, Kogame made another and most extravagant low bow in the direction of the shogun's loge. As a man the entire congregation, even the courtiers and high priests nearest to the shogun's loge, threw up their fans and arms, expressing thanks with cheers and applause for what they interpreted as the shogun's own decision. With all eyes fixed on him, Yoshinori could not do otherwise but irresolutely nod and acknowledge the ovation and remain seated; besides, he had never had the opportunity to see this famed dance of a holy bird which by strict tradition had to be danced only by either boys before puberty or men over seventy, in both cases unmasked. If he had to see it one day, he might as well see it danced by . . . well, by *this one,* he ruminated, and glared at the Flat Earth having a convulsive fit of laughter as Kogame performed a short kyogen piece in order to give Zeami time to change costume.

In the dressing area, the moment Zeami had uttered, "the heron," Toyosaburo gasped: "But what about the heron wig, and the costume, Master?"

Zeami casually pointed at one of the baskets piled up along the far wall. "In the red one. I told Kogame to put them in, just in case . . ."

He searched out Saburo Motoshige's eye and gave him an amused little grin before the young Raiman and Raizen brothers pounced on him to strip off his *Obasute* costume.

Saburo Motoshige for once did not try to interpret Zeami's smile: he was incapable of coping with anything anymore. Looking resigned and dreadfully exhausted, he dried his sweat-spangled forehead and, mindful not to stand in the way, watched others work at a frenetic speed.

They piled on Zeami a voluminous yet almost weightless costume of airy white silk with wide ankle-length sleeves and above his unmasked face carefully adjusted a spreading white feather wig, topped with a pair of silvery white wings.

As Fujiwaka he had danced "The White Heron" for Yoshimitsu at his special private gatherings, and Prince Nijo used to adore the young boy dancing on his soundless small feet, with only his flushed cheeks adding color to his otherwise entirely white fairy-tale appearance. An apparition of ethereal beauty his bird indeed had been—but not holy; not quite; not then.

As the seventy-year-old Zeami slid onto the entrance bridge on the frail single voice of a flute, every breast contracted with a gasp of religious awe; there were many who were convinced they saw a slim shaft of eerie still brightness envelop Zeami as he arrived on center stage and spread his winged sleeves.

It was not a long dance, the physical concentration demanded of the dancer being much too great; and in contrast to his *Obasute* performance, Zeami intended to sweep his audience off their feet with childlike exultation. Carrying his entire public on his enchanted wings to the point where even his professional colleagues amongst the audience forgot to analyze the hideous technical difficulties involved in each of his gossamer movements, he danced with the utmost freedom.

Meiroku's flute spiraled higher; the two hand drums stunned

the air faster; then the white bird flew. People saw the trailing ends of Zeami's costume in midair. Just as they expected them to descend toward the stage floor, Zeami opened and shut his mouth just so slightly, and the heavenly bird was seen floating higher on a farther extended arc, like a wind-carried snowflake, landing halfway across the stage on one silent toe. Then, he was gone.

No one could later explain how it could have been possible for a man to fly. Almost defeated by the logical skepticism of those who had not seen Zeami fly, those who had resigned themselves to obstinately repeating: "But I tell you, he *did;* and really, that was the least of the wonder he gave us then!"

The shogun bent forward, his knees jammed right up against the panel of his loge and his eyes glued to the spot where the white airborne creature had last been seen. The surge of groaning, waillike cheers jangled his nerves and almost frightened him. Clutching at the scabbard of his sword, he leaped to his feet and strutted out of the public's view, trying hard to show as much disdain and nonchalance as he could, but succeeding only in appearing to be hounded from the theater by the ever-rising menace of the public's roar.

The day after the performance the shogun still seemed disturbed and was curt and irritable with everyone around him, even with Saburo Motoshige, who as the new Kanze master paid him a courtesy visit of thanks.

Although he would never admit it, he did have a bad taste in his mouth about exiling Zeami. —Yes, damn, damn him, he is a genius, a giant, a positive danger to be left at large.—

Saburo Motoshige he knew he could control, use, dominate; but not this one. Too big, too free. The thought that Yoshimitsu, his father, could and that he, Yoshinori, would probably be best remembered in history as the shogun who had exiled Zeami so exasperated him that he had to vigorously expectorate with no physical need whatever.

As a spiteful afterthought, Yoshinori told Saburo Motoshige to tell Zeami that he would not be allowed to have anyone, not even his daughter, come and see him off at Obama Harbor, where he was to board a boat to the exile island, and that Kogame's request to accompany his master to Sado Island was refused.*

* Seven years later, Shogun Yoshinori was murdered in cold blood by his own vassal daimyo Lord Akamatsu during a banquet at the latter's Kyoto mansion.

•

ZEAMI was particularly cheerful during the four days that separated the performances from the day of deportation and did not stop giving lessons to the young disciples. On the last day, he took Saburo Motoshige into the storehouse, a white-painted building adjacent to the main house, with small apertures for ventilation below the black-tiled roof.

"All yours, Motoshige. Take good care of this inheritance. Especially the masks. And the house, too. It has a far better and larger stage than yours. The Great Tree himself designed it when he first brought us to the capital. With the number of your disciples increasing, you'll find it much easier to work here."

Handing him a bunch of keys, Zeami added simply:

"Motoshige, I do love you as the only son able to continue the house. I am very grateful, too, and I wish you all the best. Looking back on my life, an ordinary man would cover his eyes with horror and say, 'What a life!' People may one day say the same to you. But what does it matter? For you, as it was for me, to do noh is to live. Ah, by the way, be kind to Kogame. And his wife. She's old Meisho's youngest daughter. Of course, you're too young to have known Meisho! What a flautist, Meisho! He was never quite sober, but when he put his flute to his mouth . . ."

Zeami chuckled to himself, and for a split second he looked the happiest man on earth.

AUTHOR'S NOTE

IN JAPAN today, at performances given in a major city or at a traditional festival by one of the five noh schools—Kanze, Komparu, Hosho, Kongo and Kita—half or more of the program is likely to consist of plays created by Zeami, by his father, Kanami, or by his eldest son, Motomasa. After six hundred years, books are still being written on the theatrical treatises Zeami composed and handed down in strict secrecy to his son and his son-in-law, probing into the depths of Zeami's thoughts and there constantly finding new dimensions.

William Butler Yeats and Bertolt Brecht wrote noh plays of their own, and Benjamin Britten's opera *Curlew River* was inspired by Motomasa's *Sumidagawa*. Not only have Arthur Waley's translations of prominent noh plays helped make Zeami's work accessible to Western readers, but Yukio Mishima's modern noh plays based on Zeami's masterpieces, such as *Lady Aoi* and *Burden of Love,* are frequently performed not only in Japanese but in English, French and other Western languages.

Yet about Zeami and his family not much more is reliably known than about Shakespeare, whom Zeami antedated by two centuries. Having studied the relatively scarce facts on the lives of Kanami, Zeami, his sons and the Ashikaga shoguns with whom their fortunes were so closely linked, and having taken into consideration the theories of experts, I have still had to imagine and invent a great many of the characters and events and much of the background of the story, which must be considered as historical fiction, with the emphasis on fiction.

The most flagrant invention concerns the Fourth Master of Kanze, Saburo-Motoshige, later Onami. I have made him an illegitimate grandson of Kanami and Omina—the latter inspired by the famous dancer from whom Kanami is said to have learned kusé dance and music. Otherwise I could not have dramatically substantiated the virulent hatred of Saburo-Motoshige toward Zeami, and the maniacal persecution of Zeami by the shogun Yoshinori.

To a lesser degree I have taken liberties with Zeami's wife, about whom practically nothing is known. There exists a letter written by Zeami from his exile island of Sado in which he thanks Ujinobu Komparu for taking such good care of his aging wife.

This is a small point, but as it will be bound to jar on someone who has read Motoyoshi's meticulous record of his father, Zeami's, teachings, I would like to mention that the play about which "On one silent and still night my father sighed: 'Who in a later world will be able to appreciate a play like this?'" was not Izutsu, as I have made out; it was Kinuta.

There are a few other instances in which I have also knowingly strayed from the presumed or established facts for the sake of the dramatically cogent and illuminating effects I hope they will bring to the novel.

Now, the greatest headache of all: the fact that the principal characters of the novel keep changing their names—a Japanese custom of the period which must be both confusing and irritating for the reader who is accustomed from birth to burial to keeping the same name.

Take Zeami: in my story he is called Fujiwaka as a child, then on attaining adulthood is renamed Motokiyo, only to become Zeami as a Companion-in-Arts of the shogun. He is also thought to have been called Oniyasha as a baby; and when he took the tonsure at about the age of sixty he changed his name for the last time to that of a Buddhist monk! I have pared his names down to Fujiwaka-Motokiyo-Zeami, for annoying as it is, each change of name signals a new status and development in a man's life; aesthetically, too, only a young boy could carry a name like Fujiwaka, literally meaning "young wisteria," which would hardly be suitable for a mature man; whereas Motokiyo, composed of two Chinese characters—purity and originality—would sit on him with becoming dignity. As his father, Kanami, combined the kan of Kanze and the honorific ami on being made the shogun's Companion-in-Arts, so did Zeami with the ze of Kanze and the ami. These changes in name were so much a part of their lifelong careers that I simply could not chuck them into a wastepaper basket for the sake of simplicity or easier identification.

With Zeami's three sons, close together in age and growing up under the same roof, it is hard enough not to muddle them up in their boyhood: Juro, Goro and Saburo; but when they more or less simultaneously attain adulthood, it becomes positively exasperating to keep track of their new names. Especially when all three names—Motomasa, Motoyoshi and Motoshige—start with *moto,* derived from their father's name Motokiyo, the nomenclature becomes a visual and phonetic nightmare. After months of hesitation, I decided after the three boys reach manhood to use their childhood and adulthood names together, hoping that by this means at least one of the names will ring a bell in the reader's memory.